"LOOK AT THE CLOSE-UP
OF THE THROAT, TOMMY.
HELL OF A NICE SLASH...

Too bad. Tony and you were so close, Tommy. Partners. Blood brothers, palsie walsies, right, Tommy?"

Ankles snarled as Tommy put the snapshots down and turned away.

"If you were such a palsie walsie, Ryan, why didn't you do something about it? Scared? Mob guys? Guys with white shoes, Tommy?"

"I'll find out, Ankles. My way. I don't need you."

"Let me tell you something, Tommy," Ankles said. "I've known you a long time. You're smart—big words, big mouth, big money. Now I only care about one thing—I want Tony Mauro's killer. I'm not interested in nothin' else, get it? And if I find you're holding out on Mauro's murder, I'll nail you so hard you'll think Jesus H. Christ got off easy. Remember, Tommy, I warned you. Remember."

"BRUTAL . . . HARD-HITTING . . . HAMILL BRINGS [HIS CHARACTERS] TO LIFE IN A TIGHTLY PLOTTED HORROR STORY."
—*Publishers Weekly*

STOMPING GROUND

Denis Hamill

A DELL BOOK

Published by
Dell Publishing Co., Inc.
1 Dag Hammarskjold Plaza
New York, New York 10017

Dell ® TM 681510, Dell Publishing Co., Inc.

ISBN: 0-440-17615-8

Reprinted by arrangement with Delacorte Press

Printed in the United States of America
First Dell printing—June 1981

For Shiobhion, with love,
may your blade always be sharp.

"Man is what he chooses to be. He chooses that for himself."

—John Spenkelink,
two hours before his execution,
May 25, 1979.

STOMPING
GROUND

1

Alley Boy's palms sweated inside the black leather gloves as he clenched the steering wheel. A scalding geyser of adrenaline shot up his spine, burning the worst at the nape of his neck.

Alley Boy touched the beard on his face, which hung down to the third button on his white shirt. He pressed the beard where it began at his temples.

The two men next to Alley Boy had similar beards. And all three men were dressed the same way: black coats, black pants, black gloves, black shoes, black fur hats, white shirts without ties, and, of course, white socks. The bearded man next to the door held a brown briefcase close to his chest and stared at the front doors of the bank.

It was two minutes to nine.

Tommy Ryan's watch was never wrong, so he sat

patiently, as the bright winter sun mirrored off the glass doors of the bank. In the reflection Tommy Ryan could see the yellow Econoline van he was sitting in. The Hebrew legend on the side of the van read backwards. Tommy Ryan laughed to himself: In the mirror the Hebrew read the way he was accustomed to reading—left to right. The mirror always read backwards, he thought.

The sun shifted, and Tommy Ryan could see the bank guard appear in the vestibule. The guard must have been sixty. An old cocksucker. That always made it easier. The older they get, he thought, the more they hate to die. Not out of fear. Out of resentment. The last game the old cocksuckers get to play is Beat the Clock. No winners in that game, Tommy Ryan thought. Only survivors.

The bank guard yawned as he unlocked the front doors of the bank. The high December sun spilled through the glass doors onto the fake marble floors, and the guard noticed finger smudges that the dinge window washer had missed. A dinge washes windows the way he washes himself, the bank guard thought. Half-assed. From playing with themselves.

Silvery dust hovered in the sun shafts of the vestibule. The guard touched his bulbous nose, inspecting the exposed purple vessels for leaking blood. His fingers only showed him nose oil, and he wiped it on his pistol holster for shine.

It wasn't until he bent at the waist to hook back the inside doors that the guard noticed the yellow Econoline parked out front. He knew it was one of those small school buses the Hebes used for the Yeshivas, but he couldn't understand the Hebrew writing on the side. It always looked like they write Hebrew with their sideburns, he thought.

The sun reflected off the piled snow at the curb, but even through the glare he could make out the three beards sitting up front. Hebes always traveled in bunches, the bank guard thought, like waterbugs. Especially when they carry loot. One to carry, one to count, and one to check on the other two. Fuckin' Hebes. Just like the dinges. Except one crowd's got money on the brain, and the other's sick with pussy.

The guard moved back into the bank. Fluorescent light shone from sterile plastic panels on the white ceiling. Three tellers were busy riffling crisp new bills and sipping coffee behind the barred counter. The bank guard stopped at one of the customers' writing counters and snapped off the previous day's page from the calendar and stared for a beat at the new date. December fifteenth, he thought. Another Christmas coming up. Sixty-one Christmases . . . I wish Helen was alive for this one. . . .

"Keep it running and be ready to split," Tommy Ryan told Alley Boy. "Don't worry about me and Cisco while we're in there. This is like shopping. Start worrying when we come out."

Alley Boy nodded as gas searched for release inside of him. His heart was thumping. He was afraid Tommy Ryan and Cisco might hear it.

Tommy Ryan clutched the briefcase tightly and nudged Cisco. He swung the door open and the two of them stepped out. Tommy Ryan purposely stepped on a hard chunk of ice, and it crunched noisily under his leather sole. He enjoyed that sound. It reminded him of cracking bone. Tommy Ryan and Cisco moved across the sidewalk toward the bank in a relaxed gait, the snow crunching loudly underfoot. Traffic was sparse on the quiet snowy street. Down the road a Wonder Bread truck was parked outside a super-market.

Tommy Ryan paused to breathe in the clean country air, thinking of Norman Rockwell. His father had always brought home *The Saturday Evening Post*. This street looked like a cover for that magazine, Tommy Ryan thought. Cisco nudged him on. Alley Boy sat in the van looking straight ahead, his bowels combusting.

The bank guard glanced through the front doors. The two Hebes were coming into the bank. They'd dress the same way on the Equator, he thought. Every day is Halloween. He laughed out loud. He always laughed when he saw Hasids. He remembered when he was a kid how they used to catch a Yid in town and they'd steal his beanie and cut off his sideburns. That was before the war. You couldn't do that now.

But they never fail to dress all in black with white socks, he thought. That always made him crack up. As the two Hebes came into the bank, the guard ran over to Hennessy, the bank manager, rolled his eyes toward the two Hasids, and said, "Here comes the Chicago White Sox."

Hennessy stifled a laugh and pretended to look through a pagoda of file folders on his desk. "Don't laugh," Hennessy whispered. "These mocks are sensi-tive sonsabitches."

The bank guard walked toward his permanent position at the front door. Tommy Ryan paused momentarily near the bank guard and nodded a thin smile. The bank guard returned the gesture. Tommy Ryan then looked around for the automatic security cameras. Bell and Howell, he thought to himself. Pretty good equipment. But it didn't matter if they were using a seventy-millimeter Panaflex. It wouldn't do anyone any good. He would look like any other Hasid from the diamond center. Instinctively he began to unbutton his large black overcoat. He was medium height, five foot nine, but he carried himself like a giant. At least he thought so and he worked pretty hard at it.

Cisco was a few inches shorter and had a dark complexion. He moved with a cocky swagger to one of the writing counters and took one of the forms from the counter top. Then he put it down and chose another one. He put this back, too. The bank guard noticed the little Hebe was confused, so he went over to help.

"Can I help you, sir?" the bank guard asked. Cisco looked at the bank guard's shiny holster. He saw that the snap was fastened.

"I don't know, man," Cisco said. The bank guard noticed a Hispanic inflection. A Puerto Rican Jew, he thought. A regular Hymie Rodriguez.

"Checking or savings?" the bank guard asked.

"Yeah, we're checking out the savings," Cisco said, as his eyes remained on the bank guard's sidearm. Jesus Christ, the bank guard thought, aren't all Jews supposed to be intelligent? Goes to show you what crossbreeding will do.

At the front door Tommy Ryan placed the briefcase on the floor and opened his overcoat wider. He pinpointed the manager, picked up the case again, and walked over to him. Hennessy stood up and extended his hand in greeting.

"Hi. Bill Hennessy, general manager. Pleased to meet you. What can I do for you?"

"For starters you can shut your fuckin' mouth," Tommy Ryan said as he pulled a silver-plated sawed-off shotgun from beneath the large coat. He slid his leather-clad index finger over the trigger the way a hooker might run her tongue over her lips.

At the writing counter Cisco pulled a .38 caliber Colt

from his coat pocket and pushed it against the bank guard's nose. Blood trickled from one of the exposed vessels.

"It's beginning to look a lot like Christmas," Cisco said with a cackle. The bank guard thought about Helen as the salty blood ran through his lips into his mouth. He closed his eyes and shook.

Gasps came from behind the teller cages.

"Please be calm," Hennessy shouted. "Don't do anything foolish. Stay away from the silent alarms."

Cisco took the pistol from the bank guard's holster. Hennessy, the bank manager, could not swallow with the barrel of the shotgun jammed against his throat. But he tried to talk.

"What do you want?" he croaked.

"We're here to make a withdrawal," Tommy Ryan said. Hennessy looked this Jew in the eyes and saw a lunatic. The Jew had eyes like whirlpools—deep blue, with what appeared to be a white foam running around the pupils.

"Take what you want, but please don't kill me," Hennessy said. "I have kids . . . Christmas . . . kids, a wife."

"I'm not gonna kill you," Tommy Ryan said. "But you'll be walking on stumps if you don't open that vault."

Cisco moved the bank guard over toward the teller cages while Tommy Ryan led Hennessy to the Mosler vault. He handed the bank manager the brown briefcase. Hennessy placed the briefcase down and turned three dials on the vault. Then he spun the wheel-shaped bolt release and hoisted open the foot-thick metal door. Hennessy quickly filled the briefcase with stacks of starched bills.

When the briefcase was filled Hennessy fastened the two brass clasps and handed it to Tommy Ryan. Cisco

then led the tellers and the bank guard to the vault
and marched them inside. Tommy Ryan motioned Hennessy into the vault, and when all the bank employees
were inside Tommy Ryan slammed the door shut.

Inside the yellow van Alley Boy could now smell his
fear as gas escaped from his body. The motor was rev-
ving. He saw Tommy Ryan and Cisco calmly walking
toward him from the bank. They chatted indif-
ferently as they walked. The Wonder Bread truck
was still parked up the street. It was five minutes past
nine. Cisco climbed into the van first and Tommy Ryan
entered second. Once in the van, Tommy Ryan removed
the shotgun from inside his overcoat and placed it on
his lap.

Tommy Ryan slammed the door of the van and said,
"Smells like your momma's home cooking in here."

Cisco broke up laughing. Alley Boy ignored the rib-
bing. He slid the gearshift into drive, and the eight
cylinders came to life as the van jerked from the parking spot.

"Be cool, man," Cisco said. "They're locked up inna
vault."

"There might be a silent alarm in the vault, though,"
Tommy Ryan said. "Them Mosler boxes are good.
But relax. It'll take time for them to respond."

Alley Boy slowed down. Tommy Ryan stared out at
the Wonder Bread man as they rolled past his truck.
He thought about peanut-butter-and-jelly sandwiches
on white, like Mom used to make. With freezing cold
milk. Pauper's lunch.

"Left here," Tommy Ryan said to Alley Boy. "Then
you can start making time."

Alley Boy made a sharp left and pushed his foot
down on the accelerator. Snow was piled high on both

sides of the blacktop road. Telephone poles were spaced every hundred yards. In the distance the Catskill mountains rose, their peaks hooded with snow. Pine trees glistened in the mountains. The blacktop curved continuously up the mountainside. There were no other cars on the road, and the jangle of the tire chains was very loud. A doe darted across the road, its huge wet eyes bewildered. Alley Boy honked his horn and the deer bolted into the trees. A sign on the right-hand side of the road read POUGHKEEPSIE 12 MILES.

"The turn is about another three hundred yards," Tommy Ryan said. "Slow down."

The van slowed and took a right turn onto a snow-covered path. The van bounced along the slippery path for about five hundred yards. Birds sang in the dense trees. The deeper they moved into the woods, the less snow was on the ground because of the sheltering pines. Instead the earth was covered with a shag of wet fulvous leaves and pine cones. The tall pines also blocked out most of the sun, and it grew darker and chillier in the forest.

Alley Boy took a left on a small dirt trail and followed it to a wide clearing amid the trees. A gold Cadillac Seville was parked in the clearing. From the sky, nothing could be seen. The taller trees provided a canopy over the clearing, and only small patches of sun shone through.

Alley Boy jumped out of the van and immediately rushed for a nearby tree to relieve his bowels.

"There's no time for that," Tommy Ryan said with authority. "Besides, sometimes they can tell how long you've been gone from your shit."

Alley Boy, painfully, obliged Tommy Ryan. He pulled off his coat and yanked the black gloves from his hands. Then he started peeling the bogus beard from his face. The gummy adhesive that secured the beard stuck to his skin. Alley Boy picked off little globs at a time, pulling small hairs with it.

He threw the beard into the back of the van. Then he removed the fur hat. The adhesive on his thumb stuck to the inside leather band of the hat. He shook the hat free of his thumb and tossed it into the van.

Tommy Ryan and Cisco stripped their clothes off and threw them into the van. Tommy Ryan took the briefcase and the shotgun and walked to the Cadillac and opened the trunk with a set of car keys. He took out a cardboard box filled with clothing. He lifted a lid to a secret compartment concealed by the spare tire. He placed the silver shotgun and the briefcase in the compartment and closed the hinged metal lid connected to the tire.

Alley Boy approached Tommy Ryan. He was tall, muscular and broad, but he moved like a kid trapped in the body of a man. His teeth were chattering, and he clutched occasionally at his cramped stomach.

Cisco moved toward the Cadillac almost unaffected by the cold. His hair was neatly styled over his ears, and his body was brown and small and hard.

Tommy Ryan stared at Alley Boy in mock amusement. "You are literally scared shitless, aren't you, Alley Boy?" Cisco broke up laughing as he pulled on a pair of corduroy pants.

"And look at those underpants he's wearing," Tommy Ryan said. "You can't even see where his balls are. They say your balls contract when you're scared. His are probably up near his throat by now."

"Fuck you, Tommy," Alley Boy said. "Get off my back."

"Watch your tongue," Tommy Ryan said. "Or I'll carve it out and ram it up your Guinea ass."

Alley Boy shot Tommy Ryan a severe look but kept dressing silently. From the town several miles away came the faint sound of police sirens.

"Answer me something, Alley Boy," Tommy Ryan said as he pulled on a pair of socks. "Why is it that every wop since the fall of the Roman Empire named Alley has had Boy for a middle name? Every dago named Alley I ever met was called Alley Boy. Like Shoeshine Boy."

"Come on, Tommy," Alley Boy said. "Lay off, will ya?"

"I'll lay off your mother, asshole."

Alley Boy instinctively made a move for Tommy Ryan. He stopped when he heard the metallic click of Cisco's .38.

"Get dressed, Alley Boy," Cisco said. "We don't have time for fuckin' around."

"Well I don't like nobody gettin' on my mother."

"I won't be gettin' on your mother till tonight," Tommy Ryan said. "I'll let you know how she was."

Alley Boy remained silent. His mind was red with anger; he could see red and feel red as his face flushed. He has no right talking about my mother like that, Alley Boy thought. Maybe it's just me. Tommy is always playing around. But Tommy takes care of me, too. Gave me my chance. Maybe I shouldn't have went after him like that, Alley Boy thought.

Cisco said nothing. He never crossed Tommy Ryan. Tommy Ryan was The Man. Alley Boy, well he was just that—a boy. Tommy was trying to make him a man. And Tommy was smart. He even took some of that psychology in school. Deep shit. It was better when Tony was with us, but Tony bought the big farm. Tony's dead. If Tommy thinks this Alley Boy kid will work out, I'll listen to him, Cisco thought. Shit in his pants or no.

Tommy Ryan stared at Alley Boy, goading him with a smirk. The branches of the trees quarreled in the thin wind. The faraway sirens played on.

"All right, let's go," Tommy Ryan said. He got in behind the steering wheel of the Cadillac. "If we're lucky they might not find this shit for a few days."

Cisco got in the backseat. He always sat in the backseat when there was somebody else in the car with Tommy Ryan. Tommy called him the eyes in the back of his head. Cisco wouldn't care if it was Tommy's mother in the car. If he was with him, he'd sit in the back and cover Tommy.

Alley Boy climbed into the front passenger seat. Tommy Ryan turned the key in the ignition and the engine kicked over immediately. I should smack him now instead of later, Tommy Ryan thought when he looked at Alley Boy. For being scared. Have to smack the kid out of him. Bring the adult out.

Tommy Ryan tapped Alley Boy on the shoulder. Alley Boy turned to him. "Sorry about what I said about your mother," Tommy Ryan said. Alley Boy began to grin when the right hand whacked him across the left cheek. "But not what I said about you, little boy," Tommy Ryan said.

Alley Boy was stunned. He was easily forty pounds heavier than Tommy Ryan and at least four inches taller. He tried to contain his anger. A small red cloud blew across his mind. Rage seized him and he reached for Tommy Ryan's throat. Cisco's gun cocked again. The red cloud passed. Alley Boy sat up straight and looked out the window, his nose venting gusts of rage.

"Dig yourself before you're by yourself," Cisco

said. Alley Boy collapsed back into the deep suede seat of the Cadillac. A ticking sound came from his throat. Tommy Ryan eased the car through the woods. Before he turned out onto the blacktop he listened for the sounds of traffic.

When he was certain there were no vehicles approaching, he moved out onto the road. The three of them fell silent as Tommy Ryan drove.

Cisco put the pistol under the seat as they reached the first small town. It wasn't much of a town. They could see a railroad station, a deli, and a gas station. The parking lot of the train station was half full. A small wooden sign hung over the platform; it read RHINECLIFF. Cushions of snow lay between the tracks. One citizen awaited the train. He was dressed in a blue business suit and a tweed overcoat and had a briefcase positioned between his legs. He was reading the *Daily News*. A black porter was shoveling snow from the platform and tossing it to the side of the tracks.

"You take the train back," Tommy Ryan said to Alley Boy. Alley Boy spun his head and looked at Tommy Ryan, frightened.

"Come on, Tommy," Alley Boy said. "I don't wanna. . . . Why do I have to take the train? What did I do? If I ranked on your mother you'd get pissed off too."

Tommy Ryan smiled at Alley Boy. The anger had left Tommy Ryan's eyes.

"It has nothing to do with any of that, Al," Tommy Ryan said. Alley Boy's heart was skipping fast. Tommy Ryan laid a hand on Alley Boy's shoulder. "Look, Al, I'm sorry. But you have to take the train because they'll be looking for three guys. If there's just two in the car it'll be smoother. You understand where I'm coming from?"

Alley Boy understood. As usual Tommy was right. He wished he had thought of it himself. Tommy would have liked for him to have thought that up himself. Just too scared to think, Alley Boy thought. This was my first bank. All I did was drive.

"You're right, Tommy. I'm sorry for gettin' so nervous. My first one. I didn't know what to expect. I'll be better next time."

Tommy Ryan smiled. He slapped Alley Boy affectionately on the cheek. "You did fine, Al. Just fine, Al. That's what I'm gonna call you from now on. Al. It's a man's name. No more of this Alley Boy shit. All right, Al?"

"Yeah," Alley Boy said excitedly. "Yeah, I'd like that a lot, Tommy. Al. That's what they called my old man."

"Whadda you think of it, Cisco?" Tommy Ryan asked.

"Capone liked it."

Cisco laughed. He spent half his time laughing, always at the wrong things.

"See you later, Al," Tommy Ryan said.

"Yeah. Thanks, Tommy. See you later in McCaulie's."

"Tennish."

Alley Boy waved as he watched Tommy Ryan make a U-turn and spin back toward the highway. The car moved with controlled power and grace. Like Tommy Ryan, Alley Boy thought.

Al. Fuckin' Al. Terrific. Tommy called me Al. A man's name and a bank in the same day.

He walked across the tracks and up three steps to the platform. The businessman was chatting to the porter.

"Fuckin' train is late again," Alley Boy heard the

businessman say to the porter. "I won't make it to Grand Central till it's time to go home again, at this rate. Son-of-a-bitching bastard." The businessman slapped his *Daily News* against his leg and started down the tracks looking for the train.

"That train's late all the time now," the porter said. "It's the snow, Mr. Adler. It melts down from the mountains. Floods."

"Maybe I oughta get a raft."

The porter laughed gently and moved toward the depot. Alley Boy approached him.

"Excuse me, where's your bathroom?"

"Second door to your left, my man," the porter said without really looking at Alley Boy. Alley Boy walked briskly to the bathroom. His bowels were still uneasy but the urgency had diminished. Inside the bathroom Alley Boy undid his pants and sat on the cold seat. Relief came immediately.

He looked up and read some of the graffiti on the wall of the small stall. There was one there that Tommy would like: "There are only two kinds of people in the world. The Irish and those who wish they were." He made a mental note to tell Tommy that one.

When he was done he pulled up his pants and buckled them. Now, with the physical discomfort gone and the bank job behind him, Alley Boy floated into a state of giddy euphoria. He bounded through the doors of the waiting room onto the station platform, where the businessman stood reading the sports page of the *Daily News*. Alley Boy walked directly up to the businessman and extended his right hand.

"Hi, I'm Al."

The commuter looked at Alley Boy, baffled, and thought, Big fucking deal. Gotta be a Moonie. He put his hand in Alley Boy's anyway and shook.

"Hi, Al."

"Happy December 15th," Alley Boy said.

Definitely a space cadet, the businessman thought.

"Same to you," he said and thought how ridiculous it sounded.

"What line of work are you in—uh . . . I never got your name. Mine's Al."

"Frank," the businessman said. "Frank Adler. Banking. I'm in banking."

"Hey, Frank, so am I," Alley Boy said. "What I mean is that my name isn't Frank—it's Al—and I'm in banking, too."

No wonder the ass is falling out of the dollar, thought Frank Adler as he made a head-to-toe survey of Alley Boy. A complete fucking flake.

"I'm sure you'll go a long way, Al."

They stopped at a roadblock five miles from the train station. Cisco was now in the front passenger seat. Both of them were as calm as distilled water. Tommy Ryan had the radio tuned in to a classical music station. He didn't want the news coming on in the middle of the roadblock check. The cop who approached him wore mirrored sunglasses and was trying his best to look like Clint Eastwood.

"See your license, please," the trooper said to Tommy Ryan. Tommy Ryan took out his wallet, removed the license, and handed it to the trooper.

"What's all the commotion, officer?" he asked. Strains of Bach issued from the radio.

"Somebody robbed the bank in Red Hook," the cop said. "They said it was three rabbis. Even the fucking Hasidics are doin' stickups. Probably sending the money to the JDL or some goddamned thing. Everybody has a cause."

"How much they get?" Tommy Ryan asked.

"They don't know for sure yet. Small unmarked bills. They estimate about thirty-five grand." The trooper handed back the license.

"The whole world has gone nuts. Rabbis with guns," Tommy Ryan said.

"Go ahead, you better go. The cars are backing up," the trooper said.

Tommy Ryan put the car in gear and slipped back onto the highway. After he could no longer see the roadblock in the rearview mirror, Tommy Ryan looked at Cisco and they both started laughing.

"Thirty-five big ones," Tommy Ryan said as he slapped Cisco five.

"Whole lotta ice cream," Cisco said.

Tommy Ryan punched the radio button and the car filled with rock and roll.

One and a half hours later the gold Cadillac whispered over the iron gratings of the Brooklyn Bridge, heading toward downtown Brooklyn. Tommy Ryan was silent and he thought about Alley Boy. He felt sorry for the dumb asshole. But he was certain he could bring the man out of him. Sometimes shitting in your pants helps you make that transition. It makes you realize you should still be in diapers. Sometimes that's the best jolt. Something you learn in the joint is that fear is the only thing dividing manhood and adolescence. If you beat the fear, you own it and you can put it into someone else.

Tommy Ryan realized he couldn't afford to let Alley Boy stay a kid. Alley Boy knew too much about too many things. There's nothing more dangerous than a kid with a loose tongue.

He glanced at a tug barging through the icy waters

below. The sun laid a soft sheen of gold on the water and it reflected off the large chunks of floating ice. It reminded Tommy Ryan of when he lived with his parents in the big house on the cliff overlooking the Hudson. It was a long time ago. . . .

Cisco coughed up a hocker, then rolled down the window and lunged it out into the wind. Cisco was the best, Tommy Ryan thought. He only spoke when he had to. He wasted few words. And no actions. He kept his mouth shut and did his job. Cisco approached it as a professional. Alley Boy saw it as an adventure. Adventure is for comic books, Tommy Ryan thought, and rich people who have to invent ways to spend their money and their time. Adventure was also for kids. Like Alley Boy.

Maybe it was a mistake to take him on, Tommy Ryan thought. Still, the kid had a big heart. He wrote letters to Tommy while Tommy was in the joint. And he ran errands for Carol while he was inside. When someone watches out for your woman while you're in the joint, you take care of him. Besides, the kid was pretty good at the wheel. And he was a big fuck, and easy to control. He did as he was told. The kid was all right.

But there is a difference between being an all right kid and an all right adult. Survival, Tommy Ryan reasoned.

Tommy Ryan dropped Cisco off at Biff's poolroom on the corner of Eleventh Street and Fifth Avenue in Brooklyn. Cisco usually played pool for eight hours a day. No one could understand how he could spend that much time in a poolroom and always have a pocketful of money. He had never worked in his life as far as anyone knew.

Few people knew anything about Cisco. They knew

he had no family, very few friends, no steady girls, and lots of money all the time.

When he was in the joint at Rikers Island on a three-year bit for attempted murder, no one wrote to Cisco but Tommy Ryan. So Cisco used to write letters to all the bureaucracies just to get mail in return. This made him the envy of his tier. Cisco was known as the guy who received the most mail, and in the joint this is the equivalent to being known as a cunt man on the outside. Cisco told everybody they were love letters.

As a result, most of Cisco's conversations were like verbal junk mail. Concise, distant, cold. He liked it that way. He also liked money. Money purchased clothes, beers, games of pool, and women. There was nothing else worth buying.

He liked cars and would have bought one of those, too; but he had never learned to drive because he had failed the written test for a license six times. He was twenty-eight years old now, and he had finally decided that driving was one of those things he would never do.

Cisco climbed the gray wooden steps to Biff's poolroom and opened the tin-covered door. Three tables were taken, but not Cisco's. Cisco was Biff's best customer. And old man Biff was one of the few people Cisco liked. He liked him because he never asked any questions and because he was a cranky old sonofabitch.

Off in the corner of the poolroom three teen-age truants from John Jay High School were talking to a guy named Frankie Green Eyes. Cisco didn't like Green Eyes. Cisco thought Green Eyes was a punk and he didn't like other Puerto Ricans to be punks. It gave his people a bad image. Besides, he sold goofballs, and Cisco didn't like them either. Goofballs made you dumb.

"What's that cocksucker doin' here, man?" Cisco asked old man Biff.

"I asked that lowlife to get out of here at least five times," Biff said. "Friedman and Nelson were up here last night looking for him. They know he's peddlin' them friggin' pills. It makes the fuckin' place hot. They said they'd be back looking for him."

Cisco looked over to Frankie Green Eyes. Green Eyes had on a pair of shades that sat obnoxiously low on the bridge of his nose and he had a smoke dangling from his lips. He was counting money. His jaw hung loosely to the side, as if on a broken hinge. Cisco knew Green Eyes was high on Seconals.

"What'd he say when you tole him to split, Biff?"

"He tole me to fuck myself, the green-eyed pecker-head," Biff said.

Cisco asked nothing else. He picked up his pool cue and racked up. He knew that before he finished his first game Green Eyes would walk over to him. And he knew that if Green Eyes stayed around Biff's, then Friedman and Nelson, the same two detectives who had locked up Cisco years ago on the attempted murder charge, would be back around. And they'd ask questions. And Cisco hated questions. Especially from cops.

Cisco broke the rack of pool balls, then started running the table. After five consecutive balls dropped into their commanded pockets a shadow appeared on the green felt.

"Hey, Cisco man, *que pasa*, man?" Frankie Green Eyes said as he held out his hand to be slapped five.

Cisco didn't answer. He didn't look up. He didn't slap five. He did dunk the nine ball into a side pocket. Then Cisco stood up to reposition and to chalk the cue.

"What's hap'nin', Cisco man?" Frankie Green Eyes said, again with a voice that worked in slow motion from the barbiturates. Cisco finally looked at him evenly as he chalked the cue.

"Biff tole you before to split," Cisco said calmly.

"Fuck that old motherfucker, man," Green Eyes said. He pushed an Afro pick through his bushy hair.

"Biff is a nice man," Cisco said. "You shouldn't talk about him like that."

"He's a pain in my young ass," Frankie Green Eyes said.

"You're makin' this place hot, Green Eyes," Cisco said. "Friedman and Nelson were around looking for you. They know you're dealin' pills."

"Fuck them, too, man," Green Eyes said. "You interested in coppin' some goofballs, man?"

Cisco picked up the eight ball and flipped it up and down in his hand, feeling the weight of the ball.

"No, but you look interested in pool balls," Cisco said calmly.

Cisco heaved the ball at Green Eyes's chest with all his might. Green Eyes made a sound like a rubber raft with a puncture and collapsed onto the floor, gasping desperately for breath. Cisco walked quietly over to him. Green Eyes's mouth was wide open, sucking for air. Cisco knelt and stuck his hand into Green Eyes's coat pocket. He removed a plastic bag with about two dozen red Seconals in it. The pills were small and shaped like bullets and they had the name of the pharmaceutical house "Lilly" written on them. Cisco opened the bag and poured the pills in Green Eyes's open mouth. Then he sat Green Eyes up and slammed his back hard with his hand. The impact made Green Eyes swallow. All the little pills went down his throat.

Cisco grabbed Green Eyes by the collar and dragged him to the door. He laid him belly down on the floor with his face dangling over the top step. Then he lifted

Green Eyes's feet up in the air until he was balancing helplessly on the top of his head. His sunglasses fell onto the second step. His eyes were rolled back in their sockets like limes in the window of a slot machine. Cisco held Green Eyes's feet for a few seconds, and then with a small forward motion he cast them away, as if tossing litter in a basket. Frankie Green Eyes went down the stairs, ass over heels.

Cisco didn't watch him reach the bottom step. He walked back into the poolroom. The lamps dangling over the pool tables swung easily, their lights tagging the shadows of the poolroom. The three high-school kids stood in the back of the room, looking at Cisco in awe.

"Take a hike," Cisco said to them. "And drag the pharmacist around the corner when you go. He'll need an ambulance."

The three kids made quickly for the door and went down the stairs two at a time. Frankie Green Eyes groaned as the kids dragged him out of the vestibule.

Cisco returned to his game of pool. He sunk the eight ball that had sunk Green Eyes into a corner pocket. Biff brought over a nip of Budweiser and placed it on a ledge near Cisco's table.

"So what's new?" Biff asked.

Tommy Ryan left the car in a parking lot across the street from the dentist's office in the Williamsburg Bank Building. The Williamsburg Bank Building was his favorite structure in Brooklyn. It was the tallest building in the borough and could be seen from almost anywhere in Brooklyn. It stood thirty storeys high on the corner of Hanson Place across the street from the Brooklyn Academy of Music. At the top of its great phallic building there were huge clocks on all four sides. At night they were illuminated. It was Brooklyn's Big Ben, and the time was always right. You could see it very clearly from the House of Detention on nearby Atlantic Avenue, and for the prisoners in there the building represented the system that put them there. The Williamsburg Bank Building was the very time they were doing.

Tommy Ryan checked his watch against the time on the big clock. It was moving to dead noon. His dentist's appointment was for twelve fifteen. He went into the bank building and rode the art deco elevator to the top. In the hallway on the top floor he looked through the wire-mesh window and he could see Prospect Park to the East. It was bleached with snow and the trees were mostly bare. The monument to the Civil War looked old and foolish in the middle of Grand Army Plaza at the mouth of the park.

Prospect Park, that great five-hundred-acre emerald, was special to Tommy Ryan. It was the finest park that Frederick Law Olmsted and Calvin Vaux had ever designed. Every bit of it was so well planned—the lakes and the ponds, the rolling meadows, the crumpled hillocks, and the architecture ranging from Grecian columns to Georgian mansions and English Tudors.

Tommy Ryan could see tiny figures pulling sleds up the hills, kids escaping from the tenements which were probably colder than the park. He thought about how he had used the park when he was a kid, as a place of solace and for flight from the humiliation suffered by his parents at home. . . .

He let the thought pass. He had five minutes before the man with the white smock would stick fingers into his mouth and drill into his teeth. Tommy Ryan looked north toward St. John's University. His alma mater had produced more FBI and CIA agents than any other school in the country. Tommy Ryan chuckled to think what his old accounting professor, Mr. Whitlock, would think if he knew that his best student, the one who had made the dean's list every semester, had become a bank bandit instead of a bank president. He remembered a line Whitlock told the whole class one day that everybody thought was shocking: "If you want to succeed in banking, you have to have two thirds larceny in your heart and one third in your balls."

Tommy Ryan cupped his balls and chuckled. Old Whitlock, he sure was a pisser. Off in the distance, across the icy harbor, a Staten Island ferry eased into a slip. Tommy Ryan was horny as hell.

He checked his watch again; it was almost time for the appointment. He went down the hall and found the room marked Dr. Shipper, D.D.S. He went in. The smell of the dentist's office always bothered Tommy Ryan and his palms started to sweat. He became fidgety.

He was dying for a cigarette, but a sign asked patients not to smoke. A secretary smiled at him. She was pretty but slightly overweight. Tommy Ryan studied her lips. They were thick and moist. He thought about going up to her and saying, "Excuse me, Miss Paley, but would you mind very much getting down on your knees and sucking my prick?"

Tommy Ryan smiled at the thought of it, and Miss Paley looked up, puzzled.

"What?" Miss Paley said, a little embarrassed.

"Nothing," Tommy Ryan said, rubbing his clammy palms together. "I always laugh when I'm nervous. You know dentists, they make everybody nervous."

"I know what you mean," Miss Paley said. She was trying to be polite, but she could feel Tommy Ryan staring at her when she turned away.

Finally Dr. Shipper opened the door; it made a bell go off. The smell of the medicine circulated. Tommy

Ryan stood up quickly, startled by the bell and the odor and the doctor.

"Maybe some other time," Tommy Ryan blurted out to Miss Paley. She looked at him confused, and was about to speak when he hurried into the inner office.

"Ready for that old root canal, Tommy me boy?" Dr. Shipper said jovially. "I had a patient in here earlier today and she took her root canal like a trooper. She was only fifteen. You know, the reason so many of these things are necessary is because some dentists are so incompetent."

Tommy Ryan had always thought that Dr. Shipper's motor mouth was part of the anesthetic. He talked so much that he could put you to sleep. Even when he had his fingers in your mouth he would ask questions that required a direct answer: "How's the family?" he'd ask while drilling a molar. And he'd expect an instant reply.

Tommy Ryan sat in the chair and settled his head into the head rest. Dr. Shipper was continuing the verbal barrage. He had switched on the drill, and Tommy Ryan stared at it as the sound buzzed in his ears. He thought about the first safe he ever drilled. He was eighteen years old, and he and Tony Mauro had broken into a loft in the Ansonia Clock Factory and worked all night on a safe. When they got it open all they found were porno pictures, heavy stuff with blow jobs and ass fucking. He and Tony took turns in the bathroom whacking off to the pictures. The next day they sold the pictures for five bucks apiece at John Jay High School.

Dr. Shipper was pointing to some X rays on a light screen in front of him.

"I finally got the X rays and your dental history from your old dentist, Dr. Frankfurt," Dr. Shipper said. Tommy Ryan now tuned in. The mention of

Frankfurt's name brought back memories that Tommy Ryan hated to remember. Frankfurt was a butcher with an office on Ninth Street and Fifth Avenue in Brooklyn. He was the most inexpensive dentist in the neighborhood and all the poor mothers used to send their kids to Frankfurt even though he drilled and filled perfectly healthy teeth. He would rearrange your whole mouth all in one shebang. None of this one-or-two-teeth-a-week-for-eight-weeks shit. No, Frankfurt would just ram the ether mask over your puss and when you woke up there was enough metal in your mouth to set off an alarm at the airport. Then on the way out he'd hand you a lollipop to make sure you'd be back real soon. In fact, Frankfurt was the only dentist Tommy Ryan had ever been to who had a sign on his door that read THANK YOU, CALL AGAIN SOON.

"You wouldn't need this root canal if Frankfurt hadn't botched that tooth when you were a kid, Tommy," Dr. Shipper said. "I can't believe some of the things he did to your teeth. I have a good mind to report him. He's probably still operating the same kind of fast-food dentist shop. This guy pulled teeth the way some people pull nails. I think he should have his license lifted, to be perfectly honest."

As much as Tommy Ryan wanted to tell Shipper to shut up, he couldn't help listening to him. The guy was a hell of a dentist. He had remade Tommy Ryan's father's mouth. He serviced movie stars and politicians and mob guys. If mob guys go to a dentist he must be pretty good, Tommy Ryan thought.

"Is this guy Frankfurt still in the same place?" Tommy Ryan asked.

"Sure is," Shipper said. "There's a housing project across the street from him now. Those guys orbit poverty and make a lot of money. I wouldn't let him near the teeth of a hacksaw if I had my way."

Dr. Shipper now lifted the whirring drill and inspected it. He hung it back up. It was a temporary reprieve. Then Shipper injected Tommy Ryan's gums with a double dose of Novocain. The Novocain helped very little. Tommy Ryan clutched the arms of the chair with all his might as Shipper went to work.

A dentist is the only person alive who can hurt you and get away with it, Tommy Ryan thought to himself. You are in his hands. He has more power than you. You give him the power to tool with your mouth. He is the boss here. But nowhere else. You are the boss everywhere else but here.

This is what Hennessy the bank manager must have felt like, Tommy Ryan thought, as Shipper's little drill touched an exposed nerve. Helpless. Raped. Taken and and used and played with. Made little and petty and worthless. Begging for his boring little life. I should have made him lie on the floor and crawl around until his white shirt was the color of the soles of his shoes, Tommy Ryan thought. Hennessy, the general manager. Hennessy, the father and devoted husband. Hennessy with his body rattling inside the Brooks Brothers suit.

Shipper's drill located a nerve again and stayed with it. A white flame ignited in Tommy Ryan's head. He squirmed and clutched at the arms of the chair and might have even begged if he could have spoken.

Frankfurt had done the same thing to him when Tommy Ryan was a kid. But he had done it for greed. And now every time Shipper's drill electrified one of Tommy Ryan's nerves Frankfurt's smiling face lit up in Tommy Ryan's mind. It flashed there like neon. In color, every detail of that big swinish face. For the next twenty minutes Tommy Ryan saw so much of Frankfurt's face that he instinctively reached out with both hands for his neck. And found Dr. Shipper's throat.

Shipper wrestled away in panic.

Tommy Ryan opened his eyes. "I'm sorry, the pain . . ."

Dr. Shipper was a small man and he looked frightened. He massaged his neck.

"Calm down, Tommy," Dr. Shipper said. "I'm trying to save your tooth. I am a doctor. I don't want to hurt you purposely."

"I'm sorry, Doctor," Tommy Ryan said again.

Shipper reluctantly went back to work and finished as quickly as possible. Tommy Ryan stood up and his lips felt thicker than Miss Paley's. He paid Shipper in cash, as always, and walked into the outer office. Miss Paley looked up and smiled politely.

"Excuse me, Miss Paley," Tommy Ryan said, the words tumbling strangely from the numb mouth. "Are you doing anything tonight?"

Miss Paley tried to act surprised, but she was clearly delighted.

"As a matter of fact, no, I'm not, Tommy," she said.

"I didn't think so," Tommy Ryan said. Then he walked out of the office. Tommy Ryan, he thought. The boss.

3

The train from Rhinecliff to New York had come in an hour and a half late. Alley Boy and Frank Adler had waited in the terminal. When the train finally did arrive it was Adler who was furious. Alley Boy was still riding a wave of euphoria. Tommy Ryan had given him a man's name. He had robbed a bank. He had heart. Alley Boy was in no rush, so he didn't mind the wait. It wasn't very cold, because the sun was strong. But it was the sun that caused the delay.

"Sun started melting the snow up in the mountains," the conductor explained to an angered Frank Adler. "Caused flooding near Albany. We were delayed over an hour and a half. Can't argue with God, can you, mister?"

Frank Adler angrily handed over his discount commuter ticket. Alley Boy was laughing hysterically.

"Can't argue with God. Oh, shit, that's a pisser," Alley Boy said. "Can't argue with God." But Alley Boy's laughter came to a screeching halt when the conductor asked him for his ticket. Alley Boy didn't have a ticket.

"Oh, shit, I forgot," Alley Boy said. "I don't have a ticket."

"Then you'll have to buy one," the conductor said. "More expensive to buy the ticket on the train. I can never understand why people don't buy them beforehand."

Alley Boy reached into his pocket for his money. All that was in his pants pockets was lint. He couldn't locate his wallet. In a panic he started fumbling around in all of his clothes. His wallet was gone.

"I . . . I . . . can't seem to find my wallet," Alley Boy told the conductor.

"Well," the conductor said, "then I hope you can find your snowshoes."

Frank Adler looked at the conductor. He didn't like him. He was a wisenheimer. The conductor was smiling as he stood over the fumbling idiot he had met at the station. The conductor was enjoying the episode too much. The poor bastard probably did lose his wallet, Frank Adler thought. He obviously lost his marbles a long time ago, so it was not improbable that he had lost his wallet the same way.

"Don't worry about it, Al," Frank said. "I'll pay your ticket."

The conductor's face went sour as Frank Adler handed over the price of the ticket, which came to nine dollars and twenty-five cents. Alley Boy was relieved.

"Jesus," Alley Boy said. "Thanks, Frank. I won't forget you for this. As a matter of fact I'll give you my name and address and I'll mail you the money back." Alley Boy borrowed the pen and paper from Adler and scribbled down his name, address, and phone number. Frank Adler thought this was pretty comical. Alley Boy handed him the paper.

"Thanks, Al," Frank Adler said. "There's only one problem. Now I know your address. But how are you going to send me the money?"

Alley Boy thought for a moment and then laughed.

"Oh, yeah," Alley Boy said, "it's me who wants your address, isn't it?"

Frank Adler chuckled.

"Don't worry about it, Al," Frank Adler said. "Here, take one of my cards. You can mail the money to my home address on there."

Frank Adler put the slip of paper with Alley Boy's name and address inside his jacket pocket. He gave Alley Boy his business card. Frank Adler was beginning to like this kid named Al. He reminded him of a young Lou Costello. Sort of harmless and scatterbrained.

Adler looked up at Alley Boy's face as Alley Boy stared out of the window at the passing countryside. Cows lay cudding silage in the snow-covered fields, pine trees glistened in the bright sun, small white farmhouses with white picket fences flashed by the window as the train moved south toward New York. Frank Adler lit a cigarette and noticed something on Alley Boy's face.

"What's that white stuff on your face?" Frank Adler asked Alley Boy. Alley Boy touched his cheekbone and peeled off a gummy substance. He looked at it and rolled it between his fingers.

"Glue," Alley Boy said.

"Glue?" Frank Adler said.

"From the beard . . ." Alley Boy said and then fumbled for words. "I was playing Santa Claus and I had a fake beard."

"Santa Claus? With no money?"

"For my nephews," Alley Boy said nervously. "I won't see them on Christmas."

Adler was going to ask another question when the conductor interrupted.

"This is a nonsmoking car, friend," the conductor said. He took pleasure in having the last word in the feud.

Adler looked up and snarled at the conductor.

"Let's go get some coffee," Adler said to Alley Boy. "Down in the club car. Come on, I'll buy you a cup."

Alley Boy followed Adler through the train as it chugged noisily toward the Big Apple.

It was nearly three o'clock by the time Tommy Ryan reached Terrace Court in Brooklyn Heights. He parked the car in front of the four-storey brownstone. He opened the trunk of the car and removed the briefcase and the shotgun, which was wrapped in a copy of *The New York Times*. Tommy climbed the stone stoop to the private entrance. He put the key in the lock of the mahogany door and went into the upper duplex. The large living room had wall-to-wall burnt-orange carpeting and deep-brown suede couches. A bare brick wall was lined with thousands of books. The collected works of Hemingway, Fitzgerald, Faulkner, and Steinbeck were all on one shelf. These were the only books that were not in alphabetical order. They were from the Literary Guild book club, the editions handsome and uniform.

A mahogany grandfather clock stood in a corner and a huge illuminated parchment-colored globe stood in the window corner. On the coffee table were open-faced volumes on erotic art by the Kronhausens. Half-burnt black logs sat in the open fireplace. The large French windows led out to a sun deck that overlooked the promenade and the harbor and New Jersey. Steamers and tugs moved through the icy harbor. Below, pedestrians strolled up and down the promenade dressed warmly in winter clothes. A few fanatics were out jogging in shorts and T-shirts, their breath frosty as they puffed along.

The beach chairs on the sun deck were dripping with melting snow. Tommy yelled through the apartment, "Carol, you home?" There was no reply. Tommy moved through the dining room, where the Persian rug felt soft under his feet. He put the shotgun and the money into the compartment he had designed behind the false-front fireplace in the dining room. He locked the false fireplace back into position.

The Novocain began to wear off and his lips were coming back to life as he climbed the carpeted steps to the upstairs bedrooms.

"Carol, you here or what?"

Again there was no reply. Tommy went into the master bedroom and sat on the edge of the king-sized bed and started to undress. He took off his shoes and socks and his shirt and lay down on the bed.

She's probably still at school, Tommy thought. Or maybe visiting Tony's grave. She usually went once a week with flowers.

Tommy tried to put Tony out of his mind. Tony had been his best friend. His partner. He didn't like to think about him decaying under the earth in Greenwood Cemetery. Instead he concentrated on sex. He lay there with the shades drawn, in the dark of the room, and he pinched his nipples and thought about Miss Paley. As the images came faster and more bizarre and ridiculous, Tommy Ryan fell asleep.

And the dream was the awful one. The one where he

was a kid and he was in his room in the railroad flat lying on the small folding bed. He was staring at the tin ceiling as the headlights from the cars in the street three storeys down cast eerie broken light through the blinds.

It was the apartment on the top floor on Fourth Avenue near Fourteenth Street in Brooklyn across the street from Holy Family School. There was a pigeon coop on the rooftop that was covered in pebbles and tar. Rats nested between the ceiling and the roof—the rat holes were burrowed through the tar. You'd know when the rats were going to invade the pigeon coop because you could hear them—seven, eight, ten at a time—scurrying across the pebbles on the roof. They'd all move in on a lone bird and together they'd drag it across the pebbles to the rat hole. The bird would resist, but with ten sets of teeth dug into its soft flesh and feathers, it was helpless. Tortured screeches would come from the bird as they yanked it through the rat hole, its body dragging a hail of pebbles through the hole to dribble onto the tin ceiling. He would stare up at the ceiling and know that murder was being committed above him—inescapable murder. Once the rats had the bird between the roof and the tin ceiling there was no room for escape. The whole rat nest, and sometimes two and three nests, would converge on the scene. The long, hard, sharp toenails of the rats would scrape across the tin, and bits of chipped paint would fall on the small bed where he lay. The bird would make one final rally, a desperate grasp at freedom, and the fluttering would cease. Then came the panic of the rats fighting for the best parts of the carcass, the sounds of their mouths tearing and ripping the flesh—he imagined them with rings of blood around their pointed little mouths as they squeaked in satiated glee.

He would be up screaming for Mom, but there would

be no reply from the front room. He'd call for Dad, but there would be no answer. And he'd remember that Dad was working the night shift for the differential and his mother was up in the Pilgrim Laundry, folding laundry with a hundred other women, getting paid by the pound for the washing they did for people who had more money than they had. All through the night the rats would kill, and little Tommy would get up from his bed as the scratching continued and run into the kitchen and turn on the light. On the kitchen table the cockroaches would scatter like johns in a whorehouse busted by the vice squad. And sounds of neighbors arguing in the other flats would filter up to the top floor; and there in the kitchen, alone in the night, he'd wonder what happened to the big house on the cliff on the banks of the Hudson where the sun always seemed to shine.

He awoke in a broiling sweat. His pants were wet and he knew that he had pissed himself again. He pissed himself every time he had that dream. He pissed whenever he was frightened, and the dream was one of the few things that scared him. He jumped out of bed and stood frozen in the dark room for a moment as the warm pee rolled down his leg. And for some reason he could not immediately understand why only one word came to mind: *Frankfurt.*

4

Cisco was the first to arrive at McCaulie's. It was twenty-two degrees and the windows were clouded with frost—only silhouettes visible inside. Red neon beer-signs blinked through the frosted windows. Rock and roll blared from a jukebox. Cisco stepped inside. The saloon was crowded and smoky and warm and loud.

Bird was tending bar. Bird was a cross-eyed Polack with an infectious laugh. He laughed longer and louder than anyone Cisco had ever met. Bird could keep Cisco in stitches all night long. Sometimes Bird made side money as an audience plant at talk shows and sitcoms. He was paid to laugh at cue lines. But Bird liked bartending best. He got paid pretty good and the tips were okay and he got to laugh at the drunks all night.

When Cisco walked in, Bird was in the middle of laughing at a regular named Fabulous Murphy. Fabulous Murphy weighed two fifty and had a face like a catcher's mitt—pushed in, worn, pug-nosed—with blue eyes and a smile that resembled a seven/ten bowling spare. He had lost four teeth in a job-related injury ten years earlier.

Murphy lived up to his name. He was a first-rate Murphy artist. In places where they weren't wise to Murphy—and such places were very few now—he could sell a guy anything. Once he'd sold sixteen crates of nylons in the neighborhood to various drunks in the regular saloons. It wasn't until Murphy was long gone that the drunks realized that none of the stockings had any feet in them. Another time he sold three dozen transistor radios to guys in bars, telling them all the transistors needed was batteries. Later, when the backs were removed from the radios, the drunks found that the radios had no guts—just Gideons' bibles inside for weight.

Murphy had even sold eight-millimeter porno films to a blind newsdealer.

Murphy always kept a cigar clamped in the space where his teeth once were so no one would notice the gap. He usually spoke with the cigar in his mouth, too, and it bobbed up and down when he spoke. In front of him on the bar was a cardboard box of pornographic paraphernalia he was trying to sell. He had a stack of mimeographed price lists. Cisco picked one up and read it:

```
DILDOS   $5
FRENCH TICKLERS   $1
SPANISH FLIES   (square biz)   $20
INFLATABLE BROADS   (tight holes)   $30
AUTO SUCK   $25
FRENCH DECK OF CARDS   (ass humping
   and all)   $7
REGULAR SCUMBAGS   $3 a doz.
```

Cisco cracked up laughing. He looked over at Fabulous Murphy, who was smiling. Cisco watched as a tall muscle-bound kid purchased a dildo from Fabulous Murphy. The kid was about nineteen; he handed over the five dollars and walked to the back of the bar, where groups of teen-agers sat around tables chewing gum crazily to keep pace with the urges of the Methedrine.

A fat girl with pimples was snoozing through a feed of Seconals on a tabletop, and Cisco watched as the muscle-bound kid walked up to her. The fat girl was snoring loudly and her mouth was open. The muscle-bound kid slid the dildo into the fat girl's mouth. The fat girl reflexively adjusted her mouth around the rubber shaft as the muscle-bound kid slid the dildo in and out of her mouth.

Cisco giggled as the kid speeded up the process and the group of teen-agers began to cheer the show on. "Deep throat her," one girl yelled. The muscle-bound kid pushed the dildo further into the fat girl's mouth. The fat girl gurgled a little bit but kept sucking the rubber phallus.

Cisco turned away from the scene as Bird began goofing on Fabulous Murphy. "You know something, Fabulous?" Bird said. "You got teeth like the West. Wide open spaces." Bird went into a fit of laughter and buried his hands under his armpits and began to flap his arms like wings as the bar shook with high-pitched laughter. Fabulous laughed along with him. Cisco was slapping the bar and trying to control his convulsive laughter.

Fabulous Murphy took the goofing well. He had to. He was the quintessential coward: never in a fight he could run away from in his life. Laughing at himself kept him out of the hospital and into people's pockets.

"Gimme a Molson," Cisco said to Bird as he recaptured his breath. Bird slid a bottle of the Canadian ale to Cisco. Cisco never used a glass. In a bar a bottle was always a handier thing to have in your hand. Cisco took a long drink of the ale, leaned his back on the bar, and looked around the barroom.

Stephanie Kelly was sitting with a fiftyish drunk at one of the small tables. She was staring at Cisco when he looked her way. She made a motion with her hand toward her mouth and then pressed her tongue against the inside of her cheek to inquire whether Cisco was interested in some head. Cisco smiled and grabbed his cock and squeezed it and nodded yes. Stephanie flashed five fingers three times, indicating that it would cost Cisco fifteen bucks. Cisco nodded approval again.

Stephanie was a very pretty girl who was part Irish and part Negro. She had soft green eyes, flared nostrils, and a severe, almost vulgar mouth. She was tall and thin with a waist like a neck and boasted high, firm breasts and a round, tight ass. Cisco liked Stephanie all right, but he hated the straight jet-black wig she always wore. It made her look too much like a hooker. Actually Cisco didn't consider her a full-blown hooker. She only sucked off guys she knew, and even then she wouldn't fuck them. Strictly a cocksucker au go go. She wouldn't cop no stranger's joint. She just blew guys she knew when she needed a few extra skins. She was a good way to spend, say, a Tuesday afternoon before Biff's opened.

Under her straight wig she sported a nice medium Afro, but she claimed white guys didn't like to grab handfuls of kinky hair when they were pulling on her head and dropping their load. The wig was part of a business uniform. She didn't like it any more than the counter girls at Nathan's liked to wear those funny little hats.

Stephanie motionad toward the ladies' room, where she did business. Cisco said, "Later." Stephanie nodded.

"I got a job in a porno movie," Fabulous Murphy told Bird. Bird exploded in laughter and flapped his wings again and Cisco turned around and laughed along with Bird.

"Whadda you do in this porno, Fabulous?" Bird asked. "Whadda you do anyway? You fuck a yak or somethin'? Huh?"

"Nah," Fabulous said. "I gotta eat pussy for twenty straight minutes. None of the broads in the pitcher will blow me. All they do is let me eat them out. You know, for comic relief. Fat guy, no teeth, eats out a broad from the Sally Army. It ain't bad. Hundred balloons for it, too."

"That poor broad's twat," Bird said. "Imagine having a pussy that smells like Fabulous Murphy's breath." Bird roared laughing and flapped his wings again and crowed like a hawk. Cisco spit out a mouthful of ale, unable to control his laughter.

Laura and Connie sidled up to Cisco. Both were seventeen and wore too much makeup, but they were very pretty. Laura was short with red hair and blue eyes and small breasts. Connie had dark hair and monstrous tits and a beautiful smile.

"What time's he comin', Cisco?" Connie asked. Cisco regarded Connie momentarily, then looked at the clock. It was nine forty-five.

"Soon," Cisco said.

"But what time?" Laura insisted.

"I said soon." The two girls moved away, farther down the bar. Bird leaned over to Cisco.

"Talk about fuckin' bimbos," Bird said, laughing. "I'm thinking of installing a bimbometer over the door and if it rings when they pass through the door I'll eighty-six them."

Cisco and Bird laughed some more.

Alley Boy walked into the bar. Cisco nodded. Alley

Boy strode over to Cisco, his hands stuffed nervously into his leather coat pockets, his cheeks red with cold.

"You got any bread on you, Cisco?" Alley Boy asked. He glanced shyly around the barroom, stopping to stare longingly at Stephanie.

"How much you need?"

"Fifty," Alley Boy said.

Cisco peeled a fifty off a wad of cash and handed it to Alley Boy. Cisco noticed that Alley Boy was staring at Stephanie.

"You like that?" Cisco asked, laughing.

"Are you kidding?" Alley Boy said. "I'd kill for it."

"Never say things like that if you don't mean it, and you know you don't mean it," Cisco said.

"Well . . . I mean . . . sorry. But I'd love to have ten minutes, just ten minutes with her."

"So buy it," Cisco said.

"Buy it?" Alley Boy asked. "You mean she's . . ."

"More dicks go in and out of her than police headquarters."

"You mean just ask her how much?"

"Like you were buying cold cuts."

"Nah, you're fucking around, Cisco."

"Watch," Cisco said. Cisco motioned Stephanie over. Stephanie stood up from the table, where the drunk was now asleep with his hands lassoed around a bottle of Molson. She swaggered over to Cisco and immediately reached down and, smiling, grabbed him by the crotch. Alley Boy stood back with bulging eyes.

"I guarantee I can bring you off in less than three minutes," Stephanie said to Cisco.

Cisco was unfazed. He slugged from the bottle of Molson.

"Is that a money-back guarantee?" Cisco asked.

"Yeah," Stephanie said. "Sure. Three minutes."

"How about my friend here?" Cisco asked, pointing

with the bottle to Alley Boy. Stephanie turned and looked Alley Boy up and down and laughed.

"I already have one asshole in my pants. I don't need another one."

From behind the bar Bird went into a convulsion of laughter. Cisco held on to the bar to prevent himself from falling. Alley Boy stood there embarrassed. Cisco whispered something in Stephanie's ear. She looked back at Alley Boy. Then she turned to Cisco again.

"All right, but no money-back guarantee on him."

She turned and grabbed Alley Boy by the hand and led him toward the ladies' room. Alley Boy paused when he saw the muscle-bound kid sliding the dildo into the sleeping girl's mouth.

"Hey," Alley Boy said, "why don't you knock that off. She could be somebody's sister."

The kid shoved the dildo deeper into the girl's mouth so that it would stay there on its own.

The muscle-bound kid then stood up. There was no hair on his face but his body was overdeveloped. He was built like a weight lifter. He walked up to Alley Boy on legs that moved like goal posts.

"She your sister, motherfucker?" the big kid asked snottily.

"No," Alley Boy said, as his right knee started shaking.

"Then whadda you give a shit?" the weight lifter asked.

"Because it ain't right."

"Who says it ain't right?"

"I do."

"Maybe if you step away from that slut you're with you'd like to do something about it."

With that, Stephanie stepped away from Alley Boy and delivered a perfectly aimed foot to the weight lifter's balls. The weight lifter doubled over, clutching his crotch and moaning.

"Try lifting them in the morning, Samson," Stephanie said.

The weight lifter's friend was now on his feet. He approached Alley Boy like a sliding wall.

"Now I'm gonna kick your motherfuckin' ass, wise guy," the second weight lifter said. As he went to take off his jacket, a hand grabbed him by the ear. It was Tommy Ryan's hand. He twisted the ear around as far as he could. The weight lifter turned to see who it was. When he saw it was Tommy Ryan he went pale.

"You were saying?" Tommy Ryan said as he applied more pressure.

"I'm sorry, Tommy. This guy was—" Tommy twisted the ear more.

"You mean this *gentleman*, don't you, Harry?"

"This gentleman . . ."

"This gentleman named Al," Tommy instructed.

"This gentleman named Al . . ."

Tommy held him by the same ear he spoke into.

"This gentleman named Al," Tommy instructed further, "deserves an apology. Now let me hear you say that, Harry."

Harry repeated the sentence word for word.

"Okay, Harry," Tommy said. "Now you and that other galoot go over to that girl and take that thing out of her mouth. Then you will get down on your knees, both of you, and kiss her feet and apologize."

"How can we apologize, Tommy?" Harry asked. "She's asleep."

"You do as I say, you fuckin' punks," Tommy said.

"I'm not apologizing to nobody," said the weight lifter with the sore balls.

"Wanna bet?" Tommy said.

Cisco appeared behind Tommy with his gun bulging from his belt. Cisco laughed satanically, holding his jacket open so his gun would be seen.

"Please, Tommy," Harry pleaded. "Don't make us do that, man. Please."

"Okay, I'll tell you what," Tommy Ryan said to Harry. "I'll leave it up to Al here to decide."

Alley Boy looked at Tommy in confusion, not knowing what to do. He wondered what Tommy would do himself in the same position. He looked at the two weight lifters. Harry was terrified. The other one was also frightened, but he tried to hold a snarl on his face. Alley Boy looked at Stephanie. She shook her head no. Alley Boy saw strength in her face.

"No," Alley Boy said. "It's all right, Tommy. I just think they should stop puttin' that thing in her mouth when she's sleeping."

Tommy shrugged and let go of Harry's ear. Harry touched his sore ear gently.

"Thanks, Al," Harry said.

Alley Boy was almost embarrassed with pride.

"It's okay," Alley Boy said. "It's all right."

The other weight lifter said nothing. He was humiliated. Alley Boy walked over to him and held out his hand. The weight lifter looked at it, then at Alley Boy's face, and walked away. Alley Boy stared after him, rage mounting. Stephanie grabbed Alley Boy by the arm.

"Come on, handsome, this one's on the house."

Stephanie led Alley Boy into the ladies' room. Harry removed the dildo from the girl's mouth. When he removed it, the sleeping girl opened and closed her mouth in a chewing motion. Then she smacked her lips and shifted her head to the other side.

Tommy Ryan swaggered through the bar and the mostly teen-age crowd moved out of his way. He smiled and thought of it as the parting of the Red Sea. Laura and Connie were on either side of him, about two steps behind. Tommy approached his regular bar stool near the front end of the bar. Three teen-age boys got up from their stools to make room for Tommy Ryan and his girl friends. Cisco took the seat at the very end of the bar, at the bottom of the L, under the TV set. Bird set Tommy up with his usual—a double Bacardi and Coke with lime. Tommy handed Bird a hundred-dollar bill.

"Keep what's left at the end," Tommy Ryan said. "I'm not staying long."

Then Tommy Ryan pointed with his thumb to the jukebox. Bird acknowledged what he meant and turned the music lower. Laura put her arm through Tommy Ryan's idle arm.

"When we gonna go to Florida like you keep promisin', Tommy?" Laura asked.

"Yeah," Connie added, "you sez last week we was gonna go down Florida so we can get tanned over the Christmas vacation."

"Fort Lauderdale, you sez, Tommy—remember?" Laura said.

"School vacation for Christmas starts this weekend, Tommy, and my mother sez I could go down Florida."

Tommy was turning his head from side to side, listening to the two bims talk. You could do chin-ups on their Brooklyn accents, Tommy Ryan thought. They were annoying him. But they weren't a bad little tag team in the sack. That Connie could give Chuck Mangione tips on wind instruments.

"So when do we go, Tommy?" Connie said persistently.

Tommy leaned up very close to Connie's face and yelled as loud as he could, "You want to suck my *what*?!"

Bird stumbled to the other end of the bar folded in laughter. Connie's face blushed so red that her rouge looked pale in comparison.

"I asked you a question, bitch," Tommy Ryan said just as loud. Giggles were coming from all over the bar. Everyone was listening. Connie sat silently, feeling the hundreds of eyes focused on her.

"Come on, Tommy, huh?" Connie said as she stared at the floor. "Don't do this again in public. Please?"

Tommy Ryan grabbed Connie's wrist and twisted it a little. "I asked you what you wanted to suck, little girl," Tommy Ryan snapped.

"All right, I wanna suck your dick," Connie said.

"My *what* dick?"

"Your big beautiful dick," Connie said.

Tommy Ryan turned to Laura and said, "And what are you gonna suck while Connie sucks my big beautiful dick, Laura?"

Laura was hesitant. Her eyes darted from Tommy Ryan to the crowd. She was shaking.

"Answer me," Tommy Ryan said.

"Your ass," Laura said. "I'll be sucking your ass."

"My ass *what*, Laura?" Tommy Ryan coaxed.

"Your beautiful asshole," Laura said.

The entire crowd in the bar was giggling. Tommy Ryan looked around at the teen-age crowd and stood on a stool.

"What's so fuckin' funny?" Tommy Ryan shouted. The laughter immediately ceased. "Does anybody here think it's funny that Connie wants to suck my prick? Or that Laura wants to suck my asshole? Huh? Anyone think that's funny?"

The entire bar was silent except for the low murmur of the jukebox.

Tommy Ryan sat back down on his stool and Bird turned up the jukebox and conversations started again.

Cisco sat at the end of the bar with a wide grin. He loved it when Tommy Ryan used his clout—he knew how to do it right. He was a born leader of men. And women, Cisco thought.

Tommy turned to Connie, who was chewing gum furiously and smoking a cigarette. Her fingers were shaking and Tommy Ryan noticed it when she brought the cigarette to her mouth. Laura was more composed.

"From now on don't ask me any questions about when and where and how come we're going to whatever, you understand? You just keep your mouth shut until I tell you to open it so I can fill it up for you. If we go to Florida, we do. If we don't, we don't. I make those decisions, you understand?"

Connie shook her head, indicating that she understood.

"And you shouldn't smoke," Tommy Ryan said. "It's bad for you, stunts your growth."

Tommy Ryan gave Connie a kiss. And he put an arm around Laura's shoulder.

"Tommy, I don't know if you know how embarrassing it is for you to—you know, let everybody know what we do with—like you know—what we—you—you know, in bed, like."

Tommy Ryan asked Bird for a pencil and paper. Bird obliged. Tommy Ryan put the pencil and paper in front of Laura.

"I want to you write that sentence you just said word for word on this piece of paper, Laura. I want all the 'like you knows' in there, too. Then I want you to diagram that sentence and tell me what the verb is, what the subject is, and what the object is. That ought to keep you busy until school starts again. Never mind Florida."

Alley Boy walked over with Stephanie. Tommy looked at him and said, "Everything come out all right?" Alley

Boy was too embarrassed to answer. Tommy laughed and slugged his rum and Coke down in one gulp and asked Alley Boy again.

"Everything come out all right?" Bird refilled Tommy Ryan's glass.

"You should ask *me* that," Stephanie said. "Yeah, it did. Pure protein, five loads. All right? If you're interested in how it comes out why don't you go down on him yourself?"

Tommy Ryan turned and smacked Stephanie hard across the face. Stephanie spun. Then she smiled. Alley Boy made a lunge for Tommy Ryan, but Stephanie stopped him. She thought Tommy Ryan would kill him.

"It's all right, Al," Stephanie said. "I'm used to guys who like to hurt people. Only I usually get paid."

Tommy Ryan smiled. He peeled off a fifty-dollar bill from a roll of bills and put it down Stephanie's nylon blouse.

"We're even," Stephanie said and walked away.

Tommy Ryan turned to Laura and Connie.

"You two, wait out in the car." The two girls got up from their bar stools, put on their coats, and walked, asses wagging, outside. Cisco sat drinking Molson ale quietly. Tommy Ryan put his hand on Alley Boy's shoulder.

"Come 'ere, *Alley Boy*," Tommy Ryan said, putting emphasis on the last two words.

"*Al*, Tommy," Alley Boy said. "You said you'd call me Al."

"Yeah," Tommy Ryan said, "but that was when I thought you were gonna act like a man. Instead you turn on me twice in one day. Over a hooker you were gonna go for me? Let me tell you something, Alley Boy. I'll start calling you Al when you start acting like a man. Back there, you should have made those two germs crawl on the floor. Then you'd have their respect."

"But Tommy," Alley Boy replied, "you know, it was too much. I think they're sorry for doing what they were doing. You know, I think they learned their lesson."

"Who cares?" Tommy Ryan said. "You think I gave a fuck about that fat broad? I wouldn't care if they were shoving a pogo stick up her ass. It's the fuckin' respect you get from mutts like them two muscle-bound morons that measures your worth. That kid could probably tear me in half, but you think he'd try? Not on your life. But if I hadn't shown up he would've busted up your face so bad you wouldn't know which end of you to shave. Think about that, Alley Boy, and if you understand it by tomorrow, then maybe you'll be Al again."

"I'm sorry, Tommy," Alley Boy said, confused. He thought he had done the right thing. But Tommy was probably right again, thought Alley Boy. As usual. Shit.

"Look, I'll see you guys at the warehouse tomorrow," Tommy Ryan said. "And think about what I said, Alley Boy."

Tommy Ryan smacked Cisco five and stepped outside. Alley Boy watched him leave. Alley Boy was disgusted with himself. He thought about going back and making the weight lifters crawl. Cisco saw him staring at them with fury.

"Don't try it now, man," Cisco said. "Too late. Next time." Alley Boy leaned against the cigarette machine and stared at Stephanie. She was trying to wake up the old drunk at the table. Alley Boy was so confused that for the first time in his life he thought he was finally ready to kill. Then he looked over at Cisco and saw how calmly he sat at the bar. Alley Boy knew that a real killer never showed his anger.

Outside McCaulie's the street was icy. The wind whistled down Sixteenth Street toward Prospect Park. Tommy Ryan was amusing himself by watching Laura and Connie fight over who would sit next to him in the front seat.

"Fuck you, bitch," Laura said to Connie. "You sat next to him last time."

"So what, he asked me to," Connie said.

Tommy Ryan was chuckling when the familiar voice came from behind him. Tommy Ryan turned with a start.

"How you doin', Tommy?" the voice said.

It was Ankles, the detective. Tommy Ryan studied Ankles before he answered. He was a giant of a guy, with broad, sloping shoulders. His feet were easily size fourteens. He had a real wopola face, Tommy Ryan thought. His nose was bigger than some people's dicks and his skin was as olive as an olive. He had silver-black hair and wore a fedora, which made his ears stick out. And his hands were enormous, like a rack of prime ribs.

"Hello Ankles," Tommy Ryan said. "Boy, are you one *uhhhhhhh*glee motherfucker."

Ankles just smiled.

"How long you been out, Tommy?" Ankles asked. "Parole board never informed me."

"Three weeks, Ankles," Tommy Ryan said. "They knew that with me on the inside you'd have nothing to do but make firecracker busts. Or is it still popping guys with nickel bags of grass, Ankles?"

"Let's see," Ankles said, cocking his head in a calculative angle. "That means you only did five months out of a year. Not too bad. Your manhood still intact, or did you surrender it to some nine-foot Black Muslim with a horse's dick?"

"Nah," Tommy Ryan said, "I know you want my ass more than anyone alive, Ankles. So I'm saving it for you. Unless you thought that penny-ante five months for punching you in the puss was tantamount to nailing me, Ankles."

"Such big words for such a little punk," Ankles said. "You're readin' too much of that William Buckley, you ask me."

"Well, you know me, Ankles, I kinda take pride in my education," Tommy Ryan said. "You're the only cop I know who spells his own name wrong on arrest forms." Tommy Ryan laughed and thought about how Ankles got his nickname. He used to patrol the parkside as a uniformed beat cop, and whenever he caught anybody under age drinking beer, he used to stand him against a tree and kick with all his might at the kid's ankles with his size fourteens.

"We'll see what these spell for you, Tommy," Ankles said as he handed Tommy Ryan a package of snapshots. Tommy Ryan opened the envelope and took out the pictures. The first showed his best friend, Tony Mauro, lying on the floor of the front seat of his Lincoln Continental with his throat cut. A pack of Vantage cigarettes floated in the blood on the floor. Tommy Ryan showed no outward emotion. Ankles frowned disgustedly.

"Keep going," Ankles said. "They get better as you go along. Look at the close-up of the throat, Tommy. Hell of a nice slash. About four inches deep. You can see the severed tendons and all, Tommy. Good shots. Maybe you'd like one blown up into a poster, eh?"

"Shut up, you ugly prick," Tommy Ryan said.

"Somebody iced your best buddy while you were in

the joint gettin' bungholed, Tommy," Ankles said. "Too bad. Tony and you were so close, Tommy. Partners. Blood brothers, palsie walsies, right, Tommy?"

Ankles snarled as Tommy Ryan turned the other way. Laura and Connie were still arguing over the front seat.

"If you were such a palsie walsie, Ryan, why didn't you do something about it? Scared? Mob guys? Guys with white shoes, Tommy?"

"I'll find out, Ankles. My way. I don't need you."

"Let me tell you something, Tommy," Ankles said. "I've known you a long time. You're smart—big words, big mouth, big money. Now, I only care about one thing—I want Tony Mauro's killer. I'm not interested in nothin' else, get it? Just Mauro. And if I find out you're holding out on Mauro's murder, I'll nail you so fuckin' hard you'll think Jesus H. Christ got off easy."

Tommy regained a shield of posture.

"Jesus didn't have a middle initial," Tommy Ryan said. "Now why don't you go eat your ugly pills?"

Ankles pointed a long thick finger.

"Remember, Tommy, I fuckin' warned you. Remember."

Ankles walked back to the Plymouth Fury and got in. The car looked like a toy with him in it. Tommy Ryan watched him pull away from the curb. He could still hear Laura and Connie bitching in the background. He walked over to his Cadillac Seville and got in. Concern registered in his eyes.

"Tommy, she sat in the front the last time," Laura protested.

"You're just jealous because your tits are smaller than cupcakes," Connie said.

"Yeah, rather have 'em like that than like water balloons."

"Fuckin' bitch."

"Both of you get in the back," Tommy Ryan said. "You sound like a pair of magpies. I only have one dick. You'll have to share it."

The two girls fell silent and got into the backseat. Tommy Ryan sat with the motor running for a full minute thinking about Ankles and Tony. He tried to get the image of Tony with his throat cut out of his mind. But it was stamped there. Finally he pulled away from the curb. As he drove slowly past McCaulie's he saw Cisco watching through a hand-cleared patch in the frosted window. Cisco raised his bottle in farewell. Tommy nodded.

Tommy now sped the Cadillac along the Prospect Expressway. He put a cassette into the tape deck and the Rolling Stones' "Brown Sugar" blared from the speakers. The music eventually helped put the picture of Tony Mauro out of Tommy's mind.

Tommy opened the glove compartment and grabbed two black blindfolds. He passed them to the girls in the backseat.

"Come on, Tommy, not again," Laura said with a whine in her voice.

"I ain't wearin' that no more," Connie protested.

"Put them on or get out," Tommy said.

"But why, Tommy?" Laura asked.

"For your own good," Tommy said.

"I feel so ridiculous wearing that thing," Connie said.

"You can take them off when you're there," Tommy said.

The girls grudgingly donned the blindfolds and sat in the backseat. Tommy glanced at them in the rearview mirror and laughed. They really did look ridiculous. He turned on to the Belt Parkway and headed toward Bay Ridge. At the Sixty-fifth Street exit he rolled off the highway. At the corner he made a U-turn and got on the highway going in the opposite direction, east this time instead of west. He checked his rearview mirror regularly to be sure no one was following. Ankles had put caution into him.

He left the highway again at Thirty-sixth Street. When he stopped for a red light at the corner of Fourth Avenue he could see Greenwood Cemetery, a gaping black hole in the night, in front of him. He shuddered to think that Tony was lying somewhere in there, six feet underground, in a wooden box. The insects were probably marching through his body into the neck wound and eating him from the inside out, Tommy thought. The meat on the inside is more tender and easier for the insects to gnaw on. The driver in the car behind him honked his horn to signal that the light had turned green. Tommy looked in the rearview mirror and saw that it was a yellow taxicab. He took a last look at the bone yard and made a left turn.

The cab turned left and followed him closely along Fourth Avenue. Tommy's heart was pumping. He wondered if there were moonlighting cops in the taxi. He worried about the girls with the blindfolds in the backseat. It might look like a kidnapping, he thought.

"Lay down on the floor," Tommy said to the two girls.

The two girls ducked down low. Tommy continued to watch the taxi through the rearview mirror. But then the cab made a right turn onto Thirty-seventh Street. Tommy was relieved. At Thirty-sixth Street he made a left toward the harbor. In front of him lay Bush Terminal, a massive network of waterfront factory buildings, docks, and warehouses. Tommy rolled slowly under the elevated highway he had just exited. A few Puerto Ricans were sitting on milk boxes under the el drinking half-quarts of beer wrapped in brown paper bags. They warmed themselves with a wood fire burning in a metal oil drum. Orange sparks spat into the night. Tommy Ryan guessed that it was probably warmer out here in the street by the roaring fire than it was in the tenements where the junkies had long ago boosted the brass heat pipes.

He passed the Puerto Ricans and drove through the main gates of Bush Terminal. Except for one round-the-clock textile plant a hundred yards to the left, the terminal was closed for the night.

Tommy pulled up in front of a one-storey warehouse with a rolled-down accordian gate. He produced a Sony remote-control device from the glove compartment. He pushed a button and with an electronic whine the metal gate rolled open. Muffled sounds came from the machines in the textile plant across the terminal—familiar endless sighs of pistons. Water lapped weakly against the dock twenty yards from the warehouse.

Tommy Ryan looked out at the Statue of Liberty standing out against the inky blackness of the bay. A steamer slid silently past her, a half-dozen twinkling lights glowing near the hull.

"Christ almighty, it really stinks here, Tommy," Laura said. The gate was raised open now and Tommy Ryan eased the Cadillac into the warehouse garage. He activated the remote-control device again and the gate closed.

Tommy Ryan walked over to a stack of coffee-bean sacks and reached behind them to push a button. A cinder-block wall slid open, revealing a hidden annex. Tommy Ryan thought of this setup as a modern version of Ali Baba's cave. Boxes of coins filled to the top. Crates of television sets, stereos, air conditioners, and Nikon cameras piled to the ceiling. A trunk of jewelry sat in the center of the floor, its lid open, baring the glittering swag.

Tommy Ryan activated another button inside the annex and the sliding wall closed. He told the girls they

could remove their blindfolds. He thought about Carol;
he wished he had stayed and waited for her. But to hell
with it, her life right now was one long wake. Always
moaning on about Tony. A man needs sex, has to have
his pipes cleaned. Especially after a bit in the joint,
when you caught yourself looking at the boys' asses . . .

"Where you get alla this stuff?" Connie asked.

"People give at the office," Tommy said.

"I'll bet," Laura said.

Tommy said, "Don't ask questions."

He led them through another door. The inside room
was bathed in red light. There was a fifteen-foot bar,
a jukebox, couches, and a king-size brass bed. Connie
and Laura ran to the jukebox and started pushing
buttons. Rod Stewart came on the jukebox singing
"Hot Legs." The two girls started dancing erotically.
Tommy Ryan watched as he stood behind the bar mixing drinks. He made three rum and Cokes and then
took out a mayonnaise jar filled with cocaine. He
spooned some of the cocaine onto a mirror and chopped
it up finely with a single-edged razor blade. He separated the coke into six plump, even lines and rolled a
hundred-dollar bill up tightly into a cylinder. Connie
and Laura danced their way to the bar and snorted a
line of coke into each nostril. Tommy Ryan snorted the
remaining two lines.

"Be right back," Tommy Ryan said.

He walked back into the swag room and chose two
heavy gold chains from the jewelry trunk. Each chain
had a heart-shaped medallion on it. He looked around
the swag room, inhaled deeply, and smiled.

When he returned to the party room, the Rolling
Stones were singing "Let It Bleed" and Connie and
Laura were naked, dancing with each other in time to
the music. Connie's tits heaved up and down, her body
bathed in red light. Laura was dancing in a crouch, her

face near Connie's crotch. Tommy Ryan walked over to Connie and hooked one of the chains around her neck. She immediately put her arms around his neck, pushing her breasts against his chest, and slid her tongue into his mouth. Tommy's mouth was dry from the cocaine, but Connie's tongue was wet and tasted of rum and Coke. Tommy nudged her away and put the other chain around Laura's neck. He slid his hand down to Laura's ass and placed his middle finger into the crevice and then edged her away from him.

He walked back to the bar and began mixing himself another drink when Connie came up from behind him, kneeled on the floor, and undid his belt and the snap of his pants. She moved her hands inside his jeans, forcing the zipper open to massage his stiffening penis. Now she pulled his pants down around his ankles and began to kiss him on the ass, darting her tongue up and into him. Laura came around the front of him and kneeled and clutched his penis with the thumb and forefinger of both hands and moved her mouth onto his shaft.

"You have it backwards," Tommy said. The two girls switched positions and resumed their activity. Tommy looked at the ceiling and sipped his rum and Coke.

"Who's the boss?" Tommy said.

Both girls freed their mouths of their business long enough to say, "You are, Tommy."

Tommy Ryan smiled and sipped his drink.

5

Alley Boy left McCaulie's at three thirty in the morning. Cisco watched him leave. Cisco rarely moved from his window seat. Looking out the window was Cisco's idea of reading the paper. He got all the news he needed clocking people walking by McCaulie's window.

He watched Alley Boy stagger a little as he hit the cold air.

Alley Boy looked both ways along Tenth Avenue for a taxi, but there were none in sight.

"Need a ride, D'Agastino?"

Alley Boy was startled by the voice. Ankles sat in the front seat of the Plymouth Fury looking at him. Alley Boy knew by the car that Ankles was a cop. But he didn't know him.

"No thanks," Alley Boy said.

"You know who I am?" Ankles asked.

"You're a cop, right?"

"Gold star for you, D'Agastino."

"How you know my name?" Alley Boy asked.

"Knew your old man," Ankles said. "I used to drink with him up at Farrell's. Too bad what happened to him. He was a good iron worker, Al D'Agastino was. Good softball player, too. But accidents happen to anybody. Always thought your mother deserved the insurance. She ever get it?"

"No, she didn't," Alley Boy said. "They said he was drunk. The autopsy said there was alcohol in his system when he fell off the building site. The insurance don't cover that."

"Too bad," Ankles said. "Things must be rough home. You oughta go to work."

"How do you know I'm outta work?"

"I know a lot of things about you," Ankles said. "I know you hang around with mutts like Tommy Ryan."

"Tommy Ryan isn't a mutt. He's a—" Alley Boy held his words.

"A what?" Ankles laughed.

"He's a . . ." Alley Boy said. "He has a heart."

Ankles roared with laughter and opened the car door and got out of the Plymouth Fury. Alley Boy had to stare up to look Ankles in the eye. Ankles put his hands in his pockets and leaned back on his heels. Cisco watched through the window.

"Tommy Ryan is a slimy little punk who couldn't have sniffed your old man's socks," Ankles said.

"Leave my old man outta this," Alley Boy said.

"Look, why don't you let me give you a ride home?" Ankles said more gently. Alley Boy sensed that Ankles was softening and he interpreted this as weakness. He tried to think what Tommy might say to Ankles in the same situation. He chose the words, but he had difficulty getting them out because they weren't his.

"Fuck off, pig," Alley Boy said, jutting his face within inches of Ankles's. Cisco was still inside the bar, watching. His face was expressionless.

Ankles snarled at Alley Boy and in one motion grabbed him by the lapels with the huge hands and yanked him around the corner, out of Cisco's view, and slammed him against the stone wall. Alley Boy was big, but he looked very small next to Ankles. Ankles hoisted his leg back and kicked with all his might at Alley Boy's right ankle. Then he repeated the process with his size-fourteen thick-soled cop shoe to the left ankle. Alley Boy collapsed in pain.

Ankles laughed and lit the end of a big cigar with a Bic disposable lighter. The smoke scattered in the wind.

"Whadda you know about a guy named Tony Mauro?" Ankles asked, as he looked at the end of his cigar. Alley Boy didn't answer. Ankles kicked him in the shin of the right leg. Alley Boy grunted in pain.

"All I know is that he's dead," Alley Boy said, "I don't know nothing about it."

"Tommy Ryan ever talk about him?" Ankles asked.

"No," Alley Boy said.

Alley Boy's adrenaline was pumping. His ankles and his right shin were pounding in pain.

"I'll be seeing you, D'Agastino," Ankles said. "You should've took the ride home."

Ankles walked back around the corner toward his car. He stopped and looked at Cisco staring at him through the cleared patch in the frosted window of the saloon. Ankles walked up to the window and stared dead-eyed at Cisco through the small clearing. Cisco moved closer to the window. Their faces were separated by only a few inches on either side of the glass. Cisco smiled and then breathed heavily on the clear patch.

His breath caused the patch to frost again and Ankles's face became shrouded and then invisible.

Tommy climbed the steps to the apartment and opened the door. When he entered his living room, a few sparks still crackled in the fireplace of the otherwise darkened room. He looked at his watch, pressed the button, and the digital response was 5:30. Through the French glass doors Tommy looked out over the harbor to New Jersey. There was a sliver of dawn on the horizon. He moved clumsily through the darkened dining room and climbed the stairs to the bedroom. He could hear Carol breathing heavily in the bed.

Tommy snapped on the small night-light next to the bed. Carol awoke without Tommy noticing. She looked at him without speaking as he undressed. He stood in his shorts with his back to her.

"Not satisfied with one bimbo," Carol said. "You need two."

Tommy turned, startled.

"Whadda you talkin' about . . . ?"

"Quit the bullshit, Tommy," Carol said. "There's two different-colored lipsticks on your drawers. One's purple, one's orange."

Tommy tried ignoring the accusation. He reached into his pants pocket and took out a diamond necklace. He handed it to Carol; she studied it momentarily and then threw it across the room. Tommy watched it hop across the shag rug.

"What are you doing?" Tommy said. "That's worth five grand."

"That should buy you a month of bimbos," Carol said.

Tommy could think of nothing to say. Carol was the only person he knew who could leave him speechless.

He looked at her as if expecting to find the words written on her face. He wished he had idiot cards when he spoke to her, because he frequently felt like an idiot in these situations.

She stared straight back at him, un-blinkingly. She had large, wet brown eyes, long brunet hair, and a full mouth that looked as much like a weapon as an instrument of seduction. Her face was at its prime—beautiful, Roman, almost perfectly structured.

But the face was also rugged, as if supported by steel. When she stared at you the way she was now, you were glad she wasn't on a jury.

The bitch is crazy, Tommy thought. There's no winning. You cannot win an argument with her. You say something to get back, and she turns it around so fast you want to punch her teeth down her throat.

He thought: Why do you love this broad? You can have anyone you want. You are the boss. But Carol was different. If you tried to boss her, she walked out on you. Told you to take a scram. She picked up the two-year-old boy and split. And you want her here. You always have. Especially when you knew she was sleeping next to Tony. You wanted her the most then.

And now you have her. Or you almost do. And the kid, too—Tony's kid, the kid whose face is a clone of his old man's. He calls you Daddy, but every time he stares at you, you see Tony staring at you. And it eats at you. But you have him now, and you have her. And you ain't letting go. You'll be the boss. Patience . . .

He still couldn't think of anything to say to her.

"Did you tell them you piss in bed?" Carol said. "Did you tell those two little whores that? Huh? Or that you wake up in the middle of the night calling for your mommy? Huh?"

Rage mounted in Tommy Ryan. His fists clenched.

You should fuck up her face so bad that no one will ever have her, he thought. If you can't, nobody will. Break her nose so bad it looks like a roller coaster. Chew off her ear. Shave her head.

"All right," Tommy said with a heavy exhale. "So I was with a coupla bims. I just went five months without any sex. Night, noon, and breakfast I thought about you. I'm so horny I feel like I'm gonna blow to pieces. And I come home and you're handcuffed to a ghost. Visiting a graveyard. He's gone, Carol. Dead."

"Whoever killed him isn't."

Tommy ran his fingers through his hair.

"You know, you should see a shrink," Tommy said. "Going to a graveyard every day isn't gonna bring him back."

Carol smacked Tommy across the face. No one does that to you, he thought. He made a move for her. She didn't cower. She stood there facing him. He let the tension drain out of him and collapsed on the edge of the bed.

"The bimbos didn't mean anything," he said. "Slam, bam, thank you ma'am. Nothing else. I used them to jerk off with."

"I deserve better," Carol said. "Tony always said if anything happened to him he wanted you to raise Michael. He asked that I go to you. He called you family. Okay, and when you were in the joint I visited you every day after he got it. I made like your secretary and called your parents and told them you'd be outta town a few months on business. I made sure they received their weekly allowance from you. I sent the checks to the banks for the mortgage on their quarter-of-a-million-dollar house. I cook for you. I wash for you. I make love to you when I can get Tony off my mind. I even polish your goddamned shotgun. What the hell more do you want?"

"I want you to love me, Carol," Tommy said, without looking at her.

Carol didn't answer. Finally she put her arm around his neck and drew him to her. She kissed him long and hard and deep. Then she nudged him away gently.

"I'll try, Tommy," she said. "Now go in and wash them two dollar whores off your body and come to bed."

Ankles stood over the bed chewing on the unlit end of a cigar. He looked down at the Puerto Rican in the bed. The room smelled like the fatbins he used to have to clean as a butcher's helper when he was a kid. Intensive care. The sound of the words made him shudder.

Rubber tubing ran into the nose, mouth, and both arms of Frankie Green Eyes. Even in a coma the Puerto Rican had a snarl on his face, Ankles thought. Lowlife. All I ever meet in this racket is lowlifes. I'd like to give whoever did in this lowlife a medal, but it was probably only another lowlife. All fucking lowlifes. Lower than whale shit.

A Pakistani doctor with nutmeg-colored skin walked into the room. His chalk-white shoes squeaked as he walked, taking short straight steps on little feet. The doctor approached the bed and lifted Frankie Green Eyes's wrist to find a pulse.

The sawbones's got hands like a woman, Ankles thought. Small with thin bony fingers. He'd have to wrap Band-Aids on the back of his school ring to make it fit the thumb. Those nails—manicured and clean as a nun's.

The doctor pressed his small thumb against a blue vein on the Puerto Rican's wrist. He drew back the sleeve of his other arm with a flourish to check his watch against the pulse. But it was a digital watch that required manual operation. The doctor appeared very embarrassed when he had to ask Ankles to press the small button on the side of the watch.

"The price of success," Ankles said flatly.

The doctor smiled politely. He didn't understand what the cop meant. He saw how enormous Ankles's hands were, and the size frightened him when Ankles pressed the tiny button on the watch.

"The nurse usually does it," the doctor said softly.

The doctor timed the pulse as Ankles held in the button on the watch and beamed down at the frail doctor.

"How is the mutt?" Ankles asked.

"Mutt? No, his name is Sanchez. Francisco Sanchez."

Ankles laughed and removed the unlit cigar from his mouth. He was starting to like the doctor's naiveté. It was like talking to a kid. Yet he could probably take you apart and put you back together with a small knife and a needle and thread.

"How is he?"

"He's improving," the doctor said.

"When will he be able to talk?"

"Maybe a week. He talks in his sleep all the time. It is a good sign. He's trying to break through his sub-conscious. He keeps talking about someone, some man . . . I don't remember. The head nurse, Crowley, she knows. She spent the whole day with him. I don't know."

"Tony Mauro," Ankles said, "is that the name?"

The Pakistani doctor shrugged his shoulders and smiled in ignorance. "The head nurse . . ."

"Crowley, she would know, right? Gotcha the first time."

"I'm not good with these names," the doctor explained. "All I know is that he has two broken breastbones, a fractured ankle, a bad concussion, and was suffering from barbiturate overdose. We had to pump his stomach."

Ankles cut the doctor off with a raise of his flat palms. They were almost as big as tennis racquets.

"I don't wish anything on him Helen Keller never had," Ankles said.

"Helen who?"

"Just some eyewitness I had once."

"I'm not too good with the names," the doctor said and then started making notations on the yellow paper clasped to the metal clipboard hanging from the foot of the bed.

Ankles walked out of the intensive care unit of the Methodist Hospital. The hospital took up a square block of Park Slope. Many people in the neighborhood referred to it as the Meth Sadist. It didn't enjoy great popularity among the ERRs—emergency room regulars. The ERRs were the ones who'd check themselves into the hospital every weekend before all the beds were taken up by the Saturday-night casualties from the saloon wars.

Ankles knew a few of them, mostly nut jobs, but they knew more about health care than most of the sawbones. They were connoisseurs of everything from the food to rectal thermometers. Ankles never knew one who liked the Methodist. The cops hated this wound warehouse, too, because the administration demanded cash up front or some kind of medical insurance before they'd treat a patient. You could walk in there with a spear in your neck and they'd ask you if you had the Blue Cross. If the prisoner didn't, they'd have to take him to Kings County in East Flatbush, which was like a field hospital on a war front.

So Ankles was naturally curious to know who had paid for Green Eyes when they wheeled him in. As far as he knew, the neighborhood pill pushers hadn't yet gotten together a group medical plan.

He called down to administration and got a clerk on the phone and identified himself. The clerk explained that Mr. Sanchez had $880 on him when he was brought in, so they accepted him.

That ruled out robbery, Ankles thought. He hung up without saying thanks. He walked down to the solarium at the end of the hall to light his cigar. His big shoes smacked on the polished cracked tile. Ankles was always conscious of how big his feet were. Especially in front of women. He was conscious of how big everything was in front of women—his nose, ears, head, hands, mouth, waist. It's too late now anyway. There probably would never be another woman.

His feet kept smacking off the tile. He tried walking on his tiptoes. He didn't want to be accused of sending some old bastard into coronary arrest because of his big feet making too much noise. That bastard Tommy Ryan had once told him that if he got shot standing up he wouldn't fall down because his feet were more like stands than feet. That little bastard . . .

Ankles walked into the solarium and saw that three old men in green hospital bathrobes had taken the only seats. Friedman and Nelson, the two narcos, were standing by a barred window. Ankles had worked with Friedman and Nelson when all three were beat cops in the Seventy-second Precinct.

Now they were in a borough-wide narcotics unit. And he was working homicide.

Friedman was a short Jew with a very handsome face and a stocky frame. He didn't look like a cop. He looked more like a wise guy. He even wore a pinkie ring like all the wise guys. He dressed a little too well, and the broads went for him a little too fast. Ankles always thought Friedman was a backhander, taking C-notes from pushers. But he wasn't sure; he couldn't prove it. He really didn't give much of a shit.

Nelson was a tall blonde with thin little sideburns and a bubblegum-colored pockmarked face. He wore the kind of dentures that looked like dentures. When Nelson talked, the dentures always clacked together like castanets. It was one of those noises that Ankles loathed, like young girls snapping chewing gum. He remembered asking Nelson once if he picked up the choppers at a sale in Woolworth's. Nelson told him that he got them from a dentist in the Bronx. That was like mailing away for them through the *National Enquirer*.

But Ankles liked Nelson all right; he just didn't like looking at him. He had "cop" billboarded all over him. Ankles didn't like being reminded that he shared the same profession with him. Nelson reminded him of a grave robber.

The three cops exchanged greetings. Nelson called Ankles by his last name, Tufano. Few people called him that. He preferred Ankles. There was a warning built into that name.

"Where'd they find him?" Ankles asked Nelson.

"Front of Biff's," Nelson said.

Ankles looked through the barred window and over the rooftops toward Prospect Park. Dawn was sneaking over the trees. Ankles wondered about the bars on the window. Probably there to keep those informed of malignancies from doing swan dives onto Seventh Avenue.

"Biff's?"

"Yeah," Nelson said, "the poolroom on Fifth Avenue. Green Eyes had enough goofballs in him to OD Godzilla."

"The fuckin' poolroom," Ankles said. "People still hang around poolrooms? Adults? I thought just high-school kids majoring in hand jobs hung around pool-rooms."

"Yeah," Friedman said. "But someone's gotta sell them the pills. Willie the Spic, Green Eyes, Cisco—you know them. Mostly just Puerto Ricans."

"Cisco?" Ankles said. "You mean Cisco Diaz? Tommy Ryan's friend?"

Nelson said, "Yeah, but he don't deal dope. Ain't his bag."

"I know," Ankles said. "He's a surgeon. He'd cut off your fuckin' balls just to hear you sing soprano."

"Anyway," Nelson said, "we tossed Green Eyes's pad. Found more pills than Jimmy Carter has teeth. And we found this, too."

Nelson handed Ankles a manila envelope. Ankles opened it. Inside was a plastic baggie. Ankles removed it and stared at the straight razor inside the bag.

"You send it to the lab yet?"

"No," Friedman said, "thought you might want to check it out with forensic. It might be the one used on Tony Mauro. Green Eyes kept talking about Mauro in his sleep. He keeps saying, 'I know him, Mauro. I know, I know. . . .' I don't know what the fuck else he knows. If anything. Could be he'll be playing craps with baby blocks after he wakes up."

"We thought you might want to handle it, Anthony," Nelson said and then pushed his upper plate against his gum. "Mauro is your ticket, so we thought we'd give it to you."

"Thanks," Ankles said. He hated the name Anthony.

Ankles still couldn't bring himself to look Nelson in the eye. His face had more potholes than the West Side Highway. He stared out the window toward the park again. He remembered the night a long time ago he had spent with Marsha, fucking like mad in the dark in a rowboat on Swan Lake. But Marsha was married and the affair ended there.

Outside the snow-covered trees glistened in the dawn. The day was overcast in contrast to the sun of the day before. The slush would soon freeze. It was December sixteenth. Mauro was dead two months. Under ordinary circumstances Ankles wouldn't have become so involved. But Tony Mauro was special. Finding out who had killed Mauro meant more to Ankles than police work. It was more like housework. And Tommy Ryan was shit on the living-room rug. And now this Puerto Rican, this Frankie fucking Green Eyes and his straight razor, they were dirty dishes. But it was five thirty A.M. and Ankles needed sleep.

Alley Boy tried to be quiet going into the apartment, but he was drunk and clumsy. After being decked by Ankles he had gone back into McCaulie's and drunk tequila until five o'clock to kill the pain. Bird locked the doors at four but still served drinks until about five when he finished all his laughing.

Alley Boy knocked over the broom when he pushed open the front door and he knew that would wake his grandmother. She slept like a cat. She had hearing like a cat. She even had whiskers like a cat's growing out of a few facial moles. And if lives were measured in decades, at eighty-nine she was working on her ninth.

"Eh, Alley Boy, that's you?" the grandmother shouted from the dark cave that was her bedroom in the railroad flat on the top floor of the tenement on Seventh Avenue. Alley Boy made for the refrigerator. His ankles were aching badly with bone bruises. He groped in the dark. When he opened it, the refrigerator

supplied some light and the sound of the motor grew
louder.

"Yeah, Gramma, it's me," Alley Boy said, wolfing
down a cold meatball. The grandmother hobbled out
into the kitchen dressed in a wrinkled black dress. She
had been dressing in black since Salvator, her husband,
got it in Caporetto. She had been carrying Alley Boy's
father at the time. She groped in the dark above her
until she located the light string. She pulled it and
fluorescent light blinked on. Her face had more
wrinkles than a human brain and her short-cropped
hair was shockingly white.

"Why don't you go back to sleep, Gramma?" Alley
Boy said, wiping tomato sauce off his mouth with his
wrist. "It's late."

The grandmother asked him what time it was.

"Twenty to six."

"Then it's early, not late," the grandmother said.
"Sit down over there; I'll make you eggs."

"Ma all right?" Alley Boy asked.

"I'm fine, Alley Boy," came a voice from a darkened
room beyond. "Where you've been? Gone all day, all
night. I couldn't sleep. I don't count sheep no more. I
count car crashes and it keeps me awake."

The mother entered the kitchen tying a pink poly-
ester bathrobe around her. Her dyed orange hair was
in curlers and she looked tired.

"I was working, Ma," Alley Boy said.

"Working where? On a boat to China that you're
gone so long? Working doin' what? With who? How
much? You got paid?"

"Don't ask me so many questions at once, Ma," Alley
Boy said. "I worked. Made a lot of money. Then I made
more playing cards. I wanna move us out of this dump."

"Don't you never call my home a dump," the grandmother snapped in the middle of beating eggs. "Your father was born here and I live here over forty years, so it's not a dump. It's where we live."

"Sorry, Gramma," Alley Boy said. "I didn't mean it that way. I mean the neighborhood. The neighborhood's a dump."

"My friends live here in this neighborhood," the grandmother said. The smell of green peppers frying in olive oil spread through the apartment, followed by the sound of beaten eggs scalding onto the hot pan.

Alley Boy sat at the table. The tequila made his brain feel like a submerged sponge. He rested his head on his hands. He was almost in a zombie nod when the peppers and eggs were slid under his face. The grandmother stood on his left heaping more onto the plate.

The mother stood on his right pouring cream and sugar into a mug of coffee. On the left his grandmother ground peppercorns from a wooden mill over the eggs. On his right his mother had finished buttering toast and was cutting it into quarters.

Alley Boy looked at both of them in disgust and pushed the plate of food toward the center of the table. He stood up and took his coat from the back of the chair and pulled it on. The two women looked at him in surprise.

"What's a matter? You no like my eggs with the peppers the way you always like them?" the grandmother said.

"Alley Boy, where are you going?" the mother asked.

"My name is Al, Ma," Alley Boy said. "Like Dad—Al—and I'm a man, not a little kid. I don't need you two to milk-and-sugar and salt-and-pepper me no more."

"Whadda you, crazy or something?" the grandmother said, but she was looking at the mother.

"No," Alley Boy said. "I'm twenty-one years old. I can fetch for myself."

Alley Boy walked out of the door, slamming it behind him. Daylight peeked through the skylight in the hallway. He took the three flights of stairs two steps at a time, jarring his sore ankles as he bounded. In the street he looked for a cab but there were none in sight. He walked to Ninth Street and Seventh Avenue and got one at the cabstand. He was shivering with cold when he got in. He told the black driver to take him to Ninth Street and Fifth Avenue.

"Mind if I run it off the meter, man? Only two blocks. For an ace?"

Alley Boy agreed and paid the driver the dollar up front.

At the counter of Henry's Diner the Greek brought Alley Boy his food. Green peppers and eggs and rye toast cut in quarters. He borrowed the *Daily News* from the counterman. On page ten there was a news brief about a bank robbery in Red Hook, New York. The story said the police were looking for three Hasidic Jews who had gotten away with seventy-five thousand dollars. Alley Boy smiled.

6

The jazz whispered softly from the stereo, low enough so as not to awaken two-year-old Michael in the next room. The rhythm of the music carried the two of them in a warm, wet canter in the big bed. Tommy spoke softly into Carol's ear as he moved in a circular motion inside her.

"There's only us left, Carol," Tommy whispered. "And we should think about us."

Carol slid her tongue into Tommy's mouth and rolled it over the roof of his mouth. She withdrew it a minute later.

"Don't talk with you mouth full, Tommy," Carol teased. "You don't have to talk for me to hear you."

Tommy felt momentarily embarrassed. But Carol dug her strong fingers into his ass to pull him deeper into her. He thrust repeatedly into her, keeping a steady rhythm to the music.

Tony's wife, Tommy thought. Tony's wife . . . Tony's wife . . . I'm fucking Tony's wife. . . .

The idea of invasion, violation of the dead and the untouchable, brought it on. And as he clutched her by the buttocks, soft and ample and white against the deeper brown of the rest of her body, he emptied himself of Tony, Ankles, Alley Boy, the past. He had moved into a zone that was like a white blur. No thought he had would focus. He gulped for breath as the first rush came. And then he was in control again. And he came again, and again, and again. He held her legs straight in the air.

I'm being her man, Tommy thought. She's my receptacle, she takes me in there, takes what I am and swallows it, her ass in my hands, exploring the small private hairs, the secret orifices, the places nobody else sees, no one else touches, secret and dark, all mine now, not even Tony's, this is where I reign now, wet and hot and soft and open and deep—mine . . . her accepting me in her means it's mine.

The last thrust came and his body quivered uncontrollably. And now it was the good dream, the one outside the house on the cliff on the banks of the Hudson with the sky an expansive blue print up so high, whipped-cream clouds floating on it. And Pop coming home from work in the gold Cadillac, his face closely shaven and handsome, his hair tight to the skull, the three-piece suit without so much as a wrinkle, and the cordovan shoes highly polished and glistening in the sun. Mother running out of the white house, across the squeaky-clean grass, to kiss him hello. Pop taking off the jacket and putting on a baseball mitt and tossing the ball to Tommy—the two of them having a pitching contest, seeing who could throw the most strikes through the old rubber tire that hung from the elm tree. Pop always letting Tommy win. Down below them the great band of water twinkling in the sun. And a parade of sailboats would come by, stenciled against the blue-green of the water, and Mother would come back out of the house to tell them the pot roast was ready and they'd go inside, Tommy sitting on Pop's shoulders, and he'd say Tommy didn't have to eat the turnips if he didn't like them, and Mother's dark brown gravy, and afterwards they'd play Monopoly. And Pop would always trade him Park Place for the Reading Railroad and later at bedtime he'd discuss the plot of the newest Hardy Boys novel until Tommy was asleep.

The kid woke him in the morning with a beautiful smile pushing a peeled orange against Tommy's face. Tommy glanced at the kid through sleep-crusted eyes and momentarily saw Tony grinning at him. He took the orange and thanked little Michael, but could not look him in the face.

The kid, delighted to be of service, ran downstairs to Carol in the kitchen. The smell of frying bacon drifted up the stairs. The smell reached him as he was in the bathroom trying to scour the taste of stale sex from his mouth. He scraped his tongue with the handle of a spoon and white lather gathered on the flat metal. Tommy rinsed it under the cold-water tap.

"Breakfast," Carol shouted up the stairs.

Tommy appeared in the kitchen fifteen minutes later. His hair had been washed and blow-dried. He was dressed in a pair of tight corduroy pants, an Aryn sweater, and a pair of Frye boots. He carried a suit in a traveling suit-bag, a pair of Gucci loafers, a dark tie, and a Chinese-laundered white shirt. He placed them on a small hutch and took a seat at the table.

The kid was kneeling on a chair at the table with a plate of crisp bacon and fried tomatoes in front of him. He had a hunk of French bread in one hand and a slice of bacon in the other.

Carol smiled without speaking as Tommy took his seat. She placed a sandwich consisting of two fried eggs with four slices of bacon on French bread in front of him. Tommy lifted the sandwich and took a huge bite, tearing at the chewy bread. He preferred to eat this way, simple and good and tasty. It didn't jibe with the characters in those Fitzgerald novels on the bookshelves, but it was always what he enjoyed most. He'd rather eat a meatball hero than a plate of gourmet delicacies anytime. This was the way you ate on the street, a hero and a Coke, while sitting on a stoop.

Besides, later he'd have to put on the etiquette charade at his parents' house. He'd have to ask someone to pass the salt instead of reaching for it. That bullshit was just a pain in the ass. But it was part of the game. His only passion from that world was lobsters.

He finished the large sandwich before Carol even sat down to eat.

"So you're going to your parents' house," she said, salting fried eggs.

"How'd you know?"

"The suit," she said. "The only other time you wear that is to court."

Tommy sipped a cup of hot sweet tea with milk.

"It's their anniversary, isn't it?" Carol asked while dipping her bread in yolk.

"I would ask you to come—"

"Don't worry about it," Carol said. "Just tell them your secretary sends her congratulations."

Tommy laughed and sipped the tea. When he drained the cup, he picked up his clothes and walked over to her.

"Carol . . ." Tommy said. She put her finger to her lips.

She said, "It was good last night, real good. I felt like a woman for the first time since—well, for a long time."

She reached up and kissed him affectionately. It made Tommy glow visibly. He smiled and moved to go. At the door, he winked at her. She winked back. He stepped out gingerly and closed the door softly behind him. He paused momentarily outside. The baby began to cry. He could hear Carol speaking to Michael inside.

"Daddy has to go to work to get money."

He liked that, being called Daddy, but it frightened him. Then he remembered about the money and opened the door again.

"I almost forgot the loot," Tommy said.

"You're slipping, Dillinger."

Tommy laughed and walked to the dining room to retrieve the briefcase with the money.

7

Frank Adler was furious. The train was forty-five minutes late already. He looked at his watch again and realized that he had checked it three times in two minutes. The weather was too cold to wait out on the platform, so he was forced to sit in the waiting room. The walls were hospital green and the room had large wooden benches that looked like church pews. Besides the porter, only the ticket seller gave evidence of life. A bum was asleep on a bench. He smelled like sour towels. The waiting room looked to Frank Adler like what he imagined purgatory to be. You go in there, buy the ticket from the half-asleep cashier, and wait there until the train arrives to take you to that hell they call New York City. Five days a week he commuted between purgatory and hell, and it got worse every day.

Frank Adler hoped the same conductor was working on the train. Maybe I can take out a little aggression by ripping off his ears, he thought. Wait a minute, bankers aren't suppose to think like that, Adler reasoned. But shit, they aren't supposed to read the *Daily News*, either. Then what the hell were they supposed to read? *Barron's*? That paper could bore the balls off a stud bull. He opened the *Daily News*.

After he finished reading Jimmy Breslin's column, he thumbed through the paper. He noticed a comical news brief on page ten. Three Orthodox Jews had stuck up the bank in Red Hook for seventy-five thousand dollars. The funniest part wasn't the three Jews pulling the heist. It was expecting anyone to believe that a Red Hook bank had seventy-five thousand dollars in cash on hand. The banks were always upping the ante for the insurance coverage. The tops they would keep in a small bank like that would be maybe thirty or forty grand. But seventy-five? Oh, that's hot shit.

"Morning, Mr, Adler," the black porter said as he walked toward the bench where Adler sat.

"Morning, Jim," Adler said.

"Readin' somethin' funny?"

"Yeah, the bank robbery in Red Hook yesterday."

"Oh, yeah, I saw it on the tee vee. Three rabbis. That is a little funny."

Adler was going to tell him that he thought the other part, about the seventy-five thousand, was the funniest bit, but he thought better of it. Really shouldn't give away trade secrets. Bankers were like magicians; they dealt in illusion, he thought. You keep the tricks secret.

"People must have money to throw away," Jim said. "I just found a wallet in the toilet stall. Must be two-hundred-odd dollars in it. No identification. The first thing I check in the morning is the stall. I find wallets and checkbooks and pocket combs there all the time. They fall out of the back pockets when they sit on the bowl."

Adler chuckled. Even porters have trade secrets, he thought.

"But I always turn them in," Jim said. "Fella here before me, he lost his job for not reportin' one. They found it in his locker. It belonged to the secretary of the treasury of Amtrak. So I don't risk my job for even two hundred dollars. Can't retire on that, Mr. Adler."

Adler thought that if there were more honest people like old Jim in the finance racket, inflation would disappear in a week. Then he remembered the dumb bastard on the train the day before. That poor asshole had lost his wallet. Maybe it was his.

"If nobody claims it in thirty days, then I get it anyhow," Jim said.

"I rode to New York yesterday with a guy who said he had lost his wallet," Adler said. "I think I still have the address." He looked in his inside pocket but remembered that he was wearing a different suit the day before.

"Shit, it's in the other suit, Jim," Adler said. "But if I find his name, I'll give him a ring. He'll probably give you a reward if it's his."

"They usually do," Jim said.

"His name was Al. Al something. I can't remember."

The light above the ticket seller's booth flashed on. It meant the train was arriving. About time, Adler thought, and strutted out to the platform. The train came into the station with a roar. If they ever write my biography, it should be called *To Hell and Back, Part II*, Adler thought. The train stopped and a different, younger conductor opened the door. Adler stepped on.

"Go ahead, tell me you had a flat," Adler said sarcastically. The conductor looked at him, puzzled.

The three stacks of bills lay on top of the bar in the annex room of the warehouse. Two of the stacks were thicker than the third.

"It says right here in the paper there was seventy-five thousand," Alley Boy said.

"I'm telling you there is only thirty-eight grand," Tommy said. "Don't believe things you read in the paper. Once they said we got away in a Chevrolet when we were in a Volkswagen bus."

"Well then, how come you each get fifteen thousand and I only get eight?" Alley Boy asked indignantly.

"Because all you did was drive," Tommy said, with a blade of anger slicing off the words. "The closest you came to danger was almost running over a deer."

Alley Boy paced down the bar.

"I don't believe it; it says seventy-five."

Tommy's eyes narrowed. Cisco saw trouble and stepped into the argument.

"Hey, man, let me tell you something," Cisco said. "I been working with Tommy for four years. He never lied about a dime, man. So take your loot and scoot."

Alley Boy picked up his stack of money.

"And be careful with it," Tommy said. "Don't go showin' it off. Especially if you see Ankles again. Next time don't even talk to him. Let him kick you, but don't open your mouth. If there's one thing that spooks a cop, it's silence. Remember that, Alley Boy."

Alley Boy cringed when Tommy called him that name.

"Al," Alley Boy said.

"Maybe when you learn to count," Tommy Ryan said.

"I'm sorry about that, but the paper—"

"Newspapers are for wrapping fish," Tommy said. "I had a course in journalism once at St. John's. I got an A. They taught us to learn the four W's—who, what, where, and when. But they left one out that I figured out—whoring. Most reporters are whores who'd sell their asshole for a byline. Once you know that, the rest is easy. You make up the rest of the story just like any hooker does when she goes to court. Whoever wrote that story about seventy-five thousand is a whore. Whores never tell the truth."

Alley Boy thought about Stephanie, about her soft wet mouth, her dark nipples. About her kneeling on the floor in the ladies' room. But mostly he remembered that she treated him like a man.

"Come on, we'll share a cab," Cisco said to Alley Boy.

"See you guys later," Tommy said.

"Tommy, I'm sorry," Alley Boy said.

"You don't have to open your mouth for me to hear you," Tommy said. After he said it, he realized he was quoting Carol. It bothered him. He had never used anybody else's line before. "Go ahead. It's all right, Al."

Alley Boy liked that. He had eight grand and Tommy called him Al.

"Oh, yeah," Alley Boy said. "I read something somebody wrote on the bathroom wall at the train station yesterday that I thought you'd like. It said, 'There are two kinds of people in the world—' "

" '—the Irish and those who wish they were.' " Tommy finished the line.

Alley Boy was disappointed that Tommy already knew it.

"It's as old as your granny, Al," Tommy said, then smiled glibly. "And very true."

Alley Boy forced a laugh. Cisco nudged him and the

two of them walked through the door to the outer room. Tommy heard the wall moving back mechanically. Then he heard it close. When they were gone, Tommy undressed. Then he put on the Gucci loafers and the dark-blue suit pants and the white starched shirt. The shirt collar was very stiff. He buttoned it at the neck. Then he tied a perfect V-knot in the dark tie and put on the suit vest and buttoned it. Then he put on a pair of diamond cuff links and finally the jacket.

He went to the toilet and switched on the light. An exhaust fan worked off the same switch and it whirred on. Tommy took a bottle of Vitalis from the medicine chest and dashed a liberal portion into his palm. He spread the hair tonic through his styled hair. Then he combed it straight back in a much more conservative fashion, and looked himself over in the mirror. The barber had done a good job. The haircut allowed him to change appearance from a stylish shitkicker to that of a businessman. Tommy Ryan snicked off the light and the fan wound down to a halt. He picked up his car keys and walked outside to the loading dock and got into his Cadillac. He checked the glove compartment to make sure the gift-wrapped presents were there. Then he slid the envelope with the fifteen thousand dollars into his inside jacket pocket and put the key in the ignition. The motor kicked over with barely a sound.

Sitting in his parked car across the street from the brownstone, Ankles spotted her coming down the stoop. He thought that she was beautiful. Clean-cut, fresh looking. The kind of dame that marries into royalty. But mostly he stared at the kid. God, was he the image of Tony Mauro. It's funny how them genes work, Ankles thought. Sometimes the kid comes out looking like the father and other times it comes out looking like the downstairs janitor. Never could understand those genes.

The kid took a long time walking down the stairs. It took him two steps for each step. Ankles got out of the car and crossed the street. Carol watched him coming.

"Hiya, Carol," Ankles said.

"Don't you have anything better to do, Sherlock?"

Ankles bent down and smiled at the kid. The kid appeared frightened by Ankles's bulk and hid behind Carol's legs.

"Your breath is melting his skin."

Ankles drew back. The remark hurt him and it showed in his large face.

"I'm sorry if I frightened him, Carol, but you don't have to insult me like that. I'm a cop. I'm trying to do my job. I'm trying to find out who killed your husband."

"You're trying to win brownie points with the brass. I kinda resent you doin' that with Tony's corpse."

Blood rushed to Ankles's face.

"Don't ever say that again or I'll—"

"You'll what?" Carol said defiantly.

Ankles, realizing that he was getting nowhere, assumed an official manner.

"All right, I'll get to the point and leave you alone. Do you know a guy named Frankie Green Eyes, or Francisco Sanchez?"

"No," Carol said.

"He's in the Methodist Hospital right now—looks like somebody ran him over with a street sweeper. He's comatose but he keeps mumbling about Tony Mauro in his sleep. The cops who searched his apartment found a straight razor. It's in the lab right now to see if it was used on—if it was the murder weapon. Do you have any idea why he might know Tony, or have any reason to kill him?"

"I told you. I never heard of him," Carol said.

"You're sure?"

"You want it in writing?"

"Was Tony involved in pills—pushing pills or taking pills?"

"Tony hated swallowing One-A-Day vitamins. And he might have been a lot of things, most of them pretty wonderful, but he didn't deal in pills. No way. I'd know."

"Maybe it's nothing, then," Ankles said. "But maybe it is. One way or the other, I'll find out."

Ankles was staring at the kid again. Michael's eyes were wide and wet. He smiled shyly at Ankles. Ankles smiled back. The kid hid behind Carol again.

"Your son is beautiful," Ankles said. "He looks like his old man."

"He was pretty beautiful, too," Carol said.

"Was," Ankles said and turned and walked across the street to his car. Ankles climbed into the car and fell heavily into the front seat. He stared over at the kid once more and waved good-bye. The kid never noticed. He was following his mother up the street to her car. It was a red Corvette, sleek and sporty. She unlocked the front passenger door and put the kid in the front seat and strapped him in. Then she walked around the car and got into the driver's seat.

Captain Houlihan went out to the scene himself. A chopper had spotted the yellow van first. All they saw was a small reflection in the trees, but it had to be something bigger than a beer can for them to see it from way up there on a cloudy day. It was the same van all right, with the Hebrew legend on the side. The bank guard was there doing an ID. Houlihan thought the bank guard was picking his nose when he was introduced to him, then realized that he was only touching a small scab on the beak.

Houlihan had received over a dozen phone calls from outraged members of the Jewish community complaining that the police bulletin on the three Orthodox Jews had done great harm to their image. Six Orthodox Jews had been hauled in for questioning. One cop had even gone so far as to pull one of their beards to see if it was real. Houlihan didn't like the flak, especially from members of a religious group. It was hard enough dealing with the local college kids, never mind people with God on their side.

"You sure this is the van?" Houlihan asked the bank guard.

"Positive," said the bank guard.

"You read Hebrew?"

"No," said the bank guard.

"Then how do you know it's the same one?"

"I just know," the bank guard said.

"Terrific," Houlihan said.

The guy was probably right. I mean, how many school buses move through Red Hook on bank jobs? But a good lawyer would have this yo-yo ground to granola in a matter of seconds on a witness stand. Houlihan walked over to the fingerprint guys who were dusting inside the van.

"Anything?" Houlihan asked the head print man.

"I don't think these guys had fingers," the print man said. "I can't even find prints under the hood. I think it was three guys with hooks."

"They wore gloves," Houlihan said. "They're pros."

Houlihan looked at the black outfits spread on the ground.

"What about the buttons of the coats?" he asked the print man.

"Zip. Nothing."

Houlihan picked up the beards. He laughed to himself dryly. Ballsy bastards, he thought. He dropped the beards. His hands had contacted some of the glue. He wiped it on his trousers. He picked up one of the hats, looked it over, and put it back down. He picked up a second hat and saw that there was some gummy residue on the underside of the brim. Bingo, he thought to himself as he saw the thumbprint as clear as a signature on the inside leather band of the hat.

He carried that hat over to the print man.

"Can you lift that?" he asked, pointing to the print on the leather band. The print man smiled.

"All right then, get it down to the lab and back to me as soon as possible," Houlihan said. No wonder I'm a goddamned captain, he thought proudly to himself. I'm good at this shit.

Tommy passed the wasteland of the South Bronx as he traveled along the Major Deegan Expressway. He remembered a news story he had read about a police station in the South Bronx that had once been nicknamed Fort Apache because of the number of busts that were made there. But that had been five years ago, before the torch artists had just about cindered the entire South Bronx—for profit. The landlords would pay kids to torch the buildings so they could collect the insurance. They worked with such diligence that in five years the police station was renamed the Little House on the Prairie. There was nothing near it for thirty blocks but vacant lots. There was a joke that you no longer had to go out to patrol the streets of the South Bronx—one scout with a pair of binoculars could patrol it all from the roof.

Tommy had to pass by the South Bronx to get to Riverdale, which was, in contrast to the South Bronx, one of the last great neighborhoods in New York. There were great houses that sat on cliffs overlooking the Hudson. . . . Tommy had bought his parents one of those houses after a big score five years before.

Tommy reached the house on the cliff by noon. He pulled the car to a gentle halt on the white gravel driveway. The house was white and beautiful, with high Grecian columns shouldering the front of the house. A white dog named Madman barked at Tommy as he shut off the motor. Tommy ignored the old mutt. The dog had a hard time chewing chopped meat.

Tommy checked his image in the rearview mirror. He straightened his tie and smoothed his hair. He opened the glove compartment and removed the two gift-wrapped packages.

Tommy got out of the gold Cadillac and walked along the gravel path. The snow had been melted away from the path with rock salt—Tommy could see the salt stains on the gravel. Madman barked and wagged his tail and waddled alongside of Tommy.

"How are you, Madman, you dumb asshole?" Tommy said to the dog. He didn't pet it because he didn't want the white hairs showing up on his dark suit. He climbed the wide stoop and passed under the Grecian columns. He rang the doorbell and waited patiently.

His mother answered the door. She greeted Tommy with a hug. Tommy hugged her closely. She was a short round woman with a pleasant face.

"Thomas," she said, "God, how we missed you."

"I missed you, too, Mother," Tommy said, leaving his Brooklyn inflection behind him in Brooklyn. "But work is work. Now let me get a good look at you."

He stood back and examined his mother. She was smiling broadly.

"Not only have you lost weight, you look as if you've gotten younger. I'll never know how you do it, Mother."

"And you haven't changed a bit, Thomas," she said. "As handsome as ever."

"Oh, you know me, Mother, I just dress like this for you."

"I'll bet," his mother said. "I bet you're the best-dressed man in Washington."

"Almost," Tommy Ryan said. "But the President has a private valet."

His mother chuckled. Then his father appeared. His father looked like an older version of Tommy: his facial skin still taut, hair retreating to gray, but still slim, with eyes as clear and blue as spring water.

"Tommy, my boy, how the hell are you?"

"Just great, Pop. Just great. And you?"

"Starting shortstop for the Geriatric Giants this year."

Tommy laughed and the two men held out their arms and embraced. His father smacked him affectionately on the back.

"My God," the father said. "It's been too long, Tommy. Too long."

Tommy handed his mother one of the packages and his father the other.

"Happy anniversary to you both," Tommy said.

"Thank you, Tommy," his mother said, then kissed him on the cheek.

"Don't thank me, Mom. Feed me."

Tommy's father led him into the house with an arm draped over his shoulder.

8

Alley Boy got out of the cab at McCaulie's. He reached to give Cisco some money toward the fare, but Cisco waved him away.

"I'll take care of it," he told Alley Boy. "You just be cool with that bread. Don't go spending it like a nigger with two days to live. Don't make a tip out of yourself."

Alley Boy put the wad back into his pants pocket. The day was cold and fingers of icy wind pinched at his ears.

"See you later," Alley Boy said.

"Later."

Alley Boy watched as the cab rolled down Tenth Avenue and then right onto Windsor Place. Alley Boy knew where Cisco was going. He was going to Biff's. That's the only place he ever went. He was like a cat—

he had his turf. It might not have been much of a
stomping ground, but at least it was his. Alley Boy did
all his stomping on other people's ground. But someday, he thought, someday I'll have my own stomping
ground. A place where I'm the Man. Like Tommy in
McCaulie's. Like Cisco in Biff's. Like Robin Hood in
the forest. He laughed at the thought of Robin Hood.
Maybe he would even steal from the rich to give to the
poor. Like Grandma and Ma. They're poor. But not
anymore.

This thought moved him into McCaulie's like a car-
toon character floating on the aroma of food. A fat
daytime bartender called Ocar was tending bar. Ocar's
real name was Oscar, but he had gotten the nickname
through his own mistake. He had once done a year in
the joint for stealing a street sweeper from the Department of Sanitation. He used it to try to run over his
wife who, he thought, was cheating on him. He missed
his wife but did manage to run over a mailbox and a
fire hydrant. While in jail, Oscar had decided to give
himself a tattoo. He used india ink and a needle with
thread wound tightly around the point. He would dip
the needle into the ink and jab his arm with it, then
connect the dots to form a letter. Many cons gave themselves tattoos this way to pass the time. When Oscar did
it, he misspelled his own name, leaving out the letter *S*.
Once he had finished it, it was too late. Since then,
everyone in the neighborhood called him Ocar.

When Alley Boy walked in, Ocar was playing a game
with two patrons sitting at the bar. The game was
simple—you gave the first and last initials of a famous
movie star and the other two had to guess who it was.
The stake was two dollars. The two patrons were
stumped on the initials A.F.

"You sure it ain't Anne Francis, Ocar?" one of
the two patrons asked.

"I tole you guys twice it ain't her. It's so fuckin' obvious, you make me wanna throw up!"

"Artie Fatbuckle," said the second patron.

"That's Fatty Arbuckle, you asshole," said the first patron.

"Ocar, can I have a beer?" Alley Boy asked. Ocar moved off his chair and walked to the beer tap. He pulled a mug of Rheingold. Alley Boy reached in his pocket and felt the roll. He peeled one bill off the top of the roll. It was a twenty. He handed it to Ocar. Ocar turned around and rang up fifty cents. Alley Boy took a long swig of the beer. It was bitter and cold and did nothing to shake the chill from his body. An involuntary shiver sprinted up his spine. He belched.

"Have you seen Stephanie?" Alley Boy asked Ocar.

"That half-a-nigger broad? The bouton? I ain't seen her. She usually comes in around lunch to work the garbage men who drop by."

"Thanks," Alley Boy said. He didn't like the way Ocar talked about Stephanie, but he didn't hold it against him. After all, Stephanie was a hooker. But I'll change all that, Alley Boy thought. I'll make her a princess. I'll be Robin Hood and she'll be Maid Marian, Alley Boy thought. Alley Boy and Maid Stephanie. No, wait. Al. Al the Hood and Lady Stephanie. I'll have to tell her that.

"Is it that fat spade Aretha Franklin?" asked the first patron.

"No, she's a goddamned gospel singer. I'm talking about an actor or actress. A.F. Christ Almighty, you guys are morons. A.F."

Alley Boy finished his beer and Ocar walked over and filled it without being told. It was the New York saloon custom. If you have money up on the bar, your glass is filled as soon as it is empty. He rang up the half a buck.

"I got it," said the first customer. "It has to be Albert Finney. Right?"

"No," Ocar said. "He's from England. I'm talking about an actor here. An actor, not a fuckin' guy from England."

"Anthony Franciosa," said the second.

"No," Ocar said. "Not him. It's so obvious it'll kill ya. Absofuckinlutely lay you onna floor."

"All right, I give up," said the first patron.

"What about you?" Ocar asked the second.

"No. I'll get it if it kills me."

The first patron handed over the two-dollar wager to Ocar. Alley Boy looked at the two bucks. Peanuts, he thought. He heard the sanitation trucks pulling up outside the door of McCaulie's. Garbage men in soiled greens ambled toward the bar. Alley Boy searched for Stephanie's face. Finally he saw her. She was getting out of the cab of a sanitation truck parked across the street.

He gulped his beer nervously. Ocar filled it again. As the garbage men walked in in a stew of noise and chatter, a blast of cold wind rattled through the open door. Alley Boy felt colder inside than out. Stephanie had her hand on a sanitman's ass as she entered the bar. Another garbage man had his hand on her ass. Alley Boy's eyes were cold wet stones as he stared at her. He tried moving the glass to his mouth but he couldn't do it.

Finally Stephanie saw him. She broke into a big smile when her eyes met his, but almost instantly her lips closed and her eyes sank. She looked beautiful, framed in the furious wind of the open door. Her cheeks were two pools of red, her eyes two emeralds. Alley Boy kept staring. The only thought that went through his head was: Lady Stephanie, Al the Hood.

Stephanie kept staring, too. Finally she walked over to him, serious.

"Hi, Al," she said. "How are you?"

"I'm . . . I'm fine. How are you?"

"The same, you know . . ."

"I love you."

The words tumbled out of Alley Boy's mouth like reckless dice. Stephanie looked at him softly. Then she said, "Say what?"

"You heard me, Lady Stephanie."

Stephanie didn't know what to say. Her brain wouldn't function. It couldn't work. She felt a garbage man's passing hand slide along her ass. Alley Boy didn't even notice. He was looking straight into Stephanie's eyes, terrified of what she would say, trembling in anticipation.

"Yes, I think I did hear you," Stephanie said.

"Would you like to leave?"

"With you?"

"Yeah."

"I'd love to, Al, but I'm working."

"My Lady don't have to work."

She looked around the bar. The garbage men were drinking whiskey and beers. They joked and made wise-cracks.

"All right, I give up," said the second patron who could not guess the actor's name.

"I don't know what to say," Stephanie said. "Why do you want me? There are millions of girls. Beautiful . . ."

"None of them are you," Alley Boy said.

Stephanie stared at Ocar handing over a slip of paper to one of the two original patrons. She saw him take back two dollars. The patron unfolded the paper and read the actor's name.

"Al Falfa? Who the fuck is Al Falfa? Where did he act? In the Holy Name third-grade play? I never heard of him."

"No, I guess they're not," Stephanie said.

"None of them is Lady Stephanie," Alley Boy said. "That's us. Al the Hood and Lady Stephanie. Get it?"

"Whadda you mean you never heard of Al Falfa?" Ocar said. "From the Little Rascals, you assholes. Al Falfa. Spanky and Al Falfa. You know goddamned well who I'm talking about."

"Yeah, I do get it," Stephanie said with a smile. "You steal from the rich and give to the whore, right?"

"Something like that," Alley Boy said. "I don't care. I love you."

"I'm half-black," Stephanie said. "That bother you?"

"Bother you?"

"Sometimes."

"Why?"

"Because . . . No, it doesn't bother me so much as it bothers other people. And I guess it bothers me that it bothers other people."

"It doesn't bother me what anybody says," Alley Boy said.

"Gimme my fuckin' money back, you asshole," said the first patron. "First of all, Alfalfa is one name. And that's just his name in the show. His real name is . . . I can't fuckin' remember, but he was definitely a Jew."

"Switzer," said the second patron. "His name was Carl Switzer. Now hand over the scratch, Ocar."

"You mean to tell me Al Falfa wasn't his name?" Ocar said.

"Asshole," the first patron said.

"Where do you want to go?" Stephanie asked Alley Boy.

"I don't care," Alley Boy said.

"You want to go over my house? It isn't too far."

"Let's walk through the park. The snow."

Stephanie nodded. Alley Boy left a five-dollar tip for Ocar. He took Stephanie's hand in his. It felt very small and bony, but warm.

Cisco was on his third game of pool when Ankles walked into Biff's. He looked up and saw Ankles, but his expression never changed. He eyed up the nine ball. His stick slid through his powdered fingers and the ball dunked perfectly into a corner pocket. Cisco straightened up, chalking the end of his cue.

Ankles stood near the front door of the pool hall and surveyed the room. Pool halls, Ankles thought. Spending time in pool halls was the same as doing time. Maybe that's why they attracted so many lowlifes. The big cop stared at the people at the various tables. Most of them were teen-agers, probably kids who were here because they weren't old enough yet for the saloons.

He looked over at Cisco and Cisco returned the stare. Little bedbug, Ankles thought. As he walked over to Cisco's table the dusty floorboards groaned under him. Cisco was lining up the twelve ball, stroking his aim.

"Playing with your balls again, Cisco?"

"Better than playing with yours."

"Don't knock what you ain't tried."

"I ain't tried a lot of things."

"Ever try throwing Frankie Green Eyes down a flight of stairs?" Ankles said.

"Frankie who?"

"They found him yesterday, outside here. Looked like a train crash. But he's talkin' now. Almost, anyway. Just mumblin' a little. Another coupla days he could recite the Yellow Pages backwards. Polack names and all."

"Let his fingers do the walking."

"Maybe he'll finger who done it to him. Because I think this pill-pushing prick knows more than him tumblin' down a flight of stairs. He knows something about Tony Mauro. You knew Tony pretty good, Cisco."

"I knew him, so?"

"So maybe you know who iced him."

"Nix. Afraid I cannot help you there, my man. You're smothering my light, Mr. Tufano."

Ankles stepped out of Cisco's way. Cisco sunk the thirteen ball. Ankles hocked and spat on the floor and mashed it into the dusty wood.

"Yeah. Anyway, I'll learn plenty from this Green Eyes. He'll talk. He'll yak so loud you'll need earplugs. You see, we found plenty of pills in his house. He's facing life on this Rockefeller law. He'll turn state's evidence so fast it'll be a blur. Sounds like fun, don't it?"

"A real ball. Send me an invitation. RSVP."

"Regrets only," Ankles said and walked out the door.

Carol Mauro sat in the small playground of the Montessori School watching Michael trying to help the older kids build a snowman. It was the only job she had ever enjoyed. Kids were simple, she thought. They know nothing and everything. They know enough to make them happy. It was a shame they would have to learn more. If it weren't for the kids, for Michael, for knowing there really were happy people around her, maybe she would have followed Tony into the grave.

She was an assistant and had worked here for three and a half years. The school had let her take time off while she was pregnant, then gave her the job back when Michael was able to walk. It made her happy that she could be with Michael at the same time she was working.

Not that she needed the money—there was plenty of that. Tony always had plenty. And now Tommy. The money made her a little sick. She watched the kids pat the snow onto the snowman in uneven clumps. She wished everything was as simple as building a snowman.

But it wasn't. Not since the night three years ago when she met Tony Mauro. It was in a bar called Dem Bums in Brooklyn Heights. He was with Tommy Ryan that night, and the two of them were spending money so fast and drinking so hard she couldn't help noticing them. It was Tommy who made a move toward her, the usual asshole move: "Hey, baby, what are you drinking?" Carol remembered telling him, "Whatever you're not." Tommy had been insulted, but Tony had just stood there and stared at her. His eyes were large and soft and his nose was a little too big and there was something vaguely gawky about him. But Tony Mauro had looked at her like he really wanted her. Not just for a fast bang and a phone number for cold Wednesday nights. He looked like he wanted her for more than that.

She remembered trying to look away, but she was on her own in the bar and every time she looked away another moron came on to her, and she kept looking back to make sure Tony Mauro was still there. And he was. He never stopped staring at her. Finally he had walked over to her and said, "Get out of here." She remembered looking up at him as he stood slouched over her.

"What do you mean, get out of here?" she had said.

"If you don't leave, I will."

She told him to go ahead and leave. Which he did. He banged down his glass and stormed out of the bar.

She watched him go. At first she felt like laughing. Tommy Ryan stood beside her and said, "What did you say to my friend?"

"I didn't say anything," Carol remembered saying.

Then Carol had gotten off her stool, walked to the front door, and looked out of the glass panel. And there was Tony Mauro's face, looking at her and smiling, and she cracked up laughing. He had opened the door again and said, "Wanna go?"

And she remembered answering, "Of course." She remembered now that she couldn't think of anything else to say.

One of the older kids knocked Michael to the ground and Carol got up and picked him up. She scolded the older kid. The older kid said, "You just like him better because he's your son." And Carol said, "That's right, brat."

She remembered going with Tony Mauro that night in his Lincoln Continental. He asked her where she lived and she told him her address, then he took her there and kissed her good-night on the doorstep of the brownstone on Lincoln Place.

"Is that it?" Carol remembered saying. "That's what you wanted to do? Take me home for a kiss good-night?"

"We'll get married in two weeks," Tony had said to her. And Carol remembered laughing out loud. Tony grew serious when she laughed at him. "You'll see."

She thought at the time he was mad. And maybe he was. But so was she then, because two weeks later they were in Key West on a honeymoon. When she got home from the honeymoon, she found out she was pregnant. And even when she found out what he did for a living she didn't care. Tony kept promising her that as soon as they hit a really big score he'd get out of it and they'd move to the West Coast.

Michael was born on a roasting-hot day in August. Tony Mauro was murdered on Michael's second birthday. Tony's best friend, Tommy Ryan, who had been their best man, was in jail for assaulting a cop. All Carol had was the small job at the school and a son without a father.

Tony had always asked her to go to Tommy if anything ever happened to him—to see to it that Tommy raised Michael right. Carol had always begged Tony to stop talking like that, but Tony had made her promise. He told her he didn't want a stranger raising his son if anything happened. So Carol had promised.

It was time for lunch and it was getting colder, so Carol lined up the children and marched them into school. Steam heat hissed from three large radiators as the children took seats at a small table. Carol and another assistant helped the children unpack their lunch boxes and poured drinks from Thermos bottles into the plastic caps.

Carol sat down and watched as the kids went about their business. She thought about the big cop Ankles. She was of two minds about him. One mind hated him because he was a cop and Tony had taught her to at least mistrust them. He was the kind of cop who would lock up his own son. He was a brute and a sonofabitch and he enjoyed his job too much.

The other mind saw a big slob trying to be gentle with Michael but being too pathetically awkward to have even a small child trust him. You can tell something about people in the way they approach kids, Carol thought. And Ankles expressed a goofy but genuine affection for her son. And the guy did seem to want to catch Tony's killer. It was almost an obsession, and that seemed to be more than what Tommy offered. Tommy hated the entire subject. It was as if it terrified him, and she had never known Tommy to be afraid of anything before. Except his dreams. His dreams sucked him into some big mouth and chewed him up—tore his flesh, powdered his bones, and then spit him out like a trembling little kid.

She wondered what it was that he dreamt of. She wished she knew more about the man she shared her bed with. Outwardly there was something exciting about him. He was fearless, tough, smart, and lived on the razor's edge. He teased death. There was something sensual about that kind of man, but there was also something revolting. He wasn't like Tony. Tony was afraid—mostly of dying the way he did. He had told her that the day Michael was born. He had told her he was afraid he might die before he got a chance to be a perfect father.

The kids were finishing their lunches and tossing food around the room. Carol began collecting the trash. She looked at Michael, and at the angle he was sitting he looked the way Tony Mauro had that first night when he was staring through the glass panel in the door of the bar in Brooklyn Heights.

9

Tommy Ryan looked around at the furnishings of his parents' house. It's fucking beautiful, Tommy Ryan thought. And they have no one to thank for it but you. When they needed you, you were there. Not like when you needed them. Not like when you got up in the middle of the night hearing the rats feasting and found nobody home. You came through, gave them all this, and made them be the parents you wanted them to be —what you always wanted everyone else to see. You're not the little kid with the dirty undershirt anymore.

You gave them what *you* wanted them to have. You chose the house, the furniture. You bought the Cadillac. You even purchased a new identity for them—found them a new name. You gave them plastic cards that said O'Brian instead of Ryan. You did not want anyone to remember your father. He was a disgrace. You laid him to rest. You bought your father a new name and you paid doctors to make him look different. You did all this. You gave birth to your mother and father—they were really your children—and they did what you said. And you could take it all away again. But of course you wouldn't, because you loved them.

Tommy had been introduced to all the guests at the anniversary party. There was Bill Sweetzer, a funny fat man who made his living installing tennis courts in the yards of the rich. He liked food and baseball. He was almost real, Tommy thought. He had a pretty wife named Sharon and three kids with whom he spent as much time as he could. He was sometimes funny to the point of hilarity and liked his own jokes better than anyone else did.

Tommy met the Morgans, too, a couple who were trying desperately to cheat their way out of middle age with Perrier water, Guccis, and the Arts and Leisure section of *The New York Times*. They spoke endless shop of the Academy. Each taught college literature, and they had cornered Tommy on the subject of whether Graham Greene's entertainments should be regarded as literature. Gloria Morgan was adamant in her polemic. She insisted it was not literature but "cheap exploitative pulp that did not deal seriously with the dilemma of the human condition. Just crap churned out by a journeyman craftsman in search of a few bucks."

Tommy Ryan was sure he had once read a direct quote like that somewhere.

But Charlie Morgan disagreed. Of course he would. Unlike Gloria, Charlie laced his Perrier with Bolla Soave, and he probably didn't give a hairy rat's ass about "the dilemma of the human condition" anymore. The only question he probably ever asked anyone was "Where's the corkscrew?"

Charlie said he thought *This Gun for Hire* dealt wonderfully with character and entertained at the same damned time. So what's wrong with that? Do we have to have puns and symbolism rammed down our throats or be dazzled with cosmic consciousness every time a guy with a harelip fires a gun? Sometimes you just kill people because you don't like them. Sometimes a gun is just a gun and you use it.

The asshole had a point there, Tommy thought. Tommy wished he could just tell the both of them he really didn't give a shit what either of them thought. But he couldn't do that. He couldn't fuck up the illusion. He had worked too hard for it. This was his parents' house and the guests matched the furniture. They were respectable people. People with money. People no one looks down on, unless you've been down so far you don't know the difference between up and down. *You* know, Tommy thought. You know what is down. You know what is up. You used to be down, all the way down. Now you are up, above them all. You are the boss here and they don't even know it. Shit rolls downhill, and you're at the top of the mountain.

But he'd show them he knew what they were talking about. In the joint you can go through twenty novels a week. You read all the best ones. You'll tell them what they want to hear, he thought.

Tommy said that in some cases crime novels should be considered works of art. He pointed out W. H. Auden's contention that Raymond Chandler's books should be read as solid literature. Tommy said he agreed. He thought the same was true of Hammett. But he'd draw the line at a Mickey Spillane. He back-pedaled on Graham Greene, claiming ignorance of his entertainments, but he thought Greene's serious works like *The Power and the Glory* were among the best modern fiction.

This satisfied both Gloria and Charlie Morgan.

Bill Sweetzer asked Tommy what he was drinking.
"I never touch anything but Coke," Tommy told
him and excused himself to go to the toilet. In the bathroom he took two snorts of cocaine from a small glass
vial and swigged heavily from a flask of rum. Rum and
coke, Tommy thought. Then he giggled. Rum and coke.

Tommy inspected himself in the mirror to be sure
no granules of cocaine clung to his upper lip. He patted
his hair into place. Now you'll go back out and run
through the rest of the bullshit, Tommy thought. Out
there in the street it's necessary to let them know that
you're the boss. Here in this world it's enough for *you*
to know you are.

Outside in the dining room, a black butler hired for
the party was serving dinner. Tommy had been careful
to take only two hits of cocaine, because he didn't
want the drug to completely numb his appetite. But
he had enough in him to be indifferent to the food so
as not to eat the way he was accustomed to eating.
Like a wolf. The meal, of course, would be lobster.
Mother will have seen to that.

At the dinner table Tommy's mother and father
opened their gifts. His mother's eyes sparkled almost
as brightly as the diamond necklace in the gift box.
The necklace hung like a small chandelier when Tommy
draped it around her wrinkled neck. Tommy felt the
soft, aging flesh against his fingers as he fastened the
clasp. The guests watched Tommy Ryan snap the
clasp and then rest his hands on his mother's collar-
bones.

"It's beautiful, Thomas," his mother said. She
touched Tommy Ryan's hand with hers. Her hand is
rough, Tommy thought. Still rough from the nights
when she folded the laundry for people like this in the
Pilgrim Laundry. He looked around the room at the

guests. They were all smiling. Tommy smiled back, studying each face. All the faces look like asses with ears, Tommy thought.

His father opened his gift box and removed the diamond cuff links and matching tie clasp. "They're swell, Tommy boy," his father said. "Just swell."

His father put the new cuff links on as the butler began bringing the food, one dish at a time. The butler is the only one who would understand, Tommy thought. He knows which way the shit rolls.

When Tommy's father had finished putting on the cuff links, he shook Tommy's hand. Tommy took his hand and gripped it hard. Tommy could feel the muscles in his father's arm rippling. But there was no strength left in his father's hands. His father looked at Tommy and Tommy detected a scribble of apprehension in the old eyes. He looked at his father's shoulders and remembered when his father used to sit him up there. The shoulders were sloping now and the muscle had vanished with age.

"Happy anniversary, Dad."

"Thanks, Tommy."

They sat down to dinner and Tommy was eating small hunks of lobster dipped in butter when the question of his profession arose. They all knew he had graduated from St. John's with honors in business. But why was it Tommy was always so reluctant to talk about his work?

"Just what is it you do, Tommy?" Bill Sweetzer asked.

"Maybe Tommy isn't allowed to talk about it, Bill," Sweetzer's wife, Sharon, said.

"Well, maybe he can give us a hint or something."

Tommy looked at Bill Sweetzer and smiled. He looked at his mother and father and smiled at them. No one knows what you do, Tommy thought. Not even Mom and Dad. Mom and Dad had some wild idea about him working for the government. Tommy liked that. They will never know.

"I deal in security," Tommy said. "I test the security of certain institutions. That's all I can tell you."

"Mental institutions?" Bill Sweetzer said. Everyone chuckled.

Tommy smiled again. "Don't rule it out, Bill."

Charlie Morgan was on his feet proposing a toast. "To Mr. and Mrs. O'Brian. May you enjoy many more years together."

They all lifted glasses of champagne.

Except Tommy, who lifted his glass of Coca-Cola.

Tommy nodded his head at his mother and father. They all sipped from their glasses.

Then Tommy declared another toast. "For my parents. Who were always there when I needed them."

Tommy's mother and father stared at him, wearing fractured smiles. Tommy stared back at them and smiled.

Shit rolls downhill, Tommy Ryan thought.

10

It was going on two o'clock in the afternoon when Alley Boy and Stephanie reached the second meadow of Prospect Park. He still held Stephanie's hand and their palms sweated in spite of the cold.

They were just up from the meadow, in the sparse woods behind the manmade waterfall near Swan Lake. The ground was covered with icy leaves and the wet branches of the trees crisscrossed against the sky. The small stream where the waterfall emptied was frozen. A rubber automobile tire stood up straight in the ice.

There were no other people around. Alley Boy stopped walking. He stared at a sea gull pecking at the ice on Swan Lake. He turned to Stephanie. Her shoulders were hunched against the cold and her cheeks were reddening and her eyes tearing.

Alley Boy put his arms around her and clutched two

clumps of her suede coat. She kept her hands jammed in her pockets and let her body go limp as Alley Boy pulled her to him. She was a foot shorter than Alley Boy.

Alley Boy kissed her thick lips and pushed his tongue into her warm mouth and closed his eyes. Her tongue moved into his mouth now. Alley Boy felt a shiver working up his back. This is my place, Alley Boy thought. My woman. This is what I have. My stomping ground.

"It's freezing, Al," Stephanie said. "We're only a few blocks from my place."

"No, right here," Alley Boy said.

"In the snow?"

"Yeah, in the snow. Right here."

He kissed her deeply again. Stephanie responded.

Then, "Not here, Al. We'll freeze our asses off."

Alley Boy laughed at her.

"It'll make it special. We'll never forget it."

"You crazy bastard."

Now he felt her right hand moving down in front of him. It went up under his coat, then under his wool sweater and under the tails of his shirt. He could feel her small hand—her hand that was now his hand—against the flat board of his belly. Alley Boy was tilting hot and cold. Then her hand moved lower. Inside his pants now. This new hand clutched him by the center of his body and kneaded him. Now I am a man, Alley Boy thought. A full man. Not Alley Boy. Al. Here. In this place.

The sea gull flew off the frozen lake and Alley Boy watched it flap and sail over the trees. Then he began to lie down slowly, pulling her on top of him. He felt his buckle loosening.

"For you, Al. Not for money. For you."

"And for you?"

"And for me. Crazy bastard."

He felt his pants move down near his knees. His ass was freezing and the cold air blew over his exposed skin. He watched Stephanie move her wool skirt up around her waist. And now the heat came to him.

"For me and for you, Steph."

"Crazy bastard, Al."

Ankles gave instructions to Officer Lipinski outside the intensive care unit.

"Nobody," Ankles said. "And I mean *nobody* goes in but hospital staff. IDs. Check their tags."

"Nobody," Lipinski said. "Nobody."

Ankles shook his head at Lipinski. The uniformed cop was a tall, flabby Pole with a veiny face. Good cop. He made collars like some people made lunch dates. Mean. Like Ankles wanted.

"I gotta have a nap," Ankles said. "The sawbone says Green Eyes might be able to talk soon. I don't want anything to happen to him. You hear him sneeze, call a nurse. The lab report on the razor should be ready soon, too. I gotta have some sleep."

"So go sleep," Lipinski said.

"Yeah."

Ankles moved to the fire stairs. He hated waiting on elevators. He walked down the three flights of stairs and out to the parking lot and got into his car.

He drove along Fifth Avenue to his apartment in Bay Ridge.

He thought about Tommy Ryan. He was certain there was something that motherhumper wasn't telling. He would withhold details of his own death if he could. He hung out with that little snake-in-the-grass Cisco, who wouldn't be able to tell the truth in his diary. And that other big dumb asshole D'Agastino . . . what was he doing with those two worms? Where did he fit in?

He wouldn't even make a good bag man. He'd put on loafers and try to tie the laces. His old man was a decent enough guy. Maybe he liked his cocktails, but he wasn't a bad guy. No brain surgeon or anything, but he knew his left shoe from his right. What's his kid doing with those other two animals? Who the fuck knows? Sleep, Ankles thought. Just some sleep.

He parked his car at the curb outside the Wig Wam Bar and Grill on Sixty-ninth and Sixth. He walked up the flight of stairs and unlocked his door. The lights were on in the apartment, he always left them on because going home to a dark apartment frightened him. It wasn't the dark itself so much as the emptiness it suggested. Almost every time he came into the apartment he wished he had a wife, someone to use the light, to cook and make the place smell like somebody lived there. But there never had been a wife. Never would be.

He took a can of Budweiser out of the fridge, yanked off the pop top, and took a long gulp. The can felt small and silly in his hand and the sweat from his palm made the aluminum warm so he poured the beer into a mug.

He stared around the apartment, looking at the furniture. It was good stuff, but plain, like something in a waiting room. The wall-to-wall carpet was too clean. He wished there were some kind of candy stuck in the rug and kids' toys slapped all over the place. Something that suggested life. Kids. Some little kids with dirty feet and sticky hands smearing ice cream on the walls. Kids who would never shut up, talking and breaking a million balls.

And a wife who screamed at them. Telling them she couldn't take the noise anymore. Day in and day out, kids breaking a million balls. Driving the wife up the walls and making her hit the bottle a little. Just a little, enough so she would be loose and they could laugh and grab each other later when she got the ball-breakers into bed after an hour of screaming at them.

That's what this place needs, Ankles thought. Something normal and regular like that. Maybe even a dog that would shit on the rug when the kids got him too excited. Any fucking thing. Something that mattered a little bit. Kids who asked you what happened at work today and who lined up for allowance.

Instead, all that mattered to Ankles right now was Tony Mauro.

He sat on the couch and a long sigh came from inside him. He could hear the commotion of the people in the saloon downstairs. Senseless laughter and the jukebox. I should've been a Jew, Ankles thought. Maybe I would have had one of them mothers that make you get married. The ones who set up dates for you. I'd even take a fat one, Ankles thought. With no neck. Just somebody to have around to talk to.

Instead, you hadda be Catholic, Italian, with a mother who thought you should have been a priest. You didn't find out that she thought you should be a priest because you were so ugly until years later. You thought she wanted you to be a priest because you were chosen by God. Because you were an altar boy, even if you never did learn the Latin and got thrown off the altar boys for cracking your knuckles during the part of the Mass where they bless the host.

She told you the real reason years later. The day you went into the police academy. Then she told you to get a wife even though you were ugly. But how do you get a wife if you've only been with one girl all your life?

He took another long drink of the beer and rested the empty mug on his knee. He thought about that summer night, in the rowboat with Marsha, on the lake in the park. He remembered how excited she was, hugging him, pulling him deeper into her. And how he ruined the whole thing by coming in about twenty seconds. Then he remembered Marsha asking that he take her home. He was twenty years old that year. He felt rotten after it was over. He knew she was another man's wife and he came so quick; it wasn't like it was supposed to be.

He had plenty of chances over the years to take some pussy in trade from a lot of different broads. But even with them Ankles felt self-conscious. He wanted one of them to really want him. But he'd rather pay for it than just take it if it came down to that. And almost did a couple of times, but he got too nervous to go through with it. There had been a few drunken and sloppy one-night stands, too, but the woman was always gone by morning.

He remembered he felt better when he read in *Playboy* once that there were a lot of guys like him. Guys who go through a lifetime with hardly any pussy. It made him feel less abnormal.

He thought about Marsha and wished he was twenty years old, to do it all over again. But he was forty-eight years old now, feet dangling over the edge of the couch, and he laid his head back. In a moment he was fast asleep.

After saying good-bye to the Sweetzers and the Morgans, Tommy Ryan and his parents were finally alone. Tommy sat silently in the suede armchair and looked back and forth from his mother to his father. His parents watched, waiting for him to speak. Tommy got up from the chair, walked over to the stereo, and put on a Gregorian chant.

He turned to his parents again and said, "Is there anything either of you need?"

The mother looked at the father and they exchanged glances. The haunting chant played very loud and they had to speak over the volume.

"No, Thomas," his mother said. "You've given us so much already. There really isn't anything we need."

"How can we ever thank you, Tommy?" the father said.

"No, Dad, you don't thank me. I only give you what you deserve. What they took away from you. And me."

The mother put her hand to her mouth.

"Mom, you look so well."

"She does, doesn't she," the father said, looking at his wife.

"And you just look different, Dad," Tommy Ryan said. "But you're still dear old Dad underneath."

"That I can't change, Tommy," the father said.

"No, neither can I."

Tommy walked over to his father and looked him in the eye. The father stared back. The mother watched the two of them. Tommy reached into his pocket and took out the white envelope with the fifteen thousand dollars in cash. He handed it to his father. His father accepted it but kept staring at his son.

"I don't really need this, Tommy."

"Christmas is coming, Dad. We'll have a big party."

Tommy walked over and kissed his mother on the cheek. "Take care of yourself, Mom."

"We'll see you on Christmas Eve."

Tommy shook his father's hand.

"Good-bye, Dad."

"So long, Tommy."

When Tommy Ryan left the house, Madman ran in. The Gregorian chant was still playing. Tommy looked at the name on the bell outside the door. O'Brian. Tommy nodded his head and made for his car.

Fabulous Murphy had been working on the accordion gate with the oxyacetylene torch for twenty minutes. This was physical labor and Fabulous Murphy was not used to it—the last heavy work he had done was beating his meat.

Laura and Connie sat in the cab of the yellow Ryder rent-a-truck. Connie was fidgety and nervous.

"I don't know about this, Laura," Connie said as she watched the blue white flame of the torch searing the corrugated metal gate. "Tommy will kill us. Not jus' a beatin'. I think he'll shoot us with a gun."

"Ta hell with Tommy," Laura said. "Just think about the way he treats us and all. Makin' us say we wanna suck him off in front of all them people. He treats us like bimbos."

"Yeah, but he'll know it's us. For sure."

"If he knows we was peepin' through the blindfolds, he wouldda said somethin'."

"I hope you're right."

Connie bit off her thumbnail as she watched Fabulous Murphy pause a moment to wipe his brow.

"Just think of all the money we'll have," Laura said. "We can go down Florida."

"You trust Fabulous?"

"Yeah, he's okay. I just wish he'd stop asking me to blow him."

"That's disgusting. He's fat and greasy."

Fabulous Murphy had finally burned through the gate. The hole was big enough for a small person to crawl through.

"Connie," Fabulous Murphy yelled. "You go in and open the gate."

Connie looked at Laura and hesitated.

"Go ahead," Laura said. Connie got out of the truck and walked up to Fabulous Murphy and took a flashlight from him. Connie bent over clumsily and Fabulous Murphy pushed a finger between her legs. Connie jumped.

"The little brown eye of wonder," Fabulous Murphy said and laughed. Connie looked into the black hole between his teeth.

"Keep your hands off, Fabulous."

Connie crawled through into the warehouse. With the flashlight, she located the button activating the accordion gate and it rose up.

Fabulous Murphy backed the Ryder truck into the loading dock. Connie turned on the lights and reactivated the button to close the gate. Then Connie pressed the other button, the one that made the cinder-block wall slide open. Fabulous Murphy stepped down from the cab of the truck and stood with his hands on his hips looking around at the valuables in the room.

"Holy shit."

Soon the two girls and Fabulous Murphy were loading the stuff into the back of the truck. Fabulous Murphy made them concentrate on the most valuable things first—the jewelry, the stereos, the televisions, the cameras. He chose not to bother with the boxes of coins or the furs.

It wasn't always easy to sell furs, because potential customers usually wanted to check their authenticity and Fabulous Murphy didn't have time for that. He wanted to get out of town pronto.

Twenty minutes later they all climbed back into the cab of the truck and drove out of the warehouse. Fabulous Murphy sent Connie back in to activate the close button and the gate shut. The part of the metal gate that was peeled back looked like it had been torn open with a giant can opener.

"When will we get our money?" Laura asked Fabulous Murphy.

"It'll take a few days."

"How do we know you won't be gone by then?"

"There's plenty for everybody."

Fabulous Murphy moved the gearshift into drive and the truck moved forward, laden with the weight of the heavy goods. Connie's heart was beating fast. She was certain Tommy Ryan would find them and do terrible things. She thought about how Tommy's face would look as he coursed a knife along her breast.

"Who wants to sit on my face?" Fabulous Murphy asked.

"Don't be disgusting," Laura said.

Connie tried to get Tommy Ryan off her mind. She thought of Florida—the sun pouring down like melted butter, blond guys with deep tans and muscles and lumps in their bathing suits, and nights in hotels with champagne from room service and having doors held open for her. Guys who would treat her like a lady. She squeezed her legs together and thought about the blond guys and the sun and money to buy all the clothes she wanted, and she forgot about Tommy Ryan for the moment.

Cisco darted into the laundry room on the ground floor of the Methodist Hospital. The laundry room was never locked. Nobody paid attention to the laundry room when there was the pharmacy to guard. No one at the hospital worried much about the laundry getting stolen.

Cisco helped himself to a pair of starched whites and a pair of plastic gloves. Carrying a plastic garbage bag with the whites in it into the men's room, he undressed quickly and changed into the whites, putting his street clothes in the plastic bag and placing the bag in the trash barrel to pick up later.

He walked out of the men's room and climbed the west stairwell to the third floor. Peeking through the wired glass of the fire door on the third landing, he saw a large flabby cop sitting outside the door of intensive care. The cop was reading the Night Owl edition of the *Daily News*. The cop looked up momentarily when Cisco came through the door into the corridor, but when he saw Cisco walk in the opposite direction he buried his nose back in the newspaper.

Cisco walked into the solarium at the end of the hall. It was empty because of the hour—nearly eleven at night. Cisco gathered a bunch of magazines together and tore out pages that he crumpled into a large pile beneath one of the lounge chairs. Cisco lit a cigarette with a match from a matchbook and took several drags until the ember was long and red hot.

Then he folded the cover of the matchbook back behind the matches and stuck the cigarette between the cover and the match heads. The ember was about a quarter of an inch from the match heads so that as soon as the cigarette burned down a little farther, the matches would catch fire. A trick he had learned in his days of arson for profit in South Brooklyn.

He placed the matchbook with the lit cigarette amid the crumpled papers, then walked out of the solarium toward the fire stairs. Lipinski looked up momentarily but all he saw was another white uniform.

Cisco walked calmly down to the second floor and then across the building from the west side to the east through the second floor. A nurse at a station looked up briefly, then went back to her Gothic novel. The hospital was quiet. Cisco walked up the east fire stairwell to the third floor and stood on the landing. From inside the hallway he could see Lipinski seated outside intensive care. Lipinski twisted a finger into his nose and inspected what he discovered there. He wiped it distractedly on the bottom of his plastic chair. Lipinski was about to turn a page of the newspaper when he started sniffing. He looked west down the hallway and saw smoke coming out of the solarium. Then in another instant he saw the glow of flames.

Cisco watched with a grin as Lipinski dropped the paper and ran down the hall toward the solarium. Cisco brought out his straight razor and opened the stairwell door. When he saw Lipinski disappear into the solarium, Cisco walked briskly down the hall.

Lipinski saw the entire chair in flames and began trying to smother it with his jacket. He stomped with his foot and flailed his jacket.

Cisco entered intensive care. All the patients were asleep. He walked directly to Frankie Green Eyes's bed. Green Eyes was completely unconscious. Tubing

ran into his nose and arms. Cisco pulled Green Eyes's
chin up, making the skin of his neck taut. Then, in one
experienced slash, he cut his throat straight around.
Blood gushed from the wound. Cisco heard escaping
breath.

None of the other patients stirred. Cisco folded his
blade and walked calmly out the door. In the hallway he
looked momentarily toward the solarium. Lipinski had
his head out a window, gasping for fresh air. He was
shrouded in smoke.

Lipinski saw the silhouette of someone in white up
the hallway and yelled, "Ring the fire alarm."

"Okay," Cisco shouted back. Then he smiled and
walked back to the east stairwell and down to the men's
room. He retrieved his clothes from the wastebasket.
He placed the whites in the plastic bag and then put
the bag in the trash.

He exited on the Seventh Street side of the building.
The night was cold. There was a cabstand outside the
hospital because so many people leaving needed rides.
Cisco was tempted to get in one because of the cold.
But he decided to walk to Biff's instead.

Captain Houlihan was waiting for the fingerprint
boys to get back to him. He sat in his office at the state
troopers headquarters three extra hours, hoping. The
phone calls from the Jewish community hadn't ceased
yet. There were threats of lawsuits, and the local paper
had carried a story saying that the area's rabbis were
planning a major protest outside of Houlihan's office
unless a public apology were issued.

Houlihan had met with the head rabbi and assured
him that he would make an apology, but that to do so at
this time would hinder his case. He and the rabbi

agreed to a one-week postponement of any formal protest on the issue. By that time Houlihan was hoping he would have some kind of lead from the fingerprint.

Finally the call came at midnight. The print was a good one, the lab guys said, but it wasn't much to go on. In order to get a definite ID from the FBI you needed the prints from five fingers. A single thumbprint could serve as positive identification, but only if you had a particular suspect to compare the print against. Which Captain Houlihan didn't have. If he didn't come up with a suspect soon, he would have to go public with his apology to the Jewish community and make an appeal to the citizens to come forward with any suspects they might have.

Captain Houlihan was tired. It wasn't every day, or every year, or almost ever at all, that three guys dressed as Hasidic Jews hit a bank in his territory. He wanted to crack this case, and he was determined he would succeed. More than just solving the heist, Houlihan was looking forward to meeting the people who had that kind of audacity. It would be a pleasure, in a job that had more to do with traffic violations than with real crime.

Tommy Ryan arrived at his apartment in Brooklyn Heights at 12:30 A.M. He had stopped at a bar on the Upper West Side called the Dublin House on his way home. It was one of the few saloons in New York that served a decent pint of Guinness stout. The secret to a good glass of stout was in the way the stout was drawn from the tap. Tommy Ryan liked a few glasses of stout when he had cocaine moving around inside of him. It gave him extra energy.

He had stayed only a half hour at the Dublin House, enough time for two pints of stout. It took a good seven minutes to draw one correctly, and that left only about the same amount of time to drink it. He wanted to get home before Carol fell asleep.

Carol was wide awake when he walked into the apartment. She was sitting in front of a roaring fire and barely stirred when she heard the door unlock, open, close, and lock again. The orange hue of the fire flickered on her face as Tommy stood near the front door. The glass on the French doors leading to the sun deck mirrored the flames.

"Hello, sweetheart," Tommy said.

"Hi, Tommy," Carol answered without looking up.

"How was your day?"

"The same."

"Michael okay?"

"Yeah. Fine."

"Terrific."

"How was yours?" Carol asked.

"I had a nice time," Tommy said. "We had lobster. We talked. My parents are looking fine, healthy . . . you know. They're okay, I guess."

"The cop was around, sniffing his nose into things," Carol said.

"You mean Ankles?"

"Yeah, that big guy. He was asking me questions about some guy, some Puerto Rican guy. Frankie Green Eyes. You know him?"

"I know of him," Tommy said. "But what did Ankles want to know about him?"

"He says Frankie Green Eyes knows something about Tony. Who the hell is he?"

"A pill head," Tommy said. "A dumb spic who sells pills. Cisco knows him. He's a nobody. Believe me, it would take more than a clown like him to cut Tony. . . . I'm sorry."

"Yeah, I know," Carol said. She continued to stare

into the fire. Small sparks spat out onto the brick hearth, then expired into pebbles of ash. Tommy started taking his coat off.

"Look, how many times do I have to tell you that I will handle this thing? Huh? Whadda I have to do? Give you a case number and a daily written report on the Tony Mauro murder investigation? I said I'll find out who did it and I'll serve as judge, jury, and executioner. So stay away from this cop. He's full of shit. There's nothing he'd like better than nailing me."

"He can't be all that bad then, can he?" Carol said.

"What is that supposed to mean, huh? What?"

He was standing above Carol now, his nostrils wide and taut. He felt his hands balling into fists. He wanted to haul off and punch her face until it broke. She didn't even look up at him. She took a final drag of a filtered cigarette and nonchalantly tossed the stub over the fireplace screen into the bed of hot embers.

"Think I'll go to bed," she said and stood up. She walked with a strut toward the stairs that led to the bedroom. Tommy watched as her ass bunched the sheer nightgown and then fell softly inside it. He wanted her badly. It made him feel the way he felt in jail—unable to have what he wanted most. He watched as the hem of the nightgown disappeared up the stairs. When he could see her no more, he put his coat back on and unlocked the front door and went out. He made sure to lock the door behind him.

Ankles heard the phone ringing, and ringing, and ringing. He pushed himself up to a sitting position on the couch and mopped some sleep from his eyes. His back was damp with sweat, and as he started undoing his necktie he was thinking of a shower. There was dirt under his nails, and whenever there was dirt under his nails he felt dirty all over. It made him feel like *them*, like the lowlives. At least 95 percent of them invariably had dirt under their nails.

He finally snatched up the phone. He waited a moment before saying "Hello." The words from the other end blew into his ear fast and frantic. He couldn't string them together. His head was still foggy from sleep. He heard "razor," "fire," "throat," "Green Eyes." Then finally he put them together.

"Are you saying Frankie Green Eyes had his throat cut?" He paused a moment. "That's what I thought you said." He didn't say good-bye. He simply cradled the phone onto the receiver. These things happened so often in his line of work that they no longer shocked him. But this was more than just another lowlife with a slashed swallower. This was the only key he had to the Tony Mauro murder, and that was no ordinary matter.

He put his head in his hands and pushed his hair straight back. When he lifted his head, he looked down at his fingernails. They were black with dirt. He felt disgusting. It made him feel like one of *them*. Tommy Ryan was one of *them*, he thought, but one of the other 5 percent. There was no dirt under his nails. No, not Tommy Ryan. He's a different kind of lowlife, Ankles thought. A clean lowlife. The filthiest kind.

Ankles foresaw the scenario: The lowlife would be in the bed, almost unrecognizable because there'd be so much blood, and his head would look fake as it hung half off the body. There'd be photographers from forensic, doctors, nurses, cops, and poor Lipinski would be in pieces because he blew a major assignment. They'd all look around for clues while the corpse lay in the bed looking dumbfounded in death and everyone would be smoking cigarettes or cigars as curious patients crowded around the front door and then the press would come. It would be the usual circus. People love murder, Ankles thought. It makes them feel a part of something important.

He shrugged again and began undressing, then walked into the bathroom and turned on the shower taps. He stepped under the hot spray of water and took a nail brush and began to scrub the dirt from under his nails, determined to wash out every scrap.

The encounter in the park had been brief and very cold and wet but, as Alley Boy had promised, also un- forgettable. They had laughed about it all the way to Stephanie's apartment in the tall luxury building on Prospect Park West near Grand Army Plaza.

"Maybe I'll catch cold in my prick."

"We'll have to go up and make it warm, Al."

And now they lay in her big bed in her apartment, both exhausted. They had made love three times during the afternoon and now they were drinking their second bottle of champagne.

The sheets on the bed were satin, like the ones ad- vertised in *Playboy*. They were cool and also very moist from their activities. Alley Boy thought she was even more beautiful without the wig. Her Afro suited the shape of her head and allowed him to see more of her face.

"You've lived here long?"

"Little over a year. I was living in the Village and saw the ad for this place in the *Voice*. When I saw it I took it because it overlooks the park."

"Must cost a fortune. The governor even has a place on Prospect Park West. Must cost a fortune."

"He lives two floors up. Penthouse."

"That's why there's a cop in the lobby?"

"Twenty-four hours a day."

"Twenty-four-hour police protection!"

Alley Boy was impressed. He and Stephanie clinked glasses and sipped some more champagne.

"Not bad for a hooker."

Stephanie regretted that.

"You're not a hooker anymore, Steph. You're my girl."

"I'm sorry," Stephanie said. "I was just joking, Al."

"No, you're my lady. We'll get married and—"

"Hold on, Al," Stephanie said. "That's a little drastic."

"No it's not. We can't have kids without getting married."

"Kids."

"I have the money now."

"Hey, Al, I'm not your average housewife."

"You're not your average anything, Steph. I have the money now. For you. And for kids."

Stephanie lay silent for a moment. The only compliments she had heard in the last five years were from guys who told her she gave good face. Usually when they were five bucks short.

"Al, listen to me," she said. "We only know each other a couple of days. I think you're terrific. But you know me, Al—I mean, I'm not the White Rock girl."

"The White Rock girl was the first tit I ever seen. You're the first girl I loved."

Here was a regular guy, Stephanie thought. A regular nice guy. Unbelievable. Where'd they hide him? You can't just go take a nice guy like this and run away and marry him. Can you? I mean, how does that work? You meet a guy in a nasty-assed saloon, give him some head in the toilet, and he tells you he loves you and wants you to have his kid.

"How old are you, Al?"

"I'm a grown man. That's all."

"I love you, too, Al."

"You do?"

Stephanie nodded and smiled and bit her bottom lip. She slipped her hand down Alley Boy's body and pressed gently.

"What about Tommy Ryan?" Stephanie said.

"What about him?"

"You kinda think a lot of him, don't you?"

"Tommy's got heart. He gets respect."

"He's evil."

"Evil?" Alley Boy said. "What do you mean, evil?"

"Evil. The way he carries himself. Conceited, nasty. He doesn't get respect, Al, he gets fear."

"You don't know him," Alley Boy said. "That's all, Steph. You don't know Tommy's all. I'd be penniless except that Tommy gave me a break, Steph."

"So what is it you do when you're with him, Al?"

Alley Boy smiled.

"Come on, Steph, it's nothing like that. He's my friend, that's all."

"Crazy bastard, Al. I don't mean that. I mean how do you get money with him? You steal it or something?"

A dry white knuckle formed in Alley Boy's throat.

"Can't tell you that, Steph."

"You want me to be your wife but you won't tell me what you do to make money? You know what I do— did—whatever."

"If you were my wife I could tell you. Wife can't testify against a husband."

Stephanie laughed and sipped some more champagne.

"I suppose I have no way out of this, do I?" she said.

"Nope."

Alley Boy was growing hard again and Stephanie was nibbling his nipple.

"Buy the ring," she said. "The suspense is killing me."

She kissed him lower and wetter. Alley Boy ran his fingers through her coarse hair. It felt strange to his touch.

12

Tommy Ryan parked the gold Cadillac around the corner from Biff's. He took the vial of cocaine from his pocket and hid it under the dash. Biff's was hot with cops, and Tommy didn't even like going in there clean. There wasn't enough coke to send him away, but enough to put him in the lockup for the night to give Ankles a chance to break his balls. He locked the car and walked around the corner to the poolroom entrance looking both ways for cops. There were none in sight. The night was cold and the ivory moon moved through silver clouds. A drunk staggered out of Timbo's Bar and Grill across the street and tumbled toward a snow-drift. He fell ass-first into the big drift and slowly put his hands behind his head as if accepting his position for a night's sleep. Tommy Ryan chuckled and opened the poolroom door and climbed the stairs.

Before he reached the top of the stairs he could

hear the heavy satisfying sounds of the balls knocking against each other and the din of conversation.

He stepped into the poolroom. Cisco was at his usual table, his eye on the front door as if expecting a cop. Tommy grinned as Cisco stood up from his pool stance. He walked over to Cisco and they shook hands, intertwining thumbs in an elaborate way. They walked together to the small service bar at the back of the pool hall. Biff was asleep behind the bar with a *Daily News* folded on his lap.

"Whadda you hear about Green Eyes? I hear he's talking."

"Not anymore," Cisco said.

"Yeah?"

Tommy was excited and smiling.

"He met his maker with a whisker chaser," Cisco said.

"Tonight?"

"Yeah."

"But Biff knows you were here all night, right?"

"Of course. You too."

"Solid."

"What did Green Eyes know?"

"He picked up some wire in the joint from his cousin."

"He mentioned it to me once. I didn't pay no attention cause he's usually too stoned to make sense. Said he heard Tony was iced for being a snitch."

"That's all?" Tommy asked.

"That's all he tole me. But now he won't tell nobody nothin'."

Tommy smiled.

"Come on, play you a game."

"I break."

* * *

Ankles bummed a Pall Mall from Lipinski and lit it with his Bic disposable. He looked down at Green Eyes. His head hung from his neck at a right angle and blood covered his torso and had soaked into the bedsheets. Flashbulbs popped as forensic took their obligatory pictures. Fingerprint guys dusted the doorknobs and the bed railings.

Lipinski stood in private gloom, smoking a Pall Mall, ashamed of himself.

There were no fingerprints, Ankles thought. No weapon, no fingerprints, no calling cards—just a motive: Keep Green Eyes from talking about Tony Mauro.

A photographer moved in for a close-up of Green Eyes and nudged Ankles out of the way. Ankles turned to the photographer.

"Handsome devil, isn't he? Why don't you get him from the other profile? That's his best side."

The photographer smiled in an embarrassed way.

"I'm only trying to do my job here," the photographer said. Ankles nodded.

"Yeah," he said, "I know. We're all trying to do our jobs. Don't mind me. Go ahead."

A uniformed cop walked into the room carrying a pair of starched white hospital clothes. The pocket of the smock had blood on it. The cop handed them to Ankles and Ankles held them with thumb and forefinger like a dirty diaper. He studied the white clothes.

"Found those in a men's room on the first floor," the uniformed cop said. "They were in a plastic garbage bag."

"Send it over to the lab," Ankles said. "Tell them to check the buttons for prints. Of course there won't be any, but check it anyway. And see if the blood on the pocket matches Sanchez's type."

The uniformed cop was about to leave when Ankles

called him back. He checked the label inside the jacket
for size. It was small. The waist on the pants was a size
twenty-seven. Then Ankles handed them back.

Whoever wore them was a small guy, Ankles thought.
A guy with a little waist. A guy about Cisco's size.

Another detective walked into the room carrying a
report from the lab. He handed it over to Ankles.

Ankles handed it back and took a puff from the
Pall Mall. He looked over at Lipinski, who was sitting
with his legs wide apart on a plastic chair, his head
drooping. Ankles looked at the young detective.

"Read it to me," Ankles said. "I don't have my
glasses."

"I didn't know you wore glasses, Ankles."

"I don't. That's why I don't have them. Read it."

"Well, basically, what it says is the razor they found
in Green Eyes's apartment had a different blood type
on it than Tony Mauro's. But then Mauro was killed
several months ago so it might not show up. I don't
think it was the murder weapon."

Ankles looked at the cop and bunched up his face
and stared incredulously. "No shit, Sherlock. Where'd
you get your first clue?"

The young cop flushed with embarrassment and
faked a small laugh. He moved self-consciously toward
the door as Ankles stared at him. The photographers
were finished with their picture-taking and started
lighting cigarettes. The fingerprint guys were packing
up their cases.

"All right, everybody take a march," Ankles said.
"This ain't a communion breakfast. Amscray."

All the people in the room began to make for the
door. Lipinski moved slowly for the exit.

"Lipinski, you stay a minute, will ya?"

Lipinski halted in his tracks. The door closed,
leaving just Ankles and Lipinski. Ankles took another

puff on the Pall Mall. He stared down at Green Eyes, his back to Lipinski. He exhaled the smoke and took another quick drag, thinking, Somewhere in there, inside that neck, is a voice box, and that voice box was supposed to tell me who took Tony Mauro to the butchers. But that voice box was slit in half now. He wished he could reach into the neck wound, through the tendons and the flesh and the blood, and yank the voice box out, take out the tape recording, and play it. Hear it say who killed Tony Mauro.

"I'm sorry I blew it," Lipinski said from behind Ankles.

Ankles kept staring at Green Eye's throat.

"Fuck it," Ankles said. "I should've stayed. It's my fault. You did what a cop is supposed to do. You tried to save lives."

Ankles took another puff on the cigarette, his eyes fixed on Green Eyes.

"That sounds pretty fuckin' corny, doesn't it, Lipinski? I mean, we don't really try to save lives, do we? If nobody got murdered I'd be out of a job. And then what would I do? That's the way we should really look at it, right, Lipinski?"

Lipinski stood behind him and stared at the back of Ankles's head. Smoke clouded around Ankles's bulk and Lipinski remained silent.

"Just like exterminators don't really wanna wipe out all the roaches or else they'd have no work to do. If we wanted we could just go and blow away all the lowlifes. I mean, we could say up-your-hole-with-a-Mello-Roll to the courts. What could they do? Who'd catch us? But we don't do that, Lipinski, do we? We don't, because we want to stay this side of pink slip. Right, Lipinski?"

Lipinski didn't answer right away. He felt ashamed. He had blown a big one and it was gonna cost him.

"I'm sorry, I . . . the fire was . . ." Lipinski couldn't make the words go together.

"Don't worry about it, Lipinski," Ankles said. "I'll take the weight. Go home to your wife, your kids, your dog. That's at least something. Fuck it."

"I'm sorry," Lipinski said again, holding his hat in his hand. "Good-night."

"Yeah," Ankles said. "Great night."

Lipinski stepped out the door and closed it gently. Ankles remained in the room, staring at Frankie Green Eyes. A pool of blood had gathered in between two wrinkles in the sheets. The blood in the pool was purplish and frothy with small air bubbles bobbing in it. That's what oxygen in the blood looks like, Ankles thought. Carbonated Welchade. Ankles felt the Pall Mall burning low in his fingers. He looked at the end of the butt where a halo of yellow nicotine had gathered on the paper near the ember. He reached with the cigarette stub toward the pool of Green Eyes's blood. He looked at the face once more. The mouth was open, the mouth that was supposed to tell him who killed Tony Mauro; the teeth were dry and yellow, the lips cracked and parted like a fish on a hook; the eyes were half-opened and marbled in death.

Ankles dipped the butt into the pool of blood.

13

The phone rang at nine in the morning. After the fourth ring it stopped. Tommy Ryan reached across the bed and picked it up anyway. Carol had her back to him and he held the cord up high so it wouldn't bother her.

Tommy put the phone to his ear and said, "Yeah." He could hear Michael on the extension and Cisco on the other end of the line. Michael was blabbering and giggling into the phone.

"Get off the phone, Michael," Tommy said.

"No," Michael said and giggled.

"Tommy," Cisco said. "Hey, Tommy, been ripped off, man."

Michael was giggling into the phone.

"Been ripped off *what*? Michael, get off the fuckin' phone, will you!"

"No," Michael said and giggled again.

"I'll break your little neck," Tommy said.

"I'll put a knife in yours," Carol said when she heard Tommy threaten the two-year-old. Tommy let the cord drop and it hit Carol in the face. She snatched the cord and yanked and the phone flew out of Tommy's hand.

"Come on, Carol, for chrissakes, I'm trying to talk here. This is important."

Tommy's voice was rough from too much beer. He retrieved the phone.

"Nothing you do is important."

"Tommy, they cleaned us out," Cisco said.

"Who cleaned us?—Michael, get off that mother-fuckin' phone."

The two-year-old hung up the phone.

"Sorry, Cisco, this is like living in the Wild Kingdom. What are you talking about?"

"The warehouse has been cleaned out. Ripped off, man. Burned through the steel gate."

Tommy sat up in bed, more alert now.

"What about the annex?"

"Cleaned fuckin' out."

"Everything? They took everything?"

"But the furs and some change."

"Hadda be somebody who was there before. Just me, you, and Alley Boy knew about it."

"He's here with me."

"It wasn't him," Tommy said. "Wouldn't dare."

"Nah, not him."

"I'll be there in half an hour."

Tommy hung up the phone and got out of bed. Carol lay there with her back to him, as still as midnight. The baby came into the room eating a banana, taunting Tommy with a filthy laugh. Tommy glanced at him and felt like twisting his ear. Carol sat up and held out her arms to Michael. Michael ran to her.

Tommy looked at them both. She doesn't give a shit that you got ripped off, he thought. Doesn't say a word, but let the kid come in giggling with a banana and she comes to life.

Michael was fingering off little globs of banana and flicking them at Tommy. Carol laughed.

"Food ain't for playin'," Tommy said as he snatched the banana out of Michael's hand. Michael began crying. And now Carol was sitting up at the edge of the bed.

"You swine," Carol said. "Bullying a baby. You goddamned swine." Carol cradled Michael in her arms. "Don't mind him, sweetheart. He's a dirty swine."

Tommy flung the banana at Carol in a moment of rage. Carol caught the banana and handed it back to the baby. Michael let go with a filthy laugh again.

"Daddy swan," Michael said.

"A fucking swine," Carol said.

"Fukkaswan," Michael said and laughed.

Carol cracked up at Michael's mimicking.

"I'll ram that banana up your ass," Tommy said. "I'll ram it right up your fuckin' ass."

"Food for thought," Carol said and cracked up laughing again. Tommy was furious. He grabbed his pants and shirt and shoes and socks and stormed from the room. He dressed quickly in the living room and could still hear Carol and Michael laughing uncontrollably in the bedroom. Tommy opened the door and went down the stairs, panting with rage.

You'll make her crawl, Tommy thought. In time she'll know you are the boss. Control. Be cool. You will make her love you the way she loved Tony. The same way you have loved her from the first night. You only let Tony borrow her. You own her.

Standing at the bottom of the stoop was Ankles. Tommy stopped on the second step from the bottom. Ankles stood on the sidewalk like a roadblock. Tommy quickly controlled his anger. He wanted his fury to ebb so that he would not lose his cool. Cool was the best weapon against Ankles, Tommy thought. It unnerves him. It throws him off track.

"Hello, Mr. Tufano," Tommy said in a mock Irish brogue. "Top of the mornin' to ya, and the rest of the day fir myself. Well, now, and what brings the likes of you around here at this hour of the day, me lad?"

"I'm sightseeing," Ankles said. "Been sightseeing all night. Seen some wonderful sights, Ryan. I seen a throat that was cut. Some sight. And a lot of blood. Hell of a sight. Then I had this vision, see, and a little hand came out and gave me a tour guide. It showed me all the other places I should see in Homicideland. I seen McCaulie's bar and I seen D'Agastino's house, and then this morning I seen Biff's poolroom. But I couldn't see you in none of them places, Thomas. You wasn't anywhere around, Thomas. But the tour guide kept sayin' I should see you, too. And so here I am and isn't it just wonderful?"

"Ah, Jasus, Mr. Tufano, it's nothin' short of bleedin' brilliant. 'Tis a wonderful sight indeed. And I wish I could spend more time seeing you, but I was about to go to Killarney for messages. Perhaps if you'd've gone to Mr. Biff's billiard parlor last night you'd've seen me, mind you. But I do sleep sometimes myself, y'know."

"Yeah. Mr. Biff told me your alibi," Ankles said. "Not a good one, but an alibi just the same."

"An *alibi*, Mr. Tufano? Now, why would the likes of me need an alibi?"

"Well, Frankie Green Eyes has joined the ranks of

the underworld. Someone gave him a tight shave and his last words went something like 'Thanks, I needed that.' "

"A bloody marvelous epitaph for a bloody marvelous human being, don't you think, Mr. Tufano?"

Tommy stepped down the last two steps of the stoop and tried to brush past Ankles. Ankles grabbed him by the arm. Tommy stared into Ankle's eyes. Cool, Tommy thought. You are the boss. The boss must be cool.

"You know anything about it, Tommy?"

"I hardly knew the guy."

"Looks like the same kinda cut Tony got—well done, you know? Now, I don't really give two shits about this Green Eyes guy. But he knew something about Tony Mauro. I don't know what. But that's gone now. I'd sort of like your help."

Tommy laughed in Ankles's face. Ankles flushed.

"You want my help, Ankles? That's a switch, isn't it? We never helped each other in our lives, pal. Let's keep it that way. White hats and black hats."

"I'm only asking you to help me catch the mutt who killed your best friend," Ankles said.

"What's the great interest in Tony? Why is he so important to you?"

Ankles fell silent for a moment. He couldn't find the right answer.

"Because it's my job."

"It ain't mine," Tommy said.

Tommy tried to brush past Ankles again but the big cop stepped in front of him. He pushed out his chest to exaggerate his bulk.

"One of these days, Ryan," Ankles said, staring down at a smiling Tommy, "one of these days, I'm gonna land on you. I'm gonna rip off one of your arms and beat you with it."

"Make it the left arm, will ya? I write checks with my right."

Tommy stepped around Ankles and walked to his Cadillac. Ankles stood in front of the house thinking about Carol upstairs and the little kid who resembled Tony Mauro.

14

Connie and Laura crowded into the same phone booth and dialed Fabulous Murphy's number. It rang eight times. Laura was ready to hang up when Fabulous Murphy answered.

"Yeah? Who's this?"

"Laura and Connie. We wanna know if you sold the stuff."

"I'll have some money in the morning," Fabulous Murphy said.

"Where can we meet ya?"

"Outside the club on Twelfth and Seventh."

"What time?"

"Ten."

"All right," Laura said.

"One more thing," Fabulous said. "Neither of you get a penny until you sit on my face."

"Fabulous, stop bein' so friggin' disgusting, will ya?"

"Good-bye," Fabulous Murphy said.

Laura hung up the phone and looked at Connie and smiled.

"He'll have it in the morning. We can get a plane to Fort Lauderdale tomorrow maybe."

The two girls stepped out of the phone booth and moved toward the bar. Ocar was sitting behind the stick watching *As the World Turns*. The jukebox was playing "Heart of Stone" by the Rolling Stones. A radio was also on, giving race results.

"Two Seven and Sevens," Laura said. Ocar looked from the television to the two girls.

"You got proof?"

"What proof?" Laura asked.

"You of age?"

"Come on, Ocar, we drink here allatime, for cryin' out loud."

"Pull down your pants an' lemme see some proof."

Another patron sitting at the bar laughed.

"How come everybody we meet is so disgustin'?" Laura asked Connie.

"I don't know," Connie said. "How am I apost to know?"

Ocar mixed the drinks and put them on the bar.

Cisco and Alley Boy were seated at the bar in the warehouse when Tommy Ryan showed up. Tommy revealed no emotion as he looked around. Everything but a few racks of furs was gone. There were dustless imprints where crates of merchandise had been stacked on the floor and litter was scattered all around the place.

Alley Boy was visibly nervous as Tommy nodded to

Cisco and Alley Boy. Cisco shrugged his shoulders to Tommy while Alley Boy stared numbly.

Tommy paced the floor and said, "It can only be those two bimskis. It has to be. They're the only ones I ever brought here. You guys never brought anyone here, did you?"

"No way," Cisco said.

"Never, Tommy," Alley Boy said.

Tommy put his hands on his hips and kept looking around.

"Did they at least leave the booze?"

"Yeah," Cisco said. "All heart."

"I'm going to have a drink. Then I'm going out and I'm going to find those two bimbos. I think maybe I'll kill them."

"Don't kill them," Cisco said. "Smack 'em aroun' a little. They hadda have somebody with them. That's who we kill."

"Yeah, good idea," Tommy said.

Tommy drank a glass of straight rum and looked at Alley Boy.

"You weren't home last night, Al. Ankles was looking for you. Better get an alibi because some guy got iced and Ankles wants to talk to you about it. Where were you anyway?"

Alley Boy's throat went dry. The cops at my house, he thought. Gramma and Ma will be in a panic.

"I was with Stephanie."

"Better watch what you say to that skank."

"She's not a skank, Tommy."

"What is she? A nun?"

"We're getting married," Alley Boy said.

Tommy choked on his rum and looked at Alley Boy after he caught his breath.

"Married! Are you for fuckin' real?"

"Yeah," Alley Boy said. "I'd like you to be my best man."

Incredulous, Tommy gaped at Alley Boy.

"You're not kidding, are you?"

"No, I'm not kidding."

"When'd you decide this?"

"Yesterday. We're gettin' married in a few weeks. She went down about the licenses this morning."

Tommy looked at Cisco. Cisco raised his eyebrows and shrugged his shoulders as if to say, "Fuck it." Tommy took another long drink of the rum and let it scald down into his chest.

"Hey, Al, you know, I'm sorry. I guess I just don't really know the girl. I'm sure she's a great broad. Congratulations."

"Thanks, Tommy," Alley Boy said. "You'll be my best man?"

"Yeah, Al, sure. I'd be honored. I was only a best man once. . . ." He thought about that day in City Hall when he handed the ring to Tony and watched him slide it onto Carol's slim finger. He had wanted her more at that moment than ever before.

"But I think you better wait until we get some more dough. I want to throw a big party, Al. But we've just been hitting small banks lately. If you get married you want to have the money for a house and a car and furniture. Eight grand is nothing, Al."

Alley Boy thought about what Tommy Ryan was saying. It made sense to him. As usual.

"When do we hit the bank I told you about, Tommy?" Alley Boy asked. "That's big money."

"Be patient," Tommy said. "Be patient, Al. Right now I'm going bimbo hunting. See you guys later."

Tommy Ryan bopped out of the warehouse into his Cadillac and drove off.

As the Caddy purred along Fourth Avenue rage was mounting in Tommy's gut, pushing itself up like vomit. Not only had they robbed from him, but they made him look bad, after he had been so good to them. Those two little cunts, he thought. You will find out who was with them and make them all pay. They had no respect for you. They walked into your turf. They boogied all over your stomping ground. You must get even now, he thought.

And ran a red light.

Two cars slammed to a halt and others in the intersection at Prospect Avenue honked. Tommy Ryan drove on without stopping, lost in thought.

He thought about how they had done that to his father, too. They had walked in and pulled the chair out from under him.

You remember when Dad had come home that night to the big house on the Hudson carrying the evening paper that had his name in the headline. You remember Mom sitting at the table crying. You remember Dad telling Mom how they came in and took all those pictures from the walls; how they pried the brass nameplate off his door; how they put all the things from his desk into cardboard boxes and placed them in the hall. You remember him telling Mom that he wanted to kill himself because his name was now dirt in the business. And you remember Mom crying, sobbing uncontrollably, begging him not to talk that way. You remember him telling her that his name, his life, would never be respectable again.

Tommy took a right on Ninth Street and drove up to Fifth Avenue. This time he stopped for the red light and he remembered more. He remembered the big truck coming and taking all the things out of the house, all the paintings and the furniture and the car. And when Dad rented the apartment in Brooklyn and how Mom stayed with Dad, stuck by him, and tried to tell you everything was all right. But you knew it wasn't. You knew. And you promised yourself that someday you would make it all right. You would become the boss.

The light changed and Tommy thought about the rats in the ceiling as he drove through the intersection. He could hear the toenails of the rats on the tin and the screaming bird. . . .

Tommy Ryan caught something out of the corner of his eye. It was part of the memory, there in front of him, staring him in the face. It was not in his head. He was not just daydreaming. It was a large plastic sign in a window covered by venetian blinds. It was a white sign with black lettering that spelled DR. FRANKFURT D.D.S.

Tommy Ryan slammed on the brakes. Traffic behind him screeched to a halt. The horns of a dozen cars honked. But Tommy Ryan ignored all that and stared at the plastic sign in the window.

His rage was now at a rapid boil. He could taste the anger in his mouth, a bitter filthy taste that needed rinsing out. The traffic honked crazily, but Tommy Ryan ignored it. Cars started swerving around him and motorists shouted obscenities at him as they passed.

Tommy Ryan heard nothing. He ran his tongue over all the spots in the back of his mouth where his real teeth had once been. Now they were plastic, put there because Frankfurt had taken the real ones out for profit. He counted all the fillings in his mouth in teeth that didn't need them. He remembered the ether mask being mashed into his face and the pain of the root canal he had recently suffered through because of Frankfurt.

Tommy Ryan threw the gear into park and opened the glove compartment. He took out a blackjack and put it into his coat pocket, turned off the motor, and got out of the car. Traffic was snarled in his lane—drivers blew their horns madly. Tommy Ryan walked past them.

The Pilgrim Laundry, the rats in the ceiling, the roaches on the kitchen table, the cheap wrinkled shoes, the dirty undershirt—it all came back to him now. Images of poverty and wretchedness swam in his head, and his anger focused on one person—Frankfurt.

Tommy stepped down the three steps to the doctor's office. His rage was a blowtorch now, the flame blue and searing the roof of his skull. But you must be cool. You are the boss in here and out there and everywhere you go. You must be cool.

The waiting room was jammed with Puerto Rican and black kids. Their mothers sat with them. Poverty had passed to them, and so they inherited Frankfurt.

Tommy looked at the kids, their clothing old and worn and frayed. One kid had a dirty undershirt that looked familiar. The rage was the taste of nickel in his mouth now. Then a wave of satisfaction moved through him, like Mom adding stove-heated water to his cold bath.

A small black girl stepped out of the inner office with her chubby mother. The left side of the little girl's face was swollen, and there was blood caked on her open lips through which cotton swabs were visible. The chubby mother was leading the etherized little girl, who was carrying a lollipop. The same kind of lollipop he used to give to you, Tommy Ryan thought.

Frankfurt stuck his head through the door and

Tommy looked at the face. It was the same revolting face he remembered as a kid: bushy dark eyebrows, bug eyes hidden behind black-rimmed glasses, a pencil-line moustache, a short knob of chin. His wavy hair was receding and going gray. When Frankfurt smiled, Tommy Ryan saw the mouth full of beautiful teeth.

"Next," Frankfurt said. "Whoever is next please follow me in."

Frankfurt let the door close and went inside to wait for his next patient. A heavyset Puerto Rican woman stood up to go in with the kid with the dirty undershirt.

"I'll be right out, lady," Tommy said. He took a twenty-dollar bill from his pocket and handed it to the woman. "You should try a different dentist," Tommy said. The woman looked at the twenty in astonishment and sat back down.

Tommy walked into the surgery room and Frankfurt peered at him.

"Can I help you?" Frankfurt said. He did not recognize Tommy Ryan.

"Yeah, gimme two pounds of pork chops and three sirloin steaks."

"Excuse me?" Frankfurt said. The dentist looked baffled. "Is there something I can do for you? This is primarily a children's dentist."

"I think you're confused," Tommy said. "This ain't a dentist. It's a butcher shop. This is Frankfurt's discount meat market. Frankfurt's Frankfurt Store."

Frankfurt smiled, not knowing what else to do. Tommy took his hand out of his pocket, the hand with the blackjack in it, and in one motion he slammed the flat heavy shaft against Frankfurt's smile. A couple of teeth splattered against a wall, then bounced on the tile floor. One tooth fell on Frankfurt's desk—it was sticky with blood and bits of gum at the root. Frankfurt made a sound like a man sentenced to life. He fell

to his knees, clutching his mouth. Blood leaked through
his fingers. His eyes looked goofy, like a puppy's.

"Keep smiling, Frankfurt."

Tommy Ryan walked back into the waiting room and
glanced over the women and the kids.

"The doctor is out," he said, and made for the door.
The sign was still there on the door: THANK YOU, CALL
AGAIN SOON.

Fabulous Murphy sloshed along the slushy sidewalks of Seventh Avenue with his hands jammed in his pea coat pockets and a cigar plugging the hole in his mouth. About every thirty yards Fabulous Murphy would do a pirouette, a habit he had picked up in the pursuit of self-preservation.

Fabulous made this 360-degree turn without breaking stride; and as he did, he looked at everything that moved around him. There usually was a bookmaker, a loan shark, or a victim of one of his scams hot on his worn heels, and more than once had Fabulous Murphy staved off a blind-side lead pipe aimed at his medicine-ball-sized head this way.

Turk the Cork had almost got him one day with a machete in Prospect Park, but Fabulous Murphy had narrowly escaped decapitation by ducking just in time.

Turk the Cork followed through on the swing and the
machete banged off a lamp post, which sent violent
reverberations through Turk's body and stunned him
just long enough for Fabulous Murphy to make good
his escape.

"I fight only with my feet," Fabulous Murphy was
fond of saying.

Turk the Cork was still looking for Fabulous
Murphy even though it had been almost a year and a
half since that scam. Murphy had walked into Fitzgerald's Bar on Tenth and Seventh on a sunny Saturday
afternoon carrying a portable Sony color television.
When Fabulous walks into a bar carrying merchandise,
most people head for the nearest exit just to avoid the
sales pitch.

But that afternoon Fabulous Murphy had not tried
any pitches. He simply hoisted the portable TV onto the
bar and asked Fitz for a glass of beer. Fitz drew a mug
of Rheingold and Fabulous Murphy put a fiver on the
mahogany. This brought a great hush over the saloon.
When Fabulous Murphy actually paid cash for a glass
of beer, jaws usually drop, drunks sober up, and a
great silence prevails..

Everyone was waiting for the scam. But Fabulous
Murphy had just sat there watching the Mets losing
another one up there on the black-and-white television
that Fitz had behind the bar.

Murphy had finished his beer and ordered another
one. Whispers started echoing through the bar: "What
was the deal?" "Where's the con?" But Fabulous said
nothing as he watched the Mets go down in order.

"Okay, Fabulous," Fitz finally said. "The suspense
is killing us. So what's with the tee vee?"

Fabulous Murphy looked as innocent as baby shoes.
"What tee vee?" Fabulous said.

To which three patrons pointed and said, "That fuckin' tee vee."

And Fabulous looked at his Sony and said, "You mean this tee vee?"

And a chorus came that said, "Yeah, that tee vee."

"Oh," Fabulous said, "I just bought this offa my brother-in-law down the docks. Not a bad deal. Fifty bucks. Brand-day-new. Warranty and all."

Now all the patrons in the bar wanted to know if Fabulous Murphy could get them one of those Sony TV's for fifty bucks.

"Nah, it's just a pain in the ass," Fabulous Murphy said. "There's nothing in it for me."

The patrons in the bar agreed to give Fabulous Murphy sixty dollars each, which for ten televisions would net Fabulous a hundred bucks for himself. Fabulous sat and thought about it.

"Nah," Fabulous Murphy said. "It's too much of a pain in the ass. My brother-in-law is a little paranoid over the waterfront commission. He's packin' a Luger."

That's when Turk the Cork spoke up. "You get us a tee vee like that and we'll pay you seventy-five apiece. You make twenty-five on each set."

Finally Fabulous agreed. He said he needed cash on the line. Turk the Cork said that would be okay so long as he could ride along with Fabulous Murphy.

"Fuck it," Fabulous Murphy said. "I get the feeling you guys don't trust me. After all, I'm doing you a favor. My brother-in-law sees anyone he don't recognize and the Luger starts spittin' German bullets all over the place. Forget it."

Finally Turk the Cork convinced all the other patrons to give Fabulous the cash. Fitz insisted that Murphy leave his own Sony where it was for collateral. Fabulous Murphy agreed. He collected the $750 and asked

Fitz for two dimes. Fabulous walked into the phone booth and called a taxicab with the first dime. He called American Airlines with the second.

Then he left.

Six hours later Fabulous Murphy landed in Phoenix.

Back in Brooklyn Fitz plugged in the Sony color television. There was no picture tube. Turk the Cork vowed vengeance.

And so Fabulous Murphy did his little pirouette every thirty yards as he was walking along Seventh Avenue. But this time he wasn't worried about Turk the Cork. He could outrun him and his machete. It was Tommy Ryan that Fabulous Murphy was looking for. If those two little bimbos dropped a dime on him, he knew Tommy Ryan would mean business. Tommy Ryan had a much more colorful imagination than Turk the Cork.

At the corner of Prospect Avenue and Seventh, Fabulous Murphy made his usual 360-degree survey, his head turning like a tank turret. There were no menacing faces in the street, so he walked toward Frank's Pizza Parlor. Frank's was diagonally across the street from I.S. 10 Junior High School and a lot of kids hung out there smoking Marlboros and blowing smoke rings between classes. Prospect Avenue was a decaying street of old wood-frame houses frozen in the act of collapse. Old prewar tenements lined Seventh Avenue. Above the scrawny, littered backyards of these run-down dwellings laundry hung frozen from clotheslines. These were not people who could afford clothes dryers or the energy required to run them.

A crossing guard was directing traffic at the intersection as Fabulous Murphy walked into Frank's. He was supposed to meet Suitcase Sal here. Fabulous owed Suitcase thirty grand that had begun as a ten-thousand-dollar loan on a cockamamie scam to truck bootleg cigarettes from Virginia to New York. The scam literally went up in smoke when the ten Gs' worth of cigarettes burned to a crisp as a result of spontaneous combustion right in the middle of the New Jersey Turnpike. Suitcase Sal had had his doubts about lending Fabulous Murphy carfare to the Bronx, but he was well aware there was good money in bootleg cigarettes and so gave Fabulous Murphy the loan on a 3-percent-a-day interest rate. That loan had now grown to thirty grand. And Fabulous Murphy knew that if you ran from a guy like Suitcase Sal there was never any hope. He had agents and cousins named Noochie in almost every major American city who would get you and cut off your ears first and then ask questions you couldn't hear later.

Fabulous had delivered the Ryder truck filled with Tommy Ryan's swag to Suitcase Sal the night before, and he was to meet him here in Frank's this morning to see if he could finagle an extra two grand road cash out of the loan shark. Suitcase had told Fabulous the night before that it would take till morning to make an estimate on the merchandise.

Fabulous Murphy allowed himself a small laugh when he thought about the two girls waiting for him at ten the next morning. They would wait until they froze to death before Fabulous would show up. He would be on his way to Florida in a nice warm rented car. His debts to Suitcase would be paid, and if he was lucky he'd have a few extra Gs. He'd be heading to a new warm city where the suckers were born every minute. The old ladies in Miami would be a piece of cake after dealing with the street-smart wisenheimers of New York. They'd fall for every bunco trick conceived since the invention of the fountain pen.

Suitcase Sal was standing at the counter of Frank's

eating a piece of square Sicilian pizza when Fabulous showed up. Another piece of pizza lay in front of him on the counter, guarded by a large cup of orange soda.

Fabulous Murphy moved to the counter and leaned next to Suitcase Sal. Suitcase was staring out the window.

"Eat," Suitcase Sal said.

"Pizza for breakfast?"

"Eat."

Fabulous Murphy shrugged and picked up the second slice of pizza from the counter. He twisted a pointed corner of the pie into his mouth in such a way that he could bite with his cuspids and his molars. Without front teeth he had a hard time making a frontal assault on anything firmer than tapioca.

"Why don't you get some fuckin' teeth?" Suitcase Sal said with his mouth full of gooey pizza.

"They get in the way of my cigar."

"What about pussy?"

"Nah."

"I got an appraisal on that shit. Thirty-five thou tops. And that's a pain inna ass 'cause the fence don't like handlin' big shit like stereos and televisions."

"That means there's five G's left over," Fabulous Murphy said.

"Five grand my dago ass," Suitcase Sal said. "You were supposed to pay me cash. Instead you show up with halfa Gimbels in a fuckin' truck. You're lucky I'm taking this shit at all. Only reason I didn't chop off your feet long time ago is 'cause that don't get me no money, see?"

Fabulous Murphy did not put up an argument. It was easy to see how Suitcase got his name. He was short and stocky and built like a safe. He had arms like legs, legs like pylons, and hands like anvils. He was bald and had no discernible neck, his head sitting on his shoulders like a bowling ball on a wall. His two beady eyes shifted from side to side as if always expecting uninvited guests.

"Can you at least let me have two grand?" Fabulous Murphy asked. "I have to make myself thin for a while."

"The only thing that would ever make you thin is a guillotine."

"Whadda you say, Suitcase?"

"I'll give you a loan. One thou. No more."

Suitcase took a wad of bills thick enough to jam a door out of his pants pocket. He counted off ten one-hundred-dollar bills and handed them to Murphy. Then he turned to the Italian man behind the counter.

"Ey, goombah, two more slices over here. He's payin'."

Fabulous took some singles from his pocket and paid for the pizza.

"Where you goin' anyway?" Suitcase asked.

"Florida. Early in the morning."

"That's nice. It's a short flight."

"I'm driving."

"What an asshole," Suitcase said, and returned to his slice. "Every asshole I meet is a fuckin' asshole."

16

Ocar was behind the bar sitting on a stool watching a game show when Tommy Ryan walked into McCaulie's. He leapt off the stool and immediately began mixing a rum and Coke without being asked.

Tommy looked around the barroom and saw there was only one customer in the joint, a stew bum sleeping next to his glass of beer at the bar. Ocar slipped the rum and Coke in front of Tommy. Tommy paid for it with a twenty-dollar bill.

"You see them two bimbos?" Tommy asked.

"Connie and Laura? Yeah, they were in earlier. Made a phone call and had a drink and left me a fiver tip. Tell you, wouldn't mind stirring that Connie's fudge some day. Just put it in the old dirt road and hold onto them lung warts for dear life."

Tommy smiled.

"Say where they went?"

"Nah," Ocar said. "I was watchin' the tube."

"Left you a fiver, huh?"

"Yeah. Usually they don't leave me nothin' but lip-stick on the glass."

In his mind Tommy Ryan saw that five-dollar bill. It was his five-dollar bill. He knew what he would do to them. He would make them make each other talk. He would make it very painful.

"If you see them don't tell them I'm looking for them, Ocar. Don't tell them I was around. I'll find them first."

"Sure, Tommy," Ocar said. "Just like you sez."

Tommy left the change from the twenty on the bar and went back out to his car.

Stephanie was puffing from climbing the three flights of stairs when they reached the landing outside Alley Boy's parents' apartment. High-noon sun filtered through a skylight here on the top floor of the tene-ment. Alley Boy asked Stephanie to wait in the hallway while he went in to talk to his mother and grand-mother. Stephanie didn't want to meet any mother or grandmother. She just wanted to go down to City Hall, get married real quick, and tell them about it later in a letter.

"Al, I don't want a big Italian wedding with some guy singing Mario Lanza while everybody eats veal. Let's just go swap rings and take off somewhere. Start fresh."

"You know I can't do that to them, Steph," Alley Boy said. "It wouldn't be fair. I'm the only son. The only man left in the family. They need me, Steph, they need a man around to, you know, take care of things and like that."

"I can see it now, every Sunday over at your mom's

—pasta, squid, sausage. They'll shovel it into us till we explode." Stephanie was trying to be funny, but there was a certain reluctance in the words, too. She was not sure she could handle that kind of life.

"Once you taste Gramma's cookin' you'll look forward to Sundays."

"Guess it beats gruel at the orphanage," Stephanie said. Images of lumpy porridge, fatty bacon, instant potatoes, and chopped meat cooked sixty-six different ways filled her mind. Maybe veal scallopini wouldn't be bad after all. She had never really tasted home cooking. You never do when you grow up in a home with a capital *H*—a State Home for Wayward Orphans. Where else do they send kids whose father lammed and whose mother was fourteen when the kid was born. It's the only place to send a five-year-old kid when her nineteen-year-old mother OD's on horse.

Alley Boy was about to go into the apartment when Stephanie stopped him.

"What'll they say when they see me? Maybe I should have worn the wig. You think?"

"Stop worrying, Steph. You think everybody was born down south or somethin'? Italians are dark, too."

Alley Boy chuckled and opened the door to his mother's apartment. Stephanie waited outside, sitting on the steps. The grandmother looked up from mopping the floor when Alley Boy came in.

"Rosa, he's alive," the grandmother shouted to the mother, who was back scrubbing the bathtub. "We checked the police and the morgue and they say you're not over there. I tried to call the river to see if you was floatin' over there, but there was no answer."

"Where's Ma?" Alley Boy asked, smiling.

"I'm here, where's Ma," came the voice from the bathroom. "Where are you? That's the sixty-four-dollar question. What's a matter? You don't live here anymore that you never come home to eat or sleep or nothin'? You still my son or you here to read the meter?"

The mother was drying her hands on her apron, her eyes wrinkled as she looked at him. Alley Boy was laughing. His mother had a way of exaggerating everything she talked about. The mother was quite certain that when the end of the world came it would be implemented in her kitchen.

"I'm still your son, Ma," Alley Boy said. "And I'm still your grandson, Gramma. That's why I'm here, to tell you I'm gettin' married."

The grandmother dropped the mop and quickly sat down on a chair and blessed herself, folding her hands together in a prayer, then shaking the steepled hands at the ceiling as she stared up.

The mother leaned on the table, holding a can of Comet, and took a babushka off her head. She bit the knuckle of her right index finger hard, leaving large, deep bite marks.

"You come in when I'm dressed like this, like you're the Con Edison man, and tell me you're getting married?"

The mother turned to the grandmother, who was kneeling on the wet floor now with her elbows resting on the chair, praying.

"Mamma," the mother said to the grandmother. "Mamma, you gotta tell me. Whadda I got over here? Am I crackin' up, or what's the story over here? Am I dead and dreaming and nobody wants to tell me how much the funeral costs, Mamma? You tell me, because, me, I don't know anymore."

"Oh, my God," the grandmother said. "Oh, my God who loves Saint Anthony, please tell him to find a way to keep my heart from killing me. Tell Saint Anthony that I'm looking for him. Please, oh my God. He walks in here to tell me he's getting married and I'm thinking the next time I see you is gonna be at your wake and not a wedding. Oh, my God, my poor heart. Tell Saint Anthony to find me now."

The mother shook her head and looked evenly at Alley Boy and said, "So who is she and what does she look like and what's her name and is she Italian and if she isn't, is she Catholic at least?"

"Her name is Stephanie," Alley Boy said. "She's beautiful. She's not Italian. She is a Catholic. Her last name is Kelly."

"Mamma," the mother said to the grandmother. "Look in your book of saints and see is there a Saint Stephanie."

The grandmother stood up and smoothed her black dress and shook her hands at the ceiling again. Then she shuffled into the bedroom.

The mother turned back to Alley Boy.

"And you met her where and how old is she?"

"She's twenty-three and I met her in McCaulie's bar." The mother went silent for a moment and finally sat down. She took off her plastic gloves. Her stockings were rolled down to her knees. The grandmother came back out carrying a book called *The Saints of the Catholic Church*.

"Yeah," the grandmother said, "right over here they got a Saint Stephanie."

The mother cut the grandmother off.

"She's two years older than him and he met her inna bar named McCaulie's where you don't look for an Italian wife anyway. Kelly, she must be Irish. All right. So at least she's white."

Alley Boy's smile faded.

"She's outside in the hallway and I'm gonna bring her in to meet you both," Alley Boy said.

The grandmother bit her forearm and made a small

yelp. "Are you crazy or sumthin'? I don't have nuthin' onna stove or nuthin'. You can't just bring inna girl you're gonna marry with nuthin' onna stove or nuthin'. You nuts or wha'? Saint Anthony must be lost. So where's Saint Jude?"

"We didn't come to eat, Gramma," Alley Boy said.

"You have to eat," the grandmother said. "You haven't been home in two days. So you didn't eat in two days. I know. Don't tell me what I know."

The grandmother hurried to the refrigerator and rummaged inside. Alley Boy was about to open the front door when his mother stopped him.

"First things first, Alley Boy," the mother said.

"There's nuthin' in here but light," the grandmother yelled in the background.

"Al, Ma," Alley Boy said to his mother. "Call me Al, Ma. Not Alley Boy. Okay?"

"Okay, so I'll call you Al. I'll call you Arthur Godfrey if you want. But listen to me because there was a big cop with a big nose and big ears over here and he was Italian because his name was Tufano. He said he knew your father. He says this guy got killed inna Methodist Hospital. He says he wants to talk to you about it. He says it isn't serious but he has to talk to you about it to see if you know the boy who died. You know him or what?"

"No, Ma, I didn't know him. Don't worry about it. It has nothing to do with me."

Alley Boy opened the front door and waved Stephanie in. Stephanie looked embarrassed as she stepped into the flat. The mother stared at her, focusing on the Negroid hair. The grandmother took her head out of the fridge and was about to say something when she saw Stephanie and held her tongue.

"Ma, Gramma, this is Stephanie," Alley Boy said.

The mother and the grandmother remained mute. They just stared at Stephanie silently. Alley Boy broke the silence.

"We got the marriage license this morning," Alley Boy said. The mother kept staring. The grandmother said nothing. The mother finally spoke up.

"Your name is Kelly?" the mother said, somewhat amazed.

"Yes," Stephanie said, trying to make light of the situation. "I'm what you might call black Irish."

"This I noticed," the mother said.

The grandmother was at a loss for words. She stood staring at Stephanie and finally spoke up.

"I'm sorry, Stephanie-Black-Irish, but he brings you around over here when there's nuthin' onna stove. But I'll make something to eat now. You gotta stay and tell me how much you love my gravy. I got just the thing you'll like."

"How do you know what she likes, Gramma?" Alley Boy said, grinning.

"Eggplant," said the grandmother, "she's gotta like eggplant."

Stephanie and Alley Boy broke up laughing. The mother kept staring at Stephanie like she was a television without a picture.

17

Captain Houlihan stood in his office and stared at the blank green walls. It was one o'clock in the afternoon and the sun was spilling through the windows of his office, but he was dead tired and his muscles ached and his stomach was protesting against too much rotten coffee. He had smoked forty cigarettes in ten hours and he was opening his third pack. This bothered him because he had gotten down to a pack a day and was trying to quit the filthy habit when this bank job came up.

The last couple of days had been just like staring at a wall, so Captain Houlihan decided he might just as well stare at a wall. He was hoping it would help him relax and think of something he had missed. A nun in grammar school had told his class once that staring at

the color green was the most relaxing thing one could
do for the eyes. That was why the school had gotten
green chalkboards. Sometimes it worked, too. Captain
Houlihan had more than once fallen asleep while the
nun diagrammed sentences up there on the green chalk-
board. But right now nothing, even staring at the green
wall, was working for Captain Houlihan.

He had a perfect thumbprint, but no name to attach
to it. He needed at least a name to match it against. He
had gone over thousands of mug shots of notorious
bank robbers in the past few days. Most of them were
doing time, were dead, or were under surveillance in
other states. His investigation was as blank as the
green wall. There was not even a modus operandi like
this in the books. No one had ever stuck up a bank in
New York before dressed as a Hasidic Jew.

Houlihan had no alternative but to make an appeal
to the public. The FBI was working on the case, but all
they were doing was rousting guys that looked like
someone off a Smith Brothers' cough drop box and
interrogating them. Then they'd stuff the weight on
Houlihan, who would have to deal with an outraged
religious community. There were rumors going around
that the JDL was planning to lynch Houlihan in effigy
at Grossinger's in the Catskills.

Houlihan knew he would have to call a press conference and ask anyone with any information to please
call a special number. All names would be kept confidential. He would also have to issue that public apology
to the Jewish community. That part was easy. Coming
up with some names to match against the print would
be the bitch.

He was hoping the ten-thousand-dollar reward the
bank was offering would bring a few names out of the
woods. But it would probably also bring in a whole

flock of flakes who would swear their brother-in-law pulled the heist. They'd turn in anyone for ten grand at Christmastime.

Houlihan pressed the intercom on his desk. "Yeah, Steve, schedule a three P.M. news conference. We might still make the evening news."

Houlihan lit another cigarette. It tasted like burnt toast. Then he walked back over and stared at the blank green wall.

Tommy Ryan sat in his gold Cadillac in the parking lot in Prospect Park. The high-rise apartment building where Laura lived was directly across the street. He had been sitting here for two hours now. He was in no rush. The two bimbos would have to show up soon. The radio was turned to WRVR-FM, and he drummed his fingers on the dashboard as Herbie Hancock bared his heart and soul.

From where he was sitting Tommy could also see Park Circle, where people rode horses into the snow-covered horse paths that wound through the park. Puffs of steam blew from the nostrils of the horses as they galloped into the frosted green. The riders bounced up and down in the saddles, holding the reins tightly as they rode.

Dog walkers and diehard joggers cluttered the Parkside, and buses with steamy windows and jammed with Christmas shoppers chugged along Coney Island Avenue. A cop car inched along, making the familiar sneaky sound of patrol. It was a sound that Tommy Ryan knew well. He could pick the sound of a Plymouth Fury out of a coast-to-coast traffic jam anytime because in the streets of Brooklyn the kids who survived developed antennae that allowed them to identify a cop car before they even saw it. He watched the cop car slither by like a serpent.

A group of teen-age kids were gathered at the Grecian columns near the entrance to the park passing around a bottle of whiskey wrapped in a brown paper bag. Tommy knew the cops could see them, but the cops kept going. The cops didn't give a shit anymore if kids drank booze; it was better than finding them dead on Seconals or Tuinals, or having them climbing through somebody's window looking for enough money for a sack of horse.

Besides, cops were different now. Tommy remembered them when they were much tougher. Today cops don't get out of the car for a meatball charge like underage drinking. It was too cold out. Hard drugs and guns were the only things worth going after today.

But Tommy remembered how Ankles used to come by and break balls when Tommy was a kid drinking on the Parkside. The big motherfucker would ram his size fourteen against people's ankles and break the bottles of beer. Booze was a big deal to cops in those days. It was before the goofballs and the junk and the acid came around. It was also before the city made all the layoffs with the budget cuts. Back when there was no manpower problem. Now the cops didn't have time for bullshit like underage drinking.

And Tommy remembered that the only one who hung out on the Parkside who never got a beating from Ankles was Tony Mauro. No one ever knew why. But Ankles used to let Tony go all the time with a simple hop in the ass. Nothing more. No juvenile delinquent cards. No bringing him home to his mother and father. No broken ankles. Just a hop in the ass.

Tommy watched a taxicab going by and he thought he recognized Connie and Laura in the backseat. But

the cab went past Laura's house and made a right on
Vanderbilt Street. Tommy started the engine and rolled
the car out of the parking lot and drove down to the
corner of Vanderbilt Street. He saw Connie and Laura
getting out of the cab parked outside of the back entrance to the apartment building.

Tommy smiled. They're not as fucking dumb as you'd
think, he thought. It must have been Laura's idea to go
in the back way. Connie wouldn't come up with an idea
like that if you gave her a traveler's guide.

Tommy parked the car on Coney Island Avenue as
Laura fumbled for the cab fare in the street. He went
directly through the front door of the building and
stepped into the elevator and pushed the door-close
button and waited there.

A minute had passed when he heard Connie's voice
in the lobby and the back door of the building closing.

"You don't think he knows yet?" Connie said.

"Maybe not," Laura said. "Anyway, we'll be gone by
tomorrow."

Tommy heard one of the girls press the elevator button and he flattened himself into the far corner of the
lift, where he could not be seen. The doors opened
and Connie and Laura stepped in.

Tommy sprung through the air and landed in front
of them and yelled, "Surprise!" Both girls let out short
screams. Tommy smiled broadly. "Hello, loves of my
life! I've been searching everywhere for you. I'm as
horny as a bag of cats. And I haven't seen my little
lovelies in days. I haven't been to the warehouse in days
and wondered if my lovelies would like to join me
there."

Tommy was smiling broadly in mock fashion. But
there was nothing sinister in his demeanor. Laura held
on to the last sentence. Tommy hadn't been to the ware-

house in days. Maybe that means he doesn't know about
the rip-off yet. Connie was visibly nervous, but Laura
appeared relaxed and this helped calm Connie.

"I'm tired of goin' to the warehouse, Tommy," Laura
said.

"Me, too," Connie blurted quickly.

"Where would you like to go then, my lovelies?"

"I'd like to go up and change," Laura said.

"Me too," Connie said.

"No time for that," Tommy said. "I'm too randy
today to wait. Come on, we'll go for a drive. When was
the last time we did it in the car?"

Connie looked to Laura for reassurance. Laura
nodded hesitant approval.

"Let's go," Laura said.

"You're terrific," Tommy said.

Tommy led the girls out the yard door and around the
corner to his gold Cadillac. The girls got in the backseat
and Tommy drove down Prospect Park Southwest until
he reached the auto entrance to the park at Eleventh
Avenue. He drove quickly toward the Big Lake in the
center of the park and stopped the car on a back road
overlooking a small bridge. Sea gulls paraded over the
frozen surface of the lake beyond, and there were
two tiny figures of children way across the lake skipping stones across the ice.

Tommy turned the ignition key to auxiliary, and he
plugged a Bob Dylan tape into the music machine and
Dylan began singing "Love Minus Zero No Limit."

"Get undressed," Tommy said softly. And Laura and
Connie began taking off their clothes. Tommy rested his
chin on the headrest of the front seat as he watched
Connie remove her blouse, revealing the large plump
breasts. Laura did the same, and Tommy stared at the
delicate firmness of the protruding nipples. Now both

girls slid out of their jeans and rolled off their panties. Tommy smiled giddily as he watched.

"What about you, Tommy?" Laura said as she sat naked in the backseat.

"Good question," Tommy said. "It does take three for double murder, doesn't it?"

Tommy raised a .38 and leveled it at the two girls. Connie's mouth opened in an attempt to scream. Tommy pushed the barrel of the .38 into her open mouth. Dylan continued with his song as Tommy cocked the hammer of the pistol.

"Ready to bite the bullet, baby?"

Connie's eyes were wide and pleading.

Tommy grabbed Connie's pocketbook with his other hand and rummaged through it as he kept the barrel of the pistol in her mouth. He located a pair of earrings and a matching brooch.

"Now," Tommy said. "Don't these look familiar. Let's see. You got them on sale at the five and dime, right?"

Connie shook her head no.

"No?" Tommy said. "Oh, then you must have gotten them at Tiffany's, because these are worth several thousand dollars."

Connie shook her head no again. Tommy shoved the barrel deeper into her mouth and Connie gagged. Tommy withdrew the gun and trained it on Laura.

"Open your mouth," he said to Laura. "I said open your mouth."

Laura opened her mouth and Tommy Ryan put the barrel in her mouth.

"Give it head," Tommy said. "Suck that barrel like it was the last dick on earth."

Laura began to suck in and out on the barrel of the pistol.

"When you make this baby come it's *really* gonna shoot a load into you, Laura."

Connie was weeping: "Please, Tommy. Please. It was her idea. Her and Fabulous Murphy . . . they tole me to do it. They made up the idea, Tommy."

"Fabulous Murphy," Tommy said softly. "Good old Fabulous Murphy. How nice. Now how the fuck did you know where the warehouse was? Tell me or I'll blow both your brains out."

"Laura peeked through the blindfold lastime we was there," Connie said as she sat trembling and totally vulnerable in her nakedness.

Tommy withdrew the pistol from Laura's mouth.

"Is that true, Laura?" Tommy asked.

Laura hung her head and nodded yes.

"After I was so good to you?"

"I'm sorry, Tommy, I'm sorry I did it," Laura said.

Tommy looked at them both and thought a minute.

"All right," Tommy said. "All is forgiven. Now just tell me when you are supposed to meet Fabulous Murphy. Where can I find him?"

"We're aposta meet him tomorrow mornin' fronta Fitzgerald's at ten o'clock," Connie said.

"Well, that gives us some time," Tommy said.

Tommy opened the glove compartment and took out the two blindfolds.

"Can I trust you both to wear these and not peek this time?"

The two girls nodded positively. Tommy gave them the blindfolds and the two girls donned them.

"Where we goin'?" Laura asked.

"Somewhere very special," Tommy said. "I had to get a new place now that other people know where my old place is."

"Where is it?" Connie asked.

"No questions, Connie," Tommy said.

He drove back onto the main road and made the girls lie down on the seat so they could not be seen from outside. Tommy Ryan took the park road to Eastern Parkway and drove out toward Bedford-Stuyvesant. The further east he drove, the more the neighborhoods were in decline and the more black people there were on the street. Tommy kept going deeper east and made his way across Bedford Stuyvesant to Broadway in Bushwick. He drove down Broadway under the elevated subway tracks as a J train thundered overhead. Broadway still showed signs of the massive blackout looting of 1977; many of the stores were covered with plyboard and zinc, and buildings stood like charred monuments to neglect.

Tommy spotted a group of about a dozen young black dudes in leather coats and wide-brimmed, beaver-skin hats standing on a corner near a playground. The black dudes were standing around a garbage-can fire, warming themselves. Tommy figured they were waiting for "the man" to come so they could cop their scag for the cold night.

Tommy stopped for a red light and the black dudes stared into the car with malevolent eyes. Tommy made a right and pulled to the curb about a hundred feet from the corner where the black dudes were standing. There were sounds of bottles breaking in the playground across the street and music blaring from a radio that was the size of a suitcase.

Tommy turned around and looked at the two naked girls on the backseat. He picked up their clothes and put them on the front seat next to him.

"We're here," Tommy said to the two girls. "Don't take off the blindfolds yet. Don't worry, it's a little cold, but we'll be indoors in a minute. Just open your doors and get out."

The two girls groped and opened the back doors and

swung themselves out of the car and stood freezing and disoriented in the street.

"Tommy, I'm gonna catch ammonia," Connie said. "There's all snow on the ground."

Tommy got out and closed both of the back car doors. He left the motor running in the car. He led both girls to the sidewalk when one of the black dudes on the corner saw this "corn pone honky" leading two naked broads up the block.

"Look at this crazy muthuhfuckin' honky, man," one of the black dudes said from the corner. The others in the group rounded the corner and stood amazed at what they saw.

"Tommy, where are we?" Laura said. "Tommy, who are those people that're talkin'? They sound like niggers."

"Hey you," Tommy yelled to the black dudes.

"Watch you talkin', Whitey?"

"I'm talking to you, my man," Tommy said. "These two broads just called you all niggers. Said there ain't a jigaboo alive can cop their cakes."

"Oh, yeah, honky?" the talkative black dude said. And he and his friends began walking quickly toward Tommy and the girls.

"Tommy," Connie said. "I'm gonna get ammonia."

But Tommy never heard her. He was already in the driver's seat of the gold Cadillac spinning down the block. The last things he could hear were the sounds of two females screaming and the shouting of eager men.

18

Frank Adler saw a piece of the press conference on the four o'clock news. It was a taped telecast and there was this cop named Captain Houlihan asking anyone who had seen any suspicious characters in the Red Hook or Rhinecliff area on the morning of the bank robbery to please contact the local police. They gave a special number and assured the viewers that all calls would be kept confidential.

Adler didn't immediately think of the kid he had met on the train station. It wasn't until Captain Houlihan talked about the nature of the fingerprint that Adler's attention grew sharper.

". . . Our laboratory tests indicate that the sticky substance on the fingerprint was probably an adhesive that held the bogus beard to the face of one of the bandits. Anyone with information is urged to contact

Captain James Houlihan at state troopers headquarters in Red Hook immediately."

At this point the newscaster broke in to say that Captain Houlihan had also issued a formal apology to the Jewish community on behalf of his office. Adler turned off the television set as his wife banged pots while preparing dinner in the kitchen.

Adler remembered the white gummy substance on that goofy kid Al's face on the train. He remembered asking him about it. The kid had said something about Santa Claus.

Adler went to his clothes closet and looked for the suit he had worn the day he met that kid named Al. But he couldn't see it in the closet.

"Sarah," Adler called to his wife, "do you know where my blue tweed suit is?"

"I put it in the cleaner's, dear," Sarah yelled back.

Adler went to the kitchen. "What about the stuff in the pockets?"

"All there was was a scrap of paper and an empty gum wrapper, I think. I think I threw it out. In fact I'm sure I did."

"You what? You might just have thrown out ten thousand fucking dollars."

"Please watch your language, Frank honey," Sarah said. "The children are at the table."

"Fuck the kids," Adler yelled. "Fuck the goddamned kids."

Ankles chose the high ground, way up on top of the highest natural point in Brooklyn. This was the same spot where General George Washington had watched the tall British ships as they moved into New York Harbor. The same place where so many American soldiers of the Revolution lay buried. Here in Greenwood Cemetery. The same place where Tony Mauro was buried.

Ankles lifted the binoculars to his eyes and through them he could see New York Harbor in the distance. The skyscrapers stuck straight up like broken fingers pried from the clenched fist of the city. It was twilight and the lights in the big buildings were igniting.

But these were incidental background images. Ankles was trying to focus the glasses on the three figures below him. And when he wound the glasses into focus he could see them more clearly. Carol Mauro was holding young Michael's hand. And yes, he thought, the older woman with Carol was her. It was Tony Mauro's mother. Marsha Mauro. She looked older and bereaved. But her. No question, her face was still that same tough wall of strength. Strong and sensual and kind. The same way it had been that night in the rowboat on the Swan Lake.

Seeing Marsha made Ankle's heart race. It jumbled his thoughts. He felt vulnerable, empty, much older, and very alone. A squirrel scurried through some nearby leaves and clawed its way up a tree. Ankles became startled. He felt afraid standing there amidst the dead, spying on the only woman he had ever really known.

It made him move his thoughts to another time. He was cold, but he thought about those summers spent being "the fat kid" with the big clumsy feet; the one they always sent for a long one in touch football games—but never passed to. He thought about all the idle time he had spent sitting on cellar boards thinking how great it would have been if he had a steady girl like the rest of the guys. He remembered striking out every time he got up at bat in stickball until no one would pick him anymore when they chose up sides. But they always let Ankles play Buck-Buck-How-Many-Horns-

Are-Up because he was fat and was perfect to be used as the human pillow. And he remembered how when they used to go down to the Hotel St. George swimming pool everyone would laugh at Ankles in the dressing room because his cock was smaller than anyone else's and he remembered being told that all fat kids had small cocks.

He thought about his mother, who never learned how to speak English well, and how all the kids used to make fun of the way she spoke with her hands. And how his father, who was an Italian immigrant, had a hard time holding a job because he couldn't get into the father/son trade unions. And he remembered how he had never been with a woman until Marsha. And how he blew that one big, yet still how badly he wanted her even a quarter of a century later. But he knew he couldn't have her, because she was still someone else's wife.

Ankles took four deep breaths and turned off the movie projector in his head. Home movies always bored the guests. He watched the two women place Christmas wreaths on the grave, then they moved out of the cemetery as young Michael ran ahead kicking snow into the air.

When they had gone, Ankles walked down to the grave. He stood over the headstone and took his hat off and just looked at the wreaths. Tony Mauro was buried in that piece of earth. Tony Mauro, Ankles thought.

My son.

19

Alley Boy dropped the letter in the post office mailbox and let the metal door flap shut. Stephanie eyed him with amusement needled with a thread of jealousy. Alley Boy detected something inquisitive in her eyes. It was night and it was growing colder, with a wind swirling about the park.

"What's the matter, Steph?"

"A Christmas card to an old girl, Al?"

"Nah, come on, Steph. Just a few dollars I owed some guy. You jealous, Steph, or something?" Alley Boy was smiling. No one had ever been jealous for him before.

"No I'm not."

"Are too."

"Get outta here, crazy bastard, Al."

"You are, ain't ya? Come on, tell the truth."

Stephanie punched Alley Boy in the arm and laughed. "Who you owe money to?"

"Just nobody. Some guy."

"Yeah, sure."

"I can't believe it, Steph. You jealous . . ."

Stephanie smiled and held Alley Boy's arm. "Don't push it too far, Al. You'll wake up some morning looking for your nuts."

Alley Boy grabbed Stephanie in a mock headlock and they strolled along the Parkside. Across the street the marquee of the Sanders Theater had a sign that said it was being closed for remodeling. It had had that same sign for two years. Alley Boy heard they were going to turn it into a hardware store.

That was too bad, Alley Boy thought. He had seen some good flicks in there after they made it into a revival house. *Bonnie and Clyde*, that was the best. Except the ending. He didn't like the way they got caught. He was working as a teller in a bank in Flatbush when he saw *Bonnie and Clyde* for the first time, and he was hoping for the next eighteen months that someone would come in and rob it. Just to see how it would be in real life. No one ever bothered.

Alley Boy could never understand that. Every Monday the armored car would come and bring in two hundred thousand dollars in cash. Alley Boy figured he'd have to do it himself. Tommy Ryan had said they were going to take that bank with Alley Boy's plan. A real good plan. Alley Boy knew all the times the guards took their breaks, what time the money was delivered. That would be the big one. The one with all the money for getting married. Just me and Steph go off somewhere. Somewhere warm.

Alley Boy and Stephanie strolled along Prospect Park West toward Stephanie's apartment building. The walk was about a mile, Alley Boy figured. He heard a mile in the city was about twenty blocks.

When they reached Stephanie's house Alley Boy kissed Stephanie good-bye and told her he loved her and that he'd be back to eat dinner later. He walked toward Grand Army Plaza to the taxi rank.

Stephanie watched Alley Boy get in the cab and then she stepped down to the vestibule. The uniformed cop on sentry for the governor opened the door for her and nodded hello. Stephanie opened the second door and there was a very large man wearing a trench coat standing in the hallway.

It was Ankles.

Frank Adler tracked Jim, the porter, from the Rhinecliff train station to his home by telephone. He asked Jim to meet him at the station as six P.M. that evening. Jim, the porter, agreed to meet Adler. Unlike the train, he was in time.

Adler had paced the train depot cursing out his wife for having thrown out the important scrap of paper. He had looked through all the garbage bins outside his house, but they had been emptied that morning. All he could remember was the kid's first name—Al. He thought the last name was Italian, but it could have been Spanish, too. He wasn't sure. That probably narrowed it down to six million Spanish or Italians named Al. At least it was something.

Jim, the porter, rummaged through the shelves of the lost and found until he located the wallet. He was about to open the plastic bag to take the wallet out, but Adler stopped him.

"No, Jim," Adler cautioned. "There's enough of your prints on the wallet already. I'm sort of hoping there might be a print of his inside the wallet. In the secret compartment or something."

"Maybe there is, Mr. Adler," Jim said. "But still and all there isn't any identification in it. Nothing. I don't see how you can find the rightful owner of it."

"The rightful owner just might be the wrongful owner of an awful lot of money, Jim. And if there's a reward, you'll get to split it."

"I hope so," Jim said. "Sure would be nice for Christmas."

The word Christmas made Adler cringe. It meant that the ends of his credit cards would begin to curl and smoke from overuse. The wife would bug him. Christmas was a good time of year for banks, but not necessarily for bankers.

Stephanie was startled to see the large presence of Ankles in her hallway. Even if he was your best friend, he would have been an imposing sight. The cigar jutted from his thick moist lips, smoke curling from its lit tip.

Stephanie recovered her composure and attempted to move past Ankles. But Ankles removed his cigar from his mouth as she walked past and said, "Just a moment, Miss Kelly."

Stephanie halted.

"Something on your mind, Mr. Policeman?"

"Many things," Ankles replied. "Al D'Agastino is just one of them. But there are other things, too."

"I really don't think I have to discuss my private life with you," Stephanie said, trying to put steel in her voice.

"Well, we could always arrange for the vice squad to discuss your private life, which hasn't always been exactly so private, if you want. And that would be official business. But me, I just want to have a friendly chat. Upstairs in your apartment, say?"

"That's over, cop," Stephanie said with anger. "You and the rest of your oink friends can go get their free jollies elsewhere from now on. I happen to have changed jobs."

Ankles was genuinely embarrassed. He tried to look more pleasant as he stepped closer to a furious Stephanie.

"I'll tell you something, Stephanie," Ankles said. "I take pride in only one thing about my life as a cop. I never took penny one from nobody. I ain't about to start with skin grafts. I'm sorry if what I said came out wrong. I only want to talk to you because I know you like this D'Agastino kid. So do I. But I think he might be in big trouble. Maybe you can help him out?"

Stephanie eyed the big cop with hesitance. Maybe he was sincere, she thought. On the other hand, he was still a cop and she didn't like him.

"We can talk here."

"I'd really rather talk upstairs. This isn't what you'd call chitchat."

Stephanie finally nodded approval and Ankles followed her up to her apartment, where she motioned for him to sit on the couch.

"Look," Ankles said. "I'm not gonna bullshit around. Here's the deal. D'Agastino is running around with bad guys. Tommy Ryan. You know him. And his human icepick, Cisco. I know you know him, too. They're into everything. Coke, hijacking, banks, and maybe a little bit of murder. Ryan is smart. Not just street smart but book smart. And I don't have anything on him. Yet. But I will. And when he falls, I don't want D'Agastino to be there with him. Maybe because I knew his old man and his old man was all right by me. Maybe because I met his mother and his granny the other day and they

look like decent people. So I know you and him are
sweet on each other and maybe you can talk some sense
into him. Tell him to find new friends, because the
ones he has now are gonna fall real hard."

Stephanie had not yet taken off her coat; she sat
listening and staring directly at Ankles. "What can
I do?"

"Tell him to take a hike. Get him outta New York.
Take him to Pago Pago or Africa or to California."

"What if he won't go?" Stephanie asked.

"Drag him by the balls."

"You mentioned murder. You don't think Al is a
killer, do you?"

"The only one I think he's capable of killing is himself. And he's building up to it real nice like. Listen to
me, Stephanie, I'm not trying to play Father MacIner-
ney here. Personally I don't give a fiddler's fuck about
all the other shit. Nobody hates banks more than me. I
cheer every time a coke dealer gets ripped off. But
murder is another thing. That line of work I don't like.
Just see what you can do."

Ankles stood up and walked heavily toward the door.

"I'll do my best," Stephanie said.

"I know you will, sweetheart."

"Will you do me a favor—?" Stephanie began to ask
when Ankles cut her off.

"I think I know what you're gonna ask," Ankles said.
"I already told vice to put your file under *A* for Ancient
History."

"Thanks," Stephanie said and smiled.

"Good luck," Ankles said and made for the elevator.

Alley Boy had never seen Tommy Ryan so smashed
before. Tommy was in a drunken rage. He was swilling

straight out of the rum bottle and banging his fist on
the bar. Every time he looked around the empty warehouse he grew more furious.

"That two-bit, no good, fucking penny-ante cocksucker," Tommy Ryan screamed. "Fabulous Murphy!
How do you live that down? How can you look somebody in the eye and say, 'I got ripped off by Fabulous
Fucking Murphy'? How!? A toothless half-witted asshole like that taking off Tommy Ryan? Oh, he will die.
Most definitely. He will die. Finished. Roger. Over and
fucking out."

Tommy stopped ranting for a moment and took a
long gulp of the rum. Cisco sat on a bar stool nonchalantly peeling an apple with a straight razor.

"Cisco," Tommy yelled, "kill that scumbag. Tonight."

Cisco nodded the way someone might respond to a
request for change of a quarter.

Tommy Ryan took another long belt of the booze.
Alley Boy sat nervously with a glass of tequila in front
of him on the bar.

"Why kill him, Tommy?" Alley Boy said. "Then we'll
never get the stuff back."

Tommy Ryan walked over to Alley Boy with a
drunken snarl on his face. He pushed his face close to
Alley Boy's.

"Why kill him?" Tommy Ryan mimicked. "Why kill
him? Cisco, did I hear him right or did shit-for-brains
over here actually ask me 'Why kill him?'"

"That's what he said, Tommy."

Tommy Ryan kept his face within inches of Alley
Boy's, like a baseball manager screaming at an umpire.
Alley Boy's eyes were fidgety.

"Why kill him?" Tommy Ryan exploded with
drunken mockery. "Because he violated me. He shit on
us. On me. On Tommy Ryan. Now we have to rub his

nose in his shit. And you are gonna do it Al-leeey Boy.
You instead of Cisco."

Alley Boy felt adrenaline percolating inside.

"You wanna be a man. Here's your chance. Tonight
you kill that Murphy."

"Tommy, that's murder. . . ." Alley Boy said.

Tommy Ryan laughed a loud howl.

"Of course it is. It separates the men from the boys."

"Tommy, I can't."

"*Won't*, you mean. Afraid of shitting your pants?"

"I'm not afraid."

"Then do it. You'll see it's easier to kill than not to.
The first one's the best, too—like pussy."

"But what about the stuff he stole?" Alley Boy
said.

"That's long gone by now. Just kill him. The money
is unimportant. We'll get plenty more. So what's your
answer, Al?"

Alley Boy sat nervously at the bar. The adrenaline
was a hot lava now. He downed a shot of tequila.

"I don't know," Alley Boy said. "I guess so, Tommy."

"Good man," Tommy said. "Cisco knows where to
find him. After tonight you won't be shitting yellow
anymore. You'll earn the hairs on your balls tonight."

Tommy Ryan slugged again from the bottle and
Alley Boy poured himself another shot of tequila and
downed it straight. Cisco grinned.

Frank Adler brought the wallet in the plastic
bag to Captain Houlihan. He explained that he knew
the kid's name was Al. He couldn't remember the last
name. Houlihan said he would try to lift a print out
of the wallet. But in the meantime, Houlihan said, it

would be greatly helpful if Frank Adler would sit down with a police sketch artist for a composite of the suspect.

Frank Adler agreed. He was thinking about the ten grand. If the print from the wallet matched the print from the hat found in the van, the composite would be released. Adler was more than happy to cooperate. Besides, that little bastard never sent him the train fare in the mail like he promised. He was hoping it was him.

After Alley Boy and Cisco left, Tommy Ryan had taken an hour nap on the brass bed in the warehouse. He woke up still boozy, but he felt a lot better. He took four snorts of cocaine and this helped to sober him up. He washed up quickly and drove down to a restaurant in Park Slope called the Camperdown Elm.

The restaurant was a brightly lit place with mirror-topped tables, mirrored walls, and good food at decent prices. It was a favorite spot of the brownstone crowd from Park Slope. Upper-middle-class professionals mingled here with street people. It was a good joint and Tommy Ryan always felt comfortable here. No cops hung out in this place.

Tommy Ryan had a booth in the back and Carol was already a half-hour late. His watch told him it was eight thirty-one. Tommy was adding Sweet 'n Low to his third cup of coffee when Kurt, the German manager, showed Carol to the table.

"Enjoy your meal," Kurt said. Carol nodded, said thanks, and sat down.

"Sorry, Tommy. The baby-sitter canceled. I had to bring the baby over to Tony's mother's house."

"It's all right," Tommy said.

"What's good tonight?"

"I already ordered the duck with plum sauce for both of us. It's always good."

"Terrific," Carol said.

Tommy sat silently and stared at Carol with half-moon eyes. The silence was very loud.

"All right, Tommy," Carol said. "Enough of the mum crap. You said you had something to talk about."

"I do. That guy Frankie Green Eyes was murdered last night. Ankles says he was mumbling in his sleep about Tony Mauro and was killed the same way Tony was. Straight razor. It isn't a coincidence."

Tommy sipped his cool coffee. He wiped his mouth with a linen napkin.

"I told you I would find out who did Tony in. It was Green Eyes. Cisco got him the same way Green Eyes got Tony, last night. No reason to wait for the courts. The word was all over the street. Green Eyes and Tony were doing some pill deal. Green Eyes and him had a fight over money so he killed him. It's over now, Carol. Over. He got his the same way as Tony."

Carol sat silently with her hand over her month. The waitress came and placed two duckling dinners on the table. Carol did not even look at the food.

"I'm gonna be sick," Carol said.

"You wanna leave?"

"Yes, please, Tommy."

Tommy helped Carol to her feet as the duckling steamed on the table. Carol held the linen napkin to her mouth and Tommy put her coat over her shoulders. Tommy left a fifty-dollar bill to cover the check. On the way out the door, Kurt, the manager, stopped Tommy.

"Was there anything wrong with the duck?" Kurt asked.

"No," Tommy said. "But it should have flown south for the winter."

Kurt looked at Tommy in bewilderment as Tommy led Carol out to the car.

20

Stephanie had already buzzed Alley Boy in downstairs. She was waiting for him to arrive at the front door. She rehearsed what she was going to say to him when he came into the apartment. She wasn't going to tell him that she had met with Ankles, but she wanted to get him away from the dirty business he had no business being involved in.

The knock came on the door and all the rehearsed lines dropped from her head like a kid with stage fright first stepping onto a Broadway stage. When she opened the door, Alley Boy had his head leaning against the doorjamb.

"You smell like a cactus," Stephanie said. "How much of that tequila did you drink?"

"Not enough. I want some more," Alley Boy said. His words were not slurred and he was walking straight, but his eyes gave him away. They were clouded and distant, and his whole face appeared limp.

"I only came to tell you I love you," Alley Boy said. "I have something to do tonight. What time is it?"

"It's five after nine," Stephanie said.

"I'll have to hurry," Alley Boy said. "I have to be somewhere by ten."

"Where do you have to go, Al?" Stephanie asked.

"Out," Alley Boy said.

"Out where?"

"Out of my fucking mind, okay? What's with all the questions?"

"I'd just like to know where you go when you go out. Who you see. What you do. Is that too much to ask for someone you're gonna marry, Al?"

"Right now it is," Alley Boy said.

"You're in trouble, aren't you?"

"What kind of trouble?"

"With that Tommy Ryan and that Cisco. I know all about the things you do. The robberies and all that stuff, Alley B—" Stephanie caught herself before she finished the word.

Alley Boy looked at her. There was a tremor of betrayal in his eyes.

"Go ahead. Call me Alley Boy. Call me a boy. But if I'm a boy, what are you? You're nothing but a two-bit whore."

Stephanie took it on the chin. Alley Boy regretted his words. He walked to Stephanie. She was unmoved. Alley Boy put his arms around her and put his head against her breast.

"I'm sorry, Steph. I didn't mean anything. I'm sorry."

"Al, let's go away. Let's get out of here. Out of this city. Tonight. Take a plane."

"Can't, Steph. I can't. Not now. Next week we'll go, Steph. Promise. Not now."

Alley Boy was shaking now and he felt like crying.

"Why, Al? Why not?"

"There are certain things I have to prove to myself, Steph."

"You don't have to prove anything, Al. Let's just go."

"You don't understand, Steph. You just don't understand."

"No, I don't, Al."

She was threading her fingers through his hair as he clutched her. Alley Boy pulled away from her and walked backwards to the door. He opened the door and backed out into the hall and closed the door. He put on the overcoat and took Cisco's .38 out of his pants pocket and placed it into the overcoat pocket. It felt heavy and strong. He went downstairs to the street and walked north along the Parkside. He had a meeting with Fabulous Murphy.

Ankles stood at the bar in Farrell's Sports Bar on Prospect Park West and Sixteenth Street. Farrell's was the last great drinking man's saloon in New York. There were no stools at the bar, and this discouraged women and drunks who could no longer stand. It was a hangout for cops, firemen, construction workers, and sports fanatics.

Ankles had a copy of the *Daily News* spread out in front of him at the bar. On page three Michael Daly had the story on Frankie Green Eyes's murder in the intensive care unit of the Methodist Hospital. Ankles was shocked to see that all the quotes attributed to him were accurate. That was a switch. Most times press stories read like fiction.

Change from a twenty lay on the bar next to Ankles's empty glass. Danny Monahan, the bartender, filled the glass and picked up a quarter and stopped to chat with Ankles.

"That's some fuckin' story there about that guy in the Methodist, ain't it, Ankles?" Danny Monahan said, more as a statement than a question, but still hoping for a reply.

"It stinks, Danny. Stinks on hot ice."

"Yeah, probably one of them drug things like the story sez, huh?"

"I don't know. Wish it was that simple. How's the wife and kids there, Danny?"

"Not bad," Danny Monahan said. "I got my nine-year-old, little Danny, on a wrestlin' team out on the Eyeland. He's good. Gonna be a tough sonofabitch. And the little girl is on the gymnastics team. You know. The wife's okay, I guess. Family is family, you can't change that, so you live with it."

Ankles chuckled.

"I wouldn't complain if I was you," Ankles said. "At least you have someone to go home ta."

"Yeah, I know what you mean," Danny said.

"No you don't, Danny. You don't know what I mean."

Danny Monahan looked a little embarrassed for Ankles. Ankles downed the seven-ounce goblet of beer in a single slug and placed it on the bar. Danny Monahan refilled it again.

"I'd give everything for what you got, Danny," Ankles said. "Just for the kids and the wife and the house and the dog and the station wagon. I'd give the pension and the gold badge and everything."

"And what would you get?" Danny Monahan asked.

"Tuition, hospital bills, the mortgage, car payments, tolls on the bridge. You ain't missin' much. Believe me."

"Danny, I get paid to know when people are lying."

"All right, so I'm a fuckin' liar. Come on, drink up. I'll buy you a beer."

Ankles downed his glass and Danny Monahan grabbed it for a refill.

Alley Boy had been standing in front of Unbeatable Joe's saloon on the corner of Twelfth Street and Seventh Avenue for ten minutes. He kept the gun clenched in his fist inside his coat pocket as the punishing wind rallied up Twelfth Street from the harbor. Across the street was the old Ansonia Clock Factory, now a textile manufacturing company. Its filthy red-brick face was even colder than the wind. Upstairs from Unbeatable Joe's, Fabulous Murphy had a two-room flat. Alley Boy was supposed to walk up there, turn the radio up full blast, and put one behind Fabulous Murphy's ear.

But Alley Boy couldn't think of Fabulous Murphy. He was thinking about Stephanie, repeating in his mind what he had said to her. He wished he hadn't called her a whore. He thought about her warm body in between the cool satin sheets, about her ivory smile and glimmering eyes. He thought about how he should be there making love to her instead of standing on a freezing street corner preparing for murder.

He thought about that recent day in the park, near Swan Lake, in his turf, his stomping ground, where he had made love to her in the snow. He thought about her laughing and he thought about her sleeping with her limbs entwined with his.

And then he thought about how Fabulous Murphy would look with his brains scattered on the floor like shredded liver.

But he never thought about looking up to the third floor of the factory across the street, where Cisco sat with a pair of binoculars, alternately spying on Fabulous Murphy through his unshaded living room window and Alley Boy there on the street. He didn't think about Cisco watching Fabulous Murphy as he packed his suitcase with the cheap clothes from his clothes closet and dresser drawers.

He only thought about Stephanie.

And he knew the sooner he got rid of Fabulous Murphy, the sooner he could get back to her.

Alley Boy walked into the vestibule of the tenement where Fabulous Murphy lived. The smell of rat poison lingered on the stale air, mixed with the smell of rotting garbage, and some other putrid smell, like that of a dirty bum who had infected the hallway by sleeping there the night before.

Alley Boy put these smells out of his mind and thought instead of the smells of Stephanie Kelly. He could recall the smell of her sweat as she panted through lovemaking. He could smell the perfume she wore and the odor of her womanhood when she became aroused. These were the smells Alley Boy held as he climbed the sticky, filthy steps to murder.

Bare thirty-watt light bulbs hung from exposed wires over the stairwells. The sounds of families arguing behind tenement flat doors filtered into the hallway. The shouting was in Puerto Rican Spanish and the tones were high and panicky. Cockroaches zigzagged up and down the peeling walls and disappeared into the cracks and holes of the plaster as Alley Boy made his way to the top floor.

When he climbed the fourth flight of stairs it became colder. The roof door was open, flapping furiously in the muscular wind. The wind whistled through the hallway, making goosebumps scrimmage on his flesh. The .38 in his hand was as cold as ice.

Alley Boy stood outside Fabulous Murphy's door for a swollen moment, listening to the muffled sound of the all-news radio station. The door was fastened by a cheap lock that could be snapped by a minor shove.

The roof door banged repeatedly. Alley Boy thought of Stephanie once more, her face angelic and red from the cold, and then he shoved against the door with all his might. The lock gave way. The gun was out. Fabulous Murphy fell to his knees in a single motion and buried his head in his arms.

"No, please, no, not now! Don't kill me. Please. Please! No! I'll do anything you ask me."

Alley Boy stood frozen with the gun pointed at Fabulous Murphy's head. Alley Boy's finger was locked on the trigger. His teeth were chattering. And his bowels were loose and uproarious, as they had been the day of the bank robbery. He gaped wide-eyed at Fabulous Murphy, who had his head buried, and he thought of Stephanie—again. Fabulous Murphy was crying. His big flabby head bobbed up and down and up and down, waiting for the impact of the bullet to tear it off.

Alley Boy's throat was as dry as a blotter. He couldn't swallow and he couldn't talk. He could hear the sound of the roof door banging and the tinny, distant, ridiculous sound of the weatherman on the radio.

All Alley Boy could see was Fabulous Murphy's head bobbing up and down. He didn't see Cisco watching him from the window across the street through the spyglasses. Alley Boy approached Fabulous Murphy slowly, with the gun at arm's length. He placed the cold barrel behind Murphy's left ear. He saw the flushed red color retreating from the back of Fabulous Murphy's neck. It became pale, and Fabulous Murphy knelt there on the floor like a two-hundred-and-fifty-pound pile of tapioca.

Alley Boy felt something wet under his feet now and he saw that Fabulous Murphy had pissed himself. The smell of urine made the stuffy, steam-heated room unbearable. And Alley Boy felt like peeing too. And crying, just like Fabulous Murphy.

He managed to control his bladder, but the tears came. He could not control them. He had to grab the gun with both hands now, because his body was convulsing with sobs. His finger was frozen on the trigger. He couldn't move the finger, couldn't take it away. He couldn't lower the gun. He felt his knees begin to unlock like the legs of an ironing board.

"I won't let you make me kill you, you fat tub of shit," Alley Boy said. "I'm not going to let you make me! Get up on your feet, you pile of shit—up on your fat fucking feet." Alley Boy finally managed to free his left hand from the gun while still training the pistol with his right. He yanked Fabulous Murphy to a standing position with a single motion. He was amazed at his own strength.

Fabulous Murphy stood there, stinking and wet and crying, and looked at Alley Boy. Fabulous Murphy's face looked grotesquely large and red and fleshy and ugly, with the gaping hole in his teeth and his bare gums making him look somehow inhuman. They stood staring at each other, both crying uncontrollably.

"You fat fuck," Alley Boy said as he slapped Fabulous Murphy across the face. "You fat fuck, you fat fuck! I'm supposed to kill you right now, you fat fucking fuck! But I'm not going to let you make me kill you! You're not gonna make me do it! Not gonna make me be like you and the rest of them. I never killed nobody and you won't make me."

Alley Boy wished Stephanie were there to take him away.

"I'm not like them, you hear!" Alley Boy said as he smacked Murphy again and again and again. "I'm not like them! I'm not like Cisco and Tommy Ryan, you fat fuck! Now you get out of here—out of this city. Out of here so they don't even find you, you fat fuck!"

Alley Boy wiped his eyes with the back of his gun hand. His vision was blurry and there was something dry and aching in his throat.

"Don't even change your clothes. Get out right away. You fat fuck. I'm leaving now and you better be five minutes behind me. You understand me? . . ."

Fabulous Murphy could not speak. He nodded his head affirmatively. Alley Boy turned around and bolted out the door. The roof door was still banging and he took the four flights two steps at a time until he reached the street below.

Cisco watched as Alley Boy ran east along Seventh Avenue. Then he watched as Fabulous Murphy began undressing to change clothes. Cisco left his perch and made for the fire exit that would take him to the street.

Fabulous Murphy quickly cleaned himself and put on a new pair of pants. He fastened the snaps of his cheap suitcase, turned off all the lights, and opened the front door to go out.

Before the door was fully opened something blazingly swift and painlessly sharp slashed across his neck. Fabulous Murphy tried to scream, but the air necessary for such an endeavor was racing out of the split seam of his throat. A foot pushed him backwards into his apartment and Fabulous Murphy fell lifelessly to the floor.

Alley Boy had rung the buzzer for ten minutes, but he got no reply from Stephanie. He walked to the corner of Flatbush Avenue and Plaza Street near the all-night newsstand to call her.

As he passed the newsstand, Alley Boy saw the headline concerning Frank Green Eyes on the *Daily News*. The whole game was making him sick now. He wondered if Tommy Ryan and Cisco had anything to do with that murder. One thing he was sure of at least, Fabulous Murphy would not become a headline anytime in the near future.

The dime fell into the coin box with a jingle and Alley Boy dialed the seven digits. The phone rang three, four, five, six, seven, eight times. Finally Alley Boy heard Stephanie's soft voice say, "Hello, Al."

"How'd you know it was me, Steph?"

"No one else ever calls me."

"That's good."

"Is it?"

"Come on, Steph," Alley Boy said. "Why all this stuff? Why didn't you answer the door? I was ringing for ten minutes."

"I know, Al."

"Don't you want to see me, Steph?"

"Not tonight, Al. Not now anyway. I want time to think. I want to think about what you said, Al."

"I told you I was sorry, Steph."

"Not that, Al. I don't care what insults you throw at me. I'm used to that kind of thing. I'm talking about what you said about yourself, Al. About having to prove yourself. You're just *you*, Al. That's why I love you. Not for what you want to be."

"Steph, please . . ."

"No, Al. Maybe this whole idea is crazy, Al. I need some time to think, Al. I know I love you. But I don't know if I can love who you want to be."

"Steph, I want to see you. Now. I have to."

"Call me in a few days, Al. Not now."

Stephanie hung up the phone and Alley Boy gently placed the receiver on the hook. He looked toward Prospect Park, into the darkness and all its hiding places, and started walking to it quickly. Right now this place was all he had. My stomping ground, Alley Boy thought. This is my stomping ground! Then, with tears chasing down his face, Alley Boy started to run.

21

Near midnight. Tommy Ryan placed the needle on the record and Gladys Knight and the Pips came on doing "Midnight Train to Georgia." A fire was blazing in the fireplace, and Carol sat on the suede couch with her legs tucked under her and a snifter of brandy in her hand. She stared directly into the fire in a trance, recalling what Tommy Ryan had told her about Frankie Green Eyes.

Tommy Ryan was snapping his fingers and dancing to the music in the middle of the living room floor. He had not bothered to discuss the warehouse rip-off with Carol. It would not have gone over too well in contrast with Carol's mourning over Tony Mauro.

"Come on, Carol," Tommy Ryan said, smiling and gyrating.

Carol stared into the fire, not acknowledging him.

"Come on, sweetheart," Tommy urged. "Boogie, baby. Get your mind off things."

"Maybe we should have let the cops handle it," Carol said distractedly.

"The cops? Are you losing your marbles? The cops?"

"Then I would have known every day he was in there, that he was suffering, paying for it, watching his life tick away. Knowing he was rotting. Instead he got it easy, in his sleep. Over and done with."

"At least it's over, honey."

"But I still don't understand how somebody like Tony could let a guy like that get him. He was too smart. Too careful."

"Anyone can make a mistake, Carol, anyone."

"Yeah," Carol said. "Anyone."

The phone rang in the kitchen and Tommy danced toward it and snatched it up.

"It's your dime," Tommy said.

"Afraid I have to drop a dime on Alley Boy. He didn't do it, man."

It was Cisco on the line and Tommy stopped boogieing. The music was loud enough for Carol not to hear him from the living room.

"Whadda you mean didn't do it? You mean he blew it?"

"He froze, man. I saw the whole thing."

"That little asshole. You mean Murphy is still among the living?"

"I never said that, Tommy," Cisco said.

Tommy laughed. "We're gonna have to do something about Alley Boy."

"We best deep-six him fast, man. I think maybe he's ready to crack, Tommy."

"Not yet," Tommy said. "We need him for that Flatbush bank. Not yet anyway."

"You call the shots, Tommy."

"Yeah, I know, and you fire them."

"It's a livin', man."

"Let's just lay low for a day. See what happens about Murphy."

"Okay, man. Hey, man, you sure this phone ain't tapped?"

"Positive," Tommy said. "I've had it checked. No way."

"You wanna take that coke dealer tomorrow night? Ten minutes' work, man. Could be big cash."

"Yeah. We'll do that one. I talk to you tomorrow, Cisco."

"*Adiós.*"

"So long."

Tommy hung up. He thought about Alley Boy. He knew now that the kid had to go. One way or the other. He had to be put in the lost and found.

Tommy Ryan boogied back into the living room, and after gentle persuasion, got Carol to her feet and they danced. And finally Carol managed to laugh.

The night was freezing—fit only for sleep—and Alley Boy slept heavily in his mother's apartment.

Ankles slept, too, alone, on his Castro convertible, his belly filled with tap beer and his mouth fuzzy with the taste of cigars. His dreams were noisy with the sound of children.

Adler had spent a good portion of the night looking at mug shots and working with the police artist on a composite picture. His wife, Sarah, slept deeply, but Adler was fitful all night, trying to remember details, trying to remember the last name of the kid on the train. Knowing that if he remembered, a juicy reward might be in store in time for Christmas.

Stephanie Kelly slept alone, nothing new for her, but

her dreams were turbulent and unpleasant and the few times she woke she wished that Al was there.

Cisco slept as he always did, like a cat, his hand on his folded blade beneath the pillow, ready to awaken at the slightest sound.

Tommy Ryan slept soundly after a satisfying night of sex with Carol Mauro. Carol, too, slept easily, her vengeance somewhat satisfied, knowing that a vengeful part of her life was behind her. And hoping that a promising one lay ahead with Tommy Ryan.

Only Captain Houlihan did not sleep. He waited all night for the lab report on the wallet Frank Adler had brought him. And he waited also for the police artist to finish the composite for immediate release if the print matched. He sat there in his office all night, smoking cigarettes, and staring at the green walls.

The phone woke Ankles at one thirty in the afternoon. His head felt like someone had used it for batting practice the night before. The room smelled of his feet. The Ban-Lon socks always made his feet smell bad, and Ankles had a hell of a lot of feet.

The call was from headquarters. It said that a man named William Murphy a.k.a. Fabulous Murphy was found dead in his apartment by a neighbor a half-hour before. The neighbor had gone up to close a roof door that had banged all night and noticed that a pool of blood had leaked from under the door of Murphy's apartment into the hallway. This aroused the neighbor's suspicion and he pushed open the apartment door after noticing that the lock had been broken.

William Murphy had his neck cut wide open and a packed suitcase lay next to him. The desk sergeant at police headquarters gave Ankles the Seventh Avenue address and Ankles hung up.

"A bad address," Ankles said to himself. "Lousy place to die."

Ankles looked at his nails, which were filthy. In the bathroom he turned on the shower and let the water run as hot as he could stand it on the nape of his neck to encourage more blood to visit his brain. As the water needled his neck, Ankles scrubbed his nails with a fingernail brush and thought about the cut throat he'd be viewing in a very short time.

The wound looked just like he'd pictured it when he arrived at Fabulous Murphy's apartment forty-five minutes later. Straight as a part in a barber's hair, from ear to ear. If only he could find a butcher with such skill, he'd have the thinnest veal cutlets in Brooklyn.

The forensic crew was wrapping up; the place had been dusted for prints, but there wasn't much to go on. The downstairs neighbor, who couldn't speak one word of English, had left prints everywhere but inside the fucking toilet bowl.

Ankles recognized Fabulous Murphy now—a two-bit con man who usually dealt in nothing larger than hot transistor radios. If he was into anything bigger, the belongings in his pad certainly didn't reflect it.

None of the neighbors remembered hearing or seeing anything. Of course not, Ankles thought. If you live in a place like this all you do is dream about the palm trees in Puerto Rico. He often wondered why anyone would leave a place as warm as Puerto Rico to live in freezing hovels like this one. Fabulous Murphy was the only non–Spanish-speaking tenant in the building. And he was obviously on his way somewhere when he was killed. His suitcase was packed and part of the contents included $980 in cash and a travel brochure for Miami.

The bunco squad must have a half-acre of felled trees on the poor sonofabitch, Ankles thought.

If it weren't for the cut throat, Ankles would have thought it was a simple case of revenge for conning the wrong sucker. People have been known to kill for the smallest of reasons if they think they've been made a fool of. But the cut throat was too perfect. There were no signs of a desperate struggle. No jagged edges of ripped and tattered flesh. It was a perfect, surgical cut. Like the one given Frankie Green Eyes. And, of course, Tony Mauro.

At four in the evening Alley Boy was still in bed. He had gotten up twice to phone Stephanie, but there had been no reply. After both attempts Alley Boy just wandered back to bed like an aimless, pining puppy.

His mother and grandmother were beside themselves with worry. His grandmother had brought him three different trays of food, but Alley Boy refused them all. His mother had asked him if he needed a doctor. Alley Boy told her no.

"Well, what the hell's a matter with you then?" his mother demanded. "You lie there like an old man who just had his gallstones removed. You don't want this, you don't want that, you don't want nothin', but at four o'clock my son is still in bed with a face on him that looks like a summons. So what you expect from me? You want me to play the banjo or something? Whadda I look like over here, that you lie there like somebody else's son and not my Alley Boy? Eh? Whadda I need, a

psychiatrist? You want me to swallow pills? Whadda
you want from me?"

"I just want to be left alone, Ma, that's all. There's
nothing wrong with me. I'm okay. Just tired."

"Tired?" the grandmother screamed with her thumbs
touching the other four fingers of both hands. "Tired?
Who's ever tired at four o'clock inna afternoon? Maybe
the milkman. But not a young boy. You don't eat, you
don't do nothin'. Whatsamatter, I cook poison all of a
sudden? Hah. Am I trying to poison you?"

"No, Gramma," Alley Boy said. "You're not trying
to poison me. You and Ma are just trying to drive me
nuts."

"Me?" the mother said with pain. "Me drive you
nuts? They find a man dead with his throat cut open
three blocks away, you tell me you're getting married,
you stay in bed until four, and I'm driving you nuts?
Hah!"

Alley Boy jumped up. The mother and the grandmother recoiled with fright.

"Who did they find with his throat cut, Ma, who?"

"How am I supposed to know who? Some fat guy.
The radio sez his name is Murphy. How do I know who
he is? Three blocks from here where I live."

The mother made the sign of the cross as Alley
Boy pulled on his clothes.

"Now you gettin' up because somebody has his throat
cut," the grandmother said. "You like a cut throat better than my brogoli? Whadda I care? Someday I'll cut
my own throat and you'll see who cooks for you!"

Alley Boy finished dressing and ran out of the house.
The mother and the grandmother stood stupefied as
he dashed out the door.

"Today I do a novena for that boy," the grandmother

said. "Two novenas. Three. Bahfongool, a million novenas that he makes me use that kind of words."

Stephanie Kelly never dressed all day. She loafed around the apartment on Prospect Park West in her bathrobe and looked out over the iced silver branches of the maples and oaks and pines that were Prospect Park. She was sipping her thirteenth cup of black coffee and listening to the sounds of the snow chains on the buses as they clanked along the avenue. The phone had rung several times, but she never answered it.

She watched the ambulances pull up to the nursing home across the street every couple of hours to take away another cargo of old flesh and bones to the morgue. And not more than an hour after a corpse was removed from the nursing home, a private car would pull up and another old satchel of expiring life would be wheeled in to await death.

The nursing home was like a pit stop for those elderly folks who were racing toward the finish line of the coroner's office. And there was a waiting list to get in. A waiting list to get into this human warehouse where people were stored until they were ready to fill holes in the earth.

Stephanie Kelly watched with aversion. And she wondered how long it would be before Al would fill one of those holes in the ground. How long it would be before the ambulance would come and take him away.

She didn't know if she was ready for a life with someone like that. At least turning tricks was a way of life—not death.

She turned her back on the street and walked into the kitchen. Her coffee cup was empty.

* * *

Alley Boy stood on the corner of Twelfth Street and Seventh Avenue as the ambulance attendants from Kings County Hospital wheeled the stretcher out of the hallway into the street. Alley Boy's heart was pounding like a wrecking ball inside his breast.

A crowd of Puerto Rican children had gathered outside the tenement, joking and carrying on as the sheet-covered corpse was wheeled past them toward the ambulance.

Alley Boy was trying to make sense of the situation. Had Cisco done this? If he did, Tommy would know I didn't go through with it, he thought.

Alley Boy saw Ankles near the ambulance speaking to a young dark-haired guy in a trench coat. The young guy must be a reporter, Alley Boy thought. He's writing notes into a notebook. Without even considering that he might be a suspect, Alley Boy drifted toward Ankles and overheard the conversation between the cop and the reporter.

"So right now you're not sure if there is a link between this murder and the Sanchez one in the Methodist Hospital?" the reporter asked, as if for clarification of something he already knew.

"Not until we have an autopsy, Daly. How many times I have to tell you that?"

"It just seems strange that two murders within forty-eight hours and five blocks of each other, with the same MO, doesn't even warrant a guess on your part," Michael Daly from the *Daily News* said.

"Murder ain't a guessing game, Daly. Facts. I have to go on facts. If you want it off the record, that's another thing."

"All right, off the record."

"I think it's the same guy done this. But that's just an educated guess. I have absolutely no idea what this guy Murphy and that Francisco Sanchez have in common. One was a known drug dealer, the other a two-bit con artist. They usually don't swim in the same cesspool. But who the fuck knows? Maybe they were both in love with the same bull dyke. See what I mean? You're making me guess."

"Is it the same MO as the Tony Mauro murder?" Daly asked.

Ankles was sensitive to this.

"Look, I gave you all I could. I didn't even talk to the *Post* guys because you're the first guy who ever got the quotes straight in print. But do me a favor, will you? Gimme some time. I promise if I get anything worthwhile, I'll call you first. Okay?"

"Okay," Daly said and then drifted away.

Ankles was about to get into his Plymouth Fury when he noticed Alley Boy standing on the corner with a pale, blank look on his face. Alley Boy stared at the stretcher being hoisted into the back of the Kings County meat wagon. Ankles approached Alley Boy.

"Whadda you doin' here, D'Agastino?" Ankles said.

"I live a few blocks away," Alley Boy said.

"So does your mother, but I don't see her standing here like a gaping asshole."

"Just looking," Alley Boy said as he watched the ambulance doors being shut.

"You know that guy Murphy?" Ankles asked.

"Met him once or twice," Alley Boy said.

"What about that Frankie Green Eyes? You know, I was up around your mother's house looking for you the other day. But I know you have an alibi on that one, kid. Your girl friend told me you were with her. I buy that because I happen to think that Kelly girl is all right. You should take her and hit the road, kid. You keep hanging around with Tommy Ryan and you're gonna fall like him."

Ankles peered at Alley Boy, who was still staring at the ambulance as it pulled away from the curb.

"So long, kid," Ankles said, and walked to his detective car, got in, and pulled away.

Frank Adler had been arguing with Captain Houlihan for two hours over the police artist's composite.

"I'm telling you this doesn't look one iota like the kid I met on the train. The nose is too big. The ears are too small. The hair is too short. And the eyes look like Farrah Fawcett-Majors, for chrissake."

"But you don't understand, Adler. We have a first name and a perfectly matched print. The print is so clear from the wallet that we only have to hold a suspect ten minutes to see if he's our boy."

"Yeah, but with a composite like that, you'll go through a thousand guys who don't look anything like the kid I'm telling you about. Where did this police artist get his training? I seen kids finger painting in kindergarten who were better."

"He's the best we have," Houlihan said.

"I'm sorry, but if you issue this sketch I'm gonna have to go right to the newspapers and tell them that the composite they're carrying is not even close. I'll even go a step further if I have to. I'll even tell them you really hate Jews. How's that grab you?"

Houlihan looked evenly at Adler and took a drag of a Kool.

"I guess that grabs me by the balls, Mr. Adler."

"Good. Now let's work on another composite."

"I guess I have no choice," Houlihan said as he pressed the intercom to summon the artist once again.

* * *

Tommy Ryan parked the gold Cadillac on Fifty-sixth Street between Lexington. and Third Avenues in Manhattan. The luxury high-rise was across the street, rising thirty-two floors from the ground. Tommy pushed two shells into the chambers of the silver-plated shotgun. Cisco carried only his straight razor because he hadn't gotten the .38 back from Alley Boy yet.

"The wire you got on this guy is good, eh, Cisco?"

"Yeah, but like I said, man, he could have a lot of scratch and maybe not so much. It usually depends on what kind of business he's done that day. But he moves enough snow for a blizzard."

"Then he must have a rod with him."

"I'd say so, man, but so what. He'll never know what hit him, man," Cisco said. Cisco was busy pulling on a pair of greasy overalls in the backseat of the car. Once he had them on, he put on the workman's cap and he and Tommy Ryan stepped out of the car. Tommy opened the trunk and Cisco reached in and took out a tool box. Tommy Ryan put the shotgun into a plastic garbage bag and then placed it under his arm.

They walked into the vestibule of the high-rise and a doorman opened the door for them.

"Can I help you fellas?" the doorman asked.

"Yeah," Tommy Ryan said as he buried the plastic-wrapped shotgun in the doorman's belly. "You can ring Majeska's pad and tell him a man from the gas company is here to investigate a leak. Tell him we'll be right up."

The doorman's eyes bulged when he felt the double barrel against his soft belly. The doorman rang Majeska's apartment as instructed. Majeska was furious at being disturbed at this time of night and said he wasn't going to let the gas man up.

"Tell him if it isn't checked he might blow up in his sleep," Tommy Ryan whispered into the doorman's ear. The doorman relayed the message, and finally Majeska agreed to let them up.

Tommy Ryan led the doorman to the utility closet, bound him with adhesive tape, and locked the door. He and Cisco rode the elevator to the penthouse.

Tommy Ryan stood with his back flush against the wall next to the apartment door as Cisco rang the bell. Majeska looked through the peephole and saw the Puerto Rican in the work clothes outside. Satisfied with his looks, Majeska opened the door and immediately began to complain.

"What time of night is this for the gas company to come around?" he protested. "I don't smell any gas leaks."

Just as he finished the last sentence, Tommy Ryan pushed the shotgun into his nose.

"Good evening," Tommy Ryan said in his Bela Lugosi best.

Majeska, a man in his fifties with receding hair and a paunch beneath the silk bathrobe, backed up in horror.

"How goes the coke trade, Mr. Majeska?" Tommy continued as he and Cisco entered the apartment and closed the door behind them.

Majeska was speechless, like a puppet whose ventriloquist had gone hoarse.

"Money," Cisco said. "We want a lot of that."

"I don't have much right now," Majeska said as he fell to the floor while backing up.

Suddenly the sound of a female voice was heard from somewhere in the back of the apartment.

"Is everything all right, honey?" the female voice asked. And then she appeared through a doorway from the plush living room. A tall, beautiful blond woman of about thirty. She was wearing a silk housecoat that was buttoned down the front at full length.

When the woman saw Majeska on the floor and the shotgun trained on him, she froze in horror and stuck her fingers in her mouth and let her eyes do the screaming.

Tommy Ryan looked at her and smiled and said to Majeska in the deep bogus voice, "Things go better with coke."

Cisco laughed like a cackling witch as he put the toolbox on the floor and unfolded the straight razor.

"How much money you got, fatso?" Cisco asked Majeska.

"Two—maybe three thousand," Majeska said.

"That's not enough, friend," Cisco said.

"I also have about four ounces of pure crystal," Majeska said.

"Still not enough," Tommy Ryan said as he helped Majeska to his feet and led him toward the woman. Then they ushered both of them into the living room. Cisco made Majeska sit on his hands on the couch. He made the woman stand in the middle of the room and he walked in circles around her. She kept her eyes closed and a river of terror ran under the soft skin of her face.

"Whadda you say, baby?" Cisco said. "Is that all your lover boy has? Three grand? Huh?"

The woman said nothing. She stood there shaking. On the coffee table there was a candy dish with a lid on it. Tommy Ryan lifted the lid to reveal a mound of crystal cocaine. Tommy snorted some off the tip of his pinkie.

"Nice coke, Majeska," Tommy said as he kept the shotgun pointed at the man on the couch.

"Please take whatever you want, but don't hurt me," Majeska said, "or her."

"Oh, we're not gonna hurt her," Cisco said. "We're gonna make her feel real good, aren't we, sweetheart?"

The woman said nothing. She simply stood there, trembling, with her eyes shut tight. Cisco, in a flourish, took a swipe with the razor and with smooth, educated skill severed each button from the front of the housecoat. The buttons bounced on the thick carpet. The housecoat fell open revealing large, firm, pink-nippled breasts and a beard of dirty-blond pubic hair.

"Please," Majeska said. "Please don't."

"Be quiet," Tommy Ryan said in the deep voice. Cisco scooped some of the cocaine from the candy dish and began to rub it into the woman's vagina with his left hand.

"That feels nice, doesn't it, baby?" Cisco said. "Make your pussy feel like an air conditioner."

Still the woman said nothing, just trembled. Cisco moved around back of her and lifted her housecoat and made the woman bend over so her spread buttocks were facing Majeska.

"Nice ass you have, baby," Cisco said as he rubbed cocaine into her rectum.

Majeska sat on the couch whimpering now as he watched Cisco take down his pants and move his erected penis toward the woman.

"When I finish with her," Cisco said, "I'm gonna do the same to you, Majeska. A big dick stuck up your fat ass, man. You gonna like that, man."

Cisco made the woman grasp the coffee table as he penetrated her. A small cry issued from the woman as Cisco moved deeper into her. Majeska watched as the woman bit her lip so hard in pain that blood trickled from her mouth.

"Okay, okay," Majeska said. "I'll give you the money. Please stop it! Please stop!"

Cisco withdrew and the woman fainted to the floor. No sound came from her. Majeska walked across the living room to a bookcase and removed several books, revealing a wall safe. He turned the dial and opened the safe and took out a bundle of cash wrapped in rubber bands.

"There's fifteen thousand there," Majeska said. "Please take it and leave."

Tommy Ryan flipped through the wad of cash and then stuck his hand in the safe and withdrew two plastic baggies filled with cocaine. Tommy Ryan buried the butt of the shotgun into Majeska's belly. Majeska fell to the floor. Tommy Ryan kicked him in the ribs.

"You should have more loyalty to your woman than your filthy fucking cash," Tommy Ryan said.

Cisco zipped up his trousers and he and Tommy Ryan made for the door.

22

Ankles sat at a desk in the small office in Brooklyn police headquarters looking through the bunco file on Fabulous Murphy. He had his feet propped up on the desk and he was puffing on his cigar. He felt tired and his own body odor was bothering him. A young, red-faced cop named Daniels brought him another file on Fabulous Murphy and plopped it on his desk.

"That's what Manhattan South sent over, Lieutenant," Daniels said. "More of the same shit. Chisling old ladies out of pension checks, dealing in hot cameras, a couple of mail-order scams, even a bust on a porno distribution ring. Penny ante."

"He has no relatives," Ankles said. "None of these guys have any relatives. That Sanchez kid, Green Eyes, he has a cousin doing time in Rikers Island. That's it. Nothing else. This Murphy guy doesn't have squat."

"What the hell could be the connection between those two guys? Unless it's just some guy going around bumping off the destitute as an act of virtue?"

"No relatives, hardly any friends—where the hell do you start with these guys?" Ankles said.

"Well, at least that Mauro kid has relatives, don't he?" Daniels asked.

Ankles fell silent for a long moment. Then he said, "Yeah, he has relatives. He has relatives. Yeah."

Ankles's mind filled with the images of Tony Mauro again. Then he thought about Marsha in the rowboat that night on Swan Lake in Prospect Park.

Alley Boy was late. Tommy Ryan had told him to be at the warehouse by eleven P.M. and it was now eleven thirty. Tommy Ryan was furious, but he was trying to control his temper, because he didn't want to frighten Alley Boy off before this one last job. He wanted him to think things were normal. He needed him to drive the next day so he couldn't afford to frighten Alley Boy. Besides, after tomorrow they could get rid of the kid once and for all.

Alley Boy finally rang the outside bell at eleven thirty-five. Tommy Ryan led him in and put his arm over Alley Boy's shoulder. Alley Boy looked depressed —not afraid, not nervous, just in the dumps.

"Hey, Al, how are you, pal?" Tommy Ryan said.

"Okay, I guess," Alley Boy said.

"Something troubling you, Al?"

"No, nothing, Tommy. I'm all right."

"You ready for the big one tomorrow?"

"Yeah," Alley Boy said. "I suppose so."

"Well, me and Cisco went and got us some money tonight to pay for all the things we needed. We got the uniforms, the smoke bombs, the special car with the stolen plates. That baby can hit one twenty in thirty seconds. There's no way they'll ever come near us. It cost us plenty, but it's worth it. You see it parked out there in front?"

"Yeah," Alley Boy said. "I seen it."

"Well, whadda you think?"

"Fine. Just fine, Tommy."

Cisco sat at the bar inspecting a black explosive device. It was about four inches square. Alley Boy put Cisco's .38 on the bar. Cisco picked it up and tucked it in his belt.

"See those smoke bombs Cisco has there, Al?" Tommy Ryan said. "They'll make enough smoke to make it look like a forest fire. It's gonna be a piece of cake."

"Yeah," Alley Boy said.

"What's troubling you, Al? Come on, you can tell me."

"I didn't kill him, Tommy," Alley Boy said. "I went up there and I just couldn't kill him. I looked at the poor bastard and I just couldn't do it. But somebody did, Tommy."

"You mean that wasn't your work, Al?" Tommy said incredulously. "Shit, I thought you did him in, Al."

"I swear it wasn't me, Tommy. When I left, Murphy was alive."

"Well, it looks like somebody did our work for us then," Tommy Ryan said. "Probably somebody he conned."

"You think so, Tommy?"

"Obviously, Al. I didn't have anything to do with it. And Cisco didn't have anything to do with it. So if you didn't have anything to do with it, it must have been somebody else, right?"

"I suppose so," Alley Boy said more cheerfully. "Listen, Tommy, I have something I want to tell you.

After tomorrow I don't wanna have nothing more to do with banks. I want to just take the money and go off somewhere with Stephanie. Is that all right with you, Tommy?"

"Sure, Al," Tommy said. "Sure. Whatever you want, Al. Besides, this one tomorrow is gonna be so big that none of us will have to want for anything for a long time. That's if your information on this bank is right, which I hope it is, Al."

"Oh, it's right, Tommy. I know that place inside out. There should be anywhere between two hundred and two hundred fifty thousand."

"Well then, after tomorrow we can all retire for a while, Al."

Tommy Ryan put his hand on Alley Boy's shoulder and smiled.

"Come on, let's have a drink. By noon tomorrow we'll be rich."

Alley Boy smiled and thought about getting on an airplane with a briefcase filled with money in one hand and Stephanie in the other.

One day away.

23

At noon the next day Alley Boy pulled the gray four-door Mercedes to the curb outside the Chase Manhattan Flatbush branch on Flatbush Avenue and Cortelyou Road.

Tommy Ryan and Cisco got out of the car. They each were dressed in dark wool business suits and each carried a briefcase. Tommy Ryan had on a false beard and moustache and a pair of dark sunglasses. Cisco wore a fedora tipped low over his eyes and a pair of shades.

A Brink's truck was unloading a cargo of money into the bank with three armed guards protecting the cash. Tommy Ryan walked directly into the bank while Cisco lingered a moment longer in the street outside, watching as the Brink's men pulled the heavy dolly up a ramp to the curb.

Alley Boy pulled away from the curb and drove the

car around the block and parked it again on Flatbush Avenue—at a fire hydrant about two hundred yards down the street from the bank.

When Cisco saw Alley Boy park, he entered the bank. He walked directly over to one of the writing counters and took out a white form. Tommy Ryan was at another writing counter twenty feet away. Cisco opened his briefcase and took out two black metallic explosive devices. He pressed a delayed timer button on each of them.

Then he tipped his fedora, and Tommy Ryan, picking up the signal, pressed the delayed timer buttons on his black explosive devices. Cisco wrapped a sheet of white paper around one of the smoke bombs and tossed it into the trash basket next to him. Tommy Ryan did the same with one of his smoke bombs. Then Cisco and Tommy Ryan moved to different writing counters and repeated the process.

The black female bank guard did not notice. All her attention was turned on the Brink's shipment that was being wheeled up a ramp into the bank.

After he had finished his business, Tommy Ryan left the busy bank. Cisco hesitated for a minute and then exited. Cisco and Tommy Ryan walked back down the street to the parked Mercedes. Tommy opened the trunk and pulled out two large metal boxes that looked like footlockers. On the side was the stencil SCOTT PACKS. These were the emergency kits the New York City firemen used in fighting fires involving dense smoke. Tommy and Cisco got back into the Mercedes.

Alley Boy pulled away from the curb and drove around the corner onto Cortelyou Road. There were two abandoned buildings on the street and the snow was piled high in front of them. Tommy Ryan and Cisco took the Scott Packs and went into the abandoned building where they quickly undressed and took the

New York City Fire Department uniforms from the
footlockers and put them on. Tommy Ryan removed the
false moustache and beard and he and Cisco put on the
Scott gas masks. Tommy checked his watch.

"Two minutes," he said to Cisco.

They waited patiently inside the abandoned building
until they heard Alley Boy beep his horn three times.
This meant that the smoke-induced pandemonium had
begun in the bank.

Inside the bank great billows of black smoke rushed
from the four wastebaskets. The customers, tellers,
manager, officers, bank guard, and even the Brink's
men made a mad rush for the street.

When Tommy Ryan and Cisco heard the sirens of
the approaching fire engines, they ran out of the abandoned building, each carrying one of the footlockers.

When they stepped outside, they saw that the fire
engines were parked on the corner in a swirl of
commotion and red lights. Tommy Ryan and Cisco
threw their civilian clothes into the Mercedes and
Alley Boy pulled away from the curb again, driving
slowly up Cortelyou Road.

Tommy Ryan and Cisco walked to the corner carrying the Scott boxes. Tommy Ryan's silver shotgun
clanked inside the metal box. At the corner a fire
lieutenant was leading the men into the bank with the
hose. All the firemen were wearing Scott masks. Tommy
Ryan and Cisco grabbed a piece of the hose as the
crowd swelled in the street. Four fire trucks were
parked on the corner.

Inside the bank the smoke was as thick as something
solid. Tommy Ryan and Cisco immediately dropped to
their knees and produced heavy-duty flashlights from
the footlockers. They crawled along the floor until they
located the Brink's dolly.

The other fire fighters were spraying madly at the

walls and ceiling, trying to locate the flames. There was shouting; walls were being axed, and there was much running and stumbling in the gloom.

Tommy Ryan and Cisco proceeded to fill the Scott boxes with the Brink's loot. The bills were in large cardboard boxes.

They loaded the bills into the Scott boxes. They didn't bother with the coins. When they were finished, Tommy Ryan and Cisco began crawling toward the door. Tommy Ryan carried the shotgun inside his rubber turnout coat.

Once outside, Cisco and Tommy Ryan carried the heavy boxes right past the female bank guard. She studied the two gas-masked firemen suspiciously. She watched as the two firemen approached one of the fire trucks, then passed it, and then started a mad dash for the gray Mercedes parked across the street.

The car trunk was open and Cisco and Tommy Ryan threw their metal boxes into the trunk. The bank guard dropped to one knee with her gun drawn as she saw the first fireman jump into the backseat.

"Stop!" she screamed as the car began lurching away. She fired. The bullet caught Tommy Ryan in the right shoulder, just tearing his raincoat, but with enough impact to spin him around.

"Get out of here," Tommy Ryan screamed. "Split. Move it."

The Mercedes took off and Tommy Ryan ran in the opposite direction from the Mercedes, back toward Cortelyou Road. The female bank guard was in the middle of Flatbush Avenue now, down on one knee again, and she fired. This time the bullet smashed into the top of Tommy Ryan's leg and he stumbled.

As he fell he ripped off one of the barrels of the shotgun in the direction of the bank guard. The bank guard leapt behind one of the fire trucks.

Tommy Ryan began running with all he had down
Cortelyou Road, hoping to make it to one of the abandoned buildings, where he might escape through the
backyards. But he kept stumbling from the lead lodged
at the top of his right leg. Each time he fell, he got
back up and kept running, leaving a bloody trail like
a wounded animal in the unshoveled snow outside the
abandoned buildings.

The bank guard had Tommy Ryan directly in her aim
as he pushed himself off the ground. She was about to
fire when the Mercedes made a two-wheeled turn onto
Cortelyou Road with Cisco firing madly in the direction
of the bank guard. The bank guard rolled through slush
underneath a parked car as Alley Boy screeched the
Mercedes to a halt. Alley Boy jumped out and grabbed
Tommy by the arms and dragged him to the car and
threw him into the backseat. Then Cisco fired two
more shots, and Alley Boy jumped behind the wheel
and was away like a rocket.

The bank guard slid out from under the car and
pegged two more shots in the general direction of the
fleeing Mercedes. But the car was now already a block
away.

A police car rounded the slushy corner and the bank
guard pointed toward the vanishing gray Mercedes.
The police car gave chase, but it now looked futile as
the Mercedes turned right on Ocean Avenue.

Alley Boy drilled the swift machine through red
lights in the direction of Prospect Park. The car zigzagged down the slushy avenue. At Empire Boulevard
the gray Mercedes swung into the park near the entrance to the zoo.

Alley Boy raced the car through the circular blacktop of the park and exited at Coney Island Avenue.
Sirens could be heard everywhere, but no cop cars
were visible in the rearview mirror. Then, at Park

Circle, a police car came straight at Alley Boy, trying to ram him. But Alley Boy veered the car away to the right. The police car mounted the sidewalk and rammed into one of the Grecian columns at the entrance to Prospect Park.

Alley Boy made a screaming left off Coney Island Avenue onto Vanderbilt Street and raced the car in the direction of Greenwood Cemetery. At Eleventh Avenue and Twentieth Street Alley Boy slowly entered the cemetery through the front gates.

He paused briefly at the security check as Tommy Ryan covered his bullet wound with his rubber raincoat.

"We're visiting Joey Gallo's grave," Alley Boy said.

"All right," said the security guard.

Alley Boy drove slowly into the graveyard until he was out of the security guard's view. Then he sped over the winding roads through the cemetery until he came to Tommy Ryan's gold Cadillac, which was parked down the hill from the tombstone of Joey Gallo.

They quickly changed cars, moving the Scott boxes and the clothes into the Cadillac's trunk. Tommy Ryan hobbled on the bad leg. Alley Boy then drove quietly out of the Thirty-sixth Street and Fourth Avenue exit of the cemetery and headed west toward the docks.

Five minutes later they were safely concealed inside the warehouse.

Once the accordion gate rolled down, Cisco and Alley Boy helped Tommy Ryan onto the brass bed in the back room. Cisco applied a tourniquet to the wound to stop the bleeding.

Tommy Ryan looked up from the bed in short-breathed pain at Alley Boy.

"You asshole," Tommy Ryan said. "You should never have come back."

"I had to," Alley Boy said.

"Thanks, Al," Tommy Ryan said.

Alley Boy smiled broadly.

"Get out the money and bring it in and count it, Al," Tommy Ryan instructed.

Alley Boy went out to get the money and Cisco leaned close to Tommy Ryan.

"I have to let him live, Cisco," Tommy Ryan said.

"Whatever you say, Tommy," Cisco said.

Tommy Ryan lay there grimacing with pain as Alley Boy came back in with the Scott boxes. Cisco and Alley Boy busied themselves with the counting of the money. Tommy Ryan made a phone call to a doctor in upstate New York who would take care of the bullet wound.

When they had finished counting, the take came to $217,000. Tommy Ryan was pleased.

"Take your cut, Alley Boy," Tommy Ryan said. "It's seventy-two thousand dollars."

Alley Boy jumped up excited. He thought about Stephanie and faraway places. Seventy-two thousand dollars, he thought. Oh, my God!

"Tommy, you don't mind if I leave it here until I'm ready to split, do you?"

"Of course not, Al," Tommy Ryan said. "You were terrific today, Al. The fuckin' best. I never seen anybody drive like that before in my life."

Alley Boy beamed with pride and kept repeating out loud, "Seventy-two thousand dollars. Seventy-two thousand dollars . . ."

24

The letter arrived at Frank Adler's house at one thirty P.M., the usual time the postman came. Frank Adler had spent the whole night on the new composite with the police artist again. Twice he and the artist had almost come to blows. The composite still wasn't right, as if the artist were purposely screwing it up. At four A.M. Adler had told them to shove the picture up the collective Red Hook Police Department's ass. "I'm going home to get some sleep," he said.

That morning he had told Sarah, his wife, to call the office and tell them he wouldn't be in. Adler wanted some sleep. He had decided his sleuthing days were over. He had done his bit and he didn't feel like wasting any more time.

He was still in a heavy sleep when Sarah woke him up at one forty-five P.M.

"This is funny, Frank," Sarah said.

"Nothing's fun anymore, Sarah. Not even Cheerios. Leave me alone."

"It's just this letter with ten dollars in cash in it with a note."

"Sarah, I couldn't care less about ten dollars. Ten dollars doesn't even buy a pizza anymore."

"But it pays for a train ticket to New York," Sarah said.

"Stiff price for a cattle car."

"This letter is from some kid who says you paid his fare for him and he's paying you back. It says, 'Dear Frank, Thanks for the ticket and the coffee. Merry Christmas. Al.' "

One of Frank Adler's eyes opened wide. "Sarah," Adler said softly, "did you say *Al?*"

"That's what it says, Frank."

Frank Adler jumped out of bed without bending his knees and ripped the letter out of Sarah's hand. Sarah screamed in minor fright.

"My God, Frank. It's only ten dollars," Sarah said with alarm.

"No it isn't, Sarah," Frank Adler said. "It's ten thousand dollars."

Frank Adler stood in the middle of the bedroom in his shorts and looked at the return address on the envelope. It read: AL D'AGASTINO—352 7TH AVENUE, BROOKLYN 11215.

"Sarah," Frank Adler said, "from now on you have my permission to open all my mail. Anytime you want. You're a sweetheart."

He kissed his wife on the lips. Sarah sat down, bewildered. Frank Adler picked up the telephone and dialed seven digits.

"Hello," Frank Adler said into the telephone when he heard the switchboard at the Red Hook Police De-

partment answer. "I'd like to speak with Captain Houlihan. Tell him Frank Adler is calling."

Stephanie Kelly picked up the telephone on the tenth
ring.

"Hello, Al," Stephanie said softly.

"Hi, Steph," Alley Boy said excitedly. "Christ, I'm
glad you answered, Steph. It's all over, Steph. I'm
ready to go. We'll go wherever you want. Anywhere at
all. Right now, Steph."

"Al," Stephanie said, "what are you talking about?
You mean you're ready to leave? Just you and me? No
Tommy Ryan? No Mom and Granny? Just me and
you, Al?"

"That's right, Steph," Alley Boy said. "Whadda you
say, Steph?"

"But where, when, how, Al?"

"You decide that, Steph. We'll go where you want.
Get on an airplane, Steph. Me and you. That's all. Just
meet me in my mother's house in a couple of hours. I
want to say good-bye to them, Steph. Then we'll go to
the airport and just pick a plane. Any plane."

"Al," Stephanie said.

"Yeah, Steph?"

"I love you, Al."

"I love you, too, Steph."

25

Tommy Ryan drove the Cadillac due north on the New York Thruway. The tranquility of the countryside was a contrast to the afternoon of hysteria. The pine forests were green walls on either side of the blacktop and a roof of gray clouds ladled out the dimmest of daylight.

Tommy Ryan was still in great pain. The bleeding had stopped, but the lead in his groin was beginning to infect the tissue surrounding the wound. Tommy Ryan wanted to get to the doctor's place before the infection became felonious.

Cisco, who could not drive, sat next to Tommy Ryan in the front seat.

"You sure you're all right, Tommy?" Cisco asked.

"Yeah," Tommy Ryan said. "I'll make it. I better. That's the hardest money I ever earned."

"But there's lots of it, man."

"Thank God," Tommy said. "When we go back to pick it up we better get outta town with it for a while."

"You sure it'll be all right in the warehouse like that? We already have been taken off once, man."

"Only Fabulous Murphy, the bimbos, and Alley Boy know about that place. The bims won't go near it again, believe me, and Alley Boy is satisfied with what he has."

"I hope you're doin' the right thing lettin' him slide, man," Cisco said.

"The cat saved my life," Tommy Ryan said. "Besides, he's gonna adios this afternoon with the whore. So he can't hurt us."

"I just hope he gets away all right, man," Cisco said. "If he wound up in the joint he'd crack in an hour."

"This is true," Tommy Ryan said. "But we got people inside to take care of that."

"Yeah," Cisco said.

Tommy Ryan kept his foot on the accelerator as the gold Cadillac sped north to farm country.

The call from Captain Houlihan came into Brooklyn police headquarters at four in the afternoon. Ankles was in the homicide squad office on the phone with the coroner's office when Daniels from the bunco squad came in. Daniels waited patiently while Ankles took notes on a yellow legal pad as he spoke to a deputy coroner.

"I know straight razors don't have ballistics, Ralph," Ankles was saying. "But does the gash look like it was made by the same guy to you? . . . Yeah, well, that's all I wanted to know."

Ankles hung up the telephone and lit his cigar with

the disposable lighter. Daniels was sitting on his desk.

"Nothing, huh?"

"Oon gotz."

"Well, robbery division just got something that might interest you," Daniels said. "Just got a call from a Captain Houlihan from a town called Red Hook upstate. Remember last week there was a bank job, three rabbis or rabbinical students or some shit?"

"Yeah," Ankles said wearily, "sort of. . . ."

"Well, they got a positive ID on a suspect from a print left on one of them funny fur hats. They came up with a name."

"So what's his name?" Ankles asked.

"Albert D'Agastino."

Ankles choked on a mouthful of smoke and snapped to his feet.

"Are you sure, Daniels?"

"They have an APB out on him right now. Warrant was issued an hour ago in Poughkeepsie."

Ankles ran out the door of the homicide division and down the hall to the robbery division. A detective was doing paperwork at one of the ten desks in the office.

"Who's got that D'Agastino warrant in here?" Ankles asked.

"It's still on the spindle, Lieutenant," the detective said. "All our guys are out at that Flatbush bank. We won't get to that until tonight."

"I'll take it," Ankles said.

"But it ain't your department, Lieutenant," the detective said. "It's a robbery, not a homicide."

"Look, don't give me a hard time, kid, or you'll be cashing that gold badge in for food stamps. This warrant might have to do with a homicide."

"Sure, Lieutenant," the detective said. "I didn't mean anything by it. It's right here."

The detective handed Ankles the warrant. Ankles read it and shook his head.

"The poor dumb sonofabitch," Ankles said. "I told him he'd fall."

Ankles walked briskly out of the office and made for the stairs to the street.

Stephanie Kelly fastened the clasps on the two Gucci suitcases and rang for the doorman in the lobby to come up and help her down with them. The taxicab was waiting downstairs in the street.

As she waited for the doorman to arrive, Stephanie Kelly took one last look around her apartment. There was always something nostalgic in leaving a place where you've lived part of your life. Memories lived in the dusty and shadowy corners of the room. There in the kitchen she could see herself and Al eating the first home-cooked meal she ever tried. It was franks and beans, and she burned both, but Al ate them anyway and told her they were great.

Stephanie smiled.

There in the bedroom she fell in love with him. She remembered sleeping with her arm draped over his broad shoulders. His heavy breathing in the night was a sound of comfort and security and protection. There was a big difference in spending the night next to a man who didn't leave money on the dresser in the morning.

There in the living room they had had their first fight, just a few days ago. And now she was glad that they had. Because now things with Al were fresh, like the smell of the air after a storm.

There in the bathtub they had bathed together, splashing water at each other like two reckless kids.

But that's all there was left in this place. Memories.

Not a future. Now it didn't matter where they went, so long as it was together. There would be a new place, in a new town, with good nights and much laughter. And who the hell knows, maybe there were even kids ahead of them. Maybe I'll be a mother, she thought.

She laughed and the doorbell rang.

Stephanie let the doorman in. He picked up the two bags and went out to the elevator. She looked around once more, smiled, and closed the door.

Alley Boy sat at the kitchen table twirling linguine with white clam sauce around a fork. He was stuffing the pasta into his mouth and biting off clumps of garlic bread. There was a smile cemented to his face that wouldn't go away and his grandmother and mother sat at the table staring at him in astonishment.

"Whoever heard of going on your honeymoon before you're married?" the mother said, her hands outstretched toward Alley Boy. "What did I raise over here? Did I raise you ass backwards or are you goin' senile at twenty-one years old?"

"I'm telling you, Rosa," the grandmother said, "he's crazy. Maybe we should call the doctor, that he goes on a honeymoon before he marries the girl, who isn't even Italian. No, I know what I'm gonna do. I'll call the priest. Maybe he's takin' that LSD they show you onna Eyewitness News with Bill Beutel. Maybe that's it. Maybe he should go to confession."

"Any more garlic bread, Gramma?" Alley Boy asked with the same smile.

"At least he eats," the grandmother said. "But they say they always eat a lot when they go crazy. How about that Albert Fish who used to eat the kids and bury the bones in the backyard?"

Alley Boy broke out laughing and the grandmother

came over closer to him, her face turning red, forcing out the words with desperate breaths.

"You laugh, but Albert Fish, back inna thirties, he ate little kids. Right here in Brooklyn. He buried the bones inna backyard and when they asked him how come he did it he sez to them he was hungry. You tell me, Alley Boy—he wasn't crazy eating little kids the way you eat those macaronis like you haven't been fed since the leap year? Don't laugh. I think you goin' crazy—you should see the priest from Saint Stanislaus. Even if Saint Stanislaus was a Polack like the new Pope. God forgive them over there, what they did making a Polack a Pope anyway—and from a Communist country."

The grandmother put her hands together in prayer and shook them with eyes upcast toward the ceiling.

"You don't care that your grandmother has a heart attack and I have a nervous breakdown," the mother said. "Why should you? You're not my son anymore. You're some orphan who comes around to eat when it rains. So why should you care?"

Alley Boy was twirling the fork around the last of the linguine when someone knocked at the door. Alley Boy got up to answer it. He was still chewing the last of his meal when he opened the door, expecting to see Stephanie.

Alley Boy stopped chewing when he saw Ankles standing in the doorway, looking sad and immense, slapping a folded piece of paper against his open palm.

"It's over, D'Agastino," Ankles said. "I'm sorry it had to be you first. But it's over."

Alley Boy stared long and hard at Ankles for a moment. The mother was asking who it was from inside at the kitchen table. The grandmother was mumbling in Italian as she washed dishes at the kitchen sink.

"It's for me, Ma," Alley Boy said.

Ankles shrugged his shoulders and handed Alley Boy the warrant. Alley Boy read it and his face froze as if an anesthetic had been injected into it.

"I'll get my coat," Alley Boy said and walked back into the apartment.

"I'm afraid I'll have to follow you in," Ankles said. Alley Boy opened the door wider for Ankles and let him into the apartment. The mother saw the big cop standing in the foyer as Alley Boy went to a hall closet and took his coat from a hanger.

"What's going on, Alley Boy?" the mother asked with alarm.

"Your son is being arrested for bank robbery, Mrs. D'Agastino," Ankles said calmly.

The mother's face turned to stone, the worry lines dividing her soft olive flesh. The grandmother dropped instantly to her knees and took a pair of rosary beads from her apron pocket and began to bless herself and mumble the rosary in Italian.

The mother stood from the table and slowly but steadily an animal wail rose out of her. She put her hands over her ears in an effort to block out what she had just heard. The screaming was monstrous—no words, just wails and screeches.

Alley Boy ran to her and held her in his arms.

"Ma, it'll be okay. I promise, Ma. They don't have anything on me, Ma. Believe me. It isn't bad. Believe me, Ma. Please."

But the mother kept her hands over her ears and continued to wail.

Ankles put his hand on Alley Boy's shoulder.

"We'll have to go, D'Agastino," Ankles said.

As Ankles led him out of the house, tears advanced down Alley Boy's face. In the hallway Ankles snapped a pair of handcuffs on Alley Boy, pulling his arms tightly behind his back. Then he led Alley Boy down the stairs. Alley Boy stopped at the bottom of the first flight.

"Ankles," Alley Boy said, "will you do me a favor?"

"Sure, kid," Ankles said. "What is it?"

"Wipe my eyes for me, will you?" Alley Boy asked as he took deep breaths to control the sobs.

Ankles took out a handkerchief and wiped Alley Boy's eyes.

"How do I look?" Alley Boy asked.

"Like a dumb fucking asshole."

"I was an hour late."

"I know," Ankles said. "And a dollar short."

They made their way down the next two flights of stairs. At the bottom landing Alley Boy took several more deep breaths and then Ankles led him out into the street. A detective car and a regular police radio car were parked outside. A few curious neighbors had gathered in front of the tenement. Alley Boy looked at his shoes as he walked toward the detective car. Ankles sat him in the backseat of the car.

Ankles was about to get into his car next to Alley Boy when a taxicab pulled up. Stephanie Kelly bolted from the backseat and ran to the detective car in a panic. She saw Alley Boy handcuffed in the backseat and put her knuckle between her front teeth and bit hard.

"Hello, Stephanie," Ankles said.

Stephanie couldn't talk. Her mascara ran down her cheeks with the tears, like an oil slick on a river. She bent down next to the window where Alley Boy was sitting and looked at him through the glass.

Alley Boy saw her mouth the word "Why?" from the cold outside. A puff of vapor escaped with the word. Alley Boy watched the vapor evaporate and shrugged his shoulders.

Ankles walked over to Stephanie and told her what

the charge was. Stephanie never looked at him. She stared at Alley Boy, who stared back. He tried to fake a smile, but it was the smile of a fighter who was ready for the floor.

"You can have a word with him if you want," Ankles said. Stephanie nodded yes. Ankles opened the back door and she squatted outside the open car door.

"Oh, Al—Jesus, Al—it was going to be so good. Goddamn it, Al, why?"

"It happened, Steph, that's all. It ain't that bad, Steph. It's my first arrest. All they have is circumstantial evidence, Steph. I'll get bail. Tommy Ryan will get me out."

"Tommy Ryan got you *in*, Al."

"No, Steph, this is one thing I did to myself. At least I did it on my own. At least I can say, 'Al did this.'"

Alley Boy faked the desperate smile again. Stephanie hugged him.

"Steph," Alley Boy said as Stephanie held his face in her hands.

"Yeah, Al?"

"Where'd you pick, Steph? Where were we gonna go?"

"Mexico, Al, I thought it would be warm there."

"I promise, Steph, we will."

Stephanie kissed Alley Boy and Ankles closed the door and got in the front seat. Stephanie watched the Plymouth pull away until it was out of sight. Then she took the cab back to her apartment to sit and look at the memories.

26

Tommy Ryan pulled the gold Cadillac off the main road
onto a private road that had a sign that bore the legend
HUDSON HEALTH MANOR. He followed the winding
gravel road for about a half-mile until the large white
house became visible. A gazebo was situated halfway
between the main white house and a frozen pond to the
left. Bungalows stood in a line at the bottom of the
knoll that descended from the main house.

Tommy Ryan pulled the car to a halt outside the
service entrance, out of sight of the bungalows. Cisco
got out of the car and climbed the three steps to the
door and rang the bell.

Then he came down the steps and helped Tommy
Ryan out of the car. Tommy couldn't walk on the bad
leg at all now and he had to put his arm over Cisco's

shoulder and hop on the one good leg up the three steps. When they got to the top of the stoop the door was opened by a tall, thin, healthy looking man of sixty with beautiful white teeth, thick steel-gray hair, and deeply tanned skin.

"Hi, Doc," Tommy Ryan said. "You gotta give me something soon. The pain is incredible."

"You guys'll never learn, for chrissakes," the doctor said. "You know how much trouble I can get in for doing this? Huh? Do you? Why do you have to come to me?"

"Cause you know how much trouble you'll be in if you don't help me right now," Tommy Ryan said.

"Don't threaten me, Ryan, I'm warning you."

"It ain't a threat, Doc, it's a promise."

"I'm too old for threats or promises, Ryan," the doctor said.

"Your kids ain't."

"I should kill you for even thinkin' that."

"You won't," Tommy Ryan said. "Not if Cisco can help it. Cisco, meet Dr. Sann. That is, he would be a doctor except for a little piece of history called counterfeiting when he was a goombah in Jersey. He never could get that wiped out, so the AMA wouldn't give him an M.D. He studied medicine in Italy, now he runs this little fasting farm here. The fatties come up to drink water and give him money. His customers would love to know about his background, wouldn't they, Doc?"

"Get inside, you prick," Dr. Sann said. "And shut your mouth before I stitch it shut."

"Hey, man, you don't talk like that to Tommy, man," Cisco threatened.

"If you want to live, you shut up, too."

Cisco admired the old man's balls and just giggled. Dr. Sann and Cisco helped Tommy into the house and led him up the stairs to a private room. All of the people there for fasting were downstairs getting a pep talk from the manor staff.

"Now I don't want you out of this room until you can walk, Ryan, hear?"

"Anything you say, Doc. Just knock me out. I can't take the pain."

They laid Tommy Ryan on the bed and Dr. Sann took a syringe from the night table next to the bed. It had already been prepared. Dr. Sann injected the needle into Tommy Ryan's arm just below the shoulder.

"What's in that, Doc?" Tommy Ryan asked.

"I wish it were arsenic," Dr. Sann said. "But it's sodium pentathol."

Ten seconds later Tommy Ryan was fast asleep. Dr. Sann looked Cisco up and down with contempt.

"And you, you go down and put on a pair of whites. As far as anyone around here knows, you're a new orderly, see. If you want that buddy of yours to live you'll do as I say."

Cisco shrugged.

Ankles marched Alley Boy through fingerprinting and mug shots, read him his rights, and asked him if he wanted to make a statement. Alley Boy told him no. Ankles asked him if he wanted to contact his lawyer. Alley Boy told him he didn't have a lawyer.

"Well, you certainly can afford a lawyer," Ankles said. "You must have made out pretty good on that score. How much you get?"

Alley Boy didn't answer.

"I asked you how much you got on the score?" Ankles said more sternly.

"I don't know what you're talking about," Alley Boy

told Ankles as he sat handcuffed in the Brooklyn police headquarters interrogation room.

"Don't bullshit me, wise guy," Ankles said. "Maybe I felt sorry for you this afternoon because you almost broke your mother's heart and fucked up that Stephanie Kelly's life even more than it already was. She was happier turning tricks to stew bums."

Alley Boy made a lunge for Ankles. Ankles kicked him with all his might in the right shin. Alley Boy collapsed to the floor. Ankles stood over him and lit his cigar. He didn't like what he had just said, but it had the desired effect.

"But now you're nothing more than a two-bit lowlife like the rest of them," Ankles said. "No more feeling sorry for you or wiping away the tears, asshole. You're in the big time now. You're a bona fide bank robber. Make you feel good, asshole?"

Alley Boy remained silent on the floor. Ankles bent down and yanked him to his feet and pushed him into the swivel chair. The chair slid along the floor and Alley Boy's head banged off a wall.

"Now you listen to me, lowlife," Ankles snapped. "I don't really give a shit about the bank in Rinky Dink upstate New York. I don't care about the one in Flatbush either, even though we don't have nothing on you for that yet. What I want to know about is murder. Good, old-fashioned, all-American, apple-pie, cold-blooded murder."

"Now I *really* don't know what you're talking about," Alley Boy said.

"I want to know about Frankie Green Eyes and I want to know about Fabulous Murphy," Ankles said as he nonchalantly relit his cigar. "But mostly I want to know about Tony Mauro. Because I think you know something about that. I think Tommy Ryan knows something about it. I think you know about all three of them. And believe me, you might not think so now, but you're gonna tell me, pal."

"I don't know anything about no murders," Alley Boy said.

Ankles walked around the interrogation table and wheeled Alley Boy from the wall closer to the table. Then Ankles sat down at the table and tried a softer approach.

"Listen to me, D'Agastino," Ankles said. "I told you I liked your old man. He was an ace guy. Now for his sake I'm willing to go to bat for you down at night court tonight. Later on I'll testify at your trial and I'll even talk to the D.A. before your arraignment. I have some clout downtown. They'll probably hold you here in the city until your trial date upstate. I'll get you easy time. I'll get you a kitchen job or a library gig. I know most of the screws in Rikers Island. They can make life tolerable. Or they can make life unbearable."

"I don't know nothing about no murders," Alley Boy said again.

"All right, forget the murders for a minute. How about this? You turn state's evidence on Tommy Ryan and Cisco on that bank job and you might even walk on this charge with a suspended sentence."

"Tommy Ryan and Cisco?" Alley Boy said. "I only know them to say hello to. That's all. Besides, I don't know nothing about no bank job either. They must have me mixed up."

Ankles stood up from the table and looked down at Alley Boy sitting in the swivel chair. He took the cigar out of his mouth and looked at the smoldering tip.

"Okay, moron, have it your way. This time tomorrow there'll be guys on line for your ass. They'll pin you against the bars, rub melted chocolate on your keister, and then one after the other they'll ram it up your ass.

Then maybe you'll talk, if you still have your sanity. Me, I couldn't give a hairy rat fuck what happens to you now."

Ankles put the cigar back in his mouth, grinned sinisterly, and walked out of the room. Alley Boy sat in his chair, Ankles's words repeating in his mind like a skipping record.

Dr. Sann walked down the flight of stairs and into the kitchen. Cisco was sitting at the table sipping a bowl of celery soup. Dr. Sann looked at Cisco and snarled.

"That soup is only for human consumption," Dr. Sann said. Cisco looked up and smiled and said, "Why? Won't the animals eat it? I don't blame them."

Dr. Sann dropped the shattered piece of lead into the bowl of soup. Cisco slowly looked up at him.

"There's your pal's bullet," Dr. Sann said.

Cisco fished the slug out of the bowl and shook the soup off it. He inspected the flattened lead closely.

"Thirty-eight caliber," Cisco said.

"Same as your IQ," Dr. Sann said.

Cisco laughed as he pushed the soup away.

"How is he?"

"Unfortunately, he's alive. That means he'll be back. That's the seventh slug I've taken out of that jerk since he first came here. Sounds like a hell of a great way to live."

"As a matter of fact, it is," Cisco said.

"He'll have to stay here at least a week. That infection will have to be irrigated three times a day or it will spread. Just stay out of the way. Don't talk to the guests here. Just mind your own business. I'll do everything I can to get him out of here as soon as possible. Believe me."

"If you expect me to stay here that long you'll have to do something about the food," Cisco said.

"I will," Dr. Sann said. "I'll lace it a little at a time with a poison, a slow poison, one that'll kill you on your way home."

Cisco's face looked glum as Dr. Sann went back upstairs.

27

It took Ankles an hour to get the search warrants for Cisco's apartment and Carol Mauro's place, but it took only fifteen minutes to search Cisco's pad. It was just a studio apartment with a small bed, a kitchen table, a stereo, and a color television. There was nothing in the refrigerator; the mattress was torn open and searched, but nothing was found. Not a single clue was found in Cisco's apartment to connect him with anything illegal.

Ankles stood there looking at the grim, dimly lit apartment, wondering how a human being could live like that. He figured that Cisco's old cell in Rikers Island probably had more amenities than this dump. But he remembered that guys who had done hard time the way Cisco had usually don't want much but the opportunity to walk the streets. They become accustomed to living with very little, like squirrels. But even squirrels at least keep food in their nests.

Ankles left Cisco's apartment and drove down to Terrace Court in Brooklyn Heights. He didn't like what he was about to do. But it came with the badge.

He walked up the stoop to Carol Mauro's apartment and rang the doorbell. Carol answered the door wearing tight jeans, a turtleneck sweater, and high boots with the pants tucked into them. Ankles thought she looked beautiful, her long hair cascading over the sweater.

"I already have a vacuum cleaner," Carol said as she tried to close the door in Ankles's face. But Ankles pushed his large foot in the door and showed Carol a piece of white paper.

"I'm sorry, Carol," Ankles said genuinely, "but I have a search warrant."

"What are you looking for?" Carol asked.

"Evidence in a bank robbery. Maybe even a few murders."

Carol looked nervous for the first time. Behind Ankles were two uniformed police officers waiting for Ankles to direct them.

"What murders?"

"Frankie Green Eyes, a guy named Murphy, and Tony's."

"You come around to my house to look for evidence in Tony Mauro's murder? You filthy animal."

"Please open up, Carol," Ankles said. "I don't want to make this ugly. Let's make it easy. It won't take long. I promise."

Carol flung open the door with a loud bang. Ankles walked past her, followed by the two uniformed cops.

Inside, Ankles and the two cops began searching through drawers, under the mattresses, under couch cushions, under the rugs, in closets, through books.

One cop spent several minutes looking in the fireplace in the dining room. Carol watched him cautiously. The cop kept trying to remove the false front from the fireplace, but he couldn't get it to move. He called Ankles over and Ankles gave it a try. He couldn't remove it either.

"What is this false front doing on here?" Ankles asked Carol.

"It was put on to stop the draft because we never use that fireplace," Carol said. "Want any other hot flashes?"

Ankles looked embarrassed by the whole operation. He told the two cops to wait downstairs and they exited. He stood there staring at Carol, trying his best to look gentle but knowing he was failing miserably.

"Where's Tommy Ryan?" Ankles asked.

"You have a warrant for him, too?"

"No. Not yet, anyway. But we have his friend Albert D'Agastino in the lockup for a bank score in upstate New York. And that kid is too simple to stick up a bodega on his own."

"Sorry to hear that," Carol said. "He's a nice kid."

"He was a nice kid until he met Tommy Ryan."

"Your puny search warrant doesn't entitle you to stand in my house insulting the man I live with."

"How can you live with a guy who knows something he won't say about Tony Mauro's murder?"

"Maybe he won't tell you—"

Carol cut herself off before she continued. The anger let the words fall out with rash immediacy.

"Why? What does he say to you, Carol?"

"Nothing," Carol said. "Nothing at all."

"Seems funny that the same guy who cut Tony cut Green Eyes and Fabulous Murphy. The autopsy report indicates that it was definitely the same guy."

Ankles knew he was lying, that the coroner's office

couldn't say for sure, but he figured it might trigger something in Carol.

"That's a lie!" Carol shouted. "It was Green Eyes who killed Tony."

She stopped herself again, then said, "Just get out of here. Leave me alone." Carol broke down crying softly.

"Carol, I've been a homicide detective for a long time now. Too long. But I can tell you without a doubt that Frankie Green Eyes never cut Tony. First of all he wasn't smart enough. Tony was cut from behind. So it had to be someone Tony trusted enough to let sit behind him. Someone he knew. Tony wouldn't have trusted Frankie Green Eyes as far as he could throw an old stove. Personally, I don't think Frankie Green Eyes was capable of cutting his own throat."

"Get out," Carol screamed. "Get out of my house."

"I'm going, Carol," Ankles said quietly. "But just think about what I said."

Ankles left and shut the door behind him. He stood outside the door in the vestibule for a brief moment and took a deep breath. Then he went back into the street.

Stephanie Kelly sat in the large courtroom at 110 Schermerhorn Street next to Alley Boy's mother. The mother had composed herself after taking several Valiums provided by her doctor. The night court was jammed with mostly black and Puerto Rican relatives of kids in the bull pen awaiting arraignment. The judge was a black man in his early sixties with gray hair and a tough, hard face.

Stephanie Kelly sat silently. The mother turned to Stephanie and said, "We don't even have no lawyer yet. They're not gonna let him go tonight. They're gonna keep my son in jail. I know it. I just know it."

"The court will appoint a lawyer, Mrs. D'Agastino,"
Stephanie said. "They'll probably give him bail of some
kind. He's never been in trouble before."

A court officer walked over to Stephanie and the
mother and told them to keep quiet. The mother gave
the court officer the Italian salute with her arm and
then flashed her index finger and pinkie of her right
hand at the court officer, wishing the horns of the
devil on him.

The court officer walked away.

Back in the bull pen, Alley Boy sat on the cement
floor with his back propped against the wall. He was
one of two white guys in the large, crowded bull pen.
Baloney sandwiches were being passed through the
bars by one of the screws, but Alley Boy did not take
any.

The white guy sitting with Alley Boy was in for auto
theft. He was impressed that Alley Boy was in for a
bank stickup.

"Did you really do it?" the white guy asked.

"Nah," Alley Boy said. "I just drove the car."

"No shit. Wheel man, hah? What's your name?"

"Al. Al D'Agastino."

"Mine's Mulraine. Jimmy Mulraine."

They shook hands.

"Right now I'd cut off my right ear for a cigarette,"
Mulraine said. "Both ears for a pack."

"Why don't you ask one of them?" Alley Boy asked,
indicating the other prisoners.

"No way, man," Mulraine said. "Not off a yom. You
take anything off a yom in the joint and you're shot
down. White guys won't go to bat for you. Don't ever
take nothing off a yombo."

"My girl friend is half black," Alley Boy said.

Mulraine looked at Alley Boy in disbelief.

"Your chick is half *what*?"

"Half black," Alley Boy said.

"You better keep that as classified information if you get into Rikers, man. The white guys won't even talk to you, never mind go to bat for you."

"Why's that?" Alley Boy asked.

"Cause this is the joint. White and black don't mix. Yoms is yoms and whites are whites. You better get that clear from jumpstreet, man."

The sliding steel door of the bull pen opened and a young black kid with his hair in corn rows walked through the door. He had just been before the judge for arraignment. He had a hard, contrived, somewhat aloof face. He walked with a heavy hitch in his walk, not from a physical deformity but for effect. It made him look cool.

"Look at the jiveass nigger," Mulraine said. "Look at the fuckin' hairdo. He looks like Buckwheat from the Little Rascals."

A few other black prisoners walked over to the kid with the bebop walk and asked him what had happened in the courtroom.

The kid sat down and lit a Kool and rested his head against the wall and blew out the smoke in a histrionic way.

"Man, my muvuh, man, my muvuh, she went up in fron' of that nigguh judge, man, and she tell that fuckin' nigguh judge that I come home high on pills and wine, man, and that I kick in the front door and that all the glass break on the door. Then she say I went in the house, man, and that I got me a hammer and I started bustin' up the place, man. Tole that nigguh judge that I smash all the mirrors and broke up the stereo and broke up the color tee vee, man. Then she say I went in the kitchen and lit the muthafuckin' garbage on fire and that I put a knife to my baby sistuh's throat in the crib. My muvuh, she tole that nigguh judge all that shit so he won't gimmie no fuckin' bail. Fuckin' nigguh. Sheeet."

One of the black kid's friends asked him, "You really do all that shit, man?"

The black kid took another long drag on the Kool and exhaled it dramatically. He was playing for the audience now.

"Hell, no," the black kid said. "Hell, no. I didn't break no fuckin' color tee vee."

The whole bull pen rocked with laughter. Jimmy Mulraine was in stitches in the corner long after everybody else had stopped laughing. The black kid stared at Mulraine with stony eyes.

"Hey, honky, what's so fuckin' funny, man?" the black kid said to Mulraine as a challenge.

Mulraine stood up. He was short, but he had wide shoulders and bulging muscles. He walked halfway to the black kid.

"I think *you're* funny, spook," Mulraine said. "I think you're funny cause you look like fuckin' Buckwheat from the Little Rascals. That's what I think is funny, nigger."

The black kid took another drag on his Kool and let the smoke out elaborately again.

"You gonna think *you* look funny when I make your face look a bag of assholes, whitey."

"Come on, nigger," Mulraine said. "Come on."

Alley Boy stood up quickly as a dozen sets of eyes focused on him. The black kid stood up and took off a suede coat and folded it ever so neatly and then sprang at Mulraine with a sneak punch. Mulraine stepped out of the way and delivered a right hand to the black kid's ear.

The kid flew backwards into a group of his friends who pushed him back into the middle of the bull pen.

"Never hit a nigger in the skull, Al," Mulraine yelled. "It's like punching a wall."

Now the black kid was on his feet doing the Ali Shuffle and dancing around Mulraine. He flicked jabs that didn't land and he feinted with rights he never threw. Finally Mulraine charged him and caught the kid around the waist and rammed him against the wall. The wind escaped from the black kid in a loud sigh. The black kid grabbed desperately for Mulraine's hair and pulled it. But Mulraine lifted the kid into the air and slammed him onto the ground. He was on top of the black kid now, punching his face.

One of the black kid's friends, a large man of about thirty-five, walked over and punched Mulraine in the back of the head. Mulraine groaned but stayed on top of the black kid. Alley Boy spun the large black man around and threw one punch, a straight right hand, and the black man went down and smacked his head on the cement floor.

Now the screws were opening the door, rushing in with clubs drawn. They pulled Mulraine off the black kid and dragged him out of the cell. Another screw led Alley Boy out. The blacks in the bull pen shouted after Mulraine and Alley Boy that they'd see them in Rikers.

Alley Boy and Mulraine were placed in a private cell together. Mulraine was rubbing the back of his neck where he'd been punched.

"That was some fuckin' shot you hit that dinge, Al," Mulraine said.

Alley Boy looked at his fist, still amazed at his own strength.

"Yeah," Alley Boy said with a smile. "It was pretty good, wasn't it?"

"A honey for the money," Mulraine said. "Now you see what I mean about the yoms in the joint? You just keep that part about your chick to yourself. Don't worry when we get to Rikers. I'll spread the word that you're good people. You're in the joint now, pal. If you ain't prejudiced on the outside, you better be in here."

Alley Boy thought about Stephanie and her smooth mulatto skin.

"There's no mixed marriages in the joint, Al," Mulraine said. "Not even between faggots."

An hour later Alley Boy was brought in front of the judge for arraignment. The legal aid lawyer who was appointed to Alley Boy pleaded with the judge to be lenient with bail because it was Albert D'Agastino's first arrest. The judge said that he would take that into consideration, but that the defense had to understand that bank robbery was a very serious crime.

On the other hand, the district attorney argued that the arresting officer in the case, Lieutenant Anthony Tufano, believed that the accused might have knowledge of certain homicides he was currently investigating. The defense argued that those charges were unfounded and that Albert D'Agastino was being arraigned only for his alleged involvement with a bank robbery in Red Hook, New York, that occurred on December fifteenth. The district attorney claimed that the murders might be connected to the bank robbery, but that he could not disclose the exact nature of the connection at this time as it might hamper the investigation.

The judge called both counselors to the bench, where he told them that bail was to be set at fifty thousand dollars. He told the defense that under ordinary circumstances it would have been one hundred thousand, but he was taking into consideration that it was Albert D'Agastino's first offense, then he added that the bail might even have gone as low as twenty-five thousand dollars had it not been for this alleged connection to murder investigations. He instructed both attorneys to accept this bail without further, as he put bluntly, "legalistic bullshit." Both attorneys agreed. Neither was in a position to argue. What the judge says goes in Brooklyn, New York.

Al D'Agastino was to be held in Rikers Island until the arraignment papers were processed in upstate New York and a court date set by authorities there.

Alley Boy looked over his shoulder at Stephanie as the judge announced the bail and winked. His mother broke into low sobs. Stephanie put her arm around the mother. Alley Boy mouthed the words "I love you" as he was led out of the courtroom in handcuffs. Stephanie mouthed the same message back.

Ankles got up from his seat near the front of the courtroom and began to walk toward the exit. Stephanie was leading the mother out of the pew as Ankles passed. The mother looked up at Ankles and said, "Why did you do this to my boy?"

Ankles said quietly, "He did it to himself, ma'am."

28

In the morning Tommy Ryan woke up to sunlight lancing through lace curtains. The sun was blinding and he put his hand over his eyes to shield them. Looking up, he thought he was still dreaming, or thought he should be.

Standing at the end of the bed was a beautiful redhead in a white nurse's uniform. She had bright blue eyes and she was smiling broadly with clean, well-formed teeth. Tommy could make out small, hard breasts underneath the tight white uniform. She wore no bra and the nipples made small dark circular impressions on the cotton fabric.

"Good morning, Tommy," the nurse said. Tommy Ryan stared at the girl, still trying to shield his eyes from the sun. Although his pupils had not yet adjusted to the harsh light, he could see that it was Gladys Sann, Dr. Sann's daughter. The last time Tommy Ryan had seen her was two years ago, when she was seventeen. She was just a skinny kid who still wore her hair in banana curls then.

"Is that you, Gladys?" Tommy asked.

"Yeah, Tommy," Gladys said. "It's me. Don't you recognize me? Have I changed that much?"

"As a matter of fact, you have," Tommy Ryan said.

"I see you haven't," Gladys said.

"A hunting accident," Tommy said.

"What utter bullshit," Gladys said. "Who hunts with a .38 caliber pistol?"

Tommy put his head back on the pillow. He wasn't about to discuss the matter with this kid. Gladys walked over to Tommy's side and pulled the covers down. Tommy had no underwear on.

"Hey, whadda you doing?" Tommy said.

"I'm checking your wound, stupid," Gladys said. "It has to be irrigated three times a day. And you have to take plenty of penicillin."

Tommy put his forearm over his eyes as Gladys removed the dressing from the leg wound. She began slowly, so that the adhesive tape wouldn't pull at the hairs. She pressed gently around the flesh of the wound, asking Tommy if certain points hurt or had any feeling. She was checking to see if the infection had spread.

But the only thing that was spreading was Tommy Ryan's penis. Gladys noticed and teasingly squeezed his penis firmly.

"Can you feel that?" Gladys asked.

Tommy Ryan yelped. "Of course I can feel that. Are you crazy or something?"

"You have to keep it down for a few days, because you don't want it drawing blood away from the wound. You need the fresh blood circulating to make it heal faster."

Tommy Ryan stared at her lustfully now.

"Only for a few days I have to keep it down?" he asked Gladys with a smile.

"Only a few days, Tommy," she said. "The infection hasn't spread. Lucky for you. I'll check in from time to time to see how you're doing."

Gladys was moving away when Tommy clutched her gently by the arm.

"Will you be checking in on me in, say, a few days?"

Gladys smiled warmly and said, "You better believe it. I'd like to see what it's like with a real-life outlaw."

"It ain't the same as with an in-law," Tommy Ryan said.

"I'll bet it isn't. Time will tell."

Tommy pulled her close to him and kissed her. She could feel him getting hard again. Gladys smiled and snapped her finger onto his penis. Tommy yelled as it went down.

"I said in a couple of days."

Tommy watched Gladys walk toward the door and imagined the softness of the ass under the skirt.

The ride across the bridge from Queens to Rikers Island was fast. Alley Boy was handcuffed to Mulraine as the Department of Corrections bus bounced across the bridge. There were a dozen other prisoners in the bus, most of them black or Puerto Rican, but none of them were the guys Alley Boy and Mulraine had fought with in the Schermerhorn Street bull pen.

There were two other white prisoners, handcuffed together, and Mulraine bummed a cigarette from one of them. The white prisoner offered one of the cigarettes to Alley Boy.

"Thanks, but I don't smoke," Alley Boy said.

"You better start," Mulraine said. "There's nothing

else to do in the joint but smoke. Cigarettes are money in the joint. You trade cigarettes for everything. Soap, toothpaste, candy, hot books, clean sheets. Everything. Some people even trade cigarettes for the loan of somebody's wife."

"Whadda you mean 'wife'?" Alley Boy asked.

"Jailhouse wife. You know. Your own private faggot."

"I don't think I'll be trading for that," Alley Boy said with a nervous laugh.

"That depends on how much time you get. A boy's ass can look almost as good as a broad's ass if you spend enough time inside. After all, an ass is an ass."

Alley Boy watched as Mulraine sucked greedily from the filtered cigarette. The images of clanging steel, the screams of violated men, the darkness of nighttime in a locked cell, the anticipation of the violence that lay ahead—all these things wound like a ball in Alley Boy's stomach.

"Go ahead, have a smoke," Mulraine advised. "It doesn't mean you're gonna fuck boys if you smoke. It gets your mind off things. It relaxes you."

Alley Boy took one of the other white prisoners' cigarettes and Mulraine gave him a light. Alley Boy took a deep drag, the smoke scorching his dry throat. The first drag made him feel lightheaded and dizzy. He took another drag and inhaled it deeper and held the smoke in.

"Breathe it out, for chrissakes," Mulraine said. "That ain't a joint you're smokin'."

Alley Boy let the smoke out. Now his head was very dizzy. He stared out of the grated back window at the necklace of lights that was the borough of Queens, then down at the dark, cold water below him. The bus kept bouncing toward the prison ahead, but Alley Boy could not see it. It was still a shadow in his mind, a place without substance, like a state of mind. A place people only spoke of when they came home from it. Rikers Island was soon to come to life for Alley Boy.

Captain Houlihan had been waiting for Ankles to come back to Brooklyn headquarters for over an hour. When Ankles finally walked in, his eyes scoured red from lack of sleep, Houlihan approached him with quick, deliberate steps.

"Lieutenant Tufano, I'm Captain Houlihan from Red Hook," he said.

"I know," Ankles muttered as he walked past Houlihan.

Houlihan followed closely, his hat in his hand, his face pinched with annoyance.

"You know," Houlihan said. "That's nice. I'm glad you know. I also hope you know that I'm here to claim a prisoner."

Ankles was busy filling a plastic cup with coffee from a Mr. Coffee machine. He turned to Houlihan and took a sip of the black java.

"Tastes like panther piss, but you're welcome to some if you want," Ankles said as he grimaced.

"No thanks," Houlihan said. "I'd like to get Albert D'Agastino and start moving along."

"The moving along I don't care about," Ankles said. "But you ain't gonna take D'Agastino with you. Not yet, anyway. We're holding him here for a while."

"Listen, Lieutenant, that's my prisoner."

"If he's your prisoner, what's he doing in my jail?"

"This is my case. The county has a bank robbery charge against him."

"I know," Ankles said. "But he's a potential material witness in a murder investigation down here in the major leagues, Captain."

"I'm not interested in what potential anything he might be," Captain Houlihan said. "We have concrete evidence upstate on him."

"Look, Captain, you look like a nice fellow. Do me a big favor, will ya? Go up and give some speeding tickets for a few weeks, then come back down and get your prisoner. Because right now he ain't goin' nowhere. If you have any more questions, I'd appreciate it if you took it up with the district attorney's office. I haven't slept in thirty-six hours, my feet hurt, all I had to eat today was a tuna sandwich, the coffee stinks, and I have three dead people on my hands. I'm not interested in jurisdictions. The day that a two-bit bank job becomes more important than triple murder I'll trade in my gold badge for a tube of Noxzema and I'll take a lifeguard's job down on Bay Twenty-two. You see, I'm not tryin' to be impolite, but would you kindly go and fuck yourself?"

Captain Houlihan stood stiffly, his eyes black and hot. He kept staring at Ankles, at a loss for words, and then turned and walked toward the door. He stopped at the door and looked at Ankles once more, but Ankles was sitting at his desk now, reading a court brief and sipping from the cup of bitter coffee. Captain Houlihan made a hasty exit and could be heard stomping down the old wooden stairs.

Alley Boy never did get to see the jail from the outside. The bus rolled off the bridge, stopped at a security check, and then disappeared inside the monolithic prison.

He was moving down the corridor of one of the tiers now, still handcuffed to Mulraine. Other prisoners shouted to them as they walked down the hall. Mulraine said hello to those he knew and cursed out those black prisoners who made wisecracks as he walked past.

A cell door was opened and Alley Boy and Mulraine were placed inside. The handcuffs were removed and Alley Boy rubbed his wrists.

"Welcome to Plaza Suite," Mulraine said.

Alley Boy looked around the gray-colored cell. There was a toilet bowl, a sink, a bunk bed. Nothing else. Graffiti marred the walls, mostly racial epithets. A dim light bulb burned inside a metal cage in the low ceiling. The cell smelled of urine and sweat and rancid semen; the smell reminded Alley Boy of Fabulous Murphy's hallway. It was very cold, and a single barred window offered a view of a concrete wall.

"Take whatever bed you want," Mulraine said. Alley Boy climbed to the top bunk.

"Whadda you do here?" Alley Boy asked Mulraine.

"You're doing it."

"I mean in the daytime."

"You eat, you read books, you get a lockout for an hour where you can fight or smoke. There ain't much to do. You take a shower in the morning, you don't bend for the soap, and you stay out of the way of a German guy they call Sauerkraut. He's the gee. On this tier anyway. He's this big weight lifter who runs the tier. This tier is mostly white, so you won't have too many problems. Sauerkraut likes to take off new guys. Watch out for him. He might try rammin' your buns. Last time I was here, about three months ago, a different guy was the gee."

"Whadda you mean 'gee'?" Alley Boy asked.

"The boss. You know, head inmate. He runs things on the tier. If he thinks you're good people you'll have easy time. If he wants your manhood you'll have bad time and a real pain in the ass."

"Who was the gee the last time you were here?"

"Some crazy motherfucker named Tommy Ryan," Mulraine said. "Nobody fucked with him. Not even Sauerkraut."

"Tommy Ryan from Park Slope?" Alley Boy asked.

"Yeah, that's him. You know him?"

"He's my best friend."

Mulraine was on his feet now, leaning on the top bunk and looking at Alley Boy.

"No shit. You're a friend of Tommy Ryan's?"

"Yeah," Alley Boy said proudly. "I hang out with him."

"If you tell Sauerkraut that, he probably won't mess with you, man. Tommy Ryan's the only guy that German ever feared. I don't know why. He's about a foot shorter than the kraut. But there's something about the way Ryan carries himself. You know what I mean?"

"Yeah," Alley Boy said. He wanted to tell Mulraine that he had saved Tommy Ryan's life, had gone back for him in the middle of a bank robbery, but he knew he couldn't tell him that. So he lay there, and then the lights went out and darkness smothered the prison.

Alley Boy stared into the darkness and smiled knowingly, and in a few minutes he was asleep.

He dreamed of Stephanie, of an airplane touching down, and Mexicans with guitars and sombreros meeting them at the airport, and a limousine waiting for them, and Alley Boy and Stephanie running past the singing Mexicans with the gold teeth and moustaches, and the Mexican women trying to grab him and Stephanie dragging him away, telling them that he was hers, and the car doors closing and the chauffeur whisking them away into Mexico. . . .

29

Cisco shook Tommy Ryan at nine thirty in the morning. The room was half-awake with bleak gray light from an ominous sky. Tommy Ryan looked at Cisco, squinting through gluey eyes. Cisco had a serious, almost concerned look on his dark face. He was holding a copy of a newspaper called the *Poughkeepsie Journal,* which he extended to Tommy, who sat up in the bed, his leg causing minor discomfort as he moved.

Tommy Ryan took the newspaper and unfolded it to the front page. A headline screamed across the top of the newspaper: SUSPECT HELD IN RED HOOK BANK ROBBERY. Tommy Ryan rubbed his sandy eyes and sat up further in the bed, oblivious now to the pain of his wound. He read the story:

Red Hook Police announced last night the arrest of a Brooklyn man in connection with last week's daring

bank robbery in which thieves dressed as Hasidic
Jews.

The suspect, Albert D'Agastino, 21, of Brooklyn,
New York, was traced through a series of leads involving a fingerprint left on the inside leather band
of a black hat found in the abandoned getaway
vehicle.

Captain James Houlihan of the Red Hook Police
Department told reporters that his office had given
Brooklyn authorities permission to hold D'Agastino
at the Rikers Island Detention Center for questioning involving certain slayings that have taken place
in Park Slope, Brooklyn, over the past several
months.

Captain Houlihan said he was not at liberty to
divulge details of those murders as they might
hamper the investigations. Houlihan was also reluctant to reveal just how D'Agastino was traced,
for fear of recriminations on the part of other
members of the holdup team who are still at large.

"One informant was most helpful in the case,"
Houlihan told the *Poughkeepsie Journal*. "But to reveal his name at this time might jeopardize that
citizen's life and the lives of his family. All we can
tell you at this time is that we definitely have a suspect, that the evidence we have is concrete and that
a trial date is being arranged by local law enforce-
ment officials."

Asked if D'Agastino, who allegedly drove the getaway vehicle, which was a yellow Yeshiva school van
stolen the night before, had implicated his alleged
partners, Houlihan answered, "No comment."

Asked further if he had any other suspects under
surveillance at this time, Houlihan again had no
comment.

The story continued, giving background on the stickup and the row that followed. Tommy Ryan read no more. He looked up at Cisco, who was grave.

"It's my fault," Tommy Ryan said. "We should've put the kibosh on him when we had the chance. I should never have let him live. The fucking asshole. Leaving a print behind like that."

"What are we gonna do, man?" Cisco asked. "I know he'll crack. He'll have to. He can't do no time, man."

"I know," Tommy Ryan said nervously. "They have him in Rikers Island. We know people in there who would adios him. I'll have to make some calls. We gotta get him outta the way before he talks."

"That's if he didn't already."

Tommy Ryan looked ashen as he nodded his head to Cisco.

Alley Boy stood behind Mulraine at the lunchtime chow line in the prison cafeteria. The cafeteria was large and similar to a high-school lunchroom except for the bars on the windows and the uniformed guards at the doors. The long tables were Formica and they were bolted to the floor. So were the long wooden benches that provided seating. This ensured that the tables and benches could not be used as weapons.

"Don't take the green peas," Mulraine told Alley Boy. "They're shot down."

"Shot down?"

"Yeah, the yoms love them. White people don't eat the things the yoms like best. The canned peaches are the same. Don't eat 'em. Yom chow."

"But I like peaches," Alley Boy said.

"Well then take them, as long as you like them better than your cakes."

"I don't like peaches," Alley Boy said. Mulraine laughed giddily. Alley Boy took a large slice of wooden-looking meat loaf, a scoop of instant mashed potatoes, and some carrots. Mulraine took the same food and they walked to a long table where six other white prisoners were already eating.

Sitting at the head of the long table was a six-foot-five, two-hundred-and-forty-pound, blond-haired man. He had a hard angular face made up of ninety-degree angles, straight lines, and a flat nose. His eyes were deep set and dark blue and they seemed to gyrate inside the sockets. His eyebrows were platinum blond and thick and they hung over his eyes likes canopies. Alley Boy looked at him and thought he looked like he was drawn by the cartoonist who drew Dick Tracy.

The large blond man wore his sweatshirt cut off up to his shoulders, revealing a set of massive, muscular arms. His shoulders had the breadth of a small anchor and Alley Boy could feel the stilettos coming from the blond man's eyes. Goose bumps ran up Alley Boy's back and he felt a strong rush of blood to his face.

Mulraine and Alley Boy sat down. Mulraine began to eat immediately, but Alley Boy just looked down at the unappetizing food like he was saying grace.

"Hello, Jimmy," the blond man said in a very deep German accent. "You're back already? You dumbbell."

"Yeah, but it's a meatball rap. Stolen car. I can do this bit standin' on my head."

The German nodded and placed a large forkful of potatoes in his mouth and swallowed without chewing.

"Who is the baby?" the German asked.

Alley Boy looked up at the German and tried hard to look into his eyes, but the eyes were set too far back to really see them well.

"This is Al D'Agastino, Sauerkraut," Mulraine said. "He's a good friend of Tommy Ryan's."

The German put his fork down and picked his teeth with the broad nail of his right thumb. Then he sucked air through the space between the teeth to dislodge the food.

"How do you know that?" the German asked.

"Well, that's what he says anyway."

The German looked at Alley Boy the way someone might inspect a used car and said, "What kind of car does Tommy drive, baby?"

"A gold Cadillac and I'm not a baby," Alley Boy said, trying to sound tough.

"Where do his parents live?" the German asked.

"Riverdale."

"What was his best friend's name?"

"Tony Mauro. Now it's Al D'Agastino," Alley Boy said with defiance. He was beginning to relax now. For once in his life he had all the answers. "Me, I'm his best friend now."

"Who killed Tony Mauro?" the German asked with a jack-o'-lantern grin.

"I don't know," Alley Boy said. "But Tommy Ryan'll find out."

The German roared with laughter and slapped a large pink palm on the tabletop. Then he looked at Alley Boy with the same gnash of teeth and said, "You're okay, kid. You need any help, you come to me. To Sauerkraut."

The German stood up and held out his hand to slap Alley Boy five. Alley Boy stood up and put out his hand to accept the slap of friendship. The German slapped Alley Boy's hand as hard as he had slapped the table earlier. Alley Boy's hand stung with needles of heat. But he did not let it register in his face. The German turned his hand over to accept Alley Boy's hand slap. Alley Boy slapped with all his might. The German withdrew his hand quickly, his face a screen of pained surprise. The German wrung his stung hand with his other hand and smiled the same menacing grin.

"You're a big boy," the German said. "You're strong. That is good. No one will fuck with you here. You probably won't need no help from me, kid. Just stay away from the niggers and you're okay with me."

"Pleased to meet you," Alley Boy said, and sat down and began cutting the meat loaf with the edge of his fork. Mulraine looked at Alley Boy and winked. Alley Boy winked back. He wished Tommy Ryan could have seen him now.

Alley Boy put a section of the meat loaf into his mouth and began to chew. The food was tasteless except for the gravy, which was 90 percent flour. The German had finished his food already and took a cigar out from behind his ear. Then he pushed a bridge of false teeth out of his mouth. The dentures had lower back teeth on either side connected by a cobalt bridge that had two hooks to snap them securely against the real lower front teeth.

Sauerkraut took the cigar and laid it on the Formica table and with the cobalt bridge he made a neat slice from the tip of the cigar. Alley Boy watched with fascination.

"He keeps that set of dentures sharp as a razor," Mulraine said. "See that metal part he just cut the cigar with? That's cut at least six throats in here. It's like carrying a blade in your mouth."

Alley Boy watched as Sauerkraut replaced the set of lower dentures into his mouth. Then he placed the cigar in his mouth and lit it. The German was looking across the lunchroom with squinty eyes.

Alley Boy turned to see who the German was watching. He saw it was a short, frail Puerto Rican who walked with a cane and a bad limp. He was washing off tabletops with a wash rag.

"That's Willie the Spic," Mulraine said. "The German tried to take him off once, but the spic beat him with his cane long enough to call the screws. They put the German in solitary for two weeks for attempted rape and finally added two years to his sentence."

"What's the German doing time for?" Alley Boy asked.

"Manslaughter."

"What's the Puerto Rican's name?"

"Willie Sanchez. He's doing time for dealin' smack. We call him Willie the Spic. They moved him to a different tier after the thing with Sauerkraut."

"What's the German's real name?"

"Grohman. Henry Grohman. But don't ever call him Henry. He hates it."

Alley Boy kept staring at Willie Sanchez as he cleaned the tabletops. He remembered that Frankie Green Eye's name was also Sanchez.

"The German never got him back?"

"Nah," Mulraine said. "He's had the opportunity. But it was Tommy Ryan who told him to leave the spic alone. I have no idea why. You should know better than me."

"Maybe. I don't think I know why."

"Tommy Ryan left word before he got out to just leave the guy alone. When a guy like Ryan tells you something, you do it, because you never know when he's coming back."

Alley Boy nodded. Then he pushed his tray of food away and drank only the milk. He kept staring at Willie Sanchez.

30

Tommy had called Carol several times during the morning to get the phone number of a Rikers Island screw named Kane. Tommy had owned Kane when he was the gee of the tier during his brief stay in Rikers Island. Kane would smuggle cocaine and rum into the joint for Tommy Ryan for a price. A stiff price. But Tommy Ryan had the money, and it was through financial manipulation and a little blackmail that he managed to run things in the tier. Money and balls, Tommy thought. That's all anyone ever needed to make it to the top.

But Carol had not answered the phone all morning. Finally the fifth time he called Carol answered the phone. They exchanged hellos and Tommy told her where he was and why.

"Wonderful way to spend Christmas," Carol said.

"I'll be home by Christmas," Tommy assured her.

Then Tommy told her he needed the number for Kane. Carol looked the number up in Tommy's private phone book and gave it to him. There was a long pause from Carol's end of the line.

"What's the matter, Carol?" Tommy asked.

"That cop, Ankles, he was around with a search warrant, but he didn't find anything here," Carol said. "He has Alley Boy in Rikers Island."

"I know that, Carol," Tommy said. "That's why I wanted Kane's number. I want him to look after Alley Boy inside. The way he looked after me."

"Or the way you looked after Frankie Green Eyes, Tommy?" Carol said acidly.

"What the hell is that supposed to mean, Carol?"

"Ankles said that the autopsy report proves that the same person who killed Green Eyes also killed Tony."

Tommy's throat went dry. But he recovered his suave instantly.

"You listen to that cop, Carol?" Tommy asked incredulously. "You believe him over me? Well, let me tell you something. There is no way an autopsy can prove it was the same person. Not with a cut throat. It isn't like a bullet where there's ballistics. Sure, it's the same method, Carol, but that's because I wanted to give that bastard a taste of his own medicine. I wanted him to go the way Tony went."

Carol became confused.

"But that cop said—"

"Don't listen to no cops," Tommy yelled. "He's tryin' to confuse you. He wants you to make mistakes. He's bluffing, Carol, believe me. Trust me. Not some cop. Christ almighty."

"I'm sorry, Tommy . . ."

"You should be. Just about accusing me of killing Tony. How do you think that makes me feel? Huh?"

Tommy Ryan slammed the phone down. His rage immediately calmed. He picked up the phone again and dialed ten digits. The long distance phone connection took several seconds to complete. Finally it rang. On the fifth ring a voice answered, "Hello."

"Kane?"

"Speaking."

"It's Tommy Ryan."

There was a long pause from the other end.

Then: "Whadda you want, Ryan?"

Tommy Ryan said, "A favor."

"What kind of favor?" Kane asked.

"I want you to deliver a message."

"Call Western Union," Kane said. "I'm not a delivery boy."

"How about if I call the Department of Corrections instead?" Tommy Ryan said. "And a few newspapers. And I tell them they have a member of the Ku Klux Klan working in Rikers Island. And that he peddles drugs, alcohol, sneaks out uncensored letters? How about that, Kane? Want me to do that?"

"You'd be hanging yourself, Ryan," Kane said defiantly.

"With an anonymous call? To a reporter? Maybe the drugs and the delivery service would be hard to prove. But not the Klan item, Kane. And even if your little racket couldn't be proved, you'd have to give it up because they'd be watching you, Kane. And then all the money you're making would go down the drain. Right, Kane?"

There was another long pause.

"Someday I'll kill you, Ryan," Kane said.

"Better wait until the master race takes over," Tommy Ryan said.

"What's the message?" Kane said.

"I want you to tell Sauerkraut that there's a new guy

in there. His name is Albert D'Agastino. Just tell him Tommy Ryan says he's a snitch. He'll know what to do. Tell him he knows what Willie Sanchez knows and he's ready to sing. That's all."

"This is the last time, Ryan," Kane said.

"That's all right."

"I don't have a shift until tomorrow," Kane said.

"Tell him first thing tomorrow then."

Tommy Ryan hung up the phone. His bedroom door opened. It was Gladys Sann. She stepped into the room and locked the door behind her. She walked over to the bed and pulled down the covers and removed the dressing from the wound. She looked at it closely and then poured peroxide over it. The peroxide foamed up like the head on a beer.

"Does it still hurt?" Gladys asked.

"Not much," Tommy Ryan said. "But it itches like mad."

"That means it's healing nicely. It's really just a flesh wound. You'll be all right soon."

"How soon?" Tommy Ryan asked.

"As soon as I get undressed," Gladys Sann said, as she reached behind her back and pulled the zipper down a few inches. She turned around and let Tommy Ryan pull the zipper down the rest of the way. She wore no underwear or bra. She pulled the dress off her shoulders and let it drop to the floor. Then she pushed the shoes off her feet. Tommy Ryan stared at the lithe, pink body. The small hard breasts, the firm strong legs, and the vee of auburn pubic hair. He reached for her, but she clasped his hands.

"Let me do the work," Gladys Sann said. "It has to be gentle or you might hurt yourself. Don't worry about me. I'll enjoy it, too."

Tommy watched her climb onto the bed and push the hair out of her face. He watched as she took him in her hand and softly stroked him. He closed his eyes and felt her take him into her mouth slowly, and then all other thoughts abandoned him as she controlled him for those few minutes.

Just before dinner chow Alley Boy was taken from his cell and led down the corridor of the tier. He was led through two security gates and then down two flights of stairs and placed in a large empty room with a long table and two chairs. The iron door was slid shut and Alley Boy sat in one of the chairs looking around the empty room.

After waiting about five minutes, the heavy iron door was rolled open again and Ankles entered the room. His ever-present cigar protruded from his lips and he walked over and sat down in the chair facing Alley Boy.

Both of them sat there staring at each other for a full minute. Neither spoke a word. Finally Ankles broke the silence after slowly removing the cigar from his mouth with a tired, bored look on his fleshy face.

"Wonderful place, isn't it, D'Agastino?"

"It's all right."

"Oh, it is now?" Ankles said. "So you like it?"

"I didn't say that."

"But it isn't as bad as you thought. Well, let me fill you in on a few things. That tier you're on is called the Garden of Eden. It's all white guys and you'll be okay there if you play by the rules. But there are other tiers here that I can have you sent to where you'd wish you were dead instead. But I'm not gonna do that to you. Not yet anyway. Because I still like you, kid. I even sort of admire your loyalty to the lowlife, Tommy Ryan. I mean, nobody really likes a rat.

"But you're worse than a rat, D'Agastino. You're a chump. The days of takin' the fall for somebody else are over. What is this whole act supposed to be? You watch *Spartacus* too many times, or what? That part where everybody takes the weight by saying they're Spartacus so that they crucify everybody? That the idea? Cause if it is, then you'll all crucify. Cause one way or the other, I'll get Tommy Ryan and that fuckin' Cisco and they'll be strung up by the balls. And you'll still be in here. So all your loyalty won't do you or them any good."

"I still don't know what you're talking about," Alley Boy said.

"I saw Stephanie and your mother in court last night," Ankles said. "They don't look too happy. Your mother looks a wreck. It must be delightful to have a kid like you for a son. Must be nothing better than to brag to the neighbors that your son's doin' five to ten for bank robbery.

"If you had any real loyalty it would be to your family and that Kelly girl. They're the ones who care about you. Not that asshole Tommy Ryan. If he was such a good friend, why aren't you out on bail yet? Huh? How come?"

"Like I said, I don't know Tommy Ryan that well. Just to say hello. That's all. I don't know about the rest."

"You think I'm stupid, don't you?" Ankles snapped. "I seen you with him a dozen times, drinking with him, hanging around with him in that McCaulie's bar. You think I'm stupid? Didn't you tell me one night you thought Tommy Ryan had heart? Huh? Didn't you?"

"Yeah, but that doesn't mean I know him real good. Maybe I think Joe Frazier has heart, but I don't know him."

Ankles peered wide-eyed at Alley Boy and then

pushed his chair back and stood up. He stared down at Alley Boy in the chair, thinking he looked very much like a little boy sitting there.

"Any message you want me to give to Kelly or your family?"

Alley Boy smiled and said, "Yeah, tell them everything's all right and that I'll see them for Christmas."

Ankles shook his head sadly and banged on the metal door for the guard.

Gladys Sann lay smoking a cigarette with her head in the crook of Tommy Ryan's arm. She was watching the smoke curl up to the ceiling. Tommy Ryan felt satiated, relaxed, like a milked cow. He held the red-haired girl close to him. Gladys blew a perfect smoke ring that moved quickly before dissipating into shapelessness.

"Do you like what you do?" Gladys asked Tommy Ryan.

"I like what you do."

"No, seriously."

"Sometimes. Not when I get shot. But the money's good."

"I mean, is it self-rewarding, fulfilling?"

"Yeah," Tommy Ryan said. "When it goes all right. When you fool them. When you walk in and take their money because you have the brains and the balls. Yeah, it's rewarding. Very rewarding."

"How does somebody get started doing something like that? What made you an outlaw, Tommy Ryan? I mean, you're intelligent."

"I'm an outlaw, Gladys Sann, because I am intelligent. It's the smartest business to be in. Most people who are involved in business are outlaws, too. Only they're not as honest about it. Nobody steals more than banks do. They gyp all their customers. They finagle with the money—other people's money. They make people pay enormous interests on loans and mortgages. They make you stand on line for your own money. Then they abuse you when you ask for it. They're outlaws. They just use fountain pens.

"Me, I'm more honest. I use a gun. It's about the same. But I make more money than most bankers."

"So one morning you just woke up and said, 'Starting today I'm gonna be a bank robber.' And then went out and got a gun and walked into the nearest First National?"

"No," Tommy Ryan said reflectively. "It wasn't really as simple as that. But I don't want to bore you with the details."

"No, really, I'm interested."

"Forget it."

"Why? Is that asking you too much? Didn't I make you feel good? Didn't I do what you wanted?"

"It isn't the same, Gladys. I never told anyone else before. It's sort of my own secret."

"Tell me, Tommy," Gladys said. "This is just a stop in the woods. You and me. It's just a weird attraction. I told you I wanted to see what it was like with an outlaw. Now I want to know what makes an outlaw. Come on. What happens here stays here. You have my dad over a barrel; I wouldn't repeat anything you told me. If I did I'd be getting him in trouble, right?"

Tommy Ryan lay there on the bed. He looked in Gladys Sann's eyes. He did not smile. Then he looked back at the ceiling.

"Promise not to laugh," Tommy Ryan said.

"Promise."

"Lobsters," Tommy Ryan said as a complete sentence.

"Lobsters what?"

"I was ten years old," Tommy Ryan said. "And it

was the first time I ever ate a lobster. It was delicious.
I was twenty-three years old before I ever ate another
one. And that was because lobsters were expensive. But
I didn't understand that. See, the first ten years of my
life we were well off. My father was a banker. A big-
shot banker for a very big New York investment bank.
He made a great salary. And we used to live in a
beautiful house on a cliff on the Hudson like this one.
My father drove a Cadillac. There was a mortgage on
the house, but it would have been his in fifteen years.

"But that year, when I was ten, my father made a
very large investment for the bank. It was a compli-
cated deal involving about fifty million dollars. But it
was a scam. My father got taken bad. And the bank
lost all that money. The bank wound up with hundreds
of thousands of shares of worthless stock.

"My father was not only fired, he was brought to
trial. He had to sell the house to pay the court ex-
penses. Then his reputation was ruined. He became a
laughingstock of the banking industry. And he couldn't
find work doing anything, because his name was black-
listed in the business world.

"He became a fucking elevator operator. And I remember that we had to move to this rat-trap apartment
in Brooklyn, filled with roaches and rats and everything. There was nothing left. He had invested all his
own savings in the same mad scam. He even borrowed
about twenty thousand dollars to invest further, because he thought it would make him rich for a lifetime.

"The courts let him off with a suspended sentence,
but he had to make good on the loans. It was a stipula-
tion of the court. And I remember as a kid watching
him get up in the morning in the rat-trap pad in Brooklyn and he would still dress in the business suits he had
left, and carry a briefcase to work. In the briefcase
were his work clothes. An elevator operator. He couldn't

get any other job. He had no skills outside of banking. That was all he knew. He started as a teller when he was eighteen.

"My mother had to take a job in a place called the Pilgrim Laundry, and both of them worked the night shift because the pay was higher.

"And my father insisted I go to business school when I got out of high school. I wanted to get a job to help them with money, but they insisted I go to Saint John's University. I won a scholarship, but I hated school. When I got out, I didn't want any part of the business world. I learned to hate it because of what it had done to my father.

"But growing up in Brooklyn made me smarter in other ways. I realized that to get ahead you had to be ruthless, even vicious. And one day me and this guy Tony Mauro, who had a father who was a cripple from Korea, we got us a couple of guns and we walked into a bank and we held it up. We only got nine thousand dollars but we couldn't believe how easy it was. And how good it made you feel. It's like they say about heroin. It's never as good as the first time, but you keep shooting it to see if it will be. It's the same with a bank robbery. The first time you walk in there, you are the judge and the jury. You are the boss. No one can tell you anything. No one can tell you that seniority is the key to the top.

"There's no waiting until you're old to hit the big time. You are right there. There's you, the gun, and the money. And you just take the fuckin' money.

"When I started getting more and more money I bought a house like the one we lived in before my father's career was ruined. I moved them in there. I got some people I know to have their names changed so they could have a new start. I got my father plastic surgery. I made them quit their jobs. They think I work for the treasury department in Washington, D.C. They think I'm a big-time agent of some kind. They don't even know what I do. I'll keep it that way, too. For as long as I can, anyway.

"But right after that very first bank job me and Tony did, the first thing I did was I went to the Palm Restaurant in Manhattan and I ordered the biggest fucking lobster you ever saw in your life. And I ate every bit of it. And nothing ever tasted better in my life."

Gladys was looking at Tommy Ryan now, her eyes soft, and she was smiling.

"Kind of simple, isn't it?" she said.

"Telling it is," Tommy said. "Living it wasn't. Now everything is easy anyway. At least for my parents. That's all that counts."

"That's sort of nice. I think I like that story."

"It's true, Gladys."

"I didn't say it wasn't. I just said I liked it."

Gladys Sann stood up from the bed and pulled the white dress on. She turned around and Tommy Ryan zipped it up for her. She stepped into her white shoes.

"I'll see you tomorrow," Gladys said. "Thanks for a nice time."

"Thank you," Tommy Ryan quickly added.

Gladys smiled weakly and left the room. Tommy Ryan lay there and tried to remember if he had left anything out of the story. It isn't important anyway, Tommy Ryan thought. I told her enough.

31

At breakfast Alley Boy sat at the table with Mulraine, the big German, and the other white prisoners. Alley Boy had a breakfast of pebbly powdered eggs, white toast, and coffee. Mulraine ate just the toast and coffee. Sauerkraut ate a double portion he had obtained by taking what Mulraine refused.

During coffee the German took out his false teeth again and snipped off the end of the cigar with the razor-sharp cobalt edge of the denture bridge. Upon seeing the false teeth, with food particles clinging to them, Alley Boy put down his fork. The sight didn't mix well with powdered eggs.

The German put the dentures back into his mouth and lit the cigar. As he leaned back in his chair, he again saw Willie Sanchez cleaning the tables. Every time the German looked at Willie Sanchez the word *murder* seemed to light up in his eyes.

Finally he turned his head away and saw a large, ham-faced screw flagging his attention. The German got up from the table and approached the screw. The two exchanged words for several minutes.

"That's Kane," Mulraine said. "He's the Pony Express. He can get you what you want from the outside if you can get through to him. Tommy Ryan made him hop like a bellboy—I heard he had some kind of political shit on Kane that could cost him his job. But he can get you anything outside."

"The only thing I want outside is me," Alley Boy said. And it made him wonder again why Tommy Ryan had not yet bailed him out. Sure Tommy was hurt, but he could have arranged bail by now. Shit, I saved his life, Alley Boy thought. What was goin' on? He looked over to Willie Sanchez and more questions came to mind. Why would Tommy Ryan take special care of a guy like that? He never mentioned no Willie Sanchez outside. Did Tommy Ryan owe Sanchez a favor? Or did Sanchez maybe have something on Tommy Ryan, the way Tommy had something on this guard named Kane? Maybe there's more to Tommy Ryan than I thought, Alley Boy reasoned. All I know is I should have been bailed out by now.

Tommy Ryan had once explained something about jail to Alley Boy. He had told Alley Boy that anybody who does even a few nights in the joint has to deal with some of his doubts. Tommy had said that for some it was doubts about God, for some it was the size of their dick or how much hair they had on their ass. For others it was doubts about their intelligence or their courage or their manhood. Some had to confront doubts about their lives that led them to the joint, about society, their family, and mankind itself. The way Tommy Ryan explained it, jail made you admit your doubts, deal with them, and become yourself, because in the joint you can rely only on yourself.

And Tommy Ryan said that sometimes doubts you had about yourself on the outside disappeared because in the joint you were tested. Even on the smallest of bits. And now for the first time Alley Boy was beginning to have fewer doubts about himself. But also for the first time Alley Boy was beginning to form doubts about Tommy Ryan.

The German walked back over to the table and sat down. He had the jack-o'-lantern grin on his puss again. Alley Boy grinned back at him, trying to look like an equal. He was doing a pretty good job of it.

"Jimmy," the German said. "I'm gonna bunk with Al here. Tommy Ryan sent word through Kane that I'm supposed to take care of Al. See that he gets everything Tommy wants him to have. Kane will arrange it."

"Anything you say," Mulraine said.

"All right with you Al?" the German asked.

"Sure," Alley Boy said.

Alley Boy stared at the German and thought, I can take care of myself. Tommy Ryan should bail me out, not send me roommates.

The bell indicating the end of chow rang and all the inmates got to their feet and began forming lines. Then in single file they exited the cafeteria.

The Christmas lights hung across Fifth Avenue in ornate designs, the reds and greens and whites sparkling against the darkness of the cloudy night. The merchants of Bay Ridge footed the bill for the Christmas decorations every year, and they strung them from building to building across the busy commercial strip to attract Christmas shoppers to their small stores.

The street was thick with people moving through the slushy sidewalks, and buses groaned heavily along the avenue with the ever-present jingle of snow chains. Christmas music issued from the outside speakers of record shops, and men dressed in warm clothing, standing around oil-barrel fires, sold Christmas trees for outrageous prices on the street corners.

Mothers pushed prams and older children splashed down the streets throwing snowballs at the Santa Clauses that rang Salvation Army bells outside the larger stores.

Ankles walked down Fifth Avenue feeling foolish. He hadn't bought anyone a Christmas present since his mother had died a decade ago. He remembered how every year he would buy his mother the same gift, a set of English/Italian records to try to teach her the English language. And he remembered how every year by February his mother would have broken every record in frustration, because she simply could not understand this language they called English, with words that meant five and six different things at the same time. And he remembered how every year he went out and bought the translation records again, and how when she died that day in her own bed she uttered one last word to Ankles. It was one of about a dozen English words she had learned before she died. She had summoned Ankles close to her and she whispered in his ear, "Hello." She had meant to say good-bye.

Ankles had to chuckle at the memory now. But he still didn't know what to buy for gifts this year. He walked into a women's boutique, feeling mammoth and ridiculous and a little embarrassed. He held his hat in his hand and waited for a salesgirl to approach. Finally a pretty young girl in pants that were much too tight came over smiling pleasantly at Ankles and asked him what he wanted.

"Something for a middle-aged woman and something for a girl in her twenties," Ankles said. The salesgirl nodded, acknowledging his ignorance of such matters. She began to show Ankles leather goods—gloves and pocketbooks, belts and boots and wallets. All Ankles could do was shake his head agreeably at each item. He didn't have a clue as to what to buy.

"Why don't you pick out something you'd want for yourself and something you'd buy for your mother," Ankles said to the salesgirl. The girl smiled the pleasant smile again and decided on a handsome leather bag for the young woman and a pair of black leather gloves for the older woman. Ankles waited while the salesgirl gift wrapped the items, his mouth begging for the taste of a good cigar.

Ankles paid for the gifts in cash, then left the store and walked farther down Fifth Avenue. He stopped in front of a toy shop. Most of the toys in the window were guns or war toys or games with outer space themes. Then he saw what he wanted. It was a set of small boxing gloves with a punching bag on a small stand.

He went into the toy store and purchased the boxing glove set and had it gift wrapped. He carried the gifts down snowy Fifth Avenue and stopped outside a bar called the Tumble Inn. Ankles went inside and ordered a double Seagram's VO and a beer chaser. The bartender delivered the drinks and Ankles gave him a five-dollar bill and told him to keep the change.

"Merry Christmas," the bartender said as he stuffed the three dollars change into his tip cup.

"Yeah," Ankles said. "Merry Christmas."

Then Ankles knocked down the double whiskey in a single gulp and chased the booze away with the cold beer. He picked up his presents and walked back into the street. The avenue was a stew of commotion, and the Christmas music and the Christmas lights and the Santa Clauses and the running children and the Christmas-tree vendors hit Ankles in a rapid-fire montage. He stood there on the busy street and for the first time in months Ankles felt happy.

He let his face divide in a long, satisfying grin, and then at the top of this lungs he yelled, "Merry Christmas, everybody!" Dozens of people turned their heads in Ankles's direction and smiled or laughed. A few even returned the good wishes. Then Ankles turned around and went back into the saloon. The bartender approached him.

"To hell with it," Ankles said. "I'm getting drunk."

Then Ankles lit a cigar.

It had upset Alley Boy that Mulraine never said so long. In fact, before Mulraine exchanged cells with the German, he wouldn't speak to Alley Boy at all. Alley Boy wondered if he'd said something that might have upset Mulraine. He could think of nothing. Perhaps Mulraine had just come down with the jimjams because he was going to be spending Christmas in the joint.

Alley Boy made a mental note to ask Mulraine in the morning if anything was wrong. He would ask him if he had done anything to insult him.

Alley Boy took a cigarette from his shirt pocket but had no matches. He hadn't learned to enjoy the cigarettes yet, but he had to agree there was very little else one could do in a cell.

"You have a match?" Alley Boy asked the German who lay on the bottom bunk.

"No," the German answered. "Stand near the bars and you'll get one from the screw when he walks by."

Alley Boy got off his top bunk and stood in front of the bars. He stood there for fifteen minutes waiting for a screw to pass, but none came. Finally the lights went out and Alley Boy knew that meant it was now ten o'clock. But he was not tired, so he stood there with his hands on the bars and the cigarette dangling from his lips, waiting for a screw to come.

Standing there in the dark, he wondered when Tommy Ryan would get him out. The money was certainly there. Alley Boy and Tommy and Cisco had all left their money in the warehouse because they were afraid of the cops searching their apartments.

Then he thought of Stephanie again. He thought about what he would buy her for Christmas when he got out. He decided he would get her a big diamond necklace, a heavy expensive necklace. It would look beautiful hanging around her neck. Maybe even earrings to match. He thought about how the earrings would look on her small little earlobes when the cold had turned them red.

He thought of Mexico and a car and traveling through the countryside and stopping off at all those small whitewashed houses they always showed you in cowboy movies. He thought about how good the tequila would be down there. Someone had told him once that they put a worm in the tequila bottles. But he'd have to see that to believe it.

These thoughts were running through his mind when the German's forearm snapped against Alley Boy's windpipe. Alley Boy made a desperate attempt to pull the massive arm from his throat, but the German was too strong. Now he felt something very sharp placed against his neck and he knew it was the German's false teeth.

Alley Boy was struggling for breath and wrestling to free himself, but the more he resisted, the more the sharp metal cut into his throat. Finally Alley Boy stood still there in the dark, and could feel the warm blood trickling down his neck toward his chest.

"Open your belt and take down your pants," the German instructed. Panic exploded in Alley Boy's head. This was it. The German is going to have me, Alley Boy thought. Alley Boy tried to think what Tommy Ryan would do in such a situation. But the thoughts wouldn't come. Then he relied on his own thoughts and they instructed him. He loosened his belt with his hands and undid the top snap of his trousers.

"Pull them down to your knees," the German said with dark laughter.

Alley Boy pushed the pants down around his knees. Then he did the same with his underwear. The German kept the neck hold on Alley Boy, but removed his hand with the dentures to undo his own pants. Alley Boy could feel the German's warm hairy flesh against the backs of his own legs now. He could feel the German's stiff penis against one of his ass cheeks. Then he could feel the German's fingers wiping something thick and gluey on his rectum.

"You like chocolate on your ass, baby?" the German asked. "Gonna take you for a ride up the Bosco Boulevard. Then down the Hershey Highway. I'm gonna stick my tongue in your ear and my cock in your ass, baby."

The German made Alley Boy move his legs back from the bars. Then Alley Boy felt the warm, soft but stiff, blunt penis at the opening of his rectum.

"As long as we're gonna do this," Alley Boy said, "let's do it so we can both enjoy it. On the bed."

"Why? You like it?" the German asked.

"Of course I like it. I knew why you were moving in with me. I'll give you the best fuck you've had in years. I'll suck you off first."

The German held Alley Boy there for a minute with the big arm on his neck. "You gonna be my wife?" the German asked.

"I'll even sew for you. But I'd rather suck you off first to make it harder."

The German laughed with menacing delight. "You give good head?"

"Excellent."

The German relaxed the grip on Alley Boy's neck and led him to the bed. The German lay down flat on the bottom bunk.

Alley Boy knelt between the German's spread legs. The German made aroused, stimulated sounds as he anticipated Alley Boy. Alley Boy could see in the gloom as the German put his own hands behind his head. He held the sharpened dentures daintily between two fingers, the way a priest holds a host.

Alley Boy felt a rush of nausea bubbling in his gut as he fingered the German's large penis. Then in one swift motion he yanked at the German's balls with all his might. The German screamed in horror. His fingers let loose of the dentures. Alley Boy snatched them up. He held the German's shaft tightly in his left hand and jabbed the large blue protruding vein with the sharpened edge of the dentures. An urgent spout of blood shot up from the slit member. The German screamed in horror.

"Turn over you motherfucker," Alley Boy commanded. "Turn over or I'll cut it off completely."

The German was whimpering now like a little boy. He rolled over on his belly. Alley Boy still held him with both hands.

"Up on your knees, Adolf," Alley Boy instructed. The big German got up to all fours, as Alley Boy held on to his cock and applied more pressure with the sharp metal.

"How do you like it, you scumbag?" Alley Boy said. "Who put you up to it? Who told you to take me off?"

"Please don't," the German said. "I was only doing what he asked."

Alley Boy made a sawing motion with the blade and the erection went flaccid in his hand. But he held onto the tip of the German's cock with his large strong hand. Blood now covered Alley Boy's hand and he could feel it rolling down his wrists and dripping onto the bedsheets. He sawed again.

"I'll cut it off and ram it up your ass," Alley Boy said. "Now tell me, you cocksucker."

"Tommy Ryan," the German said between heaving groans. "He told me to kill you. He sent word with Kane the screw. He said you were a snitch. That you knew what Willie Sanchez knew."

"You're lying," Alley Boy said as he dug the blade deeper. "Tommy Ryan is my friend. He knows I'd never talk."

"Believe me," the German said as he broke into fitful crying. "Please believe me. It was him."

"What does Willie Sanchez know that I'm supposed to know?"

"I have no idea," the German said. "All I know is Tommy says the spic has something on him. I don't know what."

Alley Boy could hear the shouting of other prisoners now. They could hear the German crying and they were calling for the screws. Alley Boy heard the heavy metal security door opening, as the lights went on in the tier. The screws were running heavily down the corridor now.

Alley Boy could see the sheets covered with blood now and the cell door being flung open. He still did not let go of the German. The screws were yelling for Alley Boy to let go, but he would not. And then he felt the heavy crack against his head and he saw himself twisting and spinning and heard the sound of a great furious wind. He saw trees toppling and roofs being lifted from the tops of houses and water collapsing like crumbling walls onto a sandy shore, and then he felt himself being sucked out, way out into the sea, by the claws of the great waves. And then he was underwater and trying to swim to the surface.

32

"Sorry, Ryan, but the big German faggot blew it," Kane said when Tommy Ryan called him the next morning. "That Al D'Agastino is a pretty bad kid. He almost cut the kraut's cock off. The German will be in King's County Hospital for at least a month. They operated through the night. Chances are he'll never bunghole anyone again."

"How the fuck did that happen?"

"The German wanted some hole before he killed him."

"Dumb asshole," Tommy Ryan said as he ran anxious fingers through his hair. "Can never trust a faggot."

"I think you underestimated this D'Agastino kid," Kane said. "Word here is he ain't sung note number one. They take him into interrogation every day but he won't talk. He must know you ordered the hit by now."

"How do you know that?"

"Some of the other inmates heard the whole thing between the German and D'Agastino. The German sang like Englebert Humperdinck and all the lyrics were about you."

"Bullshit," Tommy Ryan said.

"Whatever you say. But that's what I hear. And by the way, I wouldn't try it again on that kid on the inside. First of all they know someone is trying to waste him. Second, they have him up in the Congo now. Up on tier nine. All niggers and spics. Ain't nobody up there gonna try it. They think he's a madman. You know, you almost cut off the gee's cock, you get yourself a heavy-duty rep."

Tommy Ryan didn't want to hear any more. He slammed the telephone down and lay in the bed for a few minutes. Maybe he had underestimated Alley Boy. But if Alley Boy knew that he had ordered the hit, the kid would be even more dangerous. He might even try something stupid like revenge. That would be okay because then he could get him out of the way. But he couldn't do anything to him now on the inside. Alley Boy was in a black tier and Tommy Ryan had no connection there.

You have to get him out, Tommy Ryan thought. That's the only way to do it. Bail him out. This kid holds a major card in your life now. Tommy didn't like anyone shuffling his deck. He had to have him where he could deal with him. In the street. Where you're the boss. In your stomping ground.

When the lunchtime lockout came, Alley Boy stepped out of his cell into the corridor. There was a large Band-Aid on his neck, and there was a hefty lump on his head. But he felt okay. The black men who stepped into the hall regarded Alley Boy with caution. He saw the black man he had knocked out in the bull pen when Mulraine had fought the other black kid. The black man walked directly up to Alley Boy when he saw him and held out his hand to shake. Alley Boy accepted it, locking thumbs in greeting.

"What's happnin', bro?" the black man said.

"Hiya," Alley Boy said.

"Heard what you did to that Nazi, man. You a bad muthafuckah. That right hand you hit me with that night laid me out, man. My name's Winston Jefferson."

"You used to be a fighter, didn't you?"

"Used to be, man. No more."

Alley Boy felt confidence moving in him. He had knocked out a fighter.

Alley Boy looked down at his hands and grinned. Then he looked up and saw Willie Sanchez at the front of the line, limping heavily with his cane.

"You know that guy?" Alley Boy asked Winston.

"Willie the Spic? Yeah. He a trustee, man. I hear he ask to be put in with you."

"Why me?"

"Don't know, man. Maybe cause he know you don't cop nobody's ass, man. I don't know. Come on. Let's go greeze."

Alley Boy followed behind Winston Jefferson as the single file moved toward the cafeteria. Inside the lunchroom Alley Boy saw Mulraine about ten spots ahead of him. Alley Boy looked to see if any of the screws were watching and he advanced up the line. Now he stood behind Mulraine. Mulraine didn't notice Alley Boy's presence.

Mulraine approached the convict counterman at the food dispatch. "I'll take hamburger and potatoes."

Alley Boy stood behind him and said, "And pile on the green peas and peaches."

Mulraine turned around with a start. The counterman watched Alley Boy stare down at Mulraine. Mulraine's eyes moved from one to the other. Alley Boy
could see Mulraine's Adam's apple swelling in his
throat.

"You knew, Jimmy," Alley Boy said. "You knew and
you didn't tell me."

"Hey, man, I'm sorry—"

"I don't want to hear it, pal," Alley Boy said. The
counterman was scooping up potatoes and hamburgers
to put onto Mulraine's plate.

"Just give him green peas and peaches," Alley Boy
said firmly to the counterman. "Nothing else. Give him
triple servings."

The counterman stared, fidgeting, unable to decide
what to do.

"You heard me," Alley Boy said.

The counterman shrugged at Mulraine as if to imply
"What can I do?" Then he heaped Mulraine's plate high
with green peas and canned peaches. Mulraine took one
last, nervous look at Alley Boy and then moved to his
assigned table. The German was conspicuously absent
from the head of the table. When Mulraine sat down
with his plate of food, all the other white prisoners at
the table stared at his plate.

Then, one by one, they got up from the table and
walked away. Mulraine sat there in terror as Alley
Boy approached and sat down at the table next to him.
Alley Boy did not eat. He drank a glass of milk and
bummed a cigarette from Winston Jefferson, who was
at an adjacent table.

Mulraine was now sitting all alone, ostracized by
his white peers.

"Eat it all," Alley Boy said flatly. "You're gonna
need all the strength you can get, Mulraine."

Mulraine looked down at the food and slowly began

・ 298 ・

to shovel the peas and peaches into his mouth. There was silence in the lunchroom. All eyes were on Mulraine.

And then the hum of whispers passed around the lunchroom. The whispers reached the table of white inmates across from Mulraine. He heard the message being put around, "Mulraine's shot down."

Fear dripped from Mulraine's face like perspiration. Alley Boy leaned toward Mulraine. "I hope you know how to press pants," Alley Boy said. "Because by tomorrow you're gonna be somebody's wife."

Tommy Ryan entered her slowly, moving warmly inside. He clutched at her buttocks and grinded his way in. Gladys Sann moved with the rhythm. Then she began to gallop, bouncing Tommy Ryan on her small fit body. She dug her nails into his back, making long scratches in his flesh. But before Gladys Sann could even begin to be satisfied, Tommy Ryan let go. He could hold it no longer. He collapsed on top of Gladys Sann in a spent pile.

"That's what I call a Concorde lay," Gladys said with disappointment. "The flight is over before you know it."

"I couldn't hold it," Tommy Ryan said.

"That's life in the fast lane."

"I'll be better later. Believe me."

"What later?" Gladys said. "You said you were leaving in the morning. Your wound is okay. You'll be as good as new in a few more days."

"Tonight," Tommy Ryan said. "I'll be better tonight."

"Nah," Gladys said. "Tonight I'm going over to my boyfriend's house."

"Boyfriend?"

"Yeah," she said. "We're getting married next month."

"But what about us?" Tommy Ryan said quickly. Gladys Sann laughed out loud as she stepped out of bed.

" 'Us'? What do you mean 'us'? All I told you was that I wanted to see what it was like with an outlaw. I never mentioned the word *us*."

"But I told you everything," Tommy Ryan said.

"And I told you I liked the story. So what do you want? Royalties? Residuals? A book advance? What?"

"You don't understand," Tommy Ryan said.

"I understand," Gladys Sann said. "It's you who doesn't."

Tommy Ryan watched her put on the white dress. She turned for him to zipper it. Tommy Ryan complied.

"So what was it like?"

"What was *what* like?" Gladys said.

"Sleeping with an outlaw."

She laughed and then thought for a minute.

"It was the same as sleeping with anyone else," she said. "Only you feel yourself being pretty desperate because you're closer to death. Sort of like necrophilia, you know. It was an experience, a very short one—like a ride on a roller coaster. But I wouldn't want to do it again."

"Necrophilia? You mean like fucking the dead?"

"Something like that," Gladys Sann said. "Dead inside and just waiting for the body to follow. You know. All dick, no balls."

"You cunt."

"Mine'll do."

"You're sick," Tommy Ryan said. "A sick little spoiled twat."

"See what I mean?" Gladys said. "You must know you're dying when you hate someone who reminds you of yourself."

Gladys moved gingerly to the door. Tommy Ryan said, "Would you do it again if you had it to do all over?"

Gladys Sann wrinkled her nose, pouted her lips, and said, "Nah."

And then she walked out of the room. Tommy Ryan sat up in the bed and stared at the closed door. He put his head in his hands and began to shake his head. Then he stood up and began to dress.

Alley Boy was alone in the new cell of the tier. His cellmate had been transferred out earlier in the evening and now he lay there alone. He refused to believe what the big German had said about Tommy Ryan. Tommy would never do that to me, Alley Boy thought. He was just a horny faggot looking for someone he thought was a kid. Tommy Ryan would be bailing him out soon. He knew that. And if he did, it would mean that the German had been lying.

Alley Boy lay there staring at the light bulb inside the cage in the ceiling. He thought about his father, and how he wished he had followed his father's advice and joined the iron workers' union. The father had him work two summers as an apprentice, but Alley Boy didn't like the way the older guys pushed him around and made fun of him and called him a boy and a punk and a gofer.

Alley Boy had always wanted to be what his father was not. His father could have made a lot of money in iron work, but Alley Boy could never remember his father working more than a full week at a time. Then he'd go on a bender, get drunk, and come home and abuse Alley Boy's mother.

It was the mother who encouraged Alley Boy to go into banking. She told him that the construction trade in New York was dead. There were no longer big buildings going up. And only the iron workers with union books and years of seniority would get work unless there was a major boom again.

So Alley Boy had gone and gotten the job as a teller in the Flatbush bank. He liked the job, but the money was poor and he kept making mistakes. The bank manager accused him of pocketing cash, which Alley Boy never did, but it eventually led to the manager asking Alley Boy to resign.

Which he did. Then he hooked up with Tommy Ryan because Tommy Ryan had told him he needed a guy who could drive well. And driving was probably the one thing Alley Boy did well. He didn't know at the time that it meant driving a getaway car for bank stickups, but Tommy Ryan had told him everything was going to be all right. He told him never to worry. He told him all the things he wished his father had told him before he went up on the high iron that day with a pint of whiskey on his hip and another pint already in his gut.

He remembered being told that the fire department had to come hose most of his father away because his body had turned to Jell-O when he hit the street.

Tommy Ryan was the kind of guy who would never let Alley Boy fall. Never. So he didn't believe the kraut for one single minute.

The cell door opened and the screw held the door as Willie Sanchez limped into the cell, putting all his weight on his wooden cane. Alley Boy sat up when he saw Willie Sanchez enter and sit down on the bottom bunk. The screw slammed the door shut and walked back down the corridor.

"Never heard of nobody who kicks the gee's ass takin' the top bunk, man," Willie Sanchez said.

"I like it better on the top," Alley Boy said.

"Well, you top man aroun' here now, man," Willie Sanchez said.

"Is that what they say?"

"Of course, man. You beat up that Sauerkraut, man. Course you the top man. Ebrybody say you berry, berry bad dude, man."

"No shit?"

"Yeah, man," Willie Sanchez said. "That's what ebrybody says. They say you gonna hear that Mulraine scream tonight, man. They say his cake's as good as baked."

"It's his own fault, man."

"I know."

Alley Boy lay silent for a moment and then smelled the distinctive odor of marijuana burning. He leaned over his bunk and saw Willie Sanchez sucking deeply on a joint. Willie Sanchez offered some to Alley Boy.

"No thanks," Alley Boy said. "Cigarettes are bad enough."

"Too bad, man—this is berry, berry good shit."

Alley Boy got down from the top bunk and sat next to Willie Sanchez and watched him inhaling the grass. Alley Boy watched the little smile on Sanchez's little mouth as he closed his eyes and held the smoke in.

"To hell with it, man," Alley Boy said. "Let me have a hit."

Sanchez passed the joint to Alley Boy and he took a deep inhale. The smoke made his lungs heave and he had to fight to keep it in. Then he exhaled quickly and took another hit.

"It's gold pot, man," Willie Sanchez said. "Berry, berry good."

Sanchez and Alley Boy passed the joint back and forth for the next few minutes in silence.

When they had finished smoking, Alley Boy crawled back up onto his cot and could feel his head becoming very light, very confused. His mouth was dry. Then he began laughing with no explanation. He didn't even know what he was laughing about.

"Told you it was good shit, man," Willie Sanchez said.

Alley Boy thought this remark was hilarious and laughed so hard he broke into a coughing fit. He had to get back down from his bunk to regain control. Finally he composed himself and looked at Willie Sanchez. He thought Sanchez looked like a caricature, a sketch drawn by an artist on Bleecker Street in the Village.

"You been lucky so far," Willie Sanchez said, and then rapped his knuckles on the gimp leg. A loud, hollow, wooden sound escaped. Alley Boy looked at Sanchez with curiosity.

"Knock on wood, man," Sanchez said.

"You have a wooden leg?"

"Better than wooden nickels," Sanchez said.

Alley Boy dissolved into laughter again. Sanchez sat there with the mousy little smile on his face. To Alley Boy he looked like a hamster.

"You better watch out for termites," Alley Boy said, and laughed even harder. Sanchez giggled along with him.

"Better you have one foot in the grave than two," Sanchez said. Alley Boy stopped laughing immediately.

"Whadda you mean by that, Sanchez?"

"Tommy Ryan."

"What about Tommy Ryan?" Alley Boy said.

"He try to have you offed, man," Sanchez said. "Tried to have that big motherfucker stick his dick in your cakes."

"What makes you think Tommy Ryan had somethin' to do with that?"

"I hear things, man. Maybe I have one leg, but I have two big ears, man. I don't listen good; I don't listen at all. You don't hear too good when you dead."

"Whadda you hear . . . ?" Alley Boy's mouth was dry from the pot.

"I can't tell you what I hear, because I do and then you know and then I'm not the only one who knows, man. But I hear a lot of things, man. I know Tommy Ryan owned that German anyway. I can tell you that because ebrybody knows that. It wasn't for Tommy and I be dead right now, man. Not that he hab any lub for me, man. But he know, I know all about him."

"Like what?" Alley Boy asked, a percussion of confusion playing in his head.

"Things, man. Things he don't want nobody to know."

"Like what? What kind of thing?"

"I tole you I can't say, man. But people outside that I know, they know what I know. I tole them, man. And Tommy Ryan, he don't know who they are, man. But he knows that if anything happen to me in here, they'll let the right people know what they know. *Comprendo?*"

"What a load of horseshit," Alley Boy said. "I don't know what the fuck you're talking about. One thing Tommy Ryan is, he's smart. He don't let a guy like you know nothin'."

"He smart enough to try to get you offed by that German *maricón*, man," Sanchez said. "How come that German don't eber get me if I don't know what Tommy Ryan don't want nobody to know? You be surprised what you find out 'bout a guy you lib in a cell with him awhile, man. Tommy Ryan, he pisses in his sleep, man. He gets bad nightmares. He talk in his sleep too, man. I find out a lot 'bout Tommy Ryan, man. But I don't tell you 'cause you say you think he's still your fren. Maybe, but you better think 'bout that, man. But I gib you some adbice, man. You got somethin' on him, you better tell somebody else outside. That keep you alibe, man. Tell more than one, though, cause he might find out who that is."

"Like maybe, Frankie Green Eyes?"

"He knew. Frankie, he was my cousin, but he was stupid, man. He open up his mouth allatime. Eatin' them pills. I don't gib a fuck 'bout him, man. He would hab killed himself with the pills soon anyway. He's crazy. Was crazy. I don't care 'bout him, jus' me."

Willie Sanchez giggled again.

"I jus' wanna give you that man, as a fren," Sanchez said. "That German been looking to my buns a long time. He say he want to see what it like to fuck a dude with one leg. You ice him good, so maybe he won't get a hard-on again, man. For that I offer you some adbice. You think 'bout that, man."

Willie Sanchez stood up and shouted for the screw. The screw arrived a few minutes later. Sanchez waved his cane in a good-bye gesture and the screw slid the cell door closed.

33

The drive from upstate New York had been fast and smooth. Tommy Ryan had kept the gold Cadillac moving at an even seventy miles an hour and the ride took only an hour and a half. His wound was healing well now; there was no longer any pain—just the maddening itch. He was to keep eating penicillin for two weeks and Doctor Sann promised everything would be all right.

As he drove Tommy Ryan had a mad desire for Carol Mauro. It was more than a sexual urge. He wanted a woman who understood him, one who did not mix sex with ridicule as Gladys Sann had done. He wanted a woman who told him he was good, told him he was the boss and the best. Carol Mauro would tell him that. Carol Mauro would soon be able to forget Tony Mauro, accept that his murder had been avenged. Time would exorcise the ghost from the bed. But in order to have that time, Tommy Ryan needed to get rid of Alley Boy.

The Cadillac rumbled over the Manhattan Bridge and soon Tommy Ryan was driving up Flatbush Avenue toward Grand Army Plaza. When he reached Prospect Park West, he made a right and pulled the car to a halt outside Stephanie Kelly's apartment building.

Cisco waited in the car as Tommy Ryan walked past the cop in the lobby and rang Stephanie's bell. Stephanie answered through the intercom and Tommy Ryan asked her to come downstairs; he'd like to talk to her. There was a long pause from Stephanie's side of the conversation. Then she told Tommy Ryan she'd be right down. She told him to wait outside in the street.

Tommy Ryan leaned against the parked car, waiting for Stephanie to come down. The cop in the hallway stared out through the frosted French windowpanes at Tommy Ryan. He looked like he was trying to place the face.

Ten minutes later Stephanie appeared from the building. Her face was rock hard and her eyes stared straight ahead in blatant hatred. She walked toward Tommy Ryan and he moved toward the corner and leaned against a red fire-alarm box. Stephanie followed, an overcoat draped over her shoulders.

"What do you want, creep?" Stephanie snapped.

"Hey, let's not get carried away here, Stephanie. I'm here to help."

"You couldn't help yourself with a miracle."

"I want to bail Alley Boy out. I have the money. But I can't be the one who posts bail for obvious reasons. Now, I have a bail bondsman who is waiting for you. He says he can have Alley Boy out by morning. Tomorrow's Christmas Eve. I think we should get him out."

Stephanie's statuesque mask softened slightly.

"You have fifty thousand dollars?"

"I can have it in an hour."

"What do I have to do?"

"Just post the bond," Tommy Ryan said. "O'Hara will take care of it. Scatter O'Hara they call him. He's a bail bondsman down on Court Street. You just have to sign the papers. Tell them you had jewelry; you sold it. It'll be all right."

"Where do I meet you?"

"Just go down to O'Hara's Bail Bonds on Court Street in about an hour. I'll leave the money there. O'Hara is all right. He won't ask any questions. He just needs your signature on some forms."

"That's all there is to it?"

"That's it."

"All right, I'll do it. For Al's sake."

Tommy Ryan gave Stephanie the Court Street address and she agreed to go there in an hour. Stephanie went back up to her apartment to get her identification.

Tommy Ryan drove the Cadillac to the warehouse. Inside he and Cisco counted out fifty thousand dollars in cash. Tommy Ryan placed the cash in a brown paper bag. He took the remaining two-hundred-odd thousand dollars and placed it in a canvas bag and put it under the brass bed.

He drove down Fifth Avenue toward downtown. He dropped Cisco off at his apartment on Eleventh Street and Fifth Avenue.

"Don't forget, Cisco," Tommy Ryan said. "Don't miss her when she gets back."

"No way," Cisco said. "I'm never late for anything, Tommy."

Tommy Ryan continued to drive down Fifth Avenue and then made a left onto Flatbush Avenue. He took Flatbush down to Court Street and parked the car in

the parking lot across the street from the bail bondsman's office.

Tommy Ryan carried the paper satchel into O'Hara's
Bail Bonds. O'Hara sat behind the counter in the office
with his chin in his hand.

"What took you so long?" O'Hara, a fat man with
white hair and a face like a dolphin's, asked.

"Sorry, Scatter," Tommy Ryan said. "Traffic on
Fifth Avenue was heavy."

"You got the money?" O'Hara asked.

"It's all here," Tommy Ryan said as he handed the
paper bag to Scatter O'Hara. "In cash, so you don't
have to worry about no skip tracing."

"Oh, I don't worry about that," O'Hara said. "That's
the only fun part of this job. That and an odd knob job
from the ones who don't have enough collateral. I got a
soft heart for them little Puerto Rican girls who ain't
got enough to get their boyfriends out. A soft heart
and a hard prick."

O'Hara inspected the contents of the bag. He appeared satisfied.

"When's the broad comin'?" he asked.

"Should be here in about a half-hour," Tommy Ryan
said.

"Well, he won't get out until the mornin' anyway
cause he's in Rikers. If he was in the Brooklyn House
of Dee it would be quicker. But he'll be out in the
mornin' anyway."

Tommy Ryan thanked O'Hara and walked out onto
Court Street and made a left up the block. He walked
down the three steps to a saloon called the Verdict.
He ordered a rum and Coke. The bartender delivered
the drink and Tommy Ryan washed down two penicillin
tablets with the drink. He ordered another one. The
liquor tasted good.

Tommy Ryan stood at the end of the bar in the Verdict for about a half an hour. He was watching the menagerie of the Christmas hustle pass by. But he was not thinking about the mothers too poor to afford to buy gifts putting themselves in hock by buying tons of crap on credit. They were waiting for buses and standing in line for taxicabs, trying to escape the Downtown Brooklyn Shopping Center before the rush hour came. The downtown shopping area was the sixth largest commercial hub in the nation, and at Christmastime it was mob city.

Tommy Ryan did not consider that most of the shoppers were blacks and Puerto Ricans, because many of the white people shopped in their own neighborhoods now. Nor did it occur to him that the black neighborhoods of Brooklyn offered little in the way of commerce any longer. That the massive looting during the great 1977 blackout had wiped out miles of commercial strips in the ghettos. So that now the poor people had to take public transportation to the downtown area from neighborhoods such as Crown Heights, East Flatbush, Brownsville, Bushwick, and Bedford-Stuyvesant.

The city had lost four hundred thousand Jews in a decade to the white security of the suburbs and Miami, and the black people moved into those abandoned white neighborhoods. This mattered very little to Tommy Ryan.

The blacks brought their poverty with them, and at Christmastime every year they toted it along with them to downtown Brooklyn, where they went far enough out on a limb to assure that they'd be broke until next Christmas. They bought all the junk and overpriced gimmicks the businessmen could devise for the Christmas season and they brought it home with them.

Tommy Ryan was watching this maze of activity

when he finally saw what he did care about—outside O'Hara's Bail Bonds. Stephanie stepped out of the cab and five different women fought to get in it to escape the mounting rush hour.

When Tommy Ryan saw Stephanie step into the bail bond office, he walked to the phone and dialed Biff's poolroom. He asked for Cisco. Biff told him to hold on a minute.

It took Stephanie only ten minutes to complete all the forms. O'Hara eyed her lasciviously, but Stephanie just stared him in the eye and he retreated to a more respectful posture.

"That's it, lady," O'Hara said.

"That's all?"

"He'll be out in the A.M. Department of Corrections bus'll leave him outside the Chase Manhattan Bank at Queensboro Plaza. From there he'll have to make his own way home."

"Will you do me a favor?" Stephanie asked.

"As long as it don't cost me money."

"Will you get a message to him that I'll meet him there with a taxi?"

"Sure, lady," O'Hara said. "I'll pass the message along."

Stephanie thanked O'Hara and walked back into the street.

She thought about popping into Abraham and Straus to buy a gift for Al, but the crush of the crowd was too maddening. She would get him something tomorrow instead, she thought. Right now it would be better to get home. She would call Alley Boy's mother and tell her the good news—Al was coming home for Christmas.

Stephanie stood on the corner of Schermerhorn Street for about fifteen minutes trying to get a cab.

But all the taxis were off duty, occupied, or quickly nabbed by someone more aggressive.

Ankles strode out of the Schermerhorn Street courthouse across the street. He was about to walk up the block to his car in the NYPD lot when he saw Stephanie standing on the corner waving madly trying to hail a cab. He stopped and watched as she flailed her arms at a passing taxi and then got splattered with slush from a puddle as the cab raced by. Ankles figured she might have just come out of O'Hara's Bail Bonds, and if she had, that might mean she had posted bail for D'Agastino.

Ankles crossed the street against the red light. A car missed hitting him by inches, but Ankles never noticed. He was walking directly toward her and finally Stephanie turned and saw him. Something electric moved in her eyes. She looked from O'Hara's Bail Bonds office to Ankles as if from a judge to jury. She clutched the pocketbook with the bond receipt closer to her body. Ankles slowed down to a stop a few steps from Stephanie. His ears were bent down from his hat and his arms dangled from his sides like a gorilla's. Stephanie looked him in the eye and Ankles stared right back, studying her.

"I see you're havin' a tough time gettin' a cab," Ankles said.

"I'm all right," Stephanie said.

"Coincidence meeting you here. I mean, I'm in and out of this joint couple a times a day. And I figure you're either shoppin' or postin' D'Agastino's bond."

"I was shopping," Stephanie said.

Ankles looked at her arms. She was carrying only a small purse.

"Didn't buy much."

"No, I didn't."

"So what time is he gettin' out?"

"Who?"

"Come on, Stephanie. Don't crap with me. I make one call and I'll find out if you posted bail or not. What's the big deal if you tell me?"

"All right, so he's getting out in the morning."

"That's nice. For Christmas Eve. I'm glad for him. He's an okay kid. A dumb bastard, but okay. I'm glad for his mother and for you anyway."

"What time you coming down the chimney, Santa?"

"You're the one playing Santy Claus. I mean, fifty thousand cash bond. That's some nice piece of change. Where'd you pick up that kind of dough? Tommy Ryan been around wearing a white beard and a red suit maybe?"

Stephanie didn't answer. She stepped off the curb and flagged another taxi. The cabbie waved his hand, indicating he was off duty. Stephanie was growing angry.

"Let me give you a lift. I'm just across the street. Come on."

Stephanie hesitated and clutched the pocketbook tighter.

"Come on, no strings. I can't make you tell me where you got the money. The D.A. might later on, but he'll wait till after New Year's. It's just a ride, anyway."

"Thanks," Stephanie said and followed Ankles across the street to the NYPD parking lot. Ankles opened the passenger door and Stephanie climbed in. He closed his door after he got in the driver's side then started the car.

"If it'll make you feel any better, I can tell you this," Ankles said. "All the evidence they got on him on that bank job is circumstantial. He could get off with eighteen months. Maybe less."

"You think so?"

"Yeah," Ankles said. "He could probably walk altogether if he turned state's evidence on Ryan and Cisco. They were the trigger men for sure. D'Agastino probably just drove. That's an accomplice. It's horseshit. But he won't talk. Not yet, anyway."

Ankles put the car in drive and pulled out of the lot.

34

Alley Boy lay awake on the top bunk, smoking a Pall Mall. He was watching the smoke twist toward the nicotine-yellow ceiling and thinking about what Willie Sanchez had said to him. He wondered why Tommy Ryan had not bailed him out yet. He wondered if the big German had been sicced on him by Tommy. Did Tommy think he was a rat? A snitch?

Nah, that couldn't be.

He had just saved Tommy's life a few days ago, and Tommy was the kind of guy who would remember that. But there were all kinds of things that were not making sense. Why was Frankie Green Eyes dead? Why did Fabulous Murphy get it the same way Green Eyes did just after Alley Boy left him alive? And he wondered if Tony Mauro's murder tied in. All cut throats. And what was it that this guy Willie Sanchez had on Tommy

Ryan? Was it true that Tommy Ryan actually pissed in the bed? Was there something about Tommy Ryan he didn't know?

Alley Boy wanted to get out of there. He wanted to go home for Christmas. He wanted to be with Stephanie and his mother and his grandmother. Tomorrow night his grandmother would have eel and linguine and baked clams and stuffed shells and wine and garlic bread and Italian pastries on the table. Alley Boy wanted to be there.

If Tommy Ryan had not bailed him out by tomorrow he would have Stephanie go and get his money from the warehouse to get him bail. He had seventy-two thousand dollars—that was his Christmas ticket home.

When he got out he would have a lot of questions to ask Tommy Ryan.

Stephanie answered the phone on the first ring. It was Cisco and he was talking fast and frantic telling Stephanie that Alley Boy might not get out because the D.A. was questioning the source of the bail money. He said that it could all be straightened out, but she would have to meet him right away. Tommy Ryan had figured the whole thing out and if she met him immediately Alley Boy would still get out in the morning.

"What do you mean questioning the source of the money?" Stephanie asked.

"They want you to sign a sworn statement that the money was yours. It isn't that unusual. But you have to deal with it right away before anyone goes on their Christmas leave."

"Where should I meet you?" Stephanie asked. She didn't really know what the hell Cisco was talking about, but if it was going to help get Al out by morning she would go and meet him.

"I'm down on Twelfth and Seventh," Cisco said. "Come down here right away. But walk so that you can be sure nobody is following you. Meet me on Twelfth Street, in between Seventh and Eighth Avenue."

"Near the factory?" Stephanie asked. "Why the hell do I have to meet you there? It's dark and empty there this time of night."

"Well, that way we can be sure no one sees us. We don't want anyone to know you're talking to us. If the D.A.'s people see me or Tommy with you they'll know we gave you the money."

"All right," Stephanie said. "How long will it take?"

"Just a few minutes. Tommy has some paperwork that'll say you owned a lot of jewelry and you sold it. That's all. He has it figured out. He's doing this for Alley Boy, Stephanie."

"All right," Stephanie said. "I'll be there in about fifteen minutes."

"Good."

The screw banged open Alley Boy's cell door and motioned him out onto the tier. Alley Boy jumped off the top bunk while a new prisoner snored away on the bottom.

"You have a visitor," the screw said.

The guard made Alley Boy walk in front of him along the walkway and Alley Boy knew he was going into the interrogation room again.

Inside the interrogation room he took his familiar seat across the table from Ankles. Ankles studied Alley Boy for a few moments and then tossed Alley Boy a pack of Pall Malls.

"Merry Christmas."

"Same to you," Alley Boy said.

"So you're going home tomorrow."

Alley Boy sat straight up and looked at Ankles with excitement.

"I am?" He realized he had acted too surprised. "Yeah, I told you I'd be out by Christmas."

"Where do you think Stephanie Kelly would get fifty thousand dollars, D'Agastino?"

"Maybe she found it."

"Yeah, of course. It was just lying there on the street. Fifty even. How convenient."

"Miracles happen."

"I suppose. But so do two-hundred-thousand-dollar bank jobs. You used to work in that bank in Flatbush that got robbed the other day. I didn't tell nobody that yet. I checked that out on my own. If I told the D.A. that, your bail would probably be revoked. See, I just found out by lookin' up your record. You had to be bonded to work in a bank. That's easy to find out."

"So what does that prove?" Alley Boy said. He was nervous about that item. Ankles could revoke his bail anytime he wanted by just dropping that information on the district attorney.

"Don't worry," Ankles said. "It's Christmas. I'm not gonna tell the D.A. yet. But maybe I'll get around to it. Or maybe I could forget I ever came across it. I mean, I could just tear up your file altogether. The FBI is on the case and you can be sure they'll never figure it out. They're too fuckin' dumb. The feds rely on us to give them information. We rely on them for laughs."

Alley Boy was looking at Ankles now. Ankles had his big hands flat down on the table and his face was earnest, almost pleasant.

"Now, maybe your file will go through the shredder. I'm not interested in that Flatbush bank. I'm really not.

I couldn't give a shit one way or the other. Nobody was hurt. The money was insured. But I want one thing from you."

Alley Boy looked at Ankles as if to say, "What's that?"

"I want to know anything you know about Tony Mauro's murder."

Alley Boy leaned closer to Ankles. Worry creased his eyes.

"Ankles, I swear on my mother, on Stephanie, on anybody—my dead father's grave—I don't know anything about that. I swear to God. If I knew I would tell you."

Ankles stared for a long time at Alley Boy and then stood up. He exhaled heavily.

"I believe you, kid."

Ankles took a large, folded manila envelope out of his coat pocket. There was a white label on the upper-right-hand corner of the envelope. The name Albert D'Agastino was written on the white label. Ankles held it in front of Alley Boy long enough for Alley Boy to see his name. Then Ankles dropped it on the table. He sat on the edge of the table closer to Alley Boy. He spoke quickly in a whisper.

"Look, I don't know why you're protecting Tommy Ryan. Maybe he did put up the money for the bail. I don't know, but I'd say so. But let me tell you something. You don't know how lucky you are. This bank charge upstate is a total meatball. With a good lawyer you might even walk. Take my advice, get yourself the best mouthpiece there is and you probably will walk. But when you get out of here, you better stay away from Tommy Ryan or you'll go down with him, kid. Take that dame of yours and split."

Alley Boy sat silently eyeing the envelope on the table. Ankles picked it up and saw that Alley Boy was staring at it.

"This could put you away," Ankles said, shaking the envelope. "You know that, don't you?"

Alley Boy swallowed hard, his Adam's apple bunching in his neck.

"Yeah," Alley Boy said.

Ankles took the envelope and tore it in half. Then he tore it again and again and again, until it was in little pieces. He dropped the torn shreds into the wastebasket and dropped in a lit match. The flames flickered inside the basket. Alley Boy watched as the paper turned to ashes.

"Thanks," Alley Boy said.

"Merry Christmas, kid."

Ankles banged for the guard and in a moment he was gone. Alley Boy felt like crying.

Tommy Ryan stood on the stepladder and placed the angel snugly on the top of the Christmas tree. Carol was draping the tree with tinsel and young Michael was tossing handfuls of it at the naked branches. Johnny Mathis was on the stereo singing about a winter wonderland and Carol and Tommy Ryan were singing along.

Tommy stepped down from the ladder and stumbled on his bum leg. Carol caught him before he fell and Tommy Ryan smiled. He kissed Carol on the lips and she slid her tongue into his mouth. It felt warm and slippery and hungry. Tommy pulled her closer to him.

"Why don't you get Michael to sleep and we can knock a piece off?"

"You're always so romantic," Carol said with a smile.

"It's been a while. I thought of you the whole time upstate."

"I better change that bandage for you, too."

"You might as well wait until after we've knocked a piece off."

Carol pushed him gently and laughed.

"Let him stay up for a while, Tommy," Carol said. "This is the first Christmas he can sort of understand. He's excited about the tree."

"What did you get him for Christmas?"

"All he ever wants is Batman toys. I got him everything I could with Batman."

"All right, let him stay up. But afterwards, we knock off a few pieces?"

Carol winked and slid her tongue back in Tommy Ryan's mouth.

The street was dark, the snow lay unshoveled, and she could hear her own footsteps. No cars moved on the street. A fluorescent streetlight hummed. Icicles hung from the ledges of the factory's windowsills. The wind was singing a high falsetto up Twelfth Street and she had trouble with her footing as she was looking down the street for Cisco.

She could not see him.

Then the hand came out of the darkness behind her. It covered her mouth and pulled her head upward from the chin, making the skin of her neck stretch tight, like a snare drum. She saw the fluorescent streetlight above her; it was still humming and the icicles hung down from the window ledges like cold fingers of death, and then she heard one long and final lisp of the wind and then the skin on her neck wasn't tight anymore. The cold blade raced across the skin, relieving the tautness. For a moment she felt the warm blood running down her chest, saturating the blouse covering her hard protruding nipples.

Stephanie thought about Al.

Then the sound of the wind died.

35

Alley Boy stepped off the green Department of Corrections bus at Queensboro Plaza nine thirty in the morning. He carried a small canvas bag containing his shaving and toilet gear. A few other cons got off with him.

A beautiful Puerto Rican girl ran past Alley Boy with tears streaming down her face and was swept up by an older guy who must have been her father. A black mother hugged her son who had just stepped off the bus and Alley Boy smiled.

He looked around for Stephanie, but she was nowhere in sight. The screw had told him that O'Hara, the bail bondsman, passed the word that Stephanie would be waiting. But it was Christmas Eve and maybe the subways weren't running so good. It was still early.

Alley Boy saw a bar called the Welcome Home across

the street and he crossed to it and went inside. He
ordered a beer from the bartender and paid him with
a five-dollar bill. The bartender gave Alley Boy his
change and Alley Boy went to the phone booth and
dialed Stephanie's number. He let the phone ring sixteen times, but there was no answer. Alley Boy hung up
the phone and dialed his mother's number and got his
grandmother on the phone.

"I knew the Virgin Mary would find a way to bring
you home for Christmas," the grandmother said. "I
knew it. I knew it even if the Pope is Polish. I knew."

Alley Boy's mother got on the phone and she was
trying to talk through sobs. Alley Boy asked her if she
knew where Stephanie was. The mother said she had
not heard from her since yesterday when Stephanie
had called to say that Alley Boy was coming home.

"She said she would be over there waiting for you.
That's why I'm not there," the mother said. "You want
me to come out there to show you how you can get home
from that Queens by the bus? You gotta take three
buses but you can get transfers. Don't take no taxicabs
because they cost too much and it's Christmas Eve. You
wait for me; I'll be there to show you how to take home
the bus from that Queens."

Alley Boy laughed and told his mother to stay where
she was. He said Stephanie was probably late and
that he would wait for her in the bar. He gave his
mother the number of the bar in case Stephanie called.
Alley Boy was about to hang up when his mother said,
"Hey, Alley Boy, Arthur Godfrey, whatever you want
—let me tell you something. That girl, Stephanie, she's
a nice girl. Maybe she isn't Italian. But she's a nice
girl. She loves you, so make sure you are good to her
and don't break her heart like you broke mine and your
grandmother who is having a convulsion onna floor
here right now."

Alley Boy laughed and hung up.

He went back to the bar and drank his beer.

On his fifth beer there was still no sight of Stephanie and it was going on eleven thirty. He called his mother again, but the mother said she had still not heard from Stephanie. He called Stephanie's number again, but there was no answer.

Alley Boy went out onto Queensboro Plaza and took a taxi to Brooklyn.

Ankles opened the gate to the areaway of the small two-storey house on Windsor Place. He strode to the doorway and pressed the bell. He saw the ramp that covered the four steps down into the house and looked away from it quickly. He waited a few moments, then he rang the bell again. His heart was beating fast and his palms were clammy and he took off his hat and put it back on and took it off again. He was about to put his hat back on once more when she stepped into the vestibule. She looked out through the wrought-iron gate at Ankles and something fond filled her eyes.

"Hello, Marsha," Ankles said.

"Hello, Anthony."

Marsha's eyes kept peering back into the house as she stood in the vestibule. Finally, shouting came from inside.

"Who is that out there, Marsha?" the voice yelled. "Another one of *them*? Another one of your men? Is it? Even Christmastime you're running around with men! I know what you're up to! I know everything you do, tramp. Don't tell me! You've been spreading your legs all over New York, from Bay Ridge to the Battery!"

Ankles could hear the wheelchair moving across the linoleum floor. Finally the man in the wheelchair appeared in the doorway. He was in his late forties and he was thin, with a face that came to a point. There wasn't much flesh over the bones of the face and blue veins protruded through the tissue-thin skin. A long vein ran across the man's forehead like a state line and the hair on his head was weedy and going gray.

He was wearing a flannel bathrobe and his legs hung lifelessly under it like thick ropes. There were no muscles in the legs and the knees looked grotesquely large, like fists.

His eyes were deep set and black and when Ankles looked into them, it was like staring into a pair of funnels.

"Go back inside, George," Marsha said. "It's cold here."

"Yeah, so you can run off with him right here in front of me! You think I don't know about what you do? When you go out shopping, you have it pushed in every hole you got. I know what you're doing. I know, tramp."

"Go back inside, George," Marsha said patiently. "You'll catch cold."

"That's what you want, isn't it? You'd like to see me get sick and die so you can bring them in and bang them in my bed. I know what you're up to. I know."

Marsha turned the man's wheelchair around and pushed it gently into the house. She closed the door and put a shawl around her shoulders and stepped out into the areaway with Ankles. The man in the wheelchair was still screaming inside the house and banging on the window. Marsha and Ankles stepped out of his view.

"How have you been, Marsha?" Ankles said nervously, turning the hat around in his hand.

"As you can see, I'm just so happily married it seems like heaven, Anthony."

"How long has he been like that?"

"The last ten years. The doctors say it's a combination of getting old and being crippled. They think there might be some syphilis, too. Total insecurity. His impotence and his total lack of hope. The only thing that keeps him alive is his paranoia."

Ankles was trying to think of things to say. He kept sniffling his nose even though he didn't have to and he was putting his index finger in his eye to scratch an itch that wasn't even there. He looked up and down the block, then at Marsha, then down to his shoes. His feet looked larger than they ever had before.

"Jeez, Marsha, you're . . . you're still looking damned good. Still as pretty as ever. Still . . . you know . . . I don't know . . . still looking damned good, Marsha."

"Getting old," Marsha said. "We're all getting old, Anthony. It's not right, is it? That we should get old like this? Isn't fair. Old George in there, crazy as a loon. Me looking like I don't know what—mutton dressed as lamb. You're still a cop and probably ready to retire. Tony—"

Marsha bit her lip. There were tears in her eyes and Ankles stood over her and wanted to take her in his arms, but he heard George banging the window and ranting away.

"I guess he was a good kid," Ankles said. "I wish— you know—I don't know. I don't know why I'm even talking. I mean, what right do I have to say anything?"

"You were his father, Anthony," Marsha said. "You have all the right in the world. But now it's Christmas and there's no reason to care anymore. This is the first Christmas in twenty-six years that I don't have a Christmas tree in the house. I only used to put it up for Tony. But now . . ."

"Marsha, you look so damn good. You really do."

Marsha fell silent for a moment and then looked up

and nodded to a passing neighbor who was pulling a shopping cart laden with groceries down the block.

"You know something, Marsha," Ankles said. "You know what? You know, I never even said I was sorry about that night. You know that? I mean that night up in the park, in the rowboat. Boy, was I terrible. I didn't even know what I was doing."

"You knew how to make a beautiful baby, Anthony."

Ankles looked up the street and watched a bus move along Seventh Avenue.

"Yeah? You think he was beautiful, Marsha?"

"Oh, he was so beautiful, Anthony. If you only coulda seen him back then. When he'd wake up in the morning, he'd smile and yell and he was so beautiful. Even George had to say so."

"Did George love him right back then, Marsha? I mean, did he love him like a father was supposed to?"

"Anthony, when George came back from Korea like that, like the way he is, a paraplegic, he wanted me to have a baby. He didn't want me to adopt a baby. He wanted me to carry one. He wanted one to come from me. But he couldn't give me one. It was his idea, Anthony. Not mine. For a year I couldn't do it. I couldn't do that after what had happened to him, Anthony. But he wanted me to have a baby so bad. So, finally, I did it."

Ankles stamped his cold feet on the cement pavement. He looked down at Marsha.

"But why'd you pick me, Marsha? Why'd you pick me outta all the guys who would have done it with you? Why did you pick me? I was the fat kid with the big ears and the big nose and the big feet."

"Because you also had a big heart, Anthony. Because you were so goddamned nice. Because I wanted a kid who would be like you. A nice kid, Anthony. And he was a nice kid. He got in trouble maybe, and it wasn't easy growing up with a cripple he thought was his father, and he was wild, but he was a really nice kid deep inside of him. Nice like you, Anthony."

"Jeesus, Marsha . . ."

"In a goddamned rowboat, Anthony. In a goddamned *row*boat! Why didn't we at least go to a hotel or something?"

"Cause back then you hadda have a marriage license or something. I don't know, Marsha. I don't know why we did it in a rowboat. I think maybe I didn't have money for a hotel."

"Nobody had money then."

"Nah."

Marsha's hair scattered around in the wind. She eyed Ankles as George kept banging on the window and shouting from inside.

"And now it's Christmas, Anthony, and he's gone. My baby is gone."

Marsha broke down and sat on the stoop. Ankles sat next to her on the stoop.

"I want to find out who did it, Marsha," Ankles said.

"I don't have any idea," Marsha said. "He would never talk to me about what he did. Who his friends were. Never. He just came and he gave me money. He always had a lot of money and he would give me a lot of it. He bought us this little house. Then he stopped coming around so much because George was so crazy and he didn't like hearing George say that he wasn't his kid and that I was a whore. So I saw him now and again. I don't know why anybody would kill him, Anthony."

"Carol might know," Ankles said.

Marsha looked up at Ankles. She wiped the tears out of her eyes.

"Carol?"

"Maybe. Listen, Marsha, I want you to tell Carol

the truth about me and you. I want her to know that
Tony was my son. I want her to know that. That's all
I want you to do for me, Marsha. I'm not too good at
that kind of thing. Besides, I don't think she'd believe
me. Will you do that for me?"

"I never told anyone before, Anthony. I never even
told George who the real father was."

"You have to tell Carol now."

"Have you seen our grandson? Little Michael? Have
you seen him, Anthony? He's so beautiful. So nice.
Like Tony was. He's your grandson, Anthony. He's
your blood."

"That's one of the reasons I want you to tell Carol,
Marsha. I want to be able to—you know, like visit that
little boy and take him to a Mets game and the fights.
Buy him things and give him—you know—a kiss or
something."

Marsha put her hand on Ankles's face. Ankles felt
warm blood racing through him.

"You're so goddamned nice, Anthony. You're still so
goddamned nice. I'll tell her."

"I got you something for Christmas, Marsha,"
Ankles said. He walked out to his car and opened the
trunk and took out some gift-wrapped presents. He
gave them to Marsha.

"There's one there for Carol and something for little
Michael. That one's for you. You can open it now if
you want."

Marsha smiled and touched Ankles's face again.
George still ranted inside, but he could not see them.
She reached over and kissed Ankles on the lips. Ankles
embraced her.

"I'll give her the gifts, Anthony. And I'll tell her
about us. You're so goddamned nice. Still so goddamned
nice."

Ankles touched her hand. It felt small and fragile and it made Ankles nervous.

"Marsha, you think that maybe—we could sometime —you know, sort of . . ."

"Sleep together again, Anthony?"

Ankles shook his head yes.

"You know something, Anthony? You were the last man I was with. Do you believe that, Anthony? George accuses me of screwing everything that moves. But I haven't, Anthony. Not since that goddamned rowboat. The doctors keep telling me that George should be in a veterans' hospital where he can get better care. But I never let him go in, Anthony. You know why? Because even though he's crazy, totally nuts, he's company. He's a voice in the house. But I'm getting old, Anthony, and I can't take it anymore. Almost thirty years like this now. I'm still a woman, Anthony. I'm entitled to get old happy, I guess. After the New Year I was gonna put him in the vets' hospital anyway. So let me put it to you this way—what are you doing Christmas?"

Ankles just stared at Marsha and let a wide grin spread across his face.

36

The scene at Alley Boy's mother's house had been filled with tears and hugs and embraces. The grandmother fed Alley Boy three plates of lasagne and then she sat down and drank four glasses of wine. It was the first time she had been drunk in twenty years. She had cried uncontrollably while she shoveled the food onto Alley Boy's plate.

The mother had hit the Scotch bottle a little too hard and she went in to sleep off the excitement and the booze. Alley Boy dialed Stephanie's house for the tenth time. There was still no answer.

Alley Boy left the house after kissing his grandmother good-bye. He got a taxi at Ninth and Seventh Avenue and rode it over to Stephanie's apartment building. It was three in the afternoon. Alley Boy asked the familiar uniformed cop if he had seen Stephanie coming or going at any time during the day. The uniformed cop said that he hadn't seen her at all, but he hadn't come on until eight A.M. Maybe she left before that.

The cop said there was a log that each shift had to keep of who came and went into the building because when the governor lived in an apartment building— he used it as his Brooklyn residence—the police had to check everyone. Residents or guests. Alley Boy explained to the cop that it was very important. The cop agreed to check the log for the last time Stephanie was seen leaving the building.

"Eight o'clock last night, friend," the cop said. "She left at eight P.M. and we don't have any entry for her returning and we're here twenty-four hours."

Alley Boy thanked the cop and got back into the waiting taxi. He told the taxi driver to take him to McCaulie's bar. Bird was behind the bar, but he said that he had not seen Stephanie in over a week. Alley Boy asked Bird if he had seen Tommy Ryan or Cisco. Bird said he hadn't. Alley Boy got back in the cab again and took it down to Biff's. Cisco was not there. Old man Biff told Alley Boy Cisco hadn't been around in about a week. And no, he hadn't seen Tommy Ryan either.

Alley Boy went to the phone booth and dialed Tommy Ryan's number.

On the fifth ring Tommy Ryan told Carol to answer the phone. "I'm out for anyone but Cisco," Tommy Ryan said to Carol. "If it's Alley Boy, you don't know where I am."

Carol told Alley Boy that she hadn't seen Tommy in over a week. There was only one other place they might be, Alley Boy thought. He took the waiting cab to Bush Terminal and paid the cabbie and gave him a five-dollar tip.

Alley Boy made his way into the warehouse. Once inside, Alley Boy activated the sliding cinder-block wall and went in. There was no sign of Tommy Ryan or Cisco. Alley Boy switched on the lights and looked around. He checked under the mattress to see if the money from the Flatbush bank was there.

It lay there in a canvas bag.

Alley Boy sat on the edge of the bed and tried to figure out where Stephanie could possibly be. He could not think of any more places. He left the warehouse and took a Third Avenue bus back to the neighborhood. He would go to his mother's house and wait for Stephanie to call.

The day had begun so beautifully for Ankles that he just knew it had to go bad by the end. Marsha was on his mind as he climbed the exterior metal steps leading to the factory roof. It was four o'clock in the afternoon and the police helicopter on routine aerial patrol had spotted the body about a half-hour ago just before darkness began to fall.

Ankles reached the rooftop and could see most of Brooklyn spread out before him. A million Christmas lights twinkled across the massive borough. Out there, two and a half million people were celebrating Christmas, Ankles thought. Give or take a few hundred thousand Jews. Tomorrow he would be with Marsha again, just the two of them. This time he would spring for a hotel.

Ankles paused for a moment to collect his breath, which he had left somewhere on the second of five flights.

Then he walked over to the huddle of uniformed cops who stood around the sheet-covered corpse on the rooftop. Ankles lit a cigar for courage and bent over and peeled back the sheet to get a look at the face.

He stared for a long moment and then closed his eyes.

"Oh, no," he said.

The long thin neck was showing white where the tendons were and the snow around the body was the color of cheap port. The eyes were open wide and Ankles closed them gently, the lids stiff from the weather and rigor mortis.

"She's been dead about eighteen to twenty-four hours," a man from the coroner's office told Ankles. "She was killed somewhere else and dumped here."

"I was with her twenty-four hours ago," Ankles said.

"Jesus," the coroner's man said.

"Yeah," Ankles said. "Tomorrow's his birthday."

Tommy Ryan dressed in his dark business suit and combed his hair back into the conservative style. Carol watched him putting on the white shirt and knotting the dark-blue tie. She was sitting in front of the roaring fire, and as she stared into the flickering flames she thought about Tony Mauro. Last Christmas they were together here in this house and Michael had just learned to walk. He would take several steps and fall into Tony's arms and Tony would toss him in the air and catch him and Michael would laugh uncontrollably.

Tony used to love to see the reflection of the Christmas tree in Michael's wide eyes. Carol remembered that last Christmas Eve; she had put Michael to bed early and she and Tony had made love on the fur rug in front of the fire while snow fluttered down outside. Later, they drank eggnog and talked about moving out to California after the big score. Bandits always talk about going away after the big score, Carol thought. But the big score never comes. The big score is just another way of saying tomorrow.

"I'm sorry I have to go, Carol," Tommy Ryan said. Carol looked up at him and smiled.

"It's all right," Carol said. "We'll be together tomorrow. Tony's mother is coming by later with some gifts for Michael, and I guess we'll have a few drinks. I'll be okay."

Tommy Ryan pulled on a long tweed overcoat and bent over and gave Carol a kiss.

"If my mother hadn't gone through the whole rigmarole of dinner and guests, I wouldn't even bother going."

"It's all right," Carol said. "Enjoy yourself."

"You too, honey."

He kissed Carol and left quickly. Carol stared back into the flames.

Ankles stood outside the tenement puffing heavily on his cigar. He was trying to figure the best way to do this disgusting little chore. Poor fucking kid is gonna flip out, Ankles thought. Christmas Eve. What kind of a fuckin' animal would do this to a kid like that on Christmas Eve?

Ankles finally decided there was no easy way to do it. He just had to open his mouth and say the words. Nothing he could say would make it any easier, any less painful. He climbed the three flights of stairs slowly; his big shoes clattered off the aluminum edges as he took each step. He used his large hand to help pull himself up by grabbing yards of the banister at a time.

When he reached the top floor, he paused another moment. He took off his hat. His ears were numb from the cold. He took a long drag of the cigar and knocked on the apartment door.

The mother answered the door and she bit her knuckle so hard that it began to bleed.

"You not comin' here onna Christmas Eve to take my boy again, I tell you that," the mother screamed. She ran to the kitchen sink and picked up a carving knife. "I'll kill you first, you big animal," the mother screamed.

Ankles shook his head and was waving his hand as the mother came toward him. Alley Boy ran into the kitchen from the bedroom. The mother was ranting and veins were popping from her neck. Her eyes were wild and flashing and she held the knife in an angle of attack. Alley Boy grabbed his mother's hand, trying to restrain her, but the mother resisted and made a lunge for Ankles. Alley Boy held her and the two of them fell to the floor.

Alley Boy pried the knife from his mother's hand.

"I'm not here to take your boy away, Mrs. D'Agastino," Ankles said. He bent down to help the sobbing woman to her feet. The grandmother hobbled into the room, dressed in black.

"What's a matter for you?" the grandmother yelled to Ankles. "You can't leave us alone onna Christmas Eve? Alley Boy no do nuthin wrong. He was here all day. You call yourself an Italian and you come around here onna Christmas Eve and make my little girl go into tears like this. Bahfongool on you, son of a pig."

"I'm sorry," Ankles said. "I wish I didn't have to come here. It's not about your son. It's about Stephanie Kelly."

Alley Boy stood motionless and closed his eyes.

"You want to come out here in the hallway, D'Agastino?" Ankles said. "I don't wanna upset your mother anymore."

Alley Boy followed Ankles on stiff legs into the hall-way. Ankles felt very awkward.

"She's dead, kid," Ankles said very quickly. "They got her the same way they got Tony Mauro, and Green Eyes, and Murphy."

Alley Boy let his weight fall against the wall. Eyes upcast toward the skylight, tears running down his cheeks, Alley Boy just stood still for a long moment.

"You sure you don't know who it was?" Ankles said. "I mean with Tony, with Murphy . . ."

Alley Boy shook his head from side to side. A spray of tears lashed off his face. His lips were trembling and his face was contorted and his hands were balling into large fists.

Alley Boy in one motion bolted from the landing and raced down the stairs two at a time. Ankles could still hear the mother sobbing inside the apartment. He heard Alley Boy take the last flight and bang open the two doors to the street. Then Ankles started slowly down the stairs, one at a time.

Tommy Ryan met Cisco in Junior's Restaurant on Flatbush Avenue. Cisco was sitting calmly at the counter devouring a piece of their famous cheesecake. Tommy Ryan paused briefly when he saw the porter mopping up spilled coffee in the aisle. The smell hit him quickly. It was the smell of ammonia and West Pine. The same concoction that his mother used to use when she mopped the halls of the tenement. It had been one of her tasks as the building super. You had to take out the garbage cans from the dark cave that was the back of the first-floor hallway. You had to mop the hallways every Saturday morning. You had to polish the broken brass mailboxes with Noxon metal polish. You and your mother, the janitors.

But it was the smell of the ammonia and West Pine that hit Tommy Ryan the hardest. It unclogged the nasal passages and let in the other smells, the smells of the urine in the hallway, the deteriorating smell of an unwashed shopping-bag lady who used to sleep in the back of the hall, the dank, musty tomblike odor that used to drift up from the wet cellar. Standing there in Junior's Restaurant, it was like smelling his own brains. And his stomach started rattling like a paint-mixing machine. He could feel fluids inside lapping at the stomach walls.

He moved quickly past Cisco into the men's room and locked the stall of the toilet. He vomited in three heavy thrusts, his eyes tearing, his nose running, his knees buckling. It was one of the most vulnerable experiences Tommy Ryan knew. It was something he could not control. He was throwing up his own self, puking up that kid he used to be, trying to spit his history out through his mouth.

When he was finished there was dizziness. He staggered to the sink and washed his face with cold water. He tried to get the taste out of his mouth with the water, but an aftertaste clung to the pit of his throat. His eyes were bloodshot, but all he could do was rinse them with water.

Finally he went back out to the restaurant and took a seat next to Cisco. Cisco looked up and nodded. Tommy Ryan ordered a tea with lemon from the waitress. The porter had finished mopping up. But the smell of the ammonia and West Pine was still there. When the waitress brought the tea Tommy bit deeply into the lemon, trying to let the sour juices take the taste from his mouth.

"They found her, you know," Tommy Ryan said.

"I know," Cisco said. "So what?"

"Maybe it's going too far."

"Just one more to go. No mouth to talk, we'll walk."

"Yeah," Tommy Ryan said. "One more."

Tommy Ryan reached for the sugar and accidentally knocked his tea off the counter with his elbow. He leapt off his stool to avoid the scalding tea. Cisco remained where he was, unfazed. The Jamaican porter came up with his pail of ammonia and West Pine again. Tommy Ryan stood there with the rage mounting and grabbed the pail of water and the mop and ran out of the door with it. He tossed it into the street in wild rage. A group of passersby looked at him with caution. The Jamaican porter ran out after him.

"Wot da fok you doin', mon?"

"Merry Christmas," Tommy Ryan said.

At the counter Cisco sat shaking his head and smiling. The customers in Junior's were mildly stunned. The Jamaican porter came back in with the mop and pail.

"Foking crazy mon, mon," he said.

Outside, Tommy Ryan was getting into the gold Cadillac for the drive to Riverdale.

Alley Boy ran all the way. He did not have a coat on, but he was not cold. He stood there just behind the manmade waterfall up from the second meadow of Prospect Park. He was standing on the very spot where he and Stephanie had done it in the snow. He looked out over the frozen lake, where a few sea gulls slept with their bills tucked into their feathers. He wondered if their feet ever got cold standing on the ice.

Stephanie would never be cold again, he thought. She always talked about going somewhere warm. Right now they probably had her in an icebox in the morgue at Kings County, but she wouldn't be cold. Alley Boy just hoped she had been warm when she got it. He hoped she was thinking about him.

He looked down at the ground. There was nothing there to suggest that he and Stephanie had lain there. Just hard snow and fallen leaves. But Alley Boy could see her. He could hear her.

"Crazy bastard, Al," she had said. "For you, Al, not for money. For you, Al."

Alley Boy tried to laugh, but the gesture was swallowed by the night wind. He could hear the sounds of small animals in the leaves. He wondered if they were looking at him and thinking, Crazy bastard, Al.

Traffic moved on the circular park highway a good distance away. Alley Boy looked at the cars spinning by, their headlights pointing at one another's backs. He thought it made no sense. They should all be home, Alley Boy thought. They should all go home.

Alley Boy scooped up some snow from the spot where he had lain under Stephanie. He put some in his mouth. It was tasteless and cold and it had no smell.

Alley Boy wanted to cry again, but no tears would come to his eyes.

"Crazy bastard, Al."

37

Marsha felt no guilt leaving George home on his own on Christmas Eve. She had now reached a point in her life where she mattered more to herself than George did. She had nursed George now since 1951. She remembered getting the telephone call about him the day that Bobby Thompson hit the home run. The rest of New York was cheering, but Marsha sat in shock.

George had been asleep in a bunker when a grenade had sailed through the cold Korean night and knocked George and two other grunts out of the bunker. The other two got off easier than George. They came home in plastic bags. George came home in a wheelchair, paralyzed from the waist down.

But Marsha stuck by him all those years. She still loved him, but later when he went mad the love turned

to pity and it was a sickening experience. Pity is something that should be used only sparingly or else you
become so addicted to it you wind up using it on yourself. Marsha had begun to pity herself on her forty-
fifth birthday. That was the big one. She was forty-
eight now and she wanted to stop pitying herself and
start loving herself again.

And, by Christ, she was determined to do it. She
felt no guilt whatsoever. After all, if George had the
syphilis the doctors said he had, he must have picked it
up over there in Korea. He sure as hell didn't get it
from his wife waiting devotedly at home.

She was looking forward to being with Anthony on
Christmas Day. She was looking forward to having sex.
After so long, it would be like the very first time again.

Marsha rang the doorbell and waited on the stoop
with the packages in a shopping bag. Now she had to
tell Carol everything. It would not be easy, but Anthony
had asked her and she had agreed.

Carol opened the door and hugged Marsha and gave
her a kiss on the cheek. She took the shopping bag from
Marsha and led her upstairs to the duplex. When
Marsha saw little Michael standing at the top of the
stairs, she scooped him up in her arms; her eyes went
juicy and soft as she hugged the little boy and carried
him into the apartment.

The fire was still blazing and Marsha took off her
coat and sat down on the couch in front of the fire.

"What are you drinking, Ma?" Carol asked her
mother-in-law.

"Not for me," Marsha said.

"Come on, it's Christmas."

"Okay, a double Scotch with a splash."

Carol chuckled and Marsha sat Michael on her knee
and brushed the hair out of his eyes. Michael was a

little shy but enjoyed the affection. He toyed with the necklace around Marsha's neck.

Carol brought in the drinks and they lifted them. Carol clinked her glass against Marsha's and they both took sips.

"So how's George?"

"He's home talking to the radio. He talks to the radio all day long. He has big fights with disc jockeys. You know George. He keeps asking me to explain the plot of *Let's Make a Deal* on the television."

"Merry Christmas, Ma."

"You too, love."

They took sips of their drinks again. Marsha put Michael on the floor and she leaned back and looked into the fire.

"You have a man, don't you?"

"Yes, Ma."

"I don't blame you. You're a beautiful girl. The little boy needs a father. I hope your man is nice."

"So do I."

Marsha laughed dryly.

"Carol," Marsha said, "I brought you some presents. I brought some from me and I brought some from someone very special to me. Someone very special to Michael."

"Who, Ma?"

Marsha handed two gift-wrapped presents to Carol. Carol looked at the labels, but they didn't say who the gifts were from.

"Who are they from, Ma?"

"Open them. I don't even know what they are."

Carol tore the paper off the larger gift and took out a set of boxing gloves and an inflatable punching bag with a picture of Popeye on it. Carol smiled.

"That will cause murder in the house," Carol said.

Then she unwrapped the other gift. It was a lovely hand-tooled leather pocketbook.

"It's beautiful, Ma," Carol said. "Who's it from?"

Marsha took a long draw from her drink and placed the glass on the coffee table.

"From Tony's father," Marsha said.

"George?" Carol said.

"No, not from George, Carol. George can't even buy the farm."

"Who, Ma? I'm a little confused. I don't understand."

"Carol, he asked me to. You know . . . you are a woman. You're a mother. You're a nice girl, and I hope you understand and don't think I'm some kind of—"

"What are you trying to say, Ma?"

Carol got up from her seat across from Marsha, came over and sat next to her, and put her arm around her.

"What do you mean, Tony's father, Ma? If not George, who, Ma?"

"Anthony," Marsha said. "Anthony Tufano."

"Who is Anthony Tufano?"

"You know him, Carol. He is the detective. The big man. He's a nice man. . . ."

Carol sat and stared at Marsha for a long moment, a little astonished.

"Ma, you don't mean Ankles?"

"That's what they call him. But he's Anthony to me."

Something eerie tingled through Carol. She looked at Michael playing with the new toys on the floor.

"Ma," Carol said, "you mean Ankles the cop is Michael's—"

"Grandfather. Yes."

"Oh, Ma. I'm so sorry for you, Ma. Why didn't you ever tell anybody, Ma?"

Carol thought about the day on the street when she had been so terse and insulting to Ankles. The big cop had tried to get a smile from Michael, she thought. Because he was his grandfather, and all he got for his efforts were insults. Carol felt very small.

"He asked me to tell you," Marsha said. "He wants to find out what happened to Tony, Carol. If you knew him, you'd know he is so goddamned nice . . ."

Carol realized now why Ankles was so obsessed with Tony's murder. She wished he was here now so she could tell him how sorry she was.

"You want to tell me all about it, Ma? Go ahead and tell me."

Tommy Ryan walked through the front door of his parents' house and kissed his mother on her cheek. She grasped his hand softly with a wrinkled, smaller hand. He thought about the ammonia and West Pine, how many times she used those hands to ring out the mop because they didn't have a pail with a roller on it since they cost more. He thought about how when she wrung out that mop she was touching all the filth and dirt and stink that was on the floors of those hallways.

"Hello, Mother," Tommy Ryan said. "Merry Christmas."

"I'm so glad you got some time off, Thomas."

Tommy's father walked up to him and put out his hand.

"Merry Christmas, son. Merry Christmas."

"Same to you, Dad."

He looked at his father's hand now, the hand that had pushed a lever on an elevator all day long, bringing people up and down, up and down, up and down, like the yo-yo they had turned him into.

The living room was filled with guests who stood in small knots and huddles. They discussed politics and oil and drank brandy and smoked cigars. Tommy Ryan said hello to Bill Sweetzer and his wife, Sharon, and then nodded to Charlie and Gloria Morgan. Tommy recognized some of the other guests but did not know their names.

You do not have to know their names. They are all rats. They have all come out of the ceiling for your food and your drink. Inside their pants there are thick tails, the length of bullwhips, and at night the whiskers come out and the ears grow big and they go to the refrigerator and they nibble the cheese with their pointy little teeth, gnawing at it with little ratty mouths.

They didn't need names. They lived in holes. Human rats that dressed up like people whenever there was a good freeload going on. These were the ones who came out of the woodwork and packed Dad's things in the cardboard box and put it in the hall. That one there, he foreclosed the mortgage on the house on the Hudson. The other one over there stuffing shrimp in his mouth, he repossessed the car. Those two in the corner drinking your Rémy Martin crossed Dad's name out of their private phone books. The fat one making with the mouth, he wouldn't give Dad a second chance.

You know these are not the same ones, but they are from the same breed. They live in the same holes and live the same rodents' lives. But you are the boss here, you are the rat catcher, you are the Pied Piper. You have lured them here so they can admire your books on the shelves. So they can envy your paintings on your walls. Minnie Mouse over there with her mouth stuffed, and the rest of the mommy rats, are admiring the furniture that is yours. They are drinking your brandy from your crystal.

"How are you, Charlie?" Tommy Ryan said to Charlie Morgan. "How's the world of letters treating you?"

"Same old malarkey, Tom," Charlie said. He was

weaving a little too heavily and Tommy noticed that he
had finally given the Perrier the heave and was slug-
ging straight bourbon. At least the pecker had the guts
to admit he was gutless.

A black bartender stood behind a service bar dis-
patching drinks to black waitresses who carried trays
of champagne and hors d'oeuvres through the crowd.
The dress was formal, although the invitations had allowed for casual.

You will stand here and watch them eat and guzzle
your food and drink and you will smile at them, Tommy
Ryan thought. You will sing along later when one of
the old biddies decides she wants to give us a belt of
Frosty the Fucking Snowman and then she'll slurp
some more eggnog. She'll get stupid drunk, maybe pass
out, throw up in the car on the way home, and in the
morning she'll have a moral hangover that will keep
her back in her rat hole and away from "company"
until all is forgotten again.

You'll watch them, Tommy Ryan thought.

You'll kiss Mom and Dad at midnight and exchange
gifts no one needs. And Dad will look at you with the
face of a stranger. And Mom will look old and her
elbows will look the oldest and her hands will always
look like they've just come out of the mop water.

You'll stay here for Christmas Eve and you'll enjoy
every minute of it. Because you made it this way, because you always promised yourself that you would
assemble the rats, the big two-footed rats with the
money, and you would be the boss. And you would
let Mom and Dad know they did not have to clean for
them anymore or take them up and down on an elevator.

Tommy breathed in deeply in a moment of self-
accomplishment. But he could still smell his own brains.
And his stomach began to slosh around again.

You must find control, here in this place, your place,

because you are the boss here. He closed his eyes for a moment and just listened to the din of the conversation. It sounded like the squeaks of rats. It soothed him.

Ankles finished typing up his report on Stephanie Kelly. He had gotten a bad chewing-out from the chief inspector of Brooklyn homicide about all these murders, these slashings with not so much as a suspect.

Ankles told the chief inspector he hoped to have something soon. Maybe even tomorrow. The chief inspector told Ankles he wanted him on the job the next day, Christmas or not.

Ankles thought about breaking his date with Marsha. Then he said the hell with it. That was too important to him now. The inspector can go and fuck himself.

After turning in his report, Ankles drove to Farrell's and had a few quick beers. The place was loud and smoky and filled with holiday drunks. It didn't mix well with the picture of Stephanie Kelly's neck that was imprinted in Ankles's mind.

He drove home to his apartment in Bay Ridge. *A Christmas Carol* was playing on television and Ankles opened a beer and sat down to watch it. The part where Scrooge sees his own gravestone always scared the hell out of Ankles, and he was awaiting it eagerly.

Alley Boy had stood there for two hours. He just stood at the spot near the waterfall like a statue, and then it started to snow. The flakes came down in small bits at first, but then they got bigger and bigger and bigger. They floated down through the branches of the trees and they were visible in the headlights of the cars still moving through the park.

Alley Boy finally began walking toward home. The

snowflakes accumulated on his hair and his shoulders as he walked and he passed kids in the street who were tossing snowballs at each other.

"It's good packin'," one kid said as he flung a snowball at his friend.

"Dynamite," said the second kid.

Alley Boy listened to their voices, but he did not really see them. His hands were jammed in his pants pockets as he walked down Tenth Street past the brownstones where gas lamps burned in the areaways. The houses were blinking wildly in a panic of colored Christmas lights. Someone had set up speakers on a windowsill and "Silent Night" played as Alley Boy crossed Eighth Avenue.

He could still hear the mournful carol halfway down the next block. The snow fell silently and gathered on the windshields of the parked cars.

Alley Boy reached his mother's tenement and lit a cigarette as he stood in the doorway. He decided he couldn't stand cigarettes and he tossed the butt onto the snowy sidewalk. He turned and went into the hallway and began climbing the first flight of stairs. The hallway smelled of ammonia and pine and the steam heat was moist in the air.

Alley Boy did not notice that the light on the third floor was out, as was the light on the top landing. Dim light came through the skylight, where snow had begun to gather.

Alley Boy could not see, but it did not matter. The less he saw right now, the better. He stepped onto the landing when the arm came around his neck. A cold circle of steel was pressed against Alley Boy's right ear. Only now did he realize how numb and cold his ears were.

"You know that song by the Drifters?" Cisco asked. " 'Up on the Roof'?"

Cisco began to sing the song in a mock whisper as he led Alley Boy backwards toward the roof stairs. Alley Boy clutched at Cisco's hand, but Cisco cocked the .38.

"I can give it to you here and your momma will run out and see your brains all over Christmas. Or we can go upstairs, sucker."

Alley Boy offered no more resistance. He let Cisco lead him up the roof stairs, backwards, while the .38 stayed screwed into his ear.

At the top of the stairs, Cisco fumbled for the roof door latch, located it, and let the door swing open.

Now Alley Boy threw all his weight against Cisco and Cisco fell across the threshold to the roof floor. Alley Boy darted past him and began running along the rooftop. He ran into a clothesline as snow fell around him. Alley Boy got back on his feet again and, running, looked over his shoulder. The traction in the snow was not good. He could see Cisco getting back to his feet, laughing.

"Hey, Alley Boy," Cisco yelled, "there's just one way to go and that's down. I have the gun, sucker."

Cisco began chasing Alley Boy across the network of rooftops. Alley Boy paused for a moment, his heart thumping, and flattened himself against a tall chimney.

"Don't make me use the gun, Alley Boy," Cisco said. "It's so much cleaner and quieter the other way."

Cisco flicked open his straight razor and snuck behind the other side of the chimney. Alley Boy saw the silver blade swipe in front of him and he began running again. Cisco laughed loudly. And he was right behind Alley Boy in a dead run across the rooftop. Alley Boy's legs were long and he leapt over the air shaft without any problem. He knew the air shaft was there. It was a game he used to play when he was a kid. See who had enough nerve to jump over the air shaft.

But Cisco had never played that game. And he didn't know the air shaft was there. You could hardly see it. It was about three feet wide, but it dropped four storeys into an alley. Cisco pushed off his left foot as he ran and brought the right foot down—into the shaft.

Terror detonated in Cisco's eyes and his left foot slid across the fresh snow and went over the lip of the air shaft. The razor fell from Cisco's right hand and in a desperate motion he grabbed the ledge of the shaft.

"Alley Boy," Cisco screamed. "Alley Boy, help me! You gotta help me, Alley Boy."

Alley Boy turned. He saw Cisco's hand wrapped over the edge of the air shaft ledge. He ran over to the air shaft and saw Cisco dangling there, his pistol still in his left hand. Cisco's fingers clawed at the ledge. He looked up at Alley Boy and tears broke out of Cisco's panicky eyes.

"Please, Alley Boy," Cisco said. "Please! I don't wanna—"

"Wanna what?" Alley Boy said as he knelt down near the edge of the air shaft. "Don't wanna die? Like Stephanie? Like Tony Mauro? Like Green Eyes and Murphy? You don't wanna die, Cisco?"

Cisco's fingers were going white and straining for survival.

"Tommy tole me. He made me, Al. You know I liked Stephanie. You know I did. He tole me what to do to her and Tony and everybody. Tony was a snitch. Help me, Alley Boy."

Alley Boy reached his hand down and grabbed Cisco's left wrist. He removed the gun from the tight fist and held him there for a minute. Cisco let his right hand go free and he was dangling in the middle of the open shaft. Alley Boy stared at him. For the first time since he had met Cisco he looked like a little boy.

"Please, Alley Boy . . ."

Alley Boy pulled Cisco up to the edge of the shaft ledge and Cisco put his elbows on the ledge and breathed deeply. Alley Boy turned around for a moment. He saw Stephanie's smiling face. "Crazy bastard, Al."

He turned around again and kicked Cisco with everything he had in the middle of his face. Cisco went over the edge with a scream. In a few seconds he lay in the alley at the bottom of the air shaft.

The snow fell silently down on top of him.

38

"But why him, Ma?" Carol asked. "Why'd you pick him? Why Ankles—Anthony?"

"If you had known him then," Marsha said. "If you had known him, how big and gentle and shy he was. He was the nicest man I ever met. We were in the same class in grammar school when they still had nuns teaching you. He wanted to be a priest then. And when George told me to find someone, I wanted someone who would not haunt me with it. I explained it to him that night, but I don't think he really understood. He was so excited. It was his first time. In a goddamned rowboat . . ."

"In a what, Ma?" Carol said, amused.

"None of your business," Marsha said, smiling. "He wasn't very good; but you know, he tried. He was ex-

cited. Maybe that's why Tony was always so wild—
because he was conceived in a fit."

Carol smiled. The doorbell rang. And rang and rang
and rang and rang. Carol was annoyed.

"Who the hell is that ringing like that?" she snapped,
and ran down the steps and opened the door. Alley
Boy was standing on the stoop, his eyes twisted and
mad-looking, his hair soaking wet and plastered to his
head.

"Where is he?" Alley Boy said, looking past Carol.

"Who?" Carol said.

Alley Boy brushed past her and ran up the stairs.
Carol saw Alley Boy take his hand out of his pants
pocket. There was a gun in it.

"Alley Boy," Carol yelled and chased him up the
stairs. Alley Boy burst into the living room and saw
Marsha sitting on the couch. She saw the pistol and
screamed. Alley Boy stalked through the rooms.

"Where is he?" he kept repeating. "Where is he?"

Carol raced into the apartment and stood in front
of Alley Boy.

"I have a baby in this house, you bastard," she said,
and slapped Alley Boy hard across the face. "If you're
looking for Tommy Ryan, he's not here. He's at his
mother's house. Now get out, you bastard."

Alley Boy began to sob. He fell against a dresser and
sank to the floor and let his body release wracking sobs.

"It was him," Alley Boy said. "It was Tommy. First
he got Tony. Then Green Eyes and Murphy. Then he
killed my girl. My lady. My Stephanie. It was him all
the time."

Alley Boy wiped away his tears with the back of the
gun hand. Carol stood stonily looking at Alley Boy.
Then she paced over and knelt in front of him.

"What do you mean, it was him?" she said to Alley

Boy. "How could Tommy have killed Tony? Tommy was in jail when Tony was killed."

Alley Boy sobbed again. Carol pulled away his arm and smacked him again, and again.

"What do you mean, Alley Boy?" Carol yelled. Michael woke up crying. Marsha sat on the couch, petrified.

"Tommy ordered it," Alley Boy said. "He told Cisco to do it. Cisco did anything Tommy told him to. Anything. He killed Stephanie and tonight he tried to kill me. Tommy told him to. Just like he told him to kill Tony."

"How do you know that, Alley Boy?"

"Cisco told me tonight," Alley Boy said. "Before I killed him. I killed him and I'm glad I killed him and I wish he was still alive so I could kill him again. And now I'm gonna kill Tommy. Nobody is gonna stop me."

Carol stood up. There was no question in her mind of what she would do. She did not shiver or shake or break down. She walked to the hall closet and pulled on a coat. She then walked into the dining room and removed the false front of the fireplace. She reached inside and took out the sawed-off, silver-plated shotgun. She grabbed a box of shells and broke the shotgun open. She pushed two cartridges into the chambers. She snapped it shut. She put some more cartridges into her coat pocket.

Marsha stood watching her in frozen disbelief.

"Carol, what are you doing?" Marsha said.

"Housework, Ma," Carol said. "This is family and I'm gonna do the housework."

Carol went into the kitchen and took out Tommy's private phone book. The one with the numbers of all his slimy friends, she thought. Carol opened the book to the initial O. There was only one entry under that letter—O'Brian. Carol memorized the Riverdale address.

"Watch Michael for me, will ya, Ma?" Carol said.

"Carol, no. You can't go. You just can't do this . . . we should call Anthony. You can't go."

"Watch me," Carol said and strode out the door.

Alley Boy stood up with sobs still racking his body.

"Who are you anyway?" Marsha asked.

"I'm really not sure, lady," Alley Boy said and ran out into the hallway and began running down the stairs.

When Alley Boy reached the top of the stoop, he saw Carol's red Corvette spin away in a snowy skid up the street. Alley Boy ran back upstairs and went into the kitchen. Marsha was still standing in the same spot. Michael was crying from a bedroom. Marsha watched Alley Boy look at the same address in the phone book as Carol had. Then Alley Boy ran out of the house.

Alley Boy ran up to Court Street and finally flagged down a taxi after waiting five minutes.

"I'm going to Riverdale," Alley Boy said.

"You must be joking, buddy," the cabbie said. "I wouldn't drive you to Riverdale on a sentence on a night like this. Riverdale's The Bronx. Nobody goes to The Bronx when it snows. Not even an arsonist."

Alley Boy jumped out of the taxi and watched as it took off. He hailed another one, but no New York cabbie ever picks up a fare that just got out of a different cab. It usually means that the fare wants to go to Staten Island or that he's a drunk. Alley Boy stood on the corner and waited for another taxi. He couldn't see any and he was growing impatient.

Ebenezer Scrooge was being led by the ghost of things to come through the graveyard. Scrooge got a fast look at his own headstone. Ankles felt a terrible tingle moving through him.

He jumped a foot when the phone rang, spilling beer all over himself. His heart was on a trampoline.

He picked up the phone and listened to Marsha run a story the length of Moby Dick past him. Ankles slowed her down. He got the part about some kid named Alley Boy with a gun. He got the part about Carol loading a shotgun. Then he got the item about Alley Boy saying it was somebody named Tommy who had ordered some guy named Cisco to kill Tony. He got all that. He also got the part about Cisco being dead. Then he got an address in Riverdale where both Carol and Alley Boy had gone to look for this guy named Tommy. Then he got his coat and his hat and his car keys. And then Ankles got the hell out of there.

Alley Boy had no luck with three cabbies. It was Christmas Eve and none of them wanted to drive through the snow to Riverdale. He got a couple of "sorry, pal" 's from the cabbies, but that was all. The gun in his pocket was hot from the sweat of his hand.

Carol raced the Corvette along Major Deegan Expressway toward The Bronx. The shotgun lay beside her on the front seat of the car. She kept looking over at it, making sure it was still there. Tony had made love to her in front of the roaring fire almost exactly this time last year. Now she was going to avenge his murder.

Tommy Ryan sniffed four hits of cocaine in his parents' bathroom and dribbled some warm water into his nostrils so that the drug would move through the mucous membranes into the bloodstream much quicker.

The evening was going just swell.

Tonight you are Santa Claus, he thought. Dashing
through the snow.

Everyone out there wishes you were his son.

They all want you.

But you own them all.

You are the boss.

Ankles soared through Manhattan toward the
Major Deegan. It was Tommy Ryan all along, he
thought. You figured he had something he was holding out. But you didn't think he'd ordered Tony's hit.
They were such good pals. Best friends. It didn't make
much sense. There had to be some reason. He hoped
Tommy Ryan lived long enough to tell him. Long
enough for him to suffer. Long enough for Ankles to
punch his face into farina. Long enough to beat him
to death for Christmas.

Another taxi pulled up and Alley Boy jumped into
the backseat.

"I'm going to Riverdale," Alley Boy said.

"A comedian," the cabbie said.

"I have to get to Riverdale," Alley Boy said.

"*You* might," the cabbie said. "*I* don't."

"I'm not getting out of the cab," Alley Boy said
through the bulletproof partition.

"Good," the cabbie said. "Then we can sit here and
sing 'Jingle Bells' 'cause I ain't moving till you get
out."

Alley Boy was sitting in the backseat on the far side
of the taxi. When he got out he left the back door wide
open. It meant the cabbie would have to get out of the
goddamned cab himself to close the door.

"Hey, buddy, it's Christmas," the cabbie said. "Have a heart. Close the fuckin' door, will ya?"

It was the one sure way of getting even with an uncooperative New York cabbie.

"Up yours," Alley Boy said as he stood on the curb.

The cabbie got out of the driver's door and left it open. He walked around the taxi to close the far passenger door. When he was around the other side, Alley Boy jumped in the driver's seat of the taxi. The motor was running. The cabbie was shouting very large "mother fuckers" into the snowy December night and Alley Boy was flooring it, spinning away toward the bridge and north toward Riverdale.

All the guests sat down at the twenty-foot mahogany table for dinner.

Tommy Ryan sat at the head of the table.

The black waitresses were placing whole lobsters in front of each guest. Gloria Morgan was bending Tommy Ryan's ear about some marvelous student in her writing class who showed not only promise, but genius.

You should tell her to shut her sloppy trap and slurp up her shit, Tommy Ryan thought. You couldn't care less about a genius in a writing class. If he was a genius, why was he taking lessons?

Tommy Ryan heard a car pull up outside of the house. Another freeloader, he thought. That is all right with you. You will sit here and watch them eat your shit and you will have owned them all.

The doorbell rang, a long, elaborate series of gongs. The black butler answered the door.

Tommy Ryan turned and saw Carol standing there, framed in the doorway against the snowy, polka-dot sky. She had the shotgun in her hands and was aiming it from the hip. Tommy Ryan stood up slowly and looked at each of the guests. Their faces were all sagging like cow tits. Tommy's mother's mouth was open and Tommy could see the half-chewed lobster in her mouth. Tommy's father remained seated, his hands clutching the edge of the table. The guests were motionless as the black butler moved backwards into the house and a long draft of cold night air rushed through the room.

"It was you, Tommy," Carol shouted. "It was you who killed Tony. It was you! You told Cisco to do it."

"Carol, you should not be here," Tommy Ryan said. "This is my place and I told you never to come here."

"You don't tell me nothing, you fucking swine," Carol Mauro said as she walked slowly toward the banquet table. "You are gonna listen to me for a change. And so are these people. So are your mother and father. They are gonna know all about Tommy Ryan. They are gonna know who you are.

"Does your mother know you still wet the bed like a little boy, Tommy? Does she know you call for her in the night when you have the bad dream, Tommy? Does she know what you do for a living, Tommy? Does she know you stick up banks and rip off drug dealers and kill people for a living, Tommy?"

Tommy Ryan's mother made a sound like a dog getting kicked.

"Tommy—" the father spoke up.

"Don't listen to her, Dad. She doesn't know what she's talking about. She's insane, Dad."

"Oh, I know what I'm talking about all right, Tommy," Carol said. "I know you killed Tony. He was my husband and you killed him. You killed my little boy's father."

Tommy's eyes skipped back and forth like loose dice.

"I owned you, Carol," Tommy said quickly. "I just loaned you to Tony. You belonged to me all along."

"You never owned me," Carol said. "You think you can just go in and take people like they were money, don't you?"

"Tony was a snitch," Tommy said. "Ankles nailed him cold on a caper and Tony walked. It meant for sure he snitched."

"No, Tommy," Carol said. "You see, you think you always have everything figured out. Tony was no snitch. Tony was Ankles's son."

Tommy Ryan's eyes grew smaller and he tried to comprehend this. He remembered that Tony was the only kid who ever drank beer on the Parkside that never caught a beating from Ankles. And then Ankles had caught him six months ago driving a truckload of furs the both of you had hijacked and Ankles just let Tony walk. Just let him march. It must have meant he was a snitch. He must have been setting you up in exchange for his own freedom. So you had to have him hit. You had no choice. He was your friend but he was in the way. He also kept Carol from you. And you owned her, not him.

But it does not matter, Tommy Ryan thought. You are the boss here. You do not have to worry here. She cannot hurt you. You own her.

Carol was circling the table with the shotgun leveled at Tommy from her hip.

"Did your mother really believe you were away on business all those months?" Carol Mauro asked. "Did

she really fall for that pile of shit, Tommy? Didn't she
know you were doing time on Rikers Island? That you
had yourself sent away on a bullshit charge so that you
couldn't be connected to Tony's murder? Did she know
that, Tommy? Huh?"

"Oh, my God," the mother said. "Oh, my God."

"And do your mother's guests here know that your
mother and father take all the dirty money you send
them? Do they know that their name isn't O'Brian,
but Ryan? William Ryan, the bank scammer? Huh?"

Carol was passing Bill Sweetzer and looking at
Tommy Ryan. Sweetzer made a sudden lunge for the
barrel of the shotgun and pushed it straight up in the
air. Carol squeezed off a round that hit the chandelier,
sending a storm of flying glass through the room.
Sweetzer wrestled the gun away from Carol.

Tommy Ryan walked to him and held out his hand
for the gun. Sweetzer hesitated. Tommy thought, Cool,
you are the boss. You must be cool.

"Bill, this has to do with the government," Tommy
Ryan said. "I cannot explain it to you. I am not allowed to."

Sweetzer looked around the room at the frightened
guests. Most of the women were crying and some of the
guests were bleeding from the flying glass. It was
darker in the room without the light from the chandelier. Sweetzer looked at Carol.

"Government!" Carol said. "He couldn't get a job
with Roto-Rooter. They don't stoop that low."

Sweetzer looked back at Tommy Ryan. Tommy Ryan
looked so cool, so collected. Like money. Sweetzer
handed over the gun and was glad to be rid of it.

Tommy Ryan heard another car pulling up outside
the house. He grabbed Carol around the throat and put
the shotgun against her head.

"Go ahead, Tommy," Carol said. "Go ahead. Show

them all how fucking brave you are. But you're not so brave without Cisco, are you? Cisco's dead, pal."

"No one gets Cisco," Tommy Ryan said.

"Alley Boy did."

"Don't make me laugh. He couldn't kill time."

Tommy Ryan looked through the window and he saw Ankles getting out of his Plymouth. Ankles had a pistol in his hand and he was slapping his feet toward the front door. Tommy Ryan put his hand over Carol's mouth. Tommy motioned for the butler to go to the door.

"Act like nothing's going on," Tommy Ryan said. "I'll explain everything later. This is government work. You have to trust me."

Tommy's mother mumbled something to the guests about Tommy working for the government. His father corroborated this. The crazy doorbell chimed again and the butler opened the door. Ankles looked into the house and saw the scattered glass.

"Is Tommy Ryan here?" Ankles asked.

"I'm afraid you have the wrong party, sir," the butler said. "This is the O'Brian residence."

Tommy Ryan was standing behind the door with the shotgun against Carol's head. She was trying to yell, but it was muffled.

"What's all that broken glass?" Ankles asked as he flashed his badge. "Detective Tufano, homicide."

"Oh, that . . ." the butler said. "The chandelier fell from the ceiling."

Ankles pushed his way into the house. He put his gun in his holster. Tommy Ryan kicked the door closed and let Carol go. He stuck the barrel of the shotgun against Ankles's head.

"Get rid of your heat," Tommy Ryan said. Ankles gingerly took the pistol from his shoulder holster and passed it back to Tommy Ryan without turning around.

"You're gonna fall, Ryan," Ankles said. "I always thought you were smart. But you're not smart. You're insane. Completely off the wall, pal."

"No, Ankles, I'm the boss. You're just another rat in my trap. Isn't that right, Dad?"

Tommy Ryan looked over at his father.

Then to his mother.

"Isn't it, Mom? I mean, I'm the one who did all this."

Tommy Ryan made a sweeping gesture of the room with his hand.

"I'm the one who took care of you," he said. "I'm the one who was there when *you* needed *me*. Where were *you* when the rats were in the ceiling, Mom? Dad? Where were you when *I* needed *you*? Out groveling around with your nose up some rat bastard's ass. Not me. No way. I became their boss. They groveled for me. Look at them all. Rats, whiskers and tails and pointy little faces. All of them. They are the same kind who did it to you, Dad. And you, Mom. And they wanted to do it to me. But they didn't get away with it. Because I did it to them first."

Tommy Ryan pointed out each guest and said, "Rat —rat—rat—rat-a-tat-tat."

Tommy Ryan cracked up laughing. His mother sat back in her chair, her arms started to shake and she closed her eyes. She was breathing short little gusts.

"See, Mom," Tommy Ryan said. "Like now. I need you now, Mom. The rats are coming out of the ceiling and you close your eyes and make believe I'm not even here. And you, Dad. You let them take you. Without even a fight. Like a big fucking faggot you let them take you. But not me. I'm the boss. I'm the one who makes the decisions. Me, Tommy Ryan. I'm the fucking boss."

* * *

Alley Boy stood outside the window and listened. A big white dog was snarling at Alley Boy, but the dog had no teeth. It was starting to growl a little bit and Alley Boy gave it a kick in the head that made it roll over with a comical look on its face.

Alley Boy watched through the window from outside as Tommy Ryan led Ankles and Carol into the living room with the other guests. He held the shotgun behind Ankles's ear. Ankles had his hands at his side. Tommy Ryan was still ranting.

Alley Boy looked at the taxi parked down the street. The motor was still running and the lights were on. He thought for a moment about getting back into it and driving off. But he looked at the still mutt at his feet and knew that only half the job was finished.

Alley Boy stepped softly up the three snowy steps to the front door. The door was slightly ajar. He pushed it open slowly. He saw Tommy Ryan with the shotgun mashed against Ankles's ear.

Now Alley Boy kicked the door open wide. Tommy Ryan spun and fired a blast of the shotgun and back-pedaled into the dining room. Alley Boy dropped flat to his stomach as the pellets smashed into the door above him. Alley Boy had the pistol trained at Tommy Ryan now and his finger was on the trigger. Tommy Ryan had Ankles's pistol in his hand, but it was not raised.

"Hey, Al," Tommy Ryan said as he backed away from the guests. "You came back, Al. You never even talked, Al. You're a real man now, Al. That's what I'm gonna call you. Al."

"Stand still, Tommy," Alley Boy said as he rose to his knees. "Just stand still."

"It's me and you, Al," Tommy Ryan said. "Partners. All I did was take the kid out of you, Al." Tommy Ryan kept backing up. Ankles made a quick move for Tommy Ryan. Tommy Ryan raised his gun to fire at Ankles.

Alley Boy pulled the trigger and the slug caught
Tommy Ryan in the stomach. He fell backwards toward
the banquet table. Alley Boy squeezed the trigger again
and again and again and again. Tommy Ryan's body
made stupid drunken lurches all over the table. He
reached out a hand and grabbed a dinner plate and
pulled it with him to the floor.

The big lobster lay next to Tommy Ryan on the thick
Persian rug.

Epilogue

It was ten o'clock in the morning on April twelfth and Alley Boy watched the sun coming up high over the desert outside of Tucson, Arizona. The Chevrolet Impala was moving south swiftly across the blacktop. Country and western music was playing on the radio. It was the only music Alley Boy could get on the radio.

He had a briefcase on the seat next to him and it contained a hundred thousand dollars in cash. It should have been more, but the legal fees that went to Jimmy LaCossa added up to almost fifty grand. The trial had lasted four weeks and the lawyer had put a whole team of attorneys on it. The evidence that Captain Houlihan had uncovered was purely circumstantial and the bank guard said that Alley Boy certainly wasn't one of the two gunmen in the Red Hook bank. He was too tall and muscular. The bandits had been shorter fellas. Even a disguise like that Hasidic Jew outfit couldn't have hidden his size, LaCossa argued.

The famous trial attorney argued that all the prosecution had was a fingerprint on a hat that could have been left there at any time prior to or after the robbery.

But what clinched it for the defense was the character witness named Anthony Tufano. He told the jury how Albert D'Agastino had saved his life on the night of December twenty-fourth after D'Agastino led him to a suspect in a series of slasher murders in Brooklyn.

Would a citizen of this caliber also participate in a bank robbery? Ankles told the jury that in his experience as a cop it was highly unlikely.

The prosecution had relied almost entirely on the fingerprint and the testimony of Frank Adler, who put Albert D'Agastino in Rhinecliff, a town twelve miles from Red Hook, on the morning of the robbery.

But LaCossa had torn that to shreds, too. The lawyer asked if citizens were not allowed to travel freely in the state of New York without being accused of capital crimes. He asked the prosecution to produce one single eyewitness that placed Albert D'Agastino in or near that bank on December fifteenth. The prosecution could not come up with such a witness.

The jury stayed out for two days.

This was the biggest trial to hit this part of the state of New York in years.

When the jury returned, the foreman looked Alley Boy in the eye and declared the verdict: Not Guilty.

After it was over, Alley Boy made sure that his mother and grandmother were taken care of. The grandmother refused to move out of the apartment on Seventh Avenue, but Alley Boy's mother accepted Alley

Boy's gift of fifty thousand dollars, which she immediately deposited in the bank under her maiden name, so the IRS would not ask questions. The grandmother said a prayer to Saint Anthony to find a way for her grandson to live a normal life again.

After the trial was over, Alley Boy had gone to say thanks and good-bye to Ankles at an address the big cop had given him on Windsor Place. The woman named Marsha answered the door and then Ankles came out after her cradling his grandson Michael in his arms and shook Alley Boy's hand. Alley Boy told Ankles he was going away. Ankles told him he should take all the money with him. "To hell with the banks," Ankles said. Alley Boy told him he didn't know what he was talking about and smiled. Then Alley Boy climbed into his brand-new Chevrolet Impala and started driving southwest from Brooklyn, New York.

Now, just outside of Tucson, Alley Boy saw the girl with her thumb out on the side of the road. She was about nineteen and she had blond hair and Alley Boy thought she was beautiful. Alley Boy stopped the car and the girl hopped into the front seat. Alley Boy tossed the briefcase into the backseat.

"Where you headed?" the girl asked Alley Boy.

"Mexico," he said.

"Me, too," she said. "Whereabouts?"

"I don't know," Alley Boy said.

"You ever been there?" the pretty girl asked.

"I was supposed to go once," Alley Boy said. "But I couldn't make it."

"You should see Mexico City just to see Mexico City," the girl said.

"That where you're going?" Alley Boy asked.

"Yup."

"Me too," Alley Boy said.

The girl laughed a little and bit her lower lip and looked at Alley Boy.

"My name is Beatrice," the girl said. "What's yours?"

"Al," Alley Boy said.

He thought a minute and looked over at Beatrice, who was smiling at him.

"But you can call me Alley Boy."